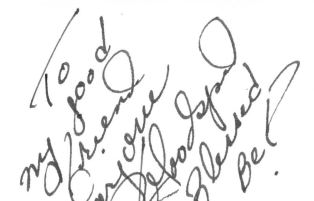

Murder On Persimmon Lane

Patricia Goodspeed and Diana Orem

Love

Diana

Cover art by Autumn Orem Paul

Kids At Heart Publishing LLC
PO Box 492
Milton, IN 47357
765-478-5873
www.kidsatheartpublishing.com

First published by Kids At Heart Publishing LLC 10/15/2015
ISBN # 978-0-9964962-5-4
Library of Congress Control Number: 2015954238

Printed in the United States of America
Milton, Indiana

This book printed on acid-free paper.

To order more copies of this book go to
www.kidsatheartpublishing.com

The books at Kids At Heart Publishing feature turn the page technology. No
batteries or charging required.

DEDICATION
We dedicate this novel to our beloved husbands, who encouraged us every day, and laughed at us for having too much fun.

In memory of co-author, Diana Orem (1946-2013).

Introduction

Grovetown, population 2,045 plus or minus a kid or two and without the inclusion of pets, is a town, not a city. In 2005, the powers that be had to approve of you to have any social life in the community. First-generation Grovetown residents weren't readily welcomed into established society. The houses had the name of their previous or original owners. If you didn't come from strong lines of old families, you might as well forget about participating in any social life. A person could be a guest of a member from the traditional clubs, literary societies, and the two sororities, but shouldn't be surprised if not invited to join. Status was even more important than being a descendant from Christopher Trinkle, the Revolutionary soldier buried out by Sinking Springs. Grovetown, was not an easy cookie to break. Either you belonged, or you didn't.

No town is exempt from secrets. Time could cooperate in building them only so long, but not forever. A stack of blocks built upon lies can only climb so high before toppling. The stress of bearing concealed knowledge finally reaches the boiling point. When these protectors fail, they allow the truth to be finally revealed, but not without consequences. Such are the secrets of Grovetown.

"In their hearts humans plan their course, but the LORD establishes their steps."
Proverbs 16:9 (NIV)

CAST OF MAJOR CHARACTERS

Beth Basford—new attorney in town

Billy Bob (William) Achsworth—twin of Donnie, handyman/plumber

Carol—waitress and girlfriend of Billy Bob, poker player, plumber

Donald (Donnie) Achsworth—twin of brother, Billy Bob, poker player, plumber

Emily Starks—daughter of Raymond Starks and Madelyn Starks Monroe, 26, teaches 3rd grade, lives in Castleton area of Indianapolis

Glenn Achsworth—2nd oldest of the Achsworth brothers, works manager, poker player

Gussy, (Gustafeson Frederick Trinkle)—murder victim, single, bachelor, substantial property owner, oldest of the Trinkle siblings, poker player

Henrietta Trinkle—middle Trinkle sibling, old maid town librarian, Gussy's estate Administratrix

Jacob (Jake) Achsworth—former Chief of Police, wife Alice, girlfriend Hope, poker player

Jayne Baldwin—new vet, working for Dr. Jeffries, girlfriend of Patrick

Judy—Nathan's girlfriend at Notre Dame

Ken Lawson—retired from lumberyard, wife deceased, and neighbor of Gussy

Madelyn Trinkle Starks Monroe—youngest Trinkle sibling, ex-wife of Raymond Starks, now married to Stuart Monroe, lives in Chicago, Mother of Emily and Nathan

Melissa Jones—owner of Melissa's Persimmon Shoppe, local florist, friend of Henrietta

Mike Petty—Grovetown Chief of Police

Nathan Stark— son of Raymond Starks and Madelyn Starks Monroe, journalism student at Notre Dame

Patrick Mattox—brother of Permelia, town General Practitioner Doctor, best friend of Nathan

Permelia Mattox Garcia—widow, son, Robbie, Wiccan, dance teacher

Raymond Starks—ex-husband of Madelyn, owner and editor of Grovetown Tribune

Ronald Green—aka Green Ron, deputy

Rosie McCorkle—beautician and owner of Rosie's Beauty Shop, town gossip

Sally Jacobs—college friend of Madelyn, wife of Samuel Jacobs, Mother of Drew

Samuel Andrew Jacobs, Jr. (Drew)—son of Sally and Samuel Jacobs

Simon Dyers—Funeral Director

Solomon Edwards—best friend of Jake, runs the Legion, poker player

Todd O'Neil—Baptist minister

1

Police Chief Mike Petty arrived at the murder scene with his Deputy, Ron Green, within minutes of the call. A crowd gathered at the crime scene, a brick building, sitting fifteen feet behind the gingerbread-trimmed back porch of the elaborate house on Persimmon Lane.

Chief Mike Petty stood six foot tall at the entrance to the workshop and completely in charge. "Everybody out, now!" he commanded. "Nobody goes back in until you glove up and bag your feet. The rest of you might as well go home. If you think you have anything to contribute, give your name, address, and phone number to Deputy Green."

Not accustomed to such explosive assertiveness from the mild-mannered Chief, everyone scurried about like startled rats chased by the snakes that were hiding in Deer Fly Creek.

The waters were rising because of the spring rains. The peony bushes were starting to bloom. The population of the entire town was abuzz. What happened? Is the body Gussy's? Is he dead? Was Gussy murdered? If it's under police inquiry, it must have been murder. Right? Do they have any suspects? Who found him? Why would anyone do such a thing? Did they find a weapon?

Ken Lawson, Gussy's neighbor, discovered the body lying in its own blood on the dirty workshop floor of the former summer kitchen of the home. Ken, shaken, still managed to call 911 to try to get his neighbor help.

The station was only a block away, and within a short period, a crowd was forming. When Dr. Mattox arrived, he quickly realized there was nothing he could do to help Gussy. The word of Gussy's unexpected demise and rumors of a murderer spread to the populace.

More townspeople were on their way. The town dispatcher, whose office was next door to the fire barn, sent out alarms to the medics and volunteer firefighters. They arrived fifteen minutes later while Petty was assessing the situation.

"What a mess, Ron. Look at all those paw prints and footprints. People and Gussy's dog walked in the blood—looks like a finger painting in red ink or a Rorschach inkblot. Secure this area ASAP. Why I even see bloody shoe prints from your shoes, too. I can hear the County Prosecutor's screams now." Chief Petty looked around as he took in the scene. "Ken told me he ran over here. Gussy's dog was whining and howling. He came in here to check Gussy's pulse, messing up more blood, and Buddy was going round and round the body—he didn't want to leave Gussy. You know the Prosecutor beat into our heads the smallest details win or lose a case in the last training meeting. We need to keep our reputations unsullied by mistakes."

Chief Petty felt disoriented and a little overwhelmed because Gussy was a close friend. He hadn't seen evidence of such violence in over ten years. He worked when he first joined the police force in Indianapolis where crime scenes like Gussy's were entirely too common.

"I'm going to call Raymond at the paper to come and take pictures. I'm sure he's still there working on this week's paper if he isn't here already. Have you seen him?"

About that time, Raymond arrived carrying his photographic equipment.

Petty saw him and immediately explained, "Now, Raymond, you have to understand this conversation is completely off the record. I know when the Peony County crime team arrives, their photographer will do their thing. However, I'll feel more comfortable if you take photos too. I trust your work."

Raymond's investigative mind took over. "This is awful! I can't believe Gussy is dead. How did this happen? Was there a break-in? Do his sisters know?"

Chief Petty replied, "We don't know much. I haven't called Henrietta. I hope she hasn't heard unreliable reports. I'll let Henrietta tell her sister."

"I'll tell Henrietta if you like. She should be home from the library by now. I pray she hasn't heard much town gossip before I get there. I know it's against police policy, but this news would be best if a friend tells her."

"We don't know the facts yet, but I would appreciate if you could talk to Henri, and keep her away from here. I don't want her to see Gussy... I think seeing him this way would tear her up."

"Yes, Henri's quite close to her brother. He's the only family she has south of Indianapolis. Her sister, Madelyn, lives in Chicago. Her nephew lives in South Bend, and a niece lives in Indianapolis. I'll ask Pastor Todd to go with me. I know Henrietta will need the Lord to lean on for comfort. Then I'll take pictures. Goodness, this is tragic! It's not going to be the same without Gussy."

Henrietta tried to be stoic when she heard the terrible news. "Oh, Pastor Todd, thank you so much for coming. Would you please lead us in prayer before Raymond goes back to the summer kitchen? I'm so glad Gussy was baptized in Jesus before he died."

She started crying, and Pastor Todd took her hand and tried to comfort her.

"Of course. I'm sure our dear Lord will be with you and your family. I'll stay this evening. I think it would be best if you didn't see Gussy yet. He's in Jesus' loving arms. Let's join hands. Let us pray."

Raymond prayed with them and then excused himself. He headed back to the crime scene.

He said to the Chief, "Pastor Todd prayed with Henri and me. The knowledge of Gussy's baptism will surely help her through this time. She's a strong woman, but the shock of Gussy's sudden death will be quite distressing. I assume she'll be in charge of handling his affairs. I hope the stress won't wear her down. At least she knows her brother is with his Lord, Jesus."

Taken aback when he saw his ex-brother-in-law on the floor, Raymond looked pale. He'd seen a corpse in a casket before, but this was a person he knew. Visibly shaken, he tried to keep his composure, and finally pulled himself together. He was Gussy's brother-in-law for years, but it wasn't until recently their relationship developed into a close and valuable friendship.

Chief Petty assigned Ron the job to maintain the crime scene.

"Raymond, I need you to take photos from all angles. Do make sure to include close-ups of Gussy's body, and the interior of the building. I know you'll know what's important."

Yes. Raymond was upset as he fulfilled his obligations to the Chief. He tried to maintain a professional distance. He hid the tears and emotions as best he could.

As the newspaper editor worked, he said to Deputy Ron, "Who would want to kill Gussy? I can't believe he's dead. I'm going to miss him." He turned towards Gussy's body. He wiped his eyes. "Oh, my God, why? Dear God, I need your continuing guidance. I thought our friendship was blossoming through Christ. Gussy started this New Year with many changes in his beliefs. You changed him so. His very nature and behavior showed you in his life." Raymond continued his task.

Chief Petty talked to the main witness, Ken Lawson. Before he sent him down to the station to sign an official statement he wanted to go over his testimony again.

Lawson said, "I don't know if I can talk about it again, but I'll try my best."

Every Tuesday Gussy and some of the neighbors come to my house for our standing weekly supper get together. We always have my special spaghetti and meatballs. He goes to his regular Tuesday poker game at the Legion. The game starts about nine o'clock. I never liked to play poker, so I stay home and watch TV. Gambling isn't my thing.

"The thunderstorm this afternoon ended in time for supper. We eat at five pm. Gussy was usually punctual but by five thirty he wasn't here. At first, I wasn't too worried. Thought he might have had a phone call or something causing him to be late. Then I heard his mutt, Buddy, howling. I recalled hearing the dog barking earlier and paid no attention. Therefore, this time I thought I should check. The commotion came from Gussy's workshop behind the house. The door to the shop was ajar, and I saw Buddy whining and howling. He was walking in circles around Gussy on the floor, so I walked over to him. There was no pulse; I tried to resuscitate him, but I realized Gussy was dead. I ran back to my house and called 911. I told the guys what I saw, and we all walked back here to wait until you guys came."

The Chief didn't reply at first. He kept writing, and he made a mental note of the blood on Ken's shoes, shirt, and pants.

He asked, "Have you seen anyone at Gussy's place today?"

"Yes. Gussy had a couple of visitors. Around one o'clock after lunch, I went out to collect the mail. I saw a man who looked like a bum. I didn't recognize him. However, Gussy often has odd visitors who've been fishing on Deer Fly Creek. Some stop by to chat. Occasionally somebody comes by wanting him to make them a box or whittle some little wood statues or something. Later on, I heard a woman's voice when I walked by. She was shrill and loud—sounded very angry, but I didn't see her. Behind the closed door, I knew it wasn't his sister by the voice. The rain started again once I got home."

"About what time?"

"Close to five, at least an hour after I saw the guy. I walked to the grocery to pick up some oregano for the spaghetti sauce and returned home before the storm. The wind had picked up."

"Before or after the first time you heard Buddy barking?"

"After."

Before Chief Petty could ask a follow-up question, the entourage of Peony County Officials arrived. The Sheriff and a deputy, some police detectives, the Coroner, Prosecutor, a stenographer, and a forensic team trudged into the now-crowded workshop. The Chief's part of the investigation was on hold while he oversaw the new arrivals. The others took charge. The Chief's mind wandered, *What if Buddy bit the murderer? A dental impression of the dog's mouth might be helpful.* He picked up the phone and told his dispatcher, "Call the dentist and the vet. Tell them to come here as soon as they can." He waved for the medic to come over. He asked her to get DNA and blood samples from Buddy. He didn't want any loose ends. The Coroner did a cursory examination. He declared Gustafeson Frederick Trinkle dead at the scene. He turned to the stenographer, "He probably died between three to four hours ago, making the time of death sometime about four pm. There are multiple wounds to his chest and abdomen."

He looked over to Chief Petty and said, "To know the details and the exact cause of death we'll have to wait for the autopsy results. The County should complete it in time. You know we don't ever have a queue of waiting bodies. However, there may be a reason to send him to Indianapolis for further tests. I'd also like to get an alcohol/drug screen."

The Sheriff looked miffed. He yelled, "How did this crime scene get so disturbed?" Nobody answered. He continued, "Oh well, I guess I have to deal with what we have—a compromised murder scene. Okay, all of you follow proper procedures."

The forensic team searched for prints, blood, clothing fibers, hair strands, and any other items that could be evidence. They examined the tools for blood to see if they could find a possible weapon. We'll send a sample of the blood in the sink to Indianapolis for testing.

"Sheriff," Petty asked, "Lawson had blood all over himself and his clothes. I took possession of his clothes. I think I should also ask him if he washed in the sink because the blood could either be his or the perpetrator.

The Sheriff nodded in agreement.

"Hey, Sheriff," said a member of the forensic team, "no one's found anything looking like a weapon, nor have the detectives found any distinguishing footprints on the floor. There's a bunch of 'em." The Chief said, "I know Gussy tried to keep his junk-filled workshop organized, but he often ignored the dirty floor."

One detective came over to the Sheriff. "I see signs of a struggle. Note the cut on the victim's right hand; I wonder if he tried to counter the weapon."

"Anything could cause this tiny cut. But we'll check if the blood matches anybody else," the Sheriff said.

One detective interjected, "They found a soda cup on the floor, and it looks like it was thrown up against the wall. See that sticky, brownish stain." He pointed to the adjacent wall.

"Get that cup! Check to see if there are prints," the Sheriff yelled.

The team complied. They bagged and labeled the cup as they did with all the other evidence. Preserving the chain of custody was imperative to protect the evidence for trial. The crew found some of the tools on the worktable out of place. Papers on the desk looked like someone rifled through them.

Chief Petty queried, "Did anybody find a cashbox? Or money?"

"Nope," they all answered in unison.

Deputy Green asked, "Could this have been a robbery gone wrong? Everybody knows Gussy stashed cash all over. Find an empty cashbox. We might have a clue. Theft could be a motive."The officers worked as the coroner completed his report. He noted the body position, body temperature, dress, and weather.

Raymond spoke privately to Chief Petty, "I'll process the photos and try to get them to you sometime tomorrow evening."

"Thanks, Raymond."

"Would it be okay if I took Buddy to my house? He's old—I think Gussy said he's eighteen years old, so he's ancient for a big dog. He'll be out of the wet air at my house, and I'm sure he'll be happier with me. I'd hate to see him shipped off to the pound or a kennel. The least I can do for old Gussy is to care for his best buddy."

Petty said, "We're not sure if Buddy bit the perp. We took DNA and blood samples from the poor dog. I've requested the dentist and the vet to come to make an impression of Buddy's mouth. We can compare it with any wound a suspect might have. You know like when you get a dental bridge. Oh, there they are."

Soon the dog and Raymond were ready to leave.

The Chief watched silently as Raymond unchained the dog. Raymond called Buddy. The old dog trotted behind his master's friend.

Deputy Green walked over to Chief Petty. "How thoughtful of Raymond to see Buddy was gone before the officials removed the body from the workshop. His actions are quite refreshing."

About nine-thirty p.m. Chief Petty concluded, "I'm going to call it a night. I know I won't get much rest until the murderer is behind bars." *I hope I'll be up to the challenge. I know Jesus will be with me. With His help, I'll do my best. I owe Gussy, his family, and the town.*

2

The weekly poker game in the private back room of the Grovetown American Legion went on as usual, but the game time was later than normal. The unlikely and improbable event of the murder of Gussy, the seventh poker player, shook the players' quiet existence. The setting for the weekly poker game was the same as other weeks, but this game was far from ordinary. Jake, deep in thought, sauntered into the room, sat down, and glanced at Gussy's vacant chair. There was no full house at the table. The silence shouted, "Gussy isn't here! He's never playing again, and one of you knows why!"

I might as well deal the cards. Jake knew they were for show. In his mind, the cards weren't the common black and red ones: spades, clubs, hearts, and diamonds. Tonight's suits were all black and sinister. He dealt six hands, instead of the usual seven.

All the poker players were a team for many years, and they would remain one in facing this new challenge. The stakes for this game weren't the usual two bits but were a loss of material possessions, money, and reputations, as well as possible arrests. This was a very serious game indeed.

Jacob Achsworth, known to everyone as Jake, was in charge of keeping the poker game alive. He was a leader and an organizer in several roles, past and present, of the community. The people of Grovetown respected Jake, the former Chief of Police. However, Jake never faced a murder investigation during his tenure of keeping the peace. He handled minor traffic offenses, vandalism, bar arguments, and an occasional theft. He protected reputations, often taking a normally sober citizen who strayed into overindulgence in drink, home instead of an arrest. Rumors in town were Jake could be bought. Extra income kept the wife and kids happy.

The four of a kind in tonights game were Jake and the other

Achsworth brothers, Glenn, and the twins, Donald (Donnie), and William (Billy Bob).

Glenn aged the best of the bunch. He retired from the Works Department. The twins were always hard to tell apart in their youth. Now there was a substantial difference in their respective weights. Both still had red facial hair to accompany their unruly graying locks. Grooming played little importance in their lifestyles. Both twins worked through the years with their friend, Gussy, on construction and repair jobs. Donnie and Billy Bob owned their small businesses in plumbing, heating, and odd jobs. Neither made much money.

Donnie complained, "Can't keep no woman happy. That's why I can't stay married." Billy Bob kept himself single but had plenty of ladies on hand.

Solomon Edwards, Jake's best friend, and confidant ran the American Legion where the players meet. Solomon's contribution to the group was in the form of information. Patrons shared their woes with the barkeeper to convince themselves by using liquor to lessen their disappointments in life. The community was abuzz about Gussy's murder. Solomon's customers would certainly want to talk to him about their own suppositions. His expertise with the rumor mill could prove invaluable.

The last man at the table was Richard Farwell, the local liquor store owner. People would be gossiping about the details of Gussy's properties and well-known investments as well as the suspected amount of cash believed hidden away. Farwell was bound to see an increase in sales. His opinions on these subjects would be on his patrons' minds. People were looking forward to hearing the latest gossip.

Farwell surveyed the group as Jake called the meeting to order, "Thanks for coming tonight, guys. We have to work on a plan of action to protect each one of us. We need to discuss alibis, preservation of the cover-ups and plan our moves. We need to get into Gussy's buildings. Protection of our past dealings is too important. We know we're facing a serious problem. Tonight, we must decide how to deal with it. First, let me speak for us all. We've been worried about Gussy's sudden feeling of guilt about our group's past actions. I know we each received a disturbing letter from Gussy saying he needed to come clean on our private affairs and we should too. He said he planned to make retribution to the community, remember. Perhaps one of us took care of the problem before he revealed our collaborations?"

In agreement, they lowered their heads and glanced around to avoid eye contact with Jake or each other. Each had his own thoughts and worries about the possible consequences of ignoring the ominous letters.

Jake continued, "I don't want to know who did it. If the cops ask, we can't tell what we don't know. Let's agree to keep secret how we make extra money, not only for the sake of the guilty one but for all of us."

There were relieved nods all around.

Glenn was the first to speak out, "We agree, Jake. You know if our friend Gussy went through with his threats in the letter, we'd be in big trouble. We didn't know his getting religion would affect any of us. But, we all need to agree on how to take care of this mess and stand together. Sure, I hate the solution was his death, but now we gotta make sure we all will be okay. We need a good plan to make sure no one can find a copy of the letter. Since we've never had a murder in town, that I know of, Chief Petty is bound to jump into a full investigation. The whole town knows we're friends. I've heard detectives look at family and friends first as 'persons of interest.' Jake, in your professional opinion, don't you think Petty will come after us as possible suspects?"

"Yeah, of course, he will," said Donnie as he hit the table with a fist. "Why, even Green Ron would think of us as suspects. We gotta get us a plan and quick. What you got in mind, Jake?"

Billy Bob jumped in, "I don't feel so good about all of this mess. I don't know what I'd say if he put me in a chair staring at a bare light bulb shining bright in my face like they do on TV."

Jake said, "Now, Billy, let's not get ahead of ourselves. Everybody calm down."

First on Jake's agenda were "straights", not the long and short poker kind but straight alibis.

"Let's go around the table talking about where we were when someone killed Gussy. Remember, we're not searching for the murderer. We're looking for a way to protect each of us, including the murderer since I guess one of us must have done it. Who else would? Let's start with me. Unfortunately, my real alibi won't work. I was with Hope this afternoon. I've kept Alice in the dark all of these years about my relationship with Hope. I'm not about to let the cat out of the bag now. If

Alice knew, she'd take me for our new house and the shirt off my back. We'll have to work on mine. Richard, were you at work?"

"Well, I closed the store for the afternoon and took care of some private business. I don't have anyone to verify my activities, either." He thought to himself, *Sure don't want them to know I'm selling under the table and was meeting with the buyers.*

Solomon interrupted, "I wasn't here at the Legion. So got no alibi, either."

Richard said, "Solomon, what if we say we were together someplace? That would cover for my time, as well as give you an alibi. How's 'bout if we say we went to Peony to check out liquor prices. You know nobody would just expect anything out of the order since I sell liquor, and I need to know what the competition's doing. The prices are usually higher in the county seat. We wouldn't have to show any receipts, 'cause we were only lookin'. Does that work for you?"

Solomon quickly mulled the idea over. "Won't the cops check out all the places in Peony?"

Richard replied, "It wouldn't do much good. We wouldn't have given anybody our names. By the time they might check it out, who's going to remember what customers were in the store buying a six-pack or just lookin' around."

"Well, the Legion employees wouldn't think anything of us hangin' out. No one will think it strange we went price checking together. We've done it before and could even make us a list of prices we found. Nobody would go to the trouble of checkin' it out, and it would make our story better. I'll get one of my Legion pads now. I can work on the list while the rest of you get your stories straight. Be right back." Solomon left the room to the confident nods of the others.

Jake watched Solomon leave, and then returned his attention to the remaining players. He looked at the twins. "Okay, Donnie and Billy Bob. What can you tell us about your day? Do you have any witnesses who can verify either of your actions? Were you on the job someplace where your customers will testify on your behalf?"

Looking at each other, Billy Bob spoke first, "Well, to be honest, I don't have any jobs goin' right now. Nobody's been needin' me, so I was just a hangin' in my trailer by myself. Didn't even have no girl with me either. Seems if you ain't got no money, no one wants to be with ya.

Anyway. Used to be good 'nuf to just have a fun afternoon alone with a gal. That don't seem to cut it anymo'. Nope, I was all alone. What about you, Donnie? Any more luck than me?"

The truth was Donnie had lots more luck than Billy Bob. He spent the day with Carol, widely known as Billy Bob's girlfriend. Billy Bob's call interrupted Donnie's liaison at Carol's, causing an early departure for Donnie. He wasn't too happy, but he wasn't going to share the embarrassing disappointment with anyone, chiefly Billy Bob. He could get angry enough to fight. There were other such instances in the past, when once revealed, led to some nasty confrontations. They were twins, but Billy Bob was much huskier. Besides, Donnie didn't want another argument with his brother over a woman. He might end up losing.

Don't want to lose face over some inky dinky deal like a wommin; he thought to himself before he said, "My business's been better than Billy Bob's but not today. I just stayed at home piddlin' around. I had a busy weekend, and I wanted to catch up on some Zzs. I guess we're going to have to come up with something for both of us."

A few seconds later, Donnie's face lit up with a touch of inspiration, "How 'bout if we say we went fishin'? Guys been sayin' the fish are bitin' out at Tucker's Bridge. Seems like today would have been a good time to try out the new pole I got last week."

"Works for me," Billy Bob piped in. "Just 'cause we went fishin' don't mean we had to catch somethin'. Could fix up a can of worms easy enuf and my boots are already muddy. I like the idea, and if someone asks if anybody saw us fishin' we'll just say the woods on Deer Fly are too thick, and we were quiet 'cause we din't wanna scare no fish. How's that sound to you, Jake?"

Jake preferred something a little more reliable, but considering the reputation of his brothers, the story was feasible. Jake was glad to get the business of their alibis under control. *He knew he needed to watch them. Sometimes they needed more time to catch on.* He had to talk to the twins on their evolving story; *I hope that the seriousness of the situation will keep them on their best behavior.*

"Sure. You two can work on some details together to make your fish tale sound true. However, don't let your imaginations work too hard. Remember, your stories must match. Don't let your egos go to your heads and make conflicting statements. Be cool! Keep it short and simple.

Don't offer info on whether or not somebody saw you. Okay? This was a lazy afternoon fishing trip, not a Canadian adventure. Solomon, give them some paper so they can each both write down the same 'facts." I'll go over your notes with you another time. You, boys, think while Glenn and I discuss our situations."

Donnie and Billy Bob energetically began arguing over the details of their "pretend" fishing trip. Jake knew he needed to watch those two. Yes, there was going to be some stern editing of their evolving tale.

Glenn dreaded any discussion of his day. He'd been busy but not with something he wanted to share with the group. His new house out in Flowering Hills Addition cost a lot more than he planned. His wife, Margaret, was being extremely unreasonable. She should be happy to be in such a beautiful, modern "mansion". Not only did she want a fantastic architectural trophy, but also wanted the décor to surpass all expectations of those welcomed inside. She wasn't a member of the elite clubs in town, but she did invite others to impress. To his mind, the extravagances were going to be the death of him, or at least lead him into bankruptcy. If he didn't find a way to appease his wife, he knew how miserable his life could be. He had been busy much of the day working out a "deal" of his own. *My friends would be quite upset if they knew about this lucrative land deal.* He needed an alibi, for sure, but one to protect him also from his comrades at the table. Considering options, he still didn't have a satisfactory plan. He had to be careful how he explained his dilemma. He didn't want to get everyone's curiosity too aroused. He decided to take the advice Jake gave the twins. *Keep it simple.*

He said to the others, "I guess I'm like everyone else but you Jake. I was by myself at home. Margaret went to visit her sister in Evansville for a few days. As big as my house is, it's still not big enough to keep us from getting on each other's nerves. She left me with a honey-do list. I was busy painting the upstairs' guest room for the fourth time. She keeps changing her mind about the color."

Glenn's story was mostly true. Before she left town, Margaret told him to paint, but he hadn't started the task yet. To validate his alibi he needed proof on the walls substantiating his following his wife's wishes, his loyalty to his friends, and his authenticity to the legal investigators.

Jake saw his brother Glenn's alibi as an opportunity for him too.

"Say, Glenn, what if I join you in your paint job? Helping my little brother just seems natural, dontcha think. I'll bring some old clothes we can smear with the paint. Why don't you pick me up in the morning, so we can explain why the neighbors didn't see my vehicle either day? Sound okay to you?"

When he got home from the Legion, Glenn planned to do enough painting to cover his alibi. *Then Jake can paint the rest tomorrow. How can I disagree?* "Sounds great. You could finish the painting, and I could pick another job off the list to do. This could help me get back in Margaret's graces. I'll pick you up about eight, and I can treat us to breakfast as part of the deal. Someone seeing us ought to add a little authenticity to our alibi."

Jake next wanted to discuss the flushes of this night's game. He advised his fellow players, "Everyone must all follow the same suit. If you still have Gussy's letter, you must flush it, or burn it. ASAP! We can't risk anyone getting hold of one of them. We need to take action immediately. Don't go to sleep tonight without destroying the evidence. We're all dependent upon each other to protect our secrets from surfacing."

Jake noted the solemn nods of agreement on the faces of his other colleagues. He could only hope they were all truly in accord with the gravity of their predicament and would stick together with his strategies.

Jake saw the lateness of the hour and decided to deal a final hand for the evening.

He was looking for pairs this time. "Before we leave tonight, we have one more thing to deal with. I want us to form pairs to conduct our investigations into Gussy's life. Yellow crime scene tape marks his workshop so we can't search it, but we'd better check out Gussy's other properties. We'll have to be careful not to leave prints or a mess. Donnie and Billy Bob you be one team, Glenn, and Richard, you guys be another, and Solomon and I will work together. I'll make a plan for each of your responsibilities and get them to you tomorrow. The sooner we look, the better our chances of keeping unwanted evidence out of the hands of the cops."

Jake continued, "I have one ace in the pocket, *me*. I plan to get real close to Green Ron during this investigation. He kinda thinks of me as a mentor. He's listened to me in the past, so I hope to get some inside information. Tomorrow, wearing my paint shirt, I'll mosey over to the crime scene to check how they're doing and see if they need a little advice from the retired chief. Let's call it a night, fellas. We have a lot of things to think about, and evidence to flush. Get rested and be ready for the busy days ahead."

Glenn bid everyone goodbye and took off. He had to find Gussy's letter and get a good start on their paint job. Glenn knew from experience he couldn't depend on his brother to help paint even though Jake talked big about helping him tomorrow. In reality, it looked like Jake's painting on Wednesday was liable to be as fanciful as it had been on Tuesday. Glenn planned to spend a couple of hours painting in case Jake backed out on his promise.

Jake double-checked the twins' story before he allowed them to leave for the night. He hoped they would remember the importance of agreeing on the essential "facts". He also felt compelled to remind them about getting rid of Gussy's letters.

"Billy Bob, make sure you and your brother burn these notes you wrote tonight, too." Jake knew the disarray in their trailers might make it difficult to find the letters and complete the task. They assured him they would find them and deal with them.

Solomon and Richard finished their price comparison lists from their alleged price-check alibi

Richard said, "Jake, we'll see you at breakfast and get our search assignments."

Jake was the last to leave the room. He looked again at the empty chair. Gussy'd been a good friend through the years, even with all of his idiosyncrasies. He hoped he had stacked the deck well enough tonight to get them all safely through the coming challenges. His sleep would be troubled tonight and every other night until the crisis passed.

3

Nathan was in a suspended dream-state of early morning. His frequent dreams were so vivid he sometimes couldn't tell if they were real or not. The other morning, he dreamed Soho, his large red tabby cat, came into his room carrying a miniscule Chihuahua in his mouth. The tiny creature wasn't hurt. Soho cuddled up with the dog and treated her like a kitten. Somehow, it seemed true, but then Nathan realized he was only dreaming of his neighbor's pets. Nathan said to himself, *Those little dogs are so cute, but they sure do yippity-yap.* He said a quick prayer, *Lord please forgive me for complaining.*

A ringing sound abruptly ended his twilight sleep, and he reached over to shut off the alarm. When the noise continued, he remembered he hadn't set it last night. Since it was Wednesday, he didn't need to race to the campus of Notre Dame. The test he was overseeing wouldn't start until one p.m. and he hadn't planned to work on that ever-consuming doctoral thesis on journalism, either. His plans to sleep in went awry. Instead, the irritating ringing didn't stop. Nathan finally realized it was the phone.

He was especially groggy today. A restless night and the fact he didn't fall asleep until a late hour after a heavy dinner date with Judy triggered his state of mind. The shrimp lo mein and egg foo yung were delicious at the Bamboo Inn, their favorite Chinese restaurant. Of course, all the meal was outstanding. As usual, he consumed two bowls of sweet and sour soup. The couple finished their meal with fortune cookies and jasmine tea. They divided their plentiful leftover delicacies.

Nathan said, "Judy, Why don't you take the vegetable fried rice and barbecued shrimp? I'll take the rest and eat the leftovers for breakfast."

The ringing brought him back to the present. *I'll let the machine get it. What time is it anyway? Eight-thirty!* Now fully awake he knew he couldn't get back to sleep. *Well, here goes.* He picked up the receiver and silenced the annoying ring tone, and he had no chance to even say, "Hello."

"Nathan, it's your mother." With frustration, she whined, "I've been trying to reach you since last night. Are you just getting in?"

Madelyn felt no need to wait for a reply. She blurted out, "Your Uncle Gussy is dead. Your Aunt Henrietta called last evening to give me the news. However, she didn't explain much, and she said she would call me today. Stuart and I had important plans last night. I didn't have much time to talk to her either. I tried to call both you and Emily before our dinner but got no answer. I decided not to leave such distressing news on your voice mail, so I tried to call again later before bedtime, but still got no answer."

She rambled on, "Aren't you kids ever home? Both of you need to go to Grovetown right away. You must make whatever necessary arrangements as needed so you can. Family members must be there to show support. We don't want any talk. What a mess! This really couldn't have happened at a worse time."

He took advantage of his mother's stop for a breath. Nathan solemnly responded, "Mom, slow down! I'm sorry. I know you and Aunt Henrietta must be very upset. Let's start over. What did Aunt Henrietta say?"

"Your Uncle Gussy *was murdered*! You have to get down to Grovetown at once."

Nathan pushed up his glasses as he did whenever he started to feel tense.

"Please explain. Did ya say 'murder'? Surely not. Who would murder my uncle? Last time I saw him, he was his usual laid back self, grouchy but quite alive."

"He was murdered. Stabbed! My brother is dead! You and Emily have to go *now*!"

"Mom, let's talk about this." He rearranged his glasses again. Soho, his cat, kept nudging his master and meowing loudly, "Feed me now!"

Madelyn kept repeating her command. "You *must* get to Grovetown immediately! Your aunt needs you. I demand you go immediately and find out what happened. Your family needs you. I have too many obligations here in Chicago to leave today. Henrietta or Emily can't handle this crisis by themselves. You're the man of our family now; it's your responsibility. You must be there to take charge of our family's interests and reputation. Who knows what kind of mess those local-yokels may make of this situation?"

"Okay, Mom, let me see what we can work out. No way can I throw some clothes in the car and leave my obligations. Is it really necessary for me to leave tonight?"

Madelyn screamed, "Yes!"

Nathan responded, "Here's my situation. Let's work with it. Okay? We're in the middle of finals. I have an exam to give this afternoon, and then a study group, one more final after that and papers to grade before I'm free. The absolute earliest I could leave is late Thursday night. Friday morning would be better. I feel sure I could change my weekly Friday thesis conference with my professor until next week. Wouldn't Friday be good enough?" He swallowed down the lump in his throat, as it began to sink in. His mother expected him to obey, not question.

"Heavens no! You must rearrange your schedule."

Soho paced nearby, wanting attention and Meow Mix.

Madelyn continued. "My brother was murdered; stabbed. There's a question of who killed him and why. I expect you to find the murderer."

His reporter's radar piqued, still wasn't convinced *he* had to be the one to go and do this work. Occupied with her own agenda, Madelyn wasn't too worried about the inconveniences she asked Nathan to make.

"Mom, remember I'll be in Grovetown for the summer working on my thesis. I can find out details then."

Madelyn's reply was as harsh and tedious as ever. She said, "Of course you can then but you should be there now. Did the police find any clues? What was the murder weapon? You have to find out everything the police know. Did he have a will? You have to go now! There's so much to do. I don't know how I'll be able to cope. I want to shop for some new things for myself. Of course, I want to buy appropriate ensembles for your aunt and your sister. Both are sure to need something in fashion. I won't be embarrassed because we look like riff-raff. I'll pick up something for you at Neiman Marcus, too. You'll need a new suit, and you *will* wear socks. I don't approve of your style of dress at the university."

They chatted for about fifteen minutes more, or rather, she chatted at him. He heard all about her accompanying his stepfather on a business trip to Geneva and then Rome. She was careful to report all of their side trips and excursions, including several late suppers at the United Nations Park near Lake Geneva.

His mother turned her conversation back to the trip to Grovetown. She said, "My intentions are to stay the weekend at the only respectable place in Grovetown, the Goodnight Bed and Breakfast. We'll drive the Caddy of course." She dwelt briefly on her concerns about how she could adequately impress her old high school acquaintances.

Nathan finally put the phone on speaker mode, all the while, his mother rambled on about her personal life. His chief concern was feeding his hungry cat. Soho rubbed his lower legs going in and out. His cat's purring was so loud he wondered if his mother could hear the cat's voice. The red tabby expected all of his needs attended to at once. His cat's green eyes demanded his breakfast.

He fed his cat and put water on for coffee since his hands were free. Barely listening to Madelyn, Nathan's mind wasn't concentrating on his mother's trivial meanderings. He wondered what happened to Uncle Gussy. Later he would call his father, Raymond, the editor of the *Grovetown Tribune* to find out the details of Gussy's death. He thought, *when is Mom going to shut up? I should remember the Ten Commandments about honoring one's parents.* After a few more comments that were insignificant to Nathan, Madelyn said her good-byes with a last command. "Get down there now!"

Now able to address Soho, "Finally, I can go on with my life. I think if I have to talk with my mother any longer, I'll go stark raving mad."

"Meow!"

He decided to shower first and then eat from the Chinese doggy bag full of leftover chicken lo mien with his freshly made coffee. He thought *I do like cold Chinese noodles.*

He sat in his cozy leather chair overlooking the duck pond relaxing after his mother's lecture. Nathan observed a colorful mallard amongst the flock. He needed to go to the university to see his professor. He would have to pack and find the plaid cat carrier for Soho, as well as, food and litter for his companion's journey.

Nathan collected his green sweats from the large walk-in closet, dressed, and put on his comfortable running shoes. He wouldn't be able to participate in the upcoming Indianapolis Mini-Marathon with the unexpected changes in plans for the weekend. He completed the training sessions in March and April. He wanted to be one of the 30,000 some participants in the ever-growing popular event.

He decided to run the mile over to the Notre Dame campus, where he hoped he could catch his professor. The professor was his mentor and adviser on his Ph.D. thesis. Nathan was studying small town investigative reporting. He needed to meet with his professor monthly during the summer to assess his progress; Nathan thought he should inform him in person about his family situation. A phone call or email was too impersonal. Nathan was relieved to find him there. He related the news about his uncle's death and his need to go to Grovetown immediately.

Nathan said, "My uncle's life has always been an enigma so it's not unusual that there would be a mystery concerning his death."

"I'm so sorry. How did he die?"

"He was stabbed. Nobody knows why anyone would want to kill Uncle Gussy. I know very little about the situation. Of course, I'm going down for the wake and the funeral. I'll probably be gone for a week or so. I'll come back to meet with if you if you have the time. Then I'm going to pack for the summer."

"I can schedule whenever you come back to campus. Please let me know. We can use that meeting as your May monthly review on your thesis."

Nathan said, "Thank you.

"Was he married? Did he leave any children?"

"He never married nor had any children. He was a bit of a loner. There are two sisters, my Aunt Henrietta, and my mother, Madelyn. My grandparents are deceased. He served in the Army in Vietnam."

"Tell me more, if you'd like."

Nathan continued, "After Nam, he did construction jobs. He was a carpenter and woodworker. He loved to whittle. He gave my sister and me a carved Noah's ark and the figures when we were born. He used oak. You should see the intricate detail in each animal. He worked hard remodeling old houses in town. He farmed the old Trinkle family farm. He was colorful and sometimes a little odd. He always wore bib overalls and a plaid flannel shirt. Apparently he seldom used the bank, so the talk around town was he stashed lots of cash."

Intrigued by Nathan's description, the professor commented, "Your uncle does sound like he was quite a character. Did he live in town or on his farm?"

"He chose to live on the old family home homestead with his dog, Buddy. Uncle Gussy was very private about his life. Perhaps his death will lead to a revelation about some of his idiosyncrasies."

Nathan proceeded to the door to leave. The professor said, "I'm so sorry you've lost your uncle. I'll certainly have your family in my thoughts and prayers this weekend. I think your summer will be a busy one."

He jogged back to his apartment. Nathan realized how sad and empty Grovetown would be without his uncle. He enjoyed Peony County in the spring. His uncle loved to hunt morel mushrooms. The blooming apple trees were one indication of mushroom season. May Apples and violets were others. Years ago, his uncle taught him the intricacies of the hunt. In addition to secret indicators, he searched for the illusive fungi, using his mushroom stick. Gussy whittled the wooden tool from white birch. He used it to push aside leaves from the mushroom growth. His ritual included singing a short parody of "If I Were a Rich Man." His lyrics were, "If I were a mushroom, daidle deedle. daidle, daidle deedle daidle dide, all day long I'd hidey-hidey-hide, or I'd be a found morel." Nathan sadly laughed at the memory.

They took empty bread bags to hold their delicious treasures. Two springs ago, Nathan and his uncle found about three dozen morels in the woods down by Sinking Springs Cemetery near Deer Fly Creek. Of course, it was a rule you never divulge where you found the rare mushrooms. How he loved to devour the delicacies soaked in milk and egg then dredged with flour and sautéed in real butter until crisp. Thinking about good times, he craved morels and hoped his father had some fresh or frozen. He knew there wouldn't be time to hunt. Also, early May was a little late in southern Indiana.

His mind continued to ramble as he ran back to his apartment. Along the way, Nathan admired the awakening foliage. He thought, *I love springtime in the mid-west. This is when I know Christ has risen!* He reflected upon springtime colors in Indiana. He loved the yellows of daffodils, whites of the paper whites, and purples of the crocus. Nathan prayed, thanking God for this season of renewal.

He was concerned about Gussy's eternal destination. Nathan was a Christian and found Jesus in his high school years during summer camp. His final thoughts about his uncle occupied his mind as he neared his apartment complex. As far back as he could remember, he never recalled his uncle worshipping with the family. Nathan hoped his uncle accepted Christ at some point in his life before he died.

He returned to the apartment where he found Soho in the middle of his morning nap, quietly snoring and tired. His toys were all over the front room. He absentmindedly picked up the tabby's toys and placed them in the toy basket.

I have to get busy. I must call Judy. He wanted to tell his girlfriend he would be out of town for the long weekend. They were in the midst of a ten -month relationship. This was the first time they would be apart for more than a week.

He planned to come back to campus to finish the semester and then pack for the summer in Grovetown working with his father. He expected to see Judy the night before leaving for the funeral. He would see her again when he came back to pack. He would miss her. They usually dated at least once a week and talked quite frequently.

Judy answered on the third ring.

"Hi. Hate to bother you at work, Judy, but something's come up," he said.

"Don't worry about it. I'm not in the middle of anything pressing. What's going on?"

"We'll have to cancel our plans for a few days. Remember me telling you about my Uncle Gussy?"

"I think so. Isn't he that odd bachelor who wears bibs all the time?"

"You got that right. Well, he died last night. My mother ordered me to change all my plans and perform the familial duty of leaving for Grovetown immediately. Someone killed my uncle. A murder."

"Oh, my goodness. What happened?"

"Someone stabbed him. The police found his body in his workshop last evening. As I said, I'll only be away for a few days, a week at most. At least we can see each other tomorrow evening. I don't intend to leave, despite my mother's insistence, until Friday morning. I'm taking Soho, and we'll be staying with my father." He gave Judy his father's home number. "I should go now. I want to call Dad and Emily and eat something before I leave for today's exam."

"Then I'll see you tomorrow at six."

"We can meet at Jo-Jo's." The small, little hole-in-the-wall café off campus was a cozy place. The specialties were giant breaded tenderloins, naked tenderloins, double-decker cheeseburgers, and according to Nathan, the best-ever onion rings.

Afternoon, he finished the rest of his Chinese cuisine with a glass of sweet tea. He decided it was time to get dressed and go to the testing room. The calls to Dad and Emily would have to wait.

4

Nathan dialed the phone. He knew his father would be available. On a Wednesday, he would publish the paper for the next day. His father, Raymond Starks, was owner and editor of the *Grovetown Tribune*, a weekly paper distributed on Thursdays.

Raymond answered the phone on the first ring, "*Grovetown Tribune*, Raymond Starks speaking. How may I be of service?"

"Hi, Dad! It's Nathan. Mom called. She said Uncle Gussy is dead. Murdered? Is it true? How can it be?"

Raymond responded, "Yes, son. Your uncle is dead. The authorities believe it was murder. I'm so sorry. I know he meant so much to you. I believe the showing is Friday night."

"Oh no! Of course, I'll be there as soon as I can. I think I can leave quite early Friday morning for sure. Maybe Thursday night if I can arrange all the details. Mom wanted me there yesterday, but I have such a heavy schedule with exams and all. I can't think of any reason someone would kill him. Must have been an outsider. Everybody in town loved him. May I stay with you? I'll be bringing Soho. I plan to stay through the weekend, come back here next Tuesday or Wednesday to pack for the summer. Then I'll return as previously scheduled."

Raymond looked forward to seeing his son. Nathan was to stay with him this summer. His son's summer goal was to work at the newspaper office researching and gathering material on small town newspapers for his thesis.

"Of course you and Soho can stay with me. I expected to hear from you and Emily. You and Soho will keep me occupied. I won't spend all the time thinking about Gussy. Oh, how we loved your Uncle Gussy."

He pushed back a tear. He realized people would say, *Real men don't cry.* He knew better. *I miss him already. If he were alive now, I'd be calling him to talk about the murder in town.*

Nathan pushed his glasses up off his nose, and continued, "Mother said Emily is staying at the Bed and Breakfast with her and Stuart."

Raymond said, "I'm glad you weren't here to see him. I only photographed his body. His soul is with Jesus; I'm going to miss the old geezer."

"I'm glad you and Uncle Gussy became close."

"Your uncle found Christ and became a whole new person. I was proud to watch his faith grow, and I do have peace knowing he is being comforted by the Lord."

"I'm pleased; I was worried about his soul. At least he's with Jesus. Dad, what do the officials think happened?"

"The murderer repeatedly stabbed him. From the pictures I took at the scene that is what it looked like to me as well. Blood everywhere. I'm afraid they don't know much more. I'm sure there's going to be an intensive investigation."

"Aunt Harriett told Mother the area was sealed off with yellow crime tape. Just like in the movies," Nathan said.

"Of course. Our police called the county sheriff's department, the coroner, and even the Prosecuting Attorney. Whenever someone is killed the authorities require a mandatory autopsy."

Raymond pushed back a tear. "The police aren't sure what could have been used to kill him. When I left, they hadn't found a viable weapon. I stayed long enough to take the requested photos and get the basic details to include in Thursday's paper. The article will be short. I brought poor old Buddy home with me."

"Will the autopsy change the times of visitation and the funeral?"

"It shouldn't. The funeral director schedules around autopsies and other necessary procedures. The showing will be Friday night.

"Did Henrietta make all the arrangements?" Nathan asked.

"Your uncle prearranged with Dyers Funeral Home to handle his final arrangements and from them I learned what I needed for the obituary. Apparently, there are no current photos of Gussy, so I used his Army photo. The Armed Forces always send the first Army photo back to the hometown paper. He didn't like having his picture taken. Well, will you come by here before the visitation?"

"Yes, just long enough to drop off Soho. Mother made plans for the immediate family to meet for supper. Would you please send me a copy of the article and obituary?"

"Sure, no problem, within the hour. You know, Nathan, all the townsfolk of Grovetown knew Gussy well. We all saw him walking about town with Buddy. His dog was always with him. I'm taking care of the poor guy for a bit. I don't know how long he's going to live without Gussy. He seems totally lost."

"Dad, his dog had so many fleas. I remember hearing Mom complain about them. She would say, 'Complements of his constant companion, Gussy and Buddy co-existed with non-paying residents, an abundance of fleas.' Do you remember his pickup truck, Ole Red? Dad, it was the first truck I ever drove. Gussy made me promise not to tell you, but I don't think he'd mind now," commented Nathan with a little tear in his eye.

"Really? I didn't know. Leave it to Gussy to have a surprise or two for me, even now."

"I remember the way he dressed. Those old flannel shirts and overalls. He always wore white socks and those awful army boots."

"The government issued those to him in the 1960s when he was drafted and shipped off to Vietnam. He kept the boots, wearing them ever since. Gussy would say, 'Why buy a new pair when they aren't worn out.' Even though there were holes in the toes and a tear on the right foot separating the leather from the sole he kept wearing them. Duct tape held them together." Raymond laughed remembering his old friend.

"Didn't he play Santa Claus at Christmas?"

"Yes, he did. He hadn't shaved in years, so the long, white beard of his made him look like Santa all year long. In fact, when he played Santa at Christmas, he wore the costume over his bibs. His eyebrows weren't bushy so he used fake ones. The children all loved him, and he really liked those kids. He didn't mind the attention, and he even told me once in a while he noticed a boy or girl who he thought could look like one of his own children if he had any."

"But he never married. Still wonder why. Oh, Dad, I haven't asked how you are," Nathan asked.

"I'm okay, I guess, but these crazy arthritic knees sure give me trouble. We'll talk more when you arrive."

"Are you sure I can bring Soho? Judy could feed him, but she has so little time, with work and all, to come over and spend quality time with him."

"No problem. I'll be happy to have him. I'm lonely without Zack," he replied. Zachariah bin Ezra, his Turkish Angora, died two years ago. His demented Border collie, Molly, had been gone five years.

"I sure enjoy sitting on the park bench where I erected a tombstone for Zack and Molly. In fact, it will be nice when you're here. Hey! You can see the new sulfide marble with the rabbit in it I bought off eBay. I have several new marbles I acquired for my marble collection."

"Yeah, I really like the colorful latticinos and St. Clair spirals."

"Well, you know I've been collecting since I was a kid."

"Oh, I know. I've heard marble stories all my life," Nathan said.

Raymond then inquired how his doctoral program was going.

"I suppose okay. I have five intense study groups I supervise per week. I also teach a class, Grammar for Reporters. They keep me hopping. I help with the Notre Dame newspaper, and some student's underground paper called *The Aardvark*. I often skim the stories to make sure what they've written won't bother people's senses or libel anyone. Nevertheless, we don't want censorship either. I try to keep them on an even keel and not to cross the line."

His father chuckled. "Well, you know college students and their colorful whims. Is the underground paper political, humorous, or plain serious news?"

"It's humorous and satirical," replied Nathan. "Oh, I forgot to tell you. My prof approved the subject matter for my thesis." He continued emphatically and with exaggerated emphasis, "*Small Town Newspapers in a Rural Society and Their Investigative Role.* Working on your Ph.D. is not all the fun and games I thought it would be."

"What a mouthful! We'll need to sit down and discuss the subject. But you know, I really think I should quit using your dime. We can catch up when you get here. Love you, Nathan."

With empathy, Nathan responded, "We'll all miss him. I'll go now and hook up the fax so I can receive the obit. I'll see you at the visitation. Love you, Dad." With the end of the conversation, he hung up the phone and walked to his home office.

Soho, ever faithful, and more like a dog than a cat, woke up, and started following him to the small office. The uniquely decorated office contained the requisite desk, chair, computer, copier, fax machine, and tiny file cabinet along with some unusual embellishments. There were large vertical blinds, an antique over-stuffed chair, and royal blue carpet on the floors. In the middle of the carpet, he placed the Turkish rug he brought back from his exchange college program in Istanbul. He studied the early history of Christianity in the area. The exotic city of Byzantium, now Istanbul was home base. He liked to sit in his overstuffed chair. Attached to the white walls were the colorful Boulanger prints of children on bicycles or trapeze-like swings. He loved the intense shades of blue, red, and turquoise. Nathan's Northwestern University diploma proudly hung framed above the desk.

While the machine received his father's info, he murmured to Soho, "Guess we'll need to take your Meow Mix in some Ball jars. Of course, we'll stash some of your toys in my bag too. Now show me which ones." Soho understood the word "toys." He started nudging his favorites. "Maybe we'll take some cat candy, too."

Nathan puttered around and gathered some blank paper along with his prized Mont Blanc pen and pencil set he received from his grandmother, on his graduation. The Trinkle family tradition was to give a fountain pen to a family member when they graduated from college. Henrietta, Madelyn, Nathan, and Emily all received a German Mont Blanc pen when they graduated. The rumor, put forth in *Shadow of the Wind,* was that Victor Hugo wrote his novels with the black over-sized writing instrument. Nathan considered them utilitarian, not ostentatious. He used his daily. *I wonder if Emily, Aunt Henrietta, and my mother still use theirs.*

Talking to the cat he said, "I always feel more creative using this fountain pen. What if I use green ink when I fill it next?" Soho looked up at him with a quizzical look.

Nathan continued talking to Soho, "I think I can afford to buy a Dell laptop computer to use at Dad's when I go there for the summer. I'll take a few minutes after I receive the faxes and go on Amazon to order one and have it delivered directly to Dad's office." He sat a little while longer thinking about his uncle. *I'm going to miss Uncle Gussy.*

5

Gustafeson Frederick Trinkle
February 19, 1945-May 3, 2005

Gustafeson Frederick Trinkle (better known as Gussy) died Tuesday, May 3, at his home in Grovetown, Indiana. He was born February 19, 1945, in Grovetown to the late Frederick and Marie (Selm) Trinkle. Mr. Trinkle never married and had no children.

The longtime resident, Trinkle owned several rental properties and other real estate in Peony County. He was self-employed working in construction and farming. The community held him in high esteem. His woodworking skills made him well known, especially for his intricately carved boxes found in the hands of many pleased owners. The wife of a former governor proudly owns one of his unique miniature chests.

Gussy was a war veteran. He served in Vietnam. He was a member of the Grovetown Lions Club, and the American Legion. Two sisters, Henrietta Marie Trinkle of Grovetown and Madelyn Trinkle Starks Monroe of Chicago, IL, survive Mr. Trinkle; one nephew, Nathan Frederick Starks of South Bend, IN; one niece, Emily Louise Starks of Indianapolis, IN; and his faithful companion of several years, his dog, Buddy.

Services will be held Friday at Dyers Funeral Home. Visitation will be from 6 pm to 8 pm. The funeral will be Saturday, 10 am, at the River Road Baptist Church.

NEWSPAPER ARTICLE
Long-Time Resident Found Dead

The Grovetown Police are investigating the suspicious death of a longtime resident of the community, Gustafeson Frederick Trinkle.

Everyone called him Gussy. Ken Lawson, a neighbor, went looking for his friend when Trinkle failed to show up for dinner at Lawson's house. He went to the workshop when he heard Gussy's dog howling. He found Gussy dead. When the police arrived, the condition of the site led them to question the circumstances of Gussy's death. They were conducting an autopsy. The investigation is ongoing and more information will be forthcoming."

These articles were published in the *Grovetown Tribune*, the *Peony Courier,* and an Indianapolis major paper.

6

Madelyn, dressed in a red satin caftan, sat alone in her cheery breakfast nook with her cup of Gevalia Costa Rican coffee. She only drank imported limited edition Gevalia made in her French coffee press. The bright nook was painted yellow and furnished with a round, antique walnut table, and chairs. A large window looking east allowed her to watch the birds at the birdfeeder. The yellow was cheerful enough, but the brilliant sun rays flowing in helped improve her dismal mood. She felt sad about her brother's death. She hadn't yet cried. Madelyn didn't grieve. She wasn't a person who showed much emotion. *There will be enough at the funeral.* Death was foreign to her. Her parents died in the 90s, but she had few other deaths in her life.

She called her daughter.

"Hello, Washington Elementary School, Secretary speaking. May I help you?"

"I certainly hope so. This is Madelyn Monroe, Emily Starks' mother." *I love saying my name.* "I have a family crisis. I need to talk with Emily immediately. I'll hold until she gets to the phone."

The secretary knew how to deal with demanding callers. She replied, "Miss Starks is busy with her class at this time. Could I please have your number and she will return your call as soon as she is able?"

Annoyed with the secretary's response, Madelyn repeated her demand loudly. "I need to speak to my daughter immediately. There is no time for me to wait for a return call. If I need to speak to your superior about this, please put her on the phone."

"That won't be necessary, Mrs. Monroe. I'll put you on hold and page Emily's room." Despite Madelyn's abruptness, the secretary admired Madelyn's daughter, Emily, and out of respect for her favorite young teacher, she agreed to have her come to the phone.

Madelyn made other "emergency" calls for her daughter in the past.

Mrs. Brown hoped this would be another useless message.

After receiving the summons and assigning an aide to oversee her students, Emily came to the office.

"Mrs. Brown, who called me away from class?"

"Your mother is on the phone."

Emily calmly picked up the receiver, apologetically smiling at the secretary.

"Hi, Mom, what's up?"

"Oh, Emily, I do hate to bother you at school. However, it's awful! I'm still in shock. Your Uncle Gussy is dead."

Emily gasped. "What? What happened? I didn't know he was ill."

"No, he wasn't ill. He was murdered. I don't know everything. The authorities said Gussy was discovered dead in his woodworking shop yesterday. Henrietta called me last night. She didn't know much except Gussy was dead and apparently murdered."

"Oh, Mom, I'm so sorry. I can only imagine how distressed you and Aunt Henrietta must be. I'll certainly be praying for you both. Please tell me what she said." With a lump in her throat, Emily held back her tears.

Ignoring Emily's words of condolence and request for further information, Madelyn got right down to her details, "I have several appointments to change. and some I'm obligated to attend before I can leave for Grovetown. Henrietta is making all the arrangements for the visitation and funeral. Stuart and I intend to leave Chicago and drive down Friday morning. We're driving so we'll have our new gold Cadillac to drive in the funeral procession. Of course, you and Nathan will ride with us in the procession. Who knows what kind of transportation they might have for the family from the funeral home to the cemetery. I'll arrange for Stuart and me and a room for you at Grovetown's quaint bed and breakfast. Nathan, I presume, will stay with your father so that you can stay with us. We'll plan to pick you up before noon. Supper is at five. We'll have more private time together going at this time of the day. I also plan to bring a couple of new outfits for you, in case you don't have anything appropriate for the occasion. The whole family will eat together at the Falls Restaurant at the Deer Fly Inn before the visitation begins."

Madelyn thought, *I love eating at the Inn by Trinkle Park. The town was correct to honor Christopher Trinkle, our illustrious ancestor, by naming the park, Trinkle Park.*

Christopher Trinkle was the area's only Revolutionary soldier buried at Sinking Spring's Cemetery.

Madelyn continued, "We can eliminate the necessity of us having to eat all the carry-in food bound to show up at Henrietta's house from the neighbors."

Even though she didn't need any new "appropriate" clothes, Emily obligingly agreed with her mother's plans. She learned it didn't pay to waste time disagreeing on non-essential matters. Best to save the controversies for more important issues. Besides, she looked forward to seeing her mother. She wouldn't mind the accommodations and arrangements. *I know Mom means well, but she is so aggravating, treating me like a ten-year-old.*

Continuing non-stop, Madelyn said, "I'm sending Nathan down earlier to be close to the investigation. I told your brother as head of the family to leave immediately. Today! Nevertheless, he seems to have conflicts and thinks Notre Dame is more important than finding his uncle's killer. Nothing the police investigator discovers should be allowed to blemish our family's good name. Surely, your father will have the decency to play down the story in the newspaper. After all, he should want to protect the reputations of his own children, even if he is no longer a part of the family." She glanced down at her Cartier gold watch. Madelyn concluded somewhat perfunctorily, "Oh, I have *so* much to do. We'll see you early Friday. Goodbye, dear."

The school secretary heard Emily's side of the conversation; she was quick to add her condolences. Emily was quite appreciative.

"Would you please contact a sub for me for Thursday, Friday, and Monday? Do try Mrs. Vogel, if possible. She does such a great job with the class. I'd better get back now and relieve my aide. She's probably finished the spelling test by now, and I didn't tell her what to start on next. I hope my class has been behaving." Emily paused to gather her thoughts. "Thank you for your help and kind words. I'll stop in after school to check on my replacement."

The rest of the day went well for Emily. Teaching was certainly where she felt God wanted her to be at this stage of her life.

Emily was relieved when she found out Mrs. Vogel would be her replacement. She took her lesson plans for the days she planned to be gone home to prepare them for her sub.

Emily returned home. She found Mr. Whiskers, her gigantic Maine Coon cat, pouting because his mistress was later than usual. His stomach informed him of his need for a bowl of sweet delicacies. A fresh bowl of cold water with the ice cubes floating in it would help his mood—so much fun to play as he drank. He used his thickly furred paw as a cup to drink. She usually had time to cater to his wishes, but tonight, she seemed to have misplaced her priorities. Emily performed the required cat-owner duties. She petted him. She opened a can of gourmet food. She refilled his water dish, without asking how many ice cubes he wanted. She talked while he ate, but without asking about his day. She ignored him. Mr. Whiskers was further confused when Emily didn't start her meal.

7

Glenn worked late into the night on his painting alibi. He brought an appropriately paint-smeared shirt for his brother. His hair, face, hands, and shirt bore evidence of his submission to Margaret's instructions to paint. The shirts reeked with perspiration.

The brothers arrived at the donut shop. The popular meeting spot was always a pot brewing with gossip, and it was at the boiling point this morning. Everyone had to speak their take on the murder, those who should be a suspect, and the investigation of Gussy's demise.

The morning clientele consisted mostly of the town's menfolk. Rarely were women customers at the donut shop. A ladies coffee group had regular tables at the café. At the donut shop, early risers were on hand to help open the doors and to claim their favorite seats. They were the first to choose from the fresh pastries, made in-house daily. By the time they left for their jobs, carrying a full coffee mug, it was eight o'clock when the lazier, retired men meandered in to visit. These latecomers were more interested in the leftover morsels of gossip than the donuts.

Many of the customers greeted Jake. He was on top of all the Grovetown news, and everyone was anxious to get his take on the matter at hand, Gussy's murder. He indifferently waved them off looking instead at Solomon, Richard, and Glenn. The twins were late as usual.

Jake loudly greeted his friends and brother "Hi, guys. Anyone know any more about last night?" Then he whispered to his buddies, "Did you find your letters and destroy them completely?"

The three men responded positively as they cautiously perused the tables closest to them for inquisitive ears. Jake decided it might be best to quietly discuss his investigative assignment. He would question the twins later.

Jake continued, "Remember Gussy owned the old hotel in town, as well as the buildings on each side. All three buildings are empty downstairs, with renters upstairs. Gussy stored stuff in locked rooms on the first floors, as we all know he was a hoarder. Glenn, you and Richard, I want you to check out all of the downstairs areas of the hotel and next-door buildings. Look for any papers linking Gussy to any of us. There might be details of our past projects. Make sure you look for copies of the letter he sent us. Tonight will be the best time. Make sure you can substantiate your activities tonight. Take care not to leave any incriminating evidence behind. Report back at the Legion when the Legion is closed for the night. Use the back door. Understand?"

Richard answered for both of them. "We'll work it out, Jake. Hopefully, we'll find something." He took a swallow of his coffee. "I think I'll go around the room to chat and see if I hear any juicy clues to help us out. I'll tell my alibi story, too, just for good measure. Talk to you guys later."

Richard got another donut and began to make the rounds. He had a good memory for details. He would remember any good crumb of gossip. Carol, the waitress, noticed Jake and Glenn for the first time. She rushed to their table, embarrassment evident on her face. She took great pride in her service to regular and prominent clients. She approached the table. Carol noticed the conversation ceased. "Morning fellers. Want the usual today?"

Glenn answered the question of the finely manicured waitress. "I can see you've been to Rosie's Beauty Shop, Carol. Lookin' good!" She smiled and nodded a thank you.

"Bring us all the full deal and a stack of pancakes with lots of red raspberry syrup. Oh, and some hash browns and plenty of hot coffee. Don't forget Tabasco Sauce for the eggs. I'm hungry after painting all evening. Jake's treatin' today, so put it on his tab."

Carol quickly placed the order and brought a pot of steaming hot coffee.

Jake quietly addressed his best friend Solomon next. "You and I can check out the old school building Gussy converted into offices and apartments. I'll meet you at the Legion after dark. We can ask the staff to give us privacy, and then slip out the back way. With any luck, they'll never know we've left." Solomon agreed.

The twins took their time reaching the table. They were busy greeting everyone they could. The two shared their regrets at the loss of their good pal, Gussy. The brothers told as many people as possible about their relaxing afternoon, fishing at Tucker's Bridge before Gussy's murder.

Jake acknowledged the guys and kept his voice low. "You're late this morning. Richard and Glenn have their marching orders. I want you boys to check out the vacant downstairs of Gussy's hotel. He stored all kinds of stuff in those locked rooms. You'll be looking for papers linking any of us to Gussy. Don't miss anything looking important. Bring your findings to the Legion, after closing tonight. Remember, be careful and don't leave any signs of a break-in. Everyone knows you both frequent the rooms there for your-ah-social purposes so your presence won't look strange."

The two agreed. They often spent time in the rooms for R&R. Hopefully, they would both be successful in finding a hotel companion and could combine work with pleasure.

"Did you both handle the letter?"

Donnie was quick with his answer. "Already took care of the situation easily. Toilet is flushing well, if you get my meaning." Donnie turned to Billy Bob. "How about you, brother, got good flushes at your place? If not, I could lend you a plunger!"

Everyone nervously chuckled at his attempt at sophomoric humor.

Jake smiled when he saw Officer Green coming in the door. "Deputy. Pull up a chair." He summoned Carol and added an order for Ron.

"Ron, we've been hoping to see you. You arrived just in time. Hope you don't mind. I ordered a full breakfast for you. Gosh, you must be tired from all your hard work. I hope you can sit with us. Eat and rest."

"Well, thanks, Jake. You always seem to know what I need. Crazy! Won't slow down till we solve this murder."

Jake made sure Ron was comfortable. He seated him so his back was to the rest of the patrons. He then loaded his coffee with cream and sugar, handed him a couple of his favorite donuts, lit his cigarette, and even allowed him a few sips, bites, and puffs, before he began grilling the deputy.

"Well, Ron, we want you to know how much confidence we have in the job you're doing. Didn't ever have anything like this happen when I was chief. Don't know if I could have handled it."

"Course you could, Jake. Everyone in town still sings your praises about what a good cop you were."

Jake continued to elevate Ron's ego. "I'm sure Chief Petty is relieved to have a competent deputy like you. At a time like this, we never can have enough good workers, you know. I'd certainly be willing to help out in any way." With sarcasm Jake thought, *Ye'll, sure. I know you'll do great and find the perp ole Green Ron.*

Ron could barely contain his excitement at the prospect of working with the well-known Chief Achsworth. "I could really use your help, Chief. The coroner sent the body to Indy for the autopsy. They are going to use special techniques for discovering evidence and Chief Petty accompanied it. They assured us the body would be back in time for the funeral. We couldn't find an obvious murder weapon, so seems they're gonna make some kind of mold of Gussy's stab wounds so they'll have it to test against possible weapons. Ain't that something? Like things they do on the TV show, *CSI*."

Glenn joined in to further Jake's plan of becoming helpful to Green Ron. "Jake, why don't you help Ron? I can finish painting by myself. Your aid in clearing up this mess is more important. Our good friend Gussy deserves the best."

Jake acted as if he was in deep thought, considering his decision. When Carol delivered the full plates, Jake steered the conversation to the subject of alibis. He began with his own. Carol was serving. Donnie's eyes roamed Carol's body from head to toe and gave her a wink, remembering their tryst. She tried not to blush.

"Deputy, I do want to help you, but I would feel guilty leaving Glenn alone on our joint project. I was helping him paint their guest bedroom. I felt sorry for Glenn when he has to paint all day. His wife ordered him to do it while she was out of town. How many times have you painted this room, Glenn?"

"Why, only the fourth. How do you like this color, Ron? I'm beyond any opinion anymore. Nothing seems to satisfy her."

Ron seriously studied the paint smears on the brothers' shirts before answering. "The color looks good to me, but you know I'm not married. And I never had no woman over to the little house I rent from Gussy. I live with the paint I've had since I moved in." Ron tipped his hat on the back of his head. *Oh my, Gussy's gone.*

He said, "I feel awful now because I kept bugging him to paint the living room of the house." *It's terrible he died like that! I hadn't even thought about loosin' my landlord. Wonder who I'll give my rent to now?* "He came and collected the cash rent every Friday, like clockwork."

"Well, Deputy, my brother's assistance is more valuable to you. Margaret will have to be satisfied with the work I put in on the painting we did yesterday. I'll try to finish it before she gets home."

Jake said, "I'll do it. Now Solomon, why don't you tell the deputy where you were during the murder yesterday? I'm sure it would help with the investigation to know where people were when Gussy was killed."

"Glad to, Deputy. Richard and I were together yesterday afternoon in the county seat. Every so often, we go into the surrounding towns to check out the prices of our competitors. We spent the whole afternoon there. We got back in town just in time for our poker game when we heard the news about Gussy."

Richard wanted to add credibility to their tale, so he told some other "facts". "By the way, Ron, I think I still have my price check paper in my pants' pocket. Yeah, here it is." After handing his notes to Ron, he turned to Solomon. "Do you have yours on you, Solomon?"

Solomon searched his pockets to no avail. He remembered he hung his jacket on a peg inside the door. He excused himself, retrieved his jacket, and returned with it and paper in hand. "Yep, I still have mine, too. I can't believe something like this happened to good ole Gussy. Goin' to miss him hangin' out around town and at our poker games. Why if he was here now I'd be so happy I think I might even let him win a game."

Everything went silent for a few moments as each thought of life without Gussy.

Donnie finished eating, while Billy Bob eyed the stack of toast and jelly.

Jake addressed the non-eating twin. "Donnie, what were you doing yesterday, when did you hear the news about Gussy?"

Donnie sat up straight as he took the spotlight. "Billy Bob and me didn't have no jobs to do yesterday, so we decided to go fishin' down at Tucker's Bridge. Was a beautiful day to be out until it started a-rainin', but not so good for fishin'. Din't catch anything worth keepin'. Just threw 'em all back for another day. We heard all the commotion, saw yellow tape, cop cars, and a crowd. Don't recollect who told us. I feel terrible about poor Gussy. Who'd want to kill him?"

Billy piped up, "Yep, we both felt real bad. Woulda thought to take Gussy with us. If we had, he'd probably still be alive. Feel real bad."

With the food all gone and the alibis served, the boys felt this was a successful morning.

"Well," Deputy Ron said, "I'm done with breakfast, so I'd better get back to the station. I'm supposed to look at the crime scene again. I also need to check Gussy's phone records. Just too much to do. Jake, I'd be honored to have your help. We could brainstorm. I'm sure the Chief will be pleased you offered your expertise."

"Glenn, sorry to desert you and the painting, but glad you've excused me. Fellows, have a productive day. Will see y'all here in the morning, if not before." Jake smiled. *I think this is going to work quite well.*

8

Henrietta was in a state of shock. *Has it been only hours since Raymond told me about Gussy? I feel like it's been days since he said he was murdered. Murdered! Who would want him dead? They say he was stabbed. This is Grovetown, not Chicago. Why Gussy? Oh, dear God, please help me. He was my only brother but why him? Why now? Only weeks ago he accepted Jesus. I know you are sovereign, but I need you to direct me. I'm your servant, but it's hard.* Henrietta sighed. *Jesus, I pray You'll be with me.*

Dr. Mattox offered her Xanax to quell her anxiousness, but she said, "No, God will provide the calm I need. I don't need drugs."

She knew it would be a difficult day. With a cup of hot Jasmine tea in hand, she sat down in her chair by the phone. She thought ahead to her morning meeting with Simon Dyers. She'd previously gone for callings and funerals at Dyers Funeral Home, but never for the reasons, nor the business she had to handle today. Her father made the necessary arrangements when her mother died; Gussy handled their fathers. She tried to keep her thoughts from drifting to what the authorities would be doing to Gussy's body. The clues an autopsy might reveal were essential in solving the crime, but realization didn't make it easier. She prayed for strength. *Dear God, please help me to understand your will.*

Henrietta picked up the phone and dialed. When Pastor Todd answered, she cried into the phone, "This is Henrietta. Will you please go with me to Dyers? I know you have other parishioners in need. However, is there any way you could come and help me? My appointment is at ten thirty. I have to arrange my brother's funeral. I've prayed for God's help but the task He's given me is like climbing up a never-ending staircase. I know God doesn't give us anything we can't handle, but I feel weak and need God's support."

Pastor Todd said, "I'll be right over. We'll talk then."

Henrietta finished putting her breakfast dishes on the drying rack. She quickly left the kitchen when she heard the doorbell. Opening the door, Henrietta collapsed in her minister's arms. In tears, she tried to talk but she couldn't think of Gussy without crying. She couldn't even say Gussy's name. She was so overwhelmed.

Pastor Todd hugged his parishioner. "Let's sit on the couch and talk for a few minutes. Were you able to sleep much last night?"

Henrietta couldn't reply. The tears kept coming. Finally, she calmed down enough to wipe her eyes with the handkerchief she pulled from her pocket.

"Thank you for coming. I didn't sleep well at all. I'm sure I must look a sight today. The calls from concerned neighbors continued until late last night. They began again early this morning. The never-ending interruptions affected my devotions and prayer time. I've decided to try to work them into my schedule later today. I think God will understand. I'm so glad you'll be with me this morning. I don't think I could do it all without help."

Knowing her well, the minister suggested, "Henri, let me pray with you before we leave." With tears in her eyes, Henrietta nodded and thankfully bowed her head.

"Father, we thank you for being our comforter. We ask you to be our solace now to the family Gussy has left behind. Be with us in the decisions we'll be making. May we glorify you through our plans. We ask for a speedy resolution to the search for the truth of Gussy's death. We leave these things in your hands. In the name of our Lord and Savior, Jesus Christ, Amen."

The two sat silently for a minute longer before departing for the funeral home. Pastor Todd helped Henri lock her house and go down her front steps. Normally she would have scoffed at such help, but this day she gratefully accepted his attentions. The morning, exceptionally beautiful, consoled them as they enjoyed the short walk. Sharing a companionable silence each thought about the evident arrival of spring and God's renewal of his awesome world.

Simon Dyers was cordial to the pair as they entered his domain. He, normally very personable, seemed even more so in his business environment. He accompanied them to a charming office, decorated in tones of mauve, blue, and ecru. Henri, impressed with the tasteful antiques, admired the masculine mahogany desk dominating the room. Upholstered Queen Anne wingbacks were available for the clients. She noticed a mahogany library table on one wall holding a lovely oil lamp, Bible, and silk roses. A beautiful floral painting hung above the table. She recognized it as an original from a local artist in town.

Simon began the meeting with a touch of hospitality. "Henrietta, may I offer you and the pastor something to drink? We have tea, coffee, colas."

"Tea would be fine, Simon. Thank you."

Simon turned towards the minister. "What about you, Pastor Todd? Would you like your usual black coffee?"

"Thanks, Simon. You know me so well. As usual, I didn't have time for my second cup this morning."

They sipped their drinks as the funeral director opened the lone file on his desk. His demeanor became very respectful as he began to discuss its contents. "Henrietta, as I told you earlier this morning, Gussy prepared the arrangements for the event of his death. I must tell you, I was as surprised at first, as you were when he approached me to make his wishes known. I've known your brother for as long as I can remember. However, while drawing up these plans, I saw a different side of him. He seemed to have made some changes in his life. He wanted his funeral service to reflect his actions. He gave you the option of making alterations. But after you hear his plans, I doubt you will."

"I've seen a difference in Gussy, too. I guess I shouldn't have been surprised to hear he'd already spoken to you. I'm sad but anxious to hear his plans. I know he couldn't have imagined they would be needed so soon." She sighed.

Simon looked at the papers and began to explain. "Gussy specifically asked for Pastor Todd to be the speaker. He said he'd be talking to him about the message he wanted. Did he?"

Henrietta looked hopefully at the pastor as he responded positively. "Yes, Gussy and I discussed a lot of what he would like said on his behalf when he passed. I can assure you, I will speak, as he would want, I feel my actions to be a privilege, and I want to publicly reveal Gussy's newly found faith, as well as his desire to be accountable to those he may have hurt in some way during his life." Pastor Todd patted Henri's hand as he spoke. She felt assured he would. She looked forward to the comfort and hope his forthcoming words promised.

Simon continued down his page of notes, "Gussy decided on the coffin and vault to be used." He handed a picture brochure to Henrietta. Simon indicated the model and continued. "His love of wood led him to choose this oak one. He came several times a week embellishing it with his carvings. He finished last month. He did such a stellar job, I know I could have kept him busy customizing others."

The rush of emotions overcame her. "I'm speechless. He was such a talented carver. What a humbling thing to do, preparing something so beautiful used only at his death."

Simon revealed yet another surprise. "Gussy loved his dog Buddy. Since the dog is so old, Gussy made plans for his burial, also. He carved a beautiful box for the entombment of his companion's cremated body. If Gussy died before Buddy, he asked me to contact the vet and have Buddy euthanized. Gussy said Buddy is so old, and he thought he would be making the decision to put Buddy down in the next few weeks and was close to making arrangements himself. He wants the dog's ashes placed in the small box he made out of oak and then placed inside his own coffin, for the viewing and for the burial. The controversy of burial of ashes of a pet with the deceased is full of opinions. The practice may not be legal. I find the action a little unusual, but I believe nothing is inappropriate. I've done it before and will again for Gussy."

Tears filled Henri's eyes. She was amazed at these new revelations into her brother's character. "I'm fine with Gussy's wishes, except about having Buddy euthanized. I want to talk to a vet and Raymond first. Of course, we'll do all we can to honor Gussy's wishes. Raymond was kind enough to take Buddy home with him, so I'll talk with him. Buddy might not last long without Gussy, but I'm not ready to end his life."

Simon continued, "I understand. We have a day or so before you have to decide. Now, in regards to Gussy's burial, his normal, everyday clothes were his choice. He said he wanted to be sure Jesus knew who he was and wasn't sure if he wore a suit, he would be recognized. He wanted his bright yellow flannel shirt and bib overalls. Rosie will do the cosmetic work. She is quite efficient and respectful in fulfilling her duties here. I'm sure she will make him look as natural as possible."

"I don't think Madelyn will approve, but if these are his wishes, it's fine with me. Gussy had a style of his own. He wore bib overalls and flannel shirts all year no matter what the weather. I may not tell Madelyn, ahead of time. I may let her see him on her own."

Simon said, "The pallbearers Gussy requested are his poker partners: the four Achsworth brothers, Solomon Edwards, and Richard Farwell. I'll contact them today. I'm sure they'll all agree."

"I know all his friends will cooperate with you on behalf of Gussy. Did he specify where he is to be buried?"

"Yes, he purchased a plot at Sinking Springs. He wanted to be close to all the relatives there, especially Christopher Trinkle, the Revolutionary War hero. If I may deviate and relate the conversation when Gussy mentioned Christopher. Henrietta, Are you familiar with Christopher Tinkle's story?"

"Not completely. Gussy was working on the genealogy of the Trinkle family. He hadn't informed me what he's found," she said.

Simon related, "Gussy told me Christopher was from Virginia. His brother, Stephen, owned a large plantation—cotton and tobacco. Stephen owned many slaves. When Gussy looked at census records of the time he discovered Stephen fathered two children with two slaves—a boy and a girl. I forget their names. Your brother seemed to think Christopher traveled west and settled in Indiana after the Revolution, because of his brother's involvement with the women slaves. Interesting theory."

This revelation didn't shock Henrietta. "How fascinating. I must tell Madelyn, Nathan, and Emily. I'll continue studying the Trinkle family. I knew the family came from Germany. I know I'll discover much more of the family's history."

"Let's continue with your brother's wishes." He consulted his notes again and said, "Gussy picked the memorial cards he wanted. This is a sample. There is a picture of a beautiful oak tree in the foreground, with a field of sheep in the background. He wanted the text on the inside to be the 23rd Psalm. He said this particular scripture become a favorite of his and would be an encouragement to his family and friends. Additionally, he asked for Ecclesiastics Chapter 3, verses 1 through 8. You know the part starting with, 'To everything there is a season and a time to every purpose under the heaven,' and to use the King James Version. He said it was lyrical. He also filled in the biographical information, except his date of death. If the information meets your approval, I'll have these printed and ready for the visitation."

"I do like his scripture choices, of course. Most certainly have them printed. You decide on how many, you know much better than I, what is appropriate. Do you need any official papers, like a birth certificate?" Henrietta was worried because she had no idea where to find such papers. Gussy was never been one for keeping very good records.

"Don't worry," Simon reassured her. "Gussy gave me copies of everything we need. He told me he loved you very much, and showed it in his actions. Grovetown will miss him. He was a fixture in the community. Do you have any more questions?"

Henrietta was touched; she could only shake her head as she wiped her eyes with her hanky.

Simon allowed Henrietta a few moments to compose herself, before he brought up a potential problem. "We'll plan to proceed with the times we've previously decided. Visitation will be Friday evening and the funeral on Saturday at ten. I don't see any reason to concern you, but I feel I must mention the autopsy may take longer than we've allowed. Usually, there is no problem. I can offer some alternatives. If Gussy's remains are not back in time, we could proceed with a closed, empty, casket. The other option is to postpone the arrangements. We would have to wait until next week. Grubby and his cemetery crew don't work on Sunday. I'll let you make the decision."

Flustered, Henrietta conscientiously said, "I'd better call my sister. This decision will affect her more than me. May I use your phone?"

"Of course. Would you like some privacy?"

"You're kind to offer, but I may need you to help answer any questions she may have."

Fortunately, Madelyn answered the phone on the third ring.

"Hello, Monroe residence, Madelyn speaking."

"Hello, Madelyn. This is Henrietta. I'm at Dyers Funeral Home. I wanted to give you the details on the visitation and funeral. We also might have a problem."

"What's wrong now? I hope it won't take too much time as I have too many things to do to deal with the arrangements. I have to shop." Madelyn made it clear she couldn't be bothered with the details of Gussy's services.

Henrietta apologized for the intrusion. She gave Madelyn the time for the visitation on Friday night and the funeral on Saturday morning.

Madelyn said, "You mean it will take two days? In Chicago, we have the showing an hour or two before the funeral on the same day."

Henrietta said, "No, it *will* be two days. Gussy made all the arrangements. He paid ahead for all services with specific instructions."

Madelyn continued to protest the two-day services.

Nevertheless, in regards to the times on Friday and Saturday, Henrietta stuck to her decision. The visitation would be one day and the service the next. Grovetown wasn't ready for the new city-style all services on one day Madelyn wanted. The uncertainty connected with Gussy's death was enough to deal with. No one needed changes in funeral traditions. This wouldn't be an easy conversation.

"I also want to consult with you about the possible need to change arrangement times. If Gussy isn't here due to the autopsy taking longer, we can postpone the services." She didn't mention the possibility of a closed casket. Henrietta continued, "A postponement would be no bother for me, but since you have a busier schedule, as well as travel time, I wanted to check with you before changing anything."

"Well, of course, I have a busier schedule than you. I cannot and will not rearrange my societal obligations again. I want the services to be at the earliest time. I insist. Can you handle the matter alone? Or do I need to talk to Mr. Dyers myself? Can't we do it in one day?"

Biting her tongue before responding, Henrietta replied, "Thank you, but it won't be necessary. I'll inform Simon of our wishes and pray Gussy's body will be here in time. We have Friday night and Saturday morning. Sorry to interrupt your busy day."

They agreed they would see each other again on Friday and said their goodbyes.

"I'll plan to see you at five Friday for our early supper at the Inn. Remember they have a fabulous buffet starting at four. Goodbye, Henrietta."

After Madelyn's quick goodbye, Henrietta returned the phone to Simon.

Simon and Pastor Todd heard Henri's side of the conversation. Neither man was surprised when she announced the decision to proceed as planned. Simon said he would take care of it and everyone stood to leave.

They walked home in silence. Henrietta marveled at the surprises she heard. She felt at peace. Gussy loved her, and demonstrated his new faith through his decisions.

The pastor helped Henri into her house, sat her down with another cup of tea, moved the phone close to her, and placed her Bible open on her lap. He left as Henrietta's phone rang. Pastor Todd gently closed the front door. His upcoming sermon was on his mind, as well as another prayer for Henri and the family. As calm as it seemed now, he was sure the next days and weeks would have revelations not as comforting as those would this morning. He knew his knees were going to get a workout before everything would be resolved.

9

Henrietta's busy day left no time to sit and process the circumstances of Gussy's demise. She spent her morning at Dyers Funeral Home and on the phone. She settled down in her favorite overstuffed chintz chair after her stressful morning. The telephone resumed its insistent ringing.

Who in town is left to call me?

At home and at the library Henrietta still used landlines. She squirmed in her chair and turned to reach for the phone. She was glad Pastor Todd was thoughtful enough to bring her the hallway phone. *I think I'm going to buy one of those carry around with you phones. I'm not spending money on a cell phone*

In an almost answering machine tone, she said, "Hello, this is Henrietta, speaking."

"Hi, Aunt Henri. I'm so sorry to hear about Uncle Gussy. How are you coping?"

Henrietta immediately recognized her niece's voice. "Oh, Emily, dear, it's so comforting to hear from you. I'm doing as well as possible considering the shock. Everyone in town has been so caring and concerned. The Lord provides in many ways. The neighbors keep bringing food. How are you doing, dear? Will I see you at the services?"

"Of course I'm coming. Mom called this morning. I've been lucky enough to make plans to be away from school on Friday and Monday. If you need me longer, I'm sure I can arrange for more time away before school's over for the summer. I know you've made the arrangements and will have more to do. Do you need me to do anything? I hope Uncle Gussy left most of his affairs in order. However, Mom said that's probably not the case. Oh, and she wants to know if he had a will." Emily sighed.

"I don't know about a will. I spent this morning with Simon Dyers arranging the services. Your Uncle Gussy's personality changed so much since last Thanksgiving. He found Jesus and became a different man, a Christian. How I wish you could have seen what happened after he accepted Christ as his Lord and Savior. He didn't make it known all over but you could tell something happened to him.

"Now about the funeral, he made all the arrangements a few months ago. I'm sure he never imagined he would die this soon, but he wanted to have these decisions made way in advance. I think Gussy knew Jesus would come for him soon. You know, one wonders if we should all have this mindset to prepare for our own deaths. He knew exactly what he wanted, even down to carving motifs on his own casket."

Emily sighed as her aunt continued. "I received a call from Raymond. Apparently, Buddy ran away last night. Raymond found him but Buddy died on the way to the vet… This all seems so unreal, because your Uncle Gussy arranged for Buddy's cremation. He wanted Buddy with him in the casket, and he had made a casket for his loyal friend. I think Gussy knew Buddy wouldn't survive without him. I'm glad I didn't have to make the decision to euthanize Gussy's friend, because I don't think I would have been able to do it, even knowing Gussy's wishes."

Henrietta paused to take a drink of her tea. "I think the situation is as under control as possible. I'll be fine. My Savior, Jesus, is with me. Let's talk about you, Emily. How are you doing?"

"Not well. How unsettling and unreal this all seems. Everything is bothering me. I can't help but wonder who would kill him. I can't imagine a murder in Grovetown, and the victim would be my uncle. This situation is incompressible. I keep hoping I'll wake up from this nightmare. I'm so sorry." She started to cry.

Her aunt wished she could hug her.

"I can't say enough about how much I'll miss Gussy. He always was a loner, but recently he seemed to make a concerted effort to spend more time with me. We were closer than we were since childhood. I felt he was preparing to share some of his long-held secrets with me. I guess I'll never know him or how he thought. Death certainly has a way of ending many things."

Emily said, "I'm sorry to hear you still have unresolved questions, but it does sound like you re-established a stable relationship, Aunt Henri. I'm glad you did. I'll see you on Friday. Mom has made reservations for me at the B&B in town. We're to have dinner at five at the Inn. I'm sure she's invited you. We'll have some time to share before the busy visitation begins. I'm sure you're exhausted from all the heart-heavy chores you've been doing today. I hope you'll be able to rest well tonight."

"I'm exhausted, dear." She sighed. "Your mother wanted to have visitation and services all on the same day, Saturday. She said having a combined showing and service is the way they do it now in Chicago, but this isn't the big city. I insisted on two days as Gussy planned. As far as the arrangements, I was going to ask Pastor Todd to officiate, but, much to my surprise, Gussy worked it out too."

"Well, I'm glad to hear you've been relieved of some of the pressures of planning. It's so very stressful. Don't let Mom intimidate you. She still thinks she can control the people in her world. I know you lead a very successful and fulfilling life, and I certainly hold you up as someone I want to emulate." Emily's call waiting rang, and disrupted her thoughts, but she didn't answer it. She thought it was rude, crude, and nasty to interrupt one call to answer another. "I'm so looking forward to our summer together. I'm happy I'll be coming to help you update the library. How much fun we'll have working and playing. I know Mr. Whiskers will enjoy exploring his new environment. How kind of you to offer to open your home to both of us."

Henrietta felt suddenly negligent. "Oh, Emily, I've been so inconsiderate. Would you like me to keep Mr. Whiskers here with me this weekend? I don't think the Goodnight Bed & Breakfast will allow pets."

Emily then felt embarrassed. "No, Aunt Henri. I didn't mean it as a cloaked plea for an invitation to bring Mr. Whiskers. He will be quite content in his own world. I have a darling neighbor girl, Jennifer, who's 'adopted' Mr. Whiskers. I'm going to ask her to pop over often. Since it's a weekend, she'll have many opportunities to disrupt his quiet domain. Oh, when I come we'll have to discuss how Mr. Whiskers came to live with me. He's quite a special companion."

Emily laughed as she thought about the power Jennifer would have over Mr. Whiskers' kingdom. *A little shake-up in his routine will do him good.*

Henrietta joined in her laughter. She'd heard enough stories about

Mr. Whiskers to imagine some of the displeasure he would have when a well-meaning child threatens his authority. "I look forward to meeting him over the summer vacation."

Emily sensed her aunt's tired demeanor and decided to end the pleasant conversation on a light note. "I'll let you go so you can, hopefully, get some rest tonight. I'm looking forward to seeing you Friday. Oh, by the way, Mom is bringing us new clothes. I'm sure we'll both be very appropriate in our new Madelyn wardrobes. I love you, Aunt Henri, and see you soon."

"I love you, too, dear. I forgot to tell you how helpful your father has been through all of this. Raymond gave me an advance copy of the paper write-up so I wouldn't be shocked or embarrassed by its contents. He'll be so glad to share time with you and Nathan this summer."

10

Chief Petty and Deputy Green needed to question some more people to see if anyone could be a suspect. They still didn't have a motive let alone opportunity, means, or weapon.

Green chain-smoked most of the morning and was already on his second pack of cigarettes since breakfast. Green thought, *I bet today will be a busy one.*

The duo checked with various renters of Gussy's properties. They discovered all of them were up to date on their payments. The two officers could find no obvious motives amongst them.

Deputy Ron asked Chief Petty, "Don't you think we should also interview the neighbors?"

"Of course. We've already talked to Ken Lawson, Gussy's next-door neighbor. But, let's see what more he can offer. I'll ask the questions, you keep notes."

They drove over to Persimmon Lane, and parked at the old house. The back of the house led down to Deer Fly Creek. They walked towards Lawson's ranch-style brick house with blue shutters on Persimmon Lane. The widower kept a well-mowed yard with a small garden of spring flowers—tulips, daffodils, and lilacs all in bloom. Ken was expecting the town police, but not today. He knew the police liked to discuss the details with a witness several times.

Ken wasn't worried as he planned to tell the police all he knew again. He would share all the information he knew about Gussy from his years of being his neighbor. Ken saw the two officers walking towards his house from a window.

He greeted them before they reached his door. "Hi guys. I knew I'd see you again. Please come in and have a seat. Would you like some sweet tea? I made it fresh this morning."

Chief Petty said, "No, thanks."

Green said, "Yes, please."

When Lawson returned he asked, "What would you like to discuss today? I think I covered it all, but is there anything else? Do you have more questions?"

Petty said, "Just a few to tie up loose ends. Can you reiterate what you were doing and what you saw and heard the day Gussy was killed?"

"Well, like I said, I was here at home in my favorite chair, reading and watching the news on CNN while waiting for Gussy to come for dinner."

"I know what you said when you found him. What were you doing earlier? Say, let's start in the morning."

"I usually awake at seven a.m., and eat my cereal with a banana. Then I sit in my easy chair and read the Louisville daily newspaper. I always shave and finish the rest of my toiletry after reading the paper anywhere from nine to ten. I watch the morning news on CNN. As far as I recall yesterday was the same. Before lunch, I went outside to weed a little in my garden. I wanted to beat the rain."

"You said you saw someone who looked like a bum. The person was a man I assume. Could you tell us more? What was he wearing? Hair length? Time?" the Chief inquired further.

"He was built a lot like Ron there but he had hair tied back in a ponytail; his clothes were a t-shirt and jeans. I didn't notice his shoes."

"Was anything written on his t-shirt?"

"There was, but I wasn't able to read it—just a bunch of letters. He looked kinda like a bum."

"What time did you see him?"

Ken answered, "About oneish. After lunch I watched some news on TV."

"Do you remember what you watched?"

"No, just news. I don't think there was a real crisis. There was another roadside bomb in Iraq. The usual and a bunch of political talk. CNN is my favorite station. I watch it all the time. I think I'm a political junkie. You know how they repeat a bunch of the news over and over. I'm afraid I don't remember the exact content. Nothing stands out in my mind. Just the usual banter."

"Then?"

"I had to walk uptown to the post office and grocery. I needed more cheese to put on top of the spaghetti."

"When did you get back home," Petty asked.

"It must have been close to three thirty. I had to get the spaghetti sauce on."

"Was anyone with you?"

"No."

"Did you talk to anyone uptown?"

"Well, the postmistress and clerks at the grocery. I said, 'Hi,' to a few people, but nobody special. I didn't hold any conversations."

Ken Lawson stood up. He said, "I need to stretch my legs a bit. My titanium knee from replacement surgery locks up if I sit too long." He walked to the window and saw the neighbor's dog. "Oh, I forgot. Scruff—he's a Border Collie. I heard him barking, and I think Buddy was barking too, making quite a racket. I know their barks but I didn't check on them. Those two, as big as they are, seem afraid of storms. Figured they'd heard the thunder and knew a storm was coming."

"What time?"

Ken replied, "I think it was after lunch."

Ken paced in front of the window as he continued. He noticed Deputy Green. *Why he's on his third cigarette!*

"You said you heard Buddy later. Again what time?"

"I was finishing up the sauce leaving it to simmer and waiting for Gussy. He was supposed to be here at five as usual, but he was late. I wasn't too worried. Hoping he had a customer for one of his boxes. He was famous for the carved ones," Ken said.

Petty asked, "Did you see anyone else yesterday afternoon?"

"Yeah, sure did. Remember? I told you about the bum and hearing a woman's voice earlier. I'm sorry I can't be of any more help to you. I didn't know who either was.

The woman's voice was loud. Maybe arguing? I know she didn't sound like his sister or anybody else I knew."

"Can you describe her?"

"No. I only heard her voice."

"What time was this?"

Ken said, "All I know is it was close to five. I was too busy to look."

Later when I heard Buddy howling and whining, the barks seemed different. I felt I should check. Then I found Gussy and called 911.”

Deputy Green noted to follow-up. *Were there any other leads on the strangers in town?*

Satisfied with his responses, Chief Petty ended the questioning. “Well, thanks for your time, Ken. I don't have any more questions for you at this time. We'll be in contact if we need any clarification.”

In the privacy of the car, Deputy Green said, “Lawson didn't appear to have a wealth of more information to share with us than he had before.”

“But his testimony did provide a clear-cut alibi.”

“I don't see Ken had any motive either, do you?”

“There was a small window of opportunity, but a pretty small one. Ken is of minor interest.” They visited several other neighbors, with little success, and stopped for the day.

11

The autopsy report arrived early Thursday morning by fax. Chief Petty and Officer Green found the report upon their arrival at the station. Green read it first and gave his interpretation to the chief.

"The report said stabbing was with a sharp object causing death. There were six stab wounds."

Chief Petty said, "Look, it states the type of wounds 'don't appear to be caused by an ice pick, flat knife, or similar tool.' The wounds are square shaped. Using casting of wounds apparently worked. The coroner thought it could have been an extra-large screwdriver because he says he's seen one or two large screwdrivers matching the description."

Deputy Green, said, "I've seen one similar in Gussy's workshop. There are quite large screwdrivers with square shanks. We didn't find one, though, did we? Access to such a weapon would have been easy. Anyone visiting Gussy would have the means to procure such a lethal weapon, but we found none matching the type of wounds."

Chief added, "The angle of the wound suggested the murderer was above average height, at least five eight and probably right-handed."

With this new information, Chief Petty and his deputy continued the investigation and talked to the local business people again. They were interested in following up on the leads of strangers like the "bum" Lawson saw.

The morning seemed fruitless. Everyone was ready to offer what he or she heard, but not what he or she knew. However, one local business owner had some information, Joe's Gas Stop.

Joe was quite willing to talk, but he had even more questions. He wanted to know, like most people in town, the details about Gussy's death.

Petty addressed Joe, "As you already know, we're investigating Gussy's death. We want to see if you can help us."

"I'll help any way I can. Gussy was a friend. Bought gas here all the time. I fixed his old truck. Don't know how we've kept his junker running all these years. Boy, I'll miss him. He was a good friend, and he spent quite a bit of time chatting with all the other fellers who came in. Occasionally they even smoked a cigar. But, I think it's my coffee bringing them in, Tim Horton's Coffee, quite a favorite brand that comes from Canada. I know a truck driver who brings it into the U.S."

Green got out his notepad and ballpoint pen. He forgot his role as "secretary" while the boss asked questions.

"Joe, we need to ask you some questions. Did you have anybody come to the station that wasn't quite the norm? You know, unusual, the day Gussy was killed?"

Joe thought carefully. "I've been thinking. There was a young guy, twenty-years-old or so. I think he was hitchhiking."

"Do you remember what time?"

Joe blinked his eyes. "It was sometime around two. I was getting hungry, but I didn't think I could run down and get a sandwich 'cause my new worker was late. He was setting up his summer school classes 'cause he flunked those high school tests. Can't graduate in Indiana if you don't pass, I guess. I saw a skinny kid who had an earring in both his ears and long hair in a ponytail. I always notice unusual people. Why do these kids today want to do such things? Tattoos covered both of his arms, too. I saw one looking like a snake. I don't think he had any money to buy anything. Said he stopped to use the restroom. I saw him trying to beg money off some of my patrons. Several people were in here at the same time. Didn't catch his name. Didn't ask either. He was hangin' around for about half an hour. I think he found a ride with the truck driver for Budweiser. You know the one who delivers to the Legion. Seen him around here before. The kid jumped in. They headed north out of town. I don't know the driver's name."

The Deputy dropped his pen and leaned over to pick it up.

"Did he use a credit card?"

"Actually, he did. I'll make a copy for you. Nobody else used one that day."

"Thanks. Could be a help." Green made a note in his notepad to follow-up with the Legion about the truck driver.

Ken continued, "Interesting day, though. Then there was this woman.

Was she a looker!" Chief Mike perked up.

Petty asked, "What stands out about her?"

"The lady didn't buy no gas, but she did get a soda. She paid cash. I remember 'cause she gave me a $50 bill. Usually check those, but she looked like she 'fit the bill'." Joe laughed at his pun. "Put it in the drawer and gave her change. Asked her if she was new to town. She said it had been a long time since she'd been to Grovetown and wanted to know if there was a map of the town available. I told her she could look at one in the phone book, but couldn't take it with her."

"Did she look at the map?"

"Yep, went right over to the phone. Saw her checking out the map. Then she left in a flurry. Didn't see her no more."

The Chief asked, "What time?"

"After four," Joe answered.

"What kind of car did she drive?"

"She caught my eye, but the car didn't. You'd think a fancy dame like her would drive a fashionable and fast car. Nope. She was in a late model silver Toyota."

"Did you notice her license plate? Was it an Indiana plate? One of those vanity plates?"

"Nah. Saw no reason."

"Can you describe her any more detail?"

"Yeah, it was very curious. She was wearing these big sunglasses with dark lenses. You know kinda strange since it was looking stormy."

"Sounds a little peculiar to me," said Green.

"She was quite tall, five foot ten, or so. I thought she might be as tall as me. She wasn't fat. Looked pretty good to me."

Chief Petty was anxious to get a description started, "What color was her hair?"

"You know what, I don't know. She had her hair pulled back and hidden under this big yellow hat. Now I think about it, she was kinda peculiar. I wish I paid more attention."

Mike looked up from his papers and pulled out a cigarette.

The officers left. They returned to the police station to work out their next plan of action and set up interviews with some of Gussy's friends, especially his poker buddies.

12

The poker buddies felt they were ready for Petty and Green to interrogate them. The breakfast meeting happened, alibis prepared, and assignments were undertaken.

Jake, Glenn, Solomon, and Richard presented their prepared statements separately. Each was flawless in their presentation to Chief Petty and Deputy Green. The officers seemed content with the alibis as provided by the men. Chief Petty noted Ron smoked more than half of his cigarettes during the questioning. Deputy Green refused to abide by the accepted social courtesy of not smoking in someone's home. He chose to ignore his boss's requests. He also thought his smoking during interrogations disoriented the suspects.

Jake's anxiousness about the twins' ability to maintain their alibis was well founded. Once apart, their stories had minor contradictions.

Petty continued his investigation with Billy Bob, the brawny member of the twins. "Can you tell me your whereabouts on the day Gussy was killed?"

"Sure. Donnie and I went fishin' together that day."

"Where'd you fish?" probed Petty.

"Donnie picked me up in his truck, and we headed to Tucker's Bridge. He brought some bologna and cheese sandwiches. We planned on spendin' the whole day out there."

"Did you see anyone else at the bridge?" questioned Petty.

"Nope, we was all alone there."

Always interested in a good fish story, Green puffed on his cigarette and asked, "What did you catch? Heard the fish were really bitin' last week. Were they this week, too?"

"I caught a couple catfish and one of 'em almost got me on the hand." Billy Bob pointed to a non-existent scar on his right hand. "Donnie didn't catch nothing. The fish just weren't bitin'. We stayed there all day like we planned. Didn't find out about Gussy 'til we got to our weekly poker game. We were shocked. Can't imagine who would do such a thing here. Must have been someone from out of town. Won't be the same without Gussy."

"Did you take any beer?"

"Nope trying to cut back," he said. He winked at Green Ron, indicating he didn't intend to cut back.

Billy Bob felt satisfied he gave a persuading interview and was happy to show it.

The Chief thanked Billy Bob for his time and told him he'd let him know if they had any further questions later.

Billy Bob left the office. He passed his twin, Donnie, going in for his interrogation. He gave his brother a big wink and smile, assuring him his answers went well in his questioning.

Petty questioned Donnie. "Tell me where you were at the time of Gussy's murder, Donnie."

"I'm not sure what time the murder occurred, but I was fishin' all day with Billy Bob. We met at Tucker's Bridge early Tuesday morning and stayed 'til it was time for our weekly poker game at the Legion. We couldn't believe the news when we heard it from the other guys. Sure put a damper on our evening."

"Did you say you met Billy Bob at Tucker's Bridge?"

"Yeah. He brought some sandwiches to spend the whole day. Salami and cheese. Had heard the fish was really bitin'. We wanted to see for ourselves."

Still wanting to be a part of this conversation, Green threw out the question, "What was bitin' Tuesday?"

"Not much really. A few young bass, but we threw everything back. Nuttin' was big enough to mess with, not even good sized catfish. Thought we'd let 'em grow some more for another time."

The Chief inquired, "Did you notice any other fishermen out that day while you were there? Someone else, besides Billy Bob, who can verify your whereabouts?"

"Na, not that I can remember. Some cars over the bridge, maybe, but no one else fishin'. Probably because the weather looked stormy."

"Well, thanks, Donnie. Know this has to be hard for you, seeing how close you were with Gussy."

"Just want to help anyway I can. I'll miss my old pal. Can't imagine anyone would have wanted to hurt him, let alone kill him. Do you have any good leads?"

"Can't really discuss that with you, but know we're going to do our best to solve this as quickly as we can," responded Petty.

After Donnie left, the Chief commented to his assistant, "Did you catch those discrepancies between their stories?"

"You're kiddin'. I didn't hear anything. What were they?"

"Billy Bob said he went *with* Donnie to the Bridge, but Donnie said they drove separately. Each related the other person brought sandwiches and one said bologna and the other said salami. Their fish stories were about different kinds of fish."

In awe of his boss, Ron stamped out his cigarette and responded, "Wow, you're good at this investigating stuff. I didn't notice nothin' at all. Do you think the differences mean anything?"

"Not sure, but we should certainly check into their fish stories further. They do smell a little fishy. Might be something else there we can catch," mused the Chief.

13

With finals over, Nathan was able to squeeze in last minute errands. He returned home early afternoon with packages. Nathan went shopping on the way home from the university. He purchased a muffin and coffee, ran into the pet store to get Soho's favorite treats and some new toys, and stopped to see Dr. Quinn, Soho's veterinarian. Nathan hoped his furry friend would be fine in the car, but to avoid having a discontented cat screaming all the way to Grovetown, Nathan picked up some tranquilizers for the tabby. Pushing up his glasses, he smiled to himself while remembering Dr. Quinn's interest in getting together for coffee. He politely turned her down, but couldn't help but be pleased. Nathan glanced at his watch, and decided it was time to pack. He found Soho's red plaid carrier and filled some Ball jars with Meow Mix.

Nathan teased his cat, "Personally, I like going to the vet, but you don't really relish the idea." Soho purred as Nathan continued, "Soho, I have a special going away surprise for you, a pack of new toy mice. Look, they have curly tails! They squeak and light up! Smell the catnip! Would you like me to pack them for you?"

Sniffing the mice, Soho meowed to answer, "Yes." Nathan tossed them in the cat carrier, and Soho dived after them.

The phone rang and interrupted Nathan's thoughts.

"Nathan here."

"Hi, Nate! It's Pat. Can you talk a bit?"

"Sure. All I'm doing now is getting things in line for the drive down to Grovetown."

Dr. Patrick Mattox was Nathan's friend from childhood. Patrick and Nathan met in Sunday school, grew up together in Grovetown, and stayed best friends through high school. They attempted to get together whenever they came home from college. Patrick was at I.U. and then in medical school. Nathan attended Northwestern University. Now they each had their own careers, but still tried to keep in touch.

Patrick continued, "Everybody in town is shocked. The people are praying for your uncle and your family."

"Thank you. We appreciate all your prayers. Our family needs them. Well, my mother wants me to investigate the murder. I would rather leave it to the police, but she's so insistent. You could help me search for information when I get there. And I thought we could hang out for a while."

Patrick replied, "I can't even imagine what your family is going through."

"I'm a bit overwhelmed with losing Gussy. I need to clear my head."

"Nate, Deer Fly Creek may be what the doctor ordered. The flowing water, fish, and birds create a peaceful atmosphere."

Patrick said, "Remember the old turtle sunning on a rock. Would you want to go?"

"What about a canoe? Would we need to rent one?"

"No, I have my old canoe, the *Gypsy Gal*, a Grumann. She's in remarkably good shape after all these years. She does have the bump in the aluminum from hitting those rocks at the falls. Remember?"

Nathan replied, "Yeah, I know. We didn't have the angle right. Would we have time this week?"

"We could go after the funeral. I've already changed my schedule to accommodate Gussy's services. In addition, I want to be there for you, whatever time you need. How about after church Sunday afternoon, we head to the creek. It'll be like the old days, even to the deer flies."

Nathan appreciated his friend's attempts at lightening his mood. "Oh, those flying nuisances! The creek got its name correctly."

"Yeah! I'm so allergic. I get huge welts from those annoying little devils. What are you doing now?"

"I'm packing for the few days I'll be in Grovetown." Nathan continued talking to Patrick, while packing.

"Nate, have you read the new novel by Cussler?'

"Not yet."

"Well, I started *The Black Wind.* You can have it when I'm through."

"Thanks, Cussler's my favorite, too. I'd like to keep talking, but I'd better get a' moving. Got a date tonight with Judy."

"Sure, I'll see you soon. Seeing you again will bring back so many memories. I'm so sorry about Gussy."

Nathan finished packing. As he packed, he noticed the wooden Noah's Ark sitting in the corner. Gussy had whittled the Ark and figures before Nathan was even born. Gussy was proud to tell Nathan it was Nathan's first present. Nathan smiled as he remembered playing with the animals, two by two. This Noah's Ark seemed always to be in his life. *Believing Gussy is dead is difficult.*

He then got ready for his date with Judy.

Nathan and Judy sat eating Jo-Jo's famous hamburgers. Their conversation remained neutral, much to Judy's consternation.

Judy watched as Nathan pushed his dirty blond hair out of his baby blue eyes, while adjusting his glasses. *Nathan is so handsome. He doesn't even realize how handsome he is. I really want to his wife. I thought he would have asked me to marry him somewhere more romantic, but we come here so often. This is our place.*

She said, "Why don't we go back to your place and watch a movie. Then we can talk for a while."

Nathan agreed to the chat but declined the movie. He told her there was too much to do.

Judy'd visited the apartment before. She said, "There Soho goes again, acting like a puppy. Meeting us at the door like we've been gone forever."

Nathan greeted the cat, picked him up, and replied to Judy, "He always greets me this way; and then he follows me around. We have a system, don't we, Soho?" Nathan scratched Soho behind the ear and placed him gently on a chair.

She sighed. "Animals are so special. I wonder if they have souls or is their behavior is all instinctive."

While they talked about souls and heaven, Nathan's thoughts returned to his uncle. *I know Uncle Gussy's soul is in heaven with Jesus.*

"Judy, Mom wants me to find out what happened in Grovetown."

"What can you do?"

"I don't know."

"How long do you think you'll be away? You are staying there for the summer, too. Please don't be gone too long. Why don't you leave a little later for your summer trip? I hoped we could spend some time together before you leave."

Judy was interested in steering the discussion to personal matters. She expected Nathan to cement their relationship. *I want the subject to be about us.*

Nathan replied, "Right now I expect to be gone no more than a long weekend. I don't foresee there'll be any reason to stay longer. I'll return to South Bend to finish some details. However, I'll be returning to Grovetown as planned for the summer. I have so many distractions right now: Gussy's death, my thesis, my family, and my job at the school."

"Oh, Nathan, you know how important you are to me, and I know this thesis is your life's work right now. I've tried hard not to be demanding and give you the space you needed. But, I want to be with you more, not less!"

Nathan saw the tears were falling down her face. "Oh, Judy please don't cry."

He kissed her tears away.

She continued, "Please, don't leave me. I know I'm demanding, but you mean the world to me. I can't imagine not seeing you all summer."

"I'll see you next week before I pack for the summer. We'll have dinner. We can have long distance phone dates while I'm in Grovetown. When I come back, we'll talk about the future."

"Nathan, why can't we talk now? I'd rather discuss all our future plans before you leave for the summer."

Judy thought, *I'm so ready for a permanent relationship.*

"Judy, it's premature. There's too much on my mind. We'll talk about us after the summer is over."

Judy dreaded the summer. She hoped he'd miss her as much as she'd miss him.

She would bring up the subject next week at dinner. She knew Nathan would be back for the Notre Dame run in June, but unfortunately, she'd planned to visit her family in Boston. Nevertheless, Judy had a special surprise for July. Nathan told her about the lively Fourth of July celebrations in Grovetown.

Judy decided. *I'll surprise him on the Fourth of July.* More than ever, she wanted to be the special spark for this year's festivities.

Judy remained silent, deep in thought. *Ten months of dating, and two and a half years of being friends, is surely enough to decide on a permanent relationship. We kiss and even play around, but we have never been intimate. I know Nathan loves me. I'm ready for more in this relationship. I want him so badly! My biological clock is ticking. We should be making some headway towards a permanent commitment. I don't know what's wrong.*

She wanted the evening to end romantically. Therefore, she took a direct move toward the physical side of their relationship. She hugged him, holding on with desperation. Nathan embraced her back. He put his arm around her soft body. She responded by nuzzling up to him. Nathan kissed her fully on the lips.

Judy thought, *See. He's attracted to me. I want to go farther. I've had other boyfriends who wanted more than a kiss and a hug.* She decided to express how she felt.

"Oh, Nathan, I love you. I want to be with you, forever."

He answered her not with, "I love you, too." Instead, he said, "Judy, I have such fond feelings for you. We'll talk again when I get back from the funeral. But for now we must pray. For the sake of any future, we need to ask God's guidance. We must find His will for us. Judy, will you pray with me?" She agreed.

Nathan took her hand and prayed, "Oh, Jesus, please guide us to find your plans for our relationship. Give us the power to ignore our physical desires until your will be known. In Jesus' name we pray."

They said in unison, "Amen."

14

Permelia was not a happy camper. She was certain something was missing from her life. She celebrated Beltane, a Wiccan ritual, a few days earlier. In her sophomore year, she took a course in comparative religions, where she learned about the ancient religions of the Celts and Wicca. She learned the basis of these pre-Christian religious traditions, originating in Ireland, Scotland, and Wales. She was attracted to the Wiccan tenets of celebrating nature, use of natural remedies, and recognizing the cycles of the sun, moon, and seasons. Wiccans believe in the Goddess, not God. She became active in a small group, the Spider Coven.

She met Steve Garcia at a fraternity party in her senior year. They were married in the Catholic Church. They couldn't have a full wedding mass with Holy Communion because she wasn't Catholic nor ready to convert to the Catholic Church. She kept her coven activities secret, but still attended clandestine meetings with her Wiccan "sorority."

The Beltane Feast or fertility festival is an important day in the Wiccan faith. Beltane Eve usually falls around May 1. Permelia invited Steve to join her at Beltane because her "sorority sisters" were having a party. Her son, Robbie was conceived on Beltane Eve.

She thought, *Did Steve realize what Beltane was?* Steve joined the Marines and died in Afghanistan after Robbie's birth. She moved back to Grovetown after he died. Robbie turned four this year.

She continued clandestinely in the Craft of Wicca but placed her young son in CCD religious classes at the local Catholic Church. After his birth, Robbie was baptized Catholic because of his father's faith.

Now as a sole practitioner, not a member of an organized coven, she was free to follow the tenets loosely. She did just that. She performed her full moon celebrations along with all the other Wiccan holidays, Summer Solstice, all Hallows Eve, Lamas, and Winter Solstice, alone.

She pondered some of the basic beliefs of Wicca: The term "Wicca" means the "wise ones." "Do what thou wilt but harm none," they would say. They believe in Reincarnation. Living in harmony with nature is important. Belief in the seven-fold law means what you do unto others would come back to you seven fold whether good or bad.

This Beltane, Permelia decorated her altar with early spring flowers from her garden, including peonies, one of her favorites. She purchased some lovely yellow roses from Melissa's Posey Shoppe. She built a bonfire in what would become the middle of the sacred circle. Purifying herself with water and salt, she cast the circle using her black spider athame. A leather case held her athame, a two-sided dagger with a pentagram engraving. Permelia used her crystal ball to invoke the moon goddess. She called on the elements of Fire, Water, Earth, and Wind to help her and requested their powers to join her in the circle ritual. Her heart wasn't in it. Still, she danced along with the chant. As the power rose, the chant gradually changed with the flow of the words. The Cone of Power in place, she tossed the flowers into the flames, proclaiming, "So mote it be." Bread and wine finished the service. She opened the circle. Although the ritual went well, she felt empty. Her life was at a standstill and void of purpose.

Permelia thought, *Do I believe in Wicca anymore? I don't know. My son is good. My business thrives. My garden is plentiful. I should be happy, but I feel so vacant? I have both old and new friends yet I feel alone and unhappy. Where am I in life? I should be content, but I'm not.*

Permelia recorded the results of meditations, dream interpretations, and Tarot readings in a journal, A Book of Shadows, writing with an old sterling silver Parker fountain pen in amethyst ink. Her last Tarot reading came up with the Death card in the future position. She interpreted it as meaning a significant change was coming in her life. *What change may happen? Will the change make me happy?*

Permelia thought, *I know I'm doing the correct parenting thing by taking Robbie to church.* He was learning to play with the other children, as well as receiving an introduction to Christianity. She remembered the sad story of a friend, another coven member from the past. Her coven "sister" told her the tale of her daughter and the "Jesus rabbit." She related, "It was very embarrassing when someone asked her four-year-old daughter who gave her an Easter basket." Her little girl replied,

"From the 'Jesus Rabbit' who comes out of his hole on Easter morning bringing baskets of candy and eggs to good little girls and boys." This revelation of confusion made the mother think her child needed religious training. The mother immediately enrolled her daughter in a Pentecostal pre-school.

Permelia said aloud, "I don't want Robbie raised a pagan."

She, herself, used the Church for both business purposes and social contacts. The Church provided an excellent cover for her Craft practices, along with an opportune place to meet students for her yoga, ballet, and belly dance classes. Many of the women were also customers for the healthy herbs thriving in her garden. She discovered church dinners were occasions to socialize. *Why, there's going to be a pitch-in this Sunday night.* She enjoyed being in the choir and being accepted as a fellow comrade in music. However, she didn't feel comfortable in some of the discussions of faith.

So what am I going to do? Who am I? What do I believe? Where am I going?

Her discontent grew like a menacing weed.

Permelia called a fellow Wiccan from the Spider Coven. Her Wicca "sister" answered. After the usual greetings, she said, "Oh, Deborah, I feel so totally lost."

"I'm so sorry. Are you still grieving for Steve?"

"Yes, I miss him terribly, especially when I see his face in Robbie. That horrendous night when two Marines came to my door was the worst thing ever to happen to me to hear the words of Steve's death. I know others go through the rush of feelings when they hear a knock, but I never dreamed it could happen to me. I feel like I live on an island far away from all civilization. I feel quite estranged from the coven."

"I understand."

"I wish I'd been with the Spider Coven May second, for Beltane, I missed sharing Beltane night with Steve. Oh well, there will come another Beltane and who knows?"

"At least you're considering celebrating Beltane in the old way. Again someday."

"Did you celebrate by yourself?"

"Tried to, and I missed the Full Moon Esbat in April. I was too tired after teaching yoga and ballet."

"What did you do to celebrate Beltane? Were you skyclad?"

"No. The night *was* cold, but the real reason I wasn't *totally* nude were the neighbors. Even with a six-foot privacy fence and being only five foot one, I didn't want anyone to see me naked. After all, my next-door neighbor *owns the* town beauty-gossip shop. I didn't want to shock Grovetown."

Then she explained the other details of her ritual.

She shared a good laugh about the dress or no dress. Deborah explained her celebration. "We had strength when we cast the circle to draw down the Cone of Power. Everyone was so energized feeling the presence of the Goddess. Why we even danced around a Maypole. I practiced alone for a while after you, and the others moved away. I submitted the necessary yearly papers with the State of Indiana to keep our status as a religion. I recently found some new Wiccans, and now, I'm in the process of training a young woman. She is so excited and anxious for her year and a day of training to end, with her initiation. Perhaps you could come to the celebration."

Permelia replied, "Make sure you let me know when and where and I'll check my calendar. I remember going through my initiation."

Permelia then changed the subject. "We had a mysterious death here Tuesday night. Emily and Nathan Starks, my old high-school friends lost their Uncle. He was murdered."

Deborah exclaimed, "Oh my!"

"I'm not sure how I'll feel talking to Emily and Nathan. Any death brings back sad memories. I'll see them when they come to town for the funeral. Oh, I just thought of Robbie. I noticed the time. I must get going. Pre-school is over for the day. We must talk more often. Please let me know the details of the upcoming initiation."

Her "sister" replied, "We'll talk again soon. Blessed Be!"

15

Emily's school was out for the day. She finished her errands and made it home in time to see the school bus drop off Susie, Emily's ten-year-old neighbor, at the corner of their apartment building.

Emily walked over to Susan's mother's apartment across the hallway. She wanted to ask Evelyn if her little friend could watch Mr. Whiskers for the few days while she was gone. Emily knocked at her neighbor's apartment, smiling as she overheard Susie talk about her exciting day at school.

"Well, hello, Emily. How nice to see you. Please, come in."

Evelyn and Emily were both elementary school teachers and shared several stories over the time they lived near each other. Emily respected the experience of her neighbor and often asked for her help in dealing with challenging students.

Evelyn continued, "Was there anything special you needed today, or did you pop over because you had a little extra time?"

Emily sadly replied, "My uncle, down in southern Indiana, died unexpectedly. I need to leave this Friday morning for the visitation and funeral. I should be back early Monday evening. I wondered if Susie would watch Mr. Whiskers."

Susie overheard the conversation from the kitchen. She ran into the hall proclaiming, "Of course! I will if mother will let me. I can feed him before and after school. On the weekend, I can play with him lots! He loves to lie on his back and have his stomach rubbed. Please, Mom? Say, yes!"

"Of course I knew she would want to, and yes, she may. Your cat will be in very good hands."

Evelyn expressed her condolences to her friend. "I'm so sorry to hear about your uncle. What was the cause of his death?"

Emily responded, "The authorities said he was stabbed."

Evelyn exclaimed, "Stabbed! How terrible!"

Emily replied, "I don't know the particulars. Details are sketchy. The police said murder. I hope they know more by the time I get down there. Uncle Gussy was the older brother of my mother and Aunt Henrietta. He never married. He was a farmer and carpenter. He loved to whittle and was very good at it. He made my brother, Nathan and me Noah's Ark sets when we were born. My animals are slightly larger than his are and made from maple, but most people think they are identical. I cherish them."

The women continued to talk, but Emily knew she still had a lot to do before she left for Grovetown. "If it's okay, I'd like to take Susie home with me now to give her instructions. She'll be back home in a few minutes. I'm sure in plenty of time for supper and homework. I'll leave the key with you when I leave."

"That's fine, Emily. Supper is about ready to come out of the oven. Why don't you stay? I'm sure you have lots to do. I hope having dinner here with us will save you the time and mess of fixing something for yourself. Please join us. My husband has to work late."

Emily agreed to return with Susie for the evening meal.

Emily encouraged Susie to join in the conversation by asking about her plans for the summer. Susie pleased Emily asked, replied, "I'll be going to Girl Scout camp, church camp, and playing softball."

After dinner, Emily volunteered to help load the dishwasher. Evelyn insisted she go home. In the morning, Emily called the school to see how the substitute was getting along with her class. The secretary answered, "No problem."

Missing her beloved class, Emily surmised, "I guess I could have come in today. since I won't leave until tomorrow. But there's so much to do—shopping, cleaning, packing, and so on."

"Emily, our prayers are with you and your family. Have a safe trip and we'll see you on Tuesday."

She thought of all the tasks she needed to do. Emily decided to clean her apartment. She remembered what her grandmother Trinkle said, "Always leave a clean house when you go away, and wear clean underwear!" She took care of her messes; next, she tackled the litter box. Mr. Whiskers wanted a clean litter box every day.

Emily warned the white cat, "Now, you be good for Susie this weekend."

As if understanding Emily, the cat blinked his emerald green eyes in response. He started toward Emily's bedroom. Seeing his intentions, Emily was quick to warn him. "Sorry, Mr. Whiskers. I'll soon be packing my suitcase in my room. I know you like to play in my suitcase as I pack, but you might prefer to stay on your chair tonight. Sitting in your chair you'll find it quieter here than in my room. I have much to do. I'll put you there, all cozy with your pillow." Emily picked him up, carried him to *his* chair, placed his head on the pillow, and offered a comforting word. "Nightie, night. Eat all those bed bugs you can find, but don't let them bite."

Emily's one bedroom rental was upstairs. The walls were all the standard white, except for the lilac bedroom. The living area sported a modern gas fireplace endearing Emily to the apartment immediately. She liked to light the gas log, cozy up in her royal blue beanbag chair for her nightly Bible study, before reading far into the night in a current novel. Sliding glass doors opened off the living room to a screened balcony. Mr. Whiskers enjoyed the balcony in spring, summer, and fall, but not during the Indiana winter. The apartment was new. She was the first tenant to live there.

Emily decorated with modern furniture, in a light blue upholstery. The carpet was dark blue. She liked the white walls. Her vibrant pictures showed up well. She kept the curtains white, but also brightened the room with colorful pillows compatible with all the blue. Her dining room table had a glass top, set on a wrought iron base. However, she liked fifties items and used vintage Fiesta Ware for eating, even for every day. The colors of the plates and bowls cheered her up. She fully believed in using them, not storing them away for special occasions.

Her vintage collection of the colorful dishware in bright shades was nearly complete. She worried about using the orange-red pieces. An old boyfriend took her to the Purdue University lab. Her friend tested a plate in the red shade for its food safety. She was shocked when the test proved positive for radioactivity. She tried not to use red ones for her cats or her own meals. She used a couple of the other hued-chipped bowls for Mr. Whiskers' food and water.

The laundry room was downstairs in the apartment building. She washed some clothes, threw them into the dryer and returned upstairs. A glass of Diet Coke helped her think what she needed to pack. Her thought, *I don't think this coke will keep me up too late, but will keep me awake to finish what I need to do.*

Emily planned to wear her navy blue, nautically inspired dress with a matching short-sleeved jacket for the showing. She figured her mother would bring her something from Chicago for the funeral. She muttered to herself, "I can dress myself, thank you, very much, Mom." Emily knew she looked smart in the short dress, navy pumps, matching handbag, and a straw hat.

In her bag, she packed a nightgown, robe, something to lounge in, and a couple of sundresses. She rarely wore pants or jeans. Emily admired her new bathing suit. She held it up to herself and studied her image in her full-length mirror. Her suit was a conservative modest two-piece, yellow and orange tankini. *I'll pack it when I go for the summer. I like Victoria Secret lingerie, but I think their swimwear is a bit skimpy.* The swimsuit cover-up came from Victoria Secret, one of her splurges, as did her ankle-length white terry cloth robe. The cover-up was a pale yellow caftan style dress with long sleeves. Orange embroidery decorated the neck and sleeves. The hem was floor length. She thought, *I think I look cute.* She purchased yellow sequined flip-flops and a canary-yellow straw hat to complete her bathing ensemble.

Of course, Emily took her red leather bound journal and her black Mont Blanc pen. She enjoyed writing with a real fountain pen and ink. She packed them as soon as she made her day's entry. Daily journaling was an enjoyable quiet time with pen and paper.

Emily remembered she would need pantyhose for the weekend. She knew her mother expected her to wear stockings. Emily's style of bare legs didn't meet Madelyn's approval, and she knew her brother would have a similar struggle wearing socks. She laughed and thanked God for the distraction her mother's standards would give to her and Nathan this weekend. She finally settled down to do her nighttime Bible studies and prayers.

16

The table by the window, the best seat in the house, overlooked Deer Fly Creek. The flowing waters gave out pleasant sounds as it rippled over the rocks. Madelyn asked the hostess to seat them immediately at the large table, where everyone could see her, and she could see everyone.

She said, "We have several people coming and will need this large table for five." The waitress ushered Madelyn, her husband Stuart, and Emily to the table.

The waitress asked Madelyn, who appeared to be in charge, "Will you be waiting for your guests to arrive before ordering?"

Madelyn was perturbed with her, for asking such a question. "Of course, we'll wait to order, but you can bring water with lemon, and two glasses of white zinfandel for my husband and me. I believe the buffet will be our meal."

The waitress turned to walk away. Henrietta entered the restaurant with a man. Madelyn waved to Henri, and while motioning her over, turned to her husband and whispered, "Of course. Leave it to Henri to bring an extra person to our family dinner."

"Hello, Madelyn."

"You're looking good under the circumstances," Madelyn exclaimed to her older sister.

"Thank you, Madelyn. What a trying time. I'm so glad to see you and Stuart."

Henrietta continued, "Madelyn, I'd like you to meet Todd O'Neil, our church pastor. I thought it would be good to have him here with us for supper before the visitation."

Pastor Todd greeted Madelyn and her husband extending his condolences. He was cordial to Henrietta's relatives who appeared unfriendly or at least aloof.

Madelyn acknowledged him with a slight smile. She was unhappy having an extra guest at dinner. Her sister's taste in clothes displeased her more. Henrietta wore a long black skirt, a white turtleneck, and a black jacket, with black leather flats. She wanted to be as prim and proper as she thought a librarian should be. She carried a large handbag with her necessities: a wallet, hairbrush, small cosmetic bag, Mont Blanc pen, paper, calendar, a novel, and her knitting. Henri carried a book and knitting in case she was required to wait somewhere. The pen and a notepad were essential for notes and lists.

Madelyn looked down from eye contact. *I'm glad I shopped and bought Henrietta some new clothes. Oh well, we'll get through the visitation. She'll look much nicer tomorrow. Such a frumpy, oversized skirt and top and with those shoes. I know Henrietta will like what I bought.*

"Henrietta, I brought you some things from Chicago. When I was out, I saw some outfits with your name on them. I found you a nice navy blue suit, white silk button-down shirt. You'll positively love the small matching wool felted hat. I hope you'll wear them for the funeral. I assume you have a pair of suitable navy pumps."

"No, not navy but I have some black patent leather flats. They should go well with your generous gifts, but you shouldn't have gone to the trouble. Thank you," Henrietta graciously replied. She thought, *I wish she wouldn't spend money on me.*

Pastor Todd addressed them, "I pray all of the funeral arrangements are fine with you. Your brother left full directions for the services. He planned and even paid for everything." Pastor Todd knew finances, and final costs are often topics causing dissension among family members, even those who have the best of relationships.

"Well, I'll examine the arrangements to make sure all is in order."

"Of course," said Henrietta.

All the others acknowledged their appearance with hugs. The pastor smiled and shook Emily and Nathan's hands.

Emily looked becoming in her navy suit dress.

Still, Madelyn complained to Emily, "Your outfit is so plain; I brought you a nice black skirt suit for the funeral with some flattering touches, a slit at the neck and fits beneath the knee. Also a pair of Mark Jacobs' black and white flats. You have the height for wearing flats.

They have a coordinating zebra-striped handbag. I thought you needed a new set of cultured pearls and drop earrings."

Emily nodded, but she felt chagrinned. She didn't like her mother's condescending tone but expected her mother's interference. Though she was prepared, it still bothered her. Out of politeness, she said, "Why, thank you, Mother. I packed black pumps and a matching black leather purse, but I'll try the new ones. I even remembered to bring my new black straw hat with the purple ostrich plume. But Mother, you spent far too much money."

Madelyn responded, "It wasn't too much for this occasion. All of Grovetown will be watching us. We must show them we have a sense of class."

Now turning her attention to Nathan, Madelyn said, "I considered buying you a new suit but I didn't have your size nor time to have you come for a fitting. I assume you own an appropriate suit. I found you a new dark blue shirt with those sharp collars in style everywhere with a matching baby blue silk tie. I'm sure you didn't bring any cufflinks, so I purchased a nice pair of plain 14-karat gold ones. You must look sharp as the main representative of our family. You needed a pair of long socks, to below the knee. I don't want you barefoot in those awful leather loafers you have on. How embarrassing."

Nathan said, "I have socks for tomorrow, but I'll take you up on the shirt and tie. Of course, I didn't bring cufflinks. I don't own any. Well, now I do. Why, thank you, Mom, for being so thoughtful." He pushed up his glasses.

Madelyn noticed Nathan's actions. She grimaced. "Nathan, must you always be pushing up your glasses? What an irritating habit! Why don't you purchase a pair that fit?"

The server arrived with an extra chair. She took drink orders for the table. Emily and Nathan exchanged glances, each happy their inspections were complete. Everyone ordered the buffet, quicker than a menu meal. They ate the tasty ham, chicken and dumplings, mashed potatoes, and green beans.

Conversation centered on Gussy. Madelyn's focus was on her son, Nathan.

"Nathan, you must find out the truth about this murder. Our family's good name depends on it."

"But, Mother, the police will handle it. Besides the local *gendarmes* may not look too kindly on my interference. Besides, I have to work on my thesis. That's why I'm coming back this summer. I'll be so busy with the thesis and my job at the newspaper."

"Nonsense, these local yokels can't solve a dog theft, let alone a murder. They don't have a clue. They'll certainly need help, and you'll have time now the University is on vacation. Your thesis shouldn't take long. Of course, you'll have plenty of time. You'll devote your off hours to the search for the truth. I'm counting on you. The family is counting on you. You have no choice. Emily can help too since she'll be working with Henrietta. You two can't spend all your time working."

Emily interjected, "I have a lot on my hands with the computer programming. How very time consuming it is to revamp the cataloguing process. Let the police handle it. State, county, and local police will do a good job."

Madelyn wouldn't give up. "But you must! I don't trust the detectives to do it right."

Nathan sighed, "Oh, Mother. Of course they can."

Emily said, "I have to spend my time helping Henrietta. I also need time to relax from school. It's been a long year with some of the students being slow in math and reading; I need the time for myself," said Emily.

Madelyn responded with a forceful gesture of the hand. "Well, we can wait until after the reading of the will for you both to start. It'll give the police some time until you return to Grovetown for the summer."

Emily and Nathan sighed.

Changing the subject, Madelyn said, "I understand Gussy planned his funeral. I wonder what songs he wanted. Does anyone know?"

Pastor Todd O'Neil was the one to respond, "Why, of course. Gussy wanted 'Amazing Grace', 'In the Garden', and 'The Old Rugged Cross'. He also wanted a more difficult hymn to sing, 'I'll Raise you Up on Angel Wings.' The fifth is 'I Love to Tell the Story'."

Henrietta said, "I knew he would want old hymns sung."

"You mean we can't choose his music? I'm shocked. I had songs that are more recent in mind. Do we have to follow his wishes?"

Henrietta stood her ground. "Of course we do and we will!"

Madelyn was not pleased Henrietta would challenge her. She said with some vehemence, "Why?"

Pastor Todd intervened, "I shall follow all of Gussy's desires."

"Well we'll see," Madelyn muttered under her breath.

The family members weren't much talkers, and the conversation dwindled as they finished the main course. Today's dessert special was fresh strawberry pie, since local strawberries were in season. The family headed for the family duty at the funeral home.

17

Madelyn insisted her sister and daughter ride with her and Stuart to the funeral home in the Cadillac. Much to his mother's dismay, Nathan insisted on going to his father's house to pick him up to join the rest of the evening's obligations. Todd O'Neil, the Baptist minister, left the dinner alone. He would join the family at Dyers and be on hand for emotional and spiritual strength for Henrietta, and anyone else in need of special consolation.

Madelyn was miffed at Nathan; silence reigned in the Monroe Cadillac. Henrietta used the quiet to prepare for the evening. She looked forward to the comfort and special memories she would share with the callers, as they came to honor her brother's life. She was especially anxious to hear of recent stories displaying the new peace Gussy found.

Pastor Todd would be available to family. His dedication to the spiritual health of the community was uplifting. Henrietta wanted to introduce him to her beloved Emily. *I hope Pastor Todd and Emily have time to learn about each other.* Emily's summer stay would offer many opportunities for them to spend time together. *They make such a nice looking couple.* Being close to six foot, Emily needed a tall gentleman friend like the six foot three Todd. *Yes,* Henrietta thought, *they made quite a striking appearance together. I think they'll both appreciate each other's dedication to the Lord.*

Madelyn dreaded the evening. Earlier on the way from Chicago, she expressed her consternation to her husband Stuart, "Why couldn't Henrietta follow my advice to only have visitation before the funeral service? You know, the coming, socially accepted way to handle funerals is one day. This extra showing is *so* inconvenient."

Stuart nodded showing he heard her comments. He knew it was useless to disagree with his opinionated spouse.

"Grovetown is so behind the times. Those backward hicks need to update their archaic funeral standards," she continued. She rued the idea of seeing all those backward townspeople. She thought, *What could I possibly have in common with them after all of these years?*

She certainly didn't want to hear about their dull lives. Their chit chat would definitely put her to sleep. Her tales of an exciting life after Grovetown would entertain them all, she was sure. She looked forward to seeing their green looks of jealousy about her escapades.

Now on the short trip to the funeral home she put on her "high society" smile. She was ready to wow them with her enviable existence in The Windy City and her "trophy husband."

Stuart preferred to relax and slip out to the local drinking establishment but knew to do so would raise Madelyn's ire. He was an obedient showpiece: an accessory with distinction. He had been guilty of using his beautiful wife as such. The worst part would be watching her as she demeaned her ex-husband. She was ruthless when Raymond was around. Stuart knew his wife could be a broken record when she went into her "impress-mode." *Wonder if she would notice if I stuffed cotton in my ears.* He was tempted.

Emily sadly anticipated this evening. She thought she might learn more about her uncle from the callers more familiar with him. His life was an enigma to her. His gruffness as a young child frightened her, but she came to overlook his demeanor as a teenager. Still, she cherished the wooden Noah's Ark he made her before she was born. She sighed. *There won't be a new set for his great niece or nephew.*

When Madelyn divorced Raymond to marry Stuart, her mother deferred primary custody of Emily and Nathan to their father. They shared hurt and disappointment when their mother not only left their father but also them, for Stuart. The teens finished their school days in Grovetown. They saw Gussy about town daily with his beard, flannel shirts, and bib overalls. He and Henrietta gave the children some additional sense of security.

Her thoughts drifted towards the present and not the past. *I like Pastor Todd. Aunt Henri sang his praises since his recent arrival in town. He seems thoughtful, and not bad to look at either. Yes, I think Grovetown has promise.*

*****

Nathan left the Falls Restaurant at the Deer Fly Creek Inn driving his beloved light green Honda Civic, endearingly called Sham, in honor of his position at Irish Notre Dame. His car was light green, not Kelly green; he felt the diminutive of "Shamrock" was appropriate. Of course, his mother and even Judy thought his humor was demeaning, but his father and sister loved his cleverness.

Nathan looked forward to this evening with mixed feelings: time with his father, sister, aunt, and boyhood best friend, Patrick Mattox. When he finished medical school, Patrick returned to Grovetown as a general practitioner. Patrick was not only competent, but also personable. Patients came from the county seat to avail themselves of the young doctor's talents. Nathan looked forward to spending lots of time with his friend this summer. Their fathers were also best friends.

He reached his dad's home at the corner of Oak and Walnut. Before he could get out of Sham, his dad closed the front door of his house and started toward the car. A stickler for time, Raymond didn't want to be the cause for a late arrival at the funeral home. He was carrying a couple of umbrellas. The weather report predicted serious weather for the evening, severe thunderstorms and possible tornados. This was ordinary for May in Indiana. The sky was already looking seriously threatening and unstable. Raymond knew Madelyn would look down on his two old beaten-up golf umbrellas. He didn't care.

"Soho is certainly making himself right at home." He greeted his son, "He's claimed the dining room bay window. He can easily watch the birds in the trees, as well as the neighborhood squirrels frequenting our walnut tree. I think he's already named them all. He speaks differently to each as they pass by. Don't know what he'll do if this predicted storm hits. Will he be frightened?"

Nathan laughed. "No, way. Soho is fascinated with storms. He might have a different opinion of storms if he'd actually been *out* in one. He's not afraid of other wildlife but then he's never faced an adversary larger than daddy-long-legs. He naively thinks he's invincible. I did hear of a cat killed by a wolf spider. Thank goodness I've never seen one in my apartment."

Raymond laughed, enjoying this time with his son even under the present circumstances. He expressed his mixed emotions about the approaching evening. "As I said on the phone. We became very good friends over the years, especially the last few months. Gussy's newfound faith was such a joy to both of us and made our friendship stronger. Gussy didn't share all of his past with me. He did let me know that because of his changed life, he was dealing with some old issues he needed to resolve. I wonder if it's possible Gussy's new resolve to make things right led to his demise. Who in his past might have been so threatened by his change of heart to kill?"

Nathan, understanding his father's inquisitive nature, responded, "I'm sure you won't rest until there are concrete answers to these questions concerning Gussy's death. I certainly will cooperate with the authorities in any way to assist in finding the perpetrator. However, I've been away from Grovetown for so long I wouldn't know where to start. Mother is certainly pressuring me to investigate, but I don't know how effective I would be. What do you suggest?"

"Well, such a crime in Grovetown is so out of character. We both should keep our eyes and minds open. Everybody is nervous. We need to have a quick resolution."

Nathan sorrowfully shook his head. He hoped the matter was soon resolved before he returned for his extended summer stay in Grovetown."Dad, I've been thinking. If the authorities haven't solved Gussy's murder by the time I get back, do you think we could use our investigation of the murder as part of my dissertation on investigative reporting? Would I be disrespecting Uncle Gussy?"

Raymond said to his son, "Let's hope the police solve my good friend's death by then, but if not, your investigation efforts might provide a hands-own insight."

18

Father and son reached the funeral home. They parked in the area reserved for family. They opened their umbrellas and dashed through the downpour into the building. Pastor Todd was inside. He saw the men as the next car entered the parking lot. The three waited at the door to greet their family. They didn't wait long before the gold Cadillac arrived at the door. One employee offered to park the car, which satisfied Stuart. He wasn't looking forward to a dash through the rain.

Emily upon seeing her father kissed him immediately. Madelyn merely nodded at her ex-husband. Stuart politely shook Raymond's hand.

Pastor Todd greeted and asked the family if they would like him to pray with them before entering the viewing area. All but Madelyn welcomed his request.

"Dear Father, we come to you now. We ask for peace and assurance for the family at this time. We ask you to bring to the minds of these family members and the friends visiting with them, stories of Gussy's uplifting to his memory. We thank you so much for the assurance his spirit is already with you because of Gussy's belief and acceptance of Jesus as his Lord and Savior. We thank you for your presence with us tonight. In the name of Jesus, our Risen Savior, we pray. Amen."

Henrietta was thankful her pastor was there to support her.

The overpowering aroma of floral condolences, still an accepted way of expressing grief, greeted the family. They entered the viewing room containing Gussy's casket.

Madelyn thought, *the local florist, Melissa, would profit well from Gussy's passing with her artful arrangement of flowers.* The family spent a lot of time looking over the floral displays. Many of the callers were there to peruse the donors' cards and offers of condolences.

Henrietta made the first move to the casket. Emily and Pastor Todd were quick to join her. Peaceful grief was evident as she lovingly touched her brother's face. She prayed silently, "Oh God. I'm so sorry to know Gussy's gone from us on earth but so thankful, Jesus, to know he is with you now in Heaven. I'm happy you had the patience to allow him time to accept you as his Savior before you took him to your loving arms. I will continue to thank you until I also join you in Heaven. Be with me tonight to show my faith and assurance in your promises to those who don't know you as I do. In Jesus' name, we pray. Amen."

Emily and Todd spoke in unison, "Amen." The three remained at Gussy's side for a few minutes, lost in their own musings about Gussy's life.

The men stepped aside to make way for Stuart. He noticed Madelyn's reluctance to approach the casket. Stuart took her arm and guided her there. Of course, Madelyn loved Gussy. He *was* family, but his lifestyle *always* upset her. His dress and actions constantly embarrassed her. How could he have been raised in the same upstanding Trinkle household as she was? Gussy would never embarrass her again. She also would lose part of her heritage. His choice to be buried in his regular attire: a yellow plaid flannel shirt opened to show a white under-shirt, and those unsophisticated bib overalls didn't surprise her.

She was disappointed Henrietta didn't override his final clothing decisions. He even requested a red bandana to be stuck in the bib pocket. *At least the clothes look clean.* The plaid shirt wasn't faded, and the undershirt was pristine. The denim bibs were stiff. His hanky even looked pressed. Her old friend, Rosie McCorkle, did a nice job on his hair and beard. Gussy held a small beautifully carved box. She knew his handiwork. He was a gifted whittler and carver of beautiful objects, one thing about her brother she always admired. She was proud of the few items she owned. Yes, Gussy in death was as he had been in life. No pretensions for Gussy, even now.

Madelyn thought, *I hate this is the last memory these people will have of him.*

She turned to Stuart, "I know this is going to be extremely boring for you, dear, so please feel free to find a comfortable spot to situate yourself. I believe even this old-fashioned facility should have a break room for the family. Ask one of the employees. If anyone of importance comes in, I feel you should meet, I'll send someone to fetch you. I want to show you off to any of my old friends who drop in tonight."

"Of course I want to meet anyone you want me to know. I think I'll stand over by the grandfather clock. I'll be close enough you can point me out, or wave me over yourself for someone special you'd like me to meet. If I feel like a cigar later, I'll give you a sign and slip outside."

Madelyn commented on the inclement weather. "I doubt if anyone will want to come out in this storm. I certainly wouldn't, if I didn't *have* to be here. Look at those people talking to Henrietta, they look like drowned rats. Look at Raymond, he's taking his umbrella outside. He's probably going to help some of those people come in from their cars."

"Should I help, too? Wouldn't want the locals to think I didn't care about their welfare." Stuart started toward the door.

Madelyn indignantly grabbed her husband's arm. "Don't you dare. The funeral director pays employees for their services. I refuse to have you lower yourself to such a thing. Moreover, think of your suit, it could be ruined. I'm sure your suit is worth a dozen of theirs."

Madelyn turned away from the door thinking her way prevailed, only to see Stuart start forward again, and he continued walking toward the door. Madelyn was relieved to see he was only helping people in the door to remove soaked coats, hats, and umbrellas. She realized these simple acts of kindness would go a long way in proving she'd chosen a good man for her second marriage.

The foyer was extremely busy with all the activity involved in removing wet items from all who entered. Henrietta, Madelyn, and Emily were the only family members. Clumps of visitors gravitated to each of the women. Henrietta drew the largest crowd. She graciously welcomed each by name.

Emily attracted an adoring group of guests. Madelyn heard bits of the conversations surrounding her daughter. All the normal questions a charming young woman has to endure, My, you've grown into such a lovely girl. What are you doing now? Where do you live? Do you have a steady boyfriend?

Madelyn looked up to see a group of women hastily approaching her. She quickly straightened her Pima shawl and put on her most sincere smile. Madelyn realized these drowned- rats were some of her friends from the past. They noisily expressed their condolences and enthusiasm at seeing Madelyn after so many years. She allowed them to babble on for a few minutes before she decided to take control of the situation.

Her friend Rosie gave her the opportunity she needed. "Maddy, you look so stunning. Such a striking outfit! Please tell us, where did you get such a shawl?"

Let us in on your shopping secrets."

Ignoring Rosie's use of her detested teenage nickname, Madelyn graciously answered, "Oh, this old thing? It's called a Pima shawl, copied after a Japanese Ainu textile. I picked it up in Japan when I was in Tokyo with my husband, Stuart, on a business trip. I loved it because it so easily spruces up a simple black dress into a pleasing fashion statement. Did you happen to see my husband, Stuart, as you came in from the rain?"

"He's such a thoughtful gentlemen. He insisted on helping everyone get out of the rain and their wet coats as quickly as possible."

Dottie, another classmate, said, "Oh, yes, we saw your yummy man when we came in. He seems as kind as he is good looking. I always wondered what kind of man would make you leave Raymond. We all thought you two would never break up. Sure looks like you got another winner. Some girls have all the luck. Wish I coulda."

Irritated by Dottie's kind comments about Raymond, Madelyn chose to elaborate on Stuart. "Stuart and I matched each other to a 'T.' Our goals and ideals are so close. Our outward appearances always complement each other. I'm sure you'll be able to notice the black and caramel of my shawl perfectly match the tweed of Stuart's suit. I always attempt to make a fashionable statement and coordinate when we're in an important public setting."

Rosie, the first to close her mouth after Madelyn's revelations, commented, "You're certainly impressive, Maddy. I can't think of another man I know who would be willing to turn the total responsibility of his clothes over to a woman. The closest we have to dress alike is his and her Hawaiian shirts or matching bowling team shirts."

Carol, the waitress at the donut shop, wanted more explanation about Madelyn's outfit. "Maddy, what about your jewelry? Is it from Tiffany's?"

"No, I picked up these gold bangle bracelets in Peru, and these gold hoop earrings and black sling sandals came from Italy. Italy has such great shoe selections. I usually try to make it over there to buy fashionable shoes at least a couple of times a year."

Madelyn glanced across the room and saw her ex-husband talking to a group of town's people. She recognized them as Gussy's poker buddies.

Emily and Nathan enjoyed friends from their youth. Nathan's friend, Patrick, had a lovely woman on each arm. One was his sister, Permelia, and the other, Patrick's new girlfriend.

Interested in the unknown attractive brunette, Nathan teased Patrick. "How does an ugly, boring doctor rate having two such intriguing women as companions? I'm sure Permelia is with you because you're her big brother, but why would this other charming lady choose to be seen with you?"

Patrick chuckled. "Permelia's with me only to avoid being alone. I hope the case with Dr. Baldwin is of a more personal nature." He was pleased to see she responded with a huge smile, not only on her mouth, but also in her beautiful brown eyes. "May I present Dr. Jayne Baldwin? Jayne, this dreadfully mannered man is Nathan Starks. This is his charming sister, Emily."

Madelyn excused herself from the group of women on the pretense of needing to speak with her children regarding family matters. She heard the introduction of a doctor. She saw her break into the conversation. "Oh. Dr. Baldwin, I'm so pleased to meet you. Do you and dear Patrick practice medicine together, or do you have a specialty?"

Patrick and Jayne enjoyed a good chuckle before Patrick asked, "Shall we tell them together?"

"Sure. Ready?" Patrick nodded and Jayne began, "My specialty is," then in unison, "veterinary medicine."

They all enjoyed an exhilarating laugh together.

Jayne went on to explain further. "Dr. Jeffries, getting close to retirement, wanted to bring someone younger to continue his practice. I saw his notice on the job opportunity board at Purdue and decided to check out the prospect. His practice was both farm and small pets. I wanted the same. I visited Grovetown and immediately fell in love with this small town. We both prayed about my decision. I felt God led me here."

"Okay, Patrick, what can you add to this story?" Emily romantically requested.

"I certainly got more from my yearly trip to the vet's this year than usual. Along with shots for Dexter, I came home with a date for dinner, my most expensive vet visit, ever," he sighed.

The visitors at Dyers Funeral Home heard the loud sirens going on repeatedly. Heads cocked as they began talking amongst themselves concerned as to what was happening. Funeral director Simon Dyers demanding attention, said, "Quiet, please. That's a tornado siren you hear meaning a tornado could be imminent or has been sighted. Stay calm. The safest place for all of you is the basement. There are several rooms downstairs. Should be plenty of room for all. Of course, if you wish to leave do so, but I feel staying here might be your best alternative. There are two sets of stairs. Jeremy will guide those in the front area to the closest stairs and will unlock the door. I'll help you to the other set. Just a reminder: the lower rooms are our working areas and usually not seen by the public. Please remember these rooms are our private areas. Please ignore the tools of our trade. One inside room is locked; it's the occupied cooler room; avoid that area out of respect for the deceased. I'm going to take care of Gussy's casket now."

Rosie quickly grabbed Madelyn's hand and pulled her towards the assigned exit. "It's not scary. I go down there all the time to do my job. I do their hair and makeup."

Madelyn wasn't sure she wanted to see Rosie's workroom. She searched the faces of the crowd to catch Stuart's eye. He nodded to her and then proceeded toward the other stairs. Madelyn was quick to take her exit from this guided tour of the funeral home and join Stuart.

Henrietta thought, *I've seen so many storms and tornados come and go. I usually go to the basement at home, but this somehow seems different. Gussy was never upset by storms, even as a child. I guess it's in character for him to stay upstairs tonight, too.*

The group of poker players/pallbearers decided to hurry to their homes or businesses, except for the twins. They thought they would be safer in the basement than in their flimsy trailers.

Permelia seemed upset. "Patrick, would you mind taking me home? I'd feel better being home with Robbie. He's with a sitter."

"No problem, Sis. Jayne, you can come too," Patrick said. Jayne shook her head.

"I'll come right back. If it's too dangerous, I'll be at Permelia's and call your cell. See you soon."

Jayne wasn't particularly happy but agreed to let Patrick take care of his sister and her family. She'd been through several tornado watches and warnings. She knew they were nothing to take lightly in this part of the country.

She told Patrick, "I think I'm going on down. I see Dr. Jeffries over there and I want to make sure he makes it safely. Avoid the cooler room." They were part of the crowd going down the front stairs and were soon enveloped in the exodus of mourners.

Once downstairs, Dr. Jeffries saw Henrietta and told Jayne he wanted to go and be with her during the storm. He politely made his way through the press of people to his dear friend. Of course, he knew everyone in the group, so he spoke to each of them on his quest to reach her. She was quite pleased to greet him when he finally arrived at her side.

His wife died several years ago. Since then, his relationship with Henri had changed. They had always been friends, but he now regarded her as more than a "friend." He was still waiting for the courage to express his feelings to her. He hated to jeopardize their relationship if she couldn't return his feelings. He offered his arm of comfort and protection in the jostling crowd, and she graciously accepted it. They began chatting in quiet conversation, despite the cacophony of sound around them. Many were loudly expressing their fears, and others were boisterously enjoying the unexpected gathering in the cellar, challenging the usual quiet mood.

Jayne, always anxious to increase her scientific experiences, glanced around the room. The "sales" room's outside walls were lined with casket choices. She reached a beautiful oak casket lined in a light blue satin fabric. Other fabric samples were on an attractive display board. She was surprised to see the brazen display of the cost, as well as the shocking cost itself. She tripped over tombstones of all sizes. The cost of some very elaborate monuments shown in pictures was also a revelation to Jayne.

As Jayne continued, she found a clothing display, like a funeral department store. The racks contained men and women's outfits, in varying sizes. She shuddered as she noticed clothes for children, including infants.

Jayne decided to investigate a different room. She ignored the

"Employees Only" sign and tried the door handle. She opened the unlocked door. The room was dark, so she felt along the wall until she found the light switch. When she glanced around the room, she correctly assessed that the room was obviously the embalming room. Now here was a room she wanted to investigate. Almost smiling she looked at the equipment. She felt very comfortable viewing the tools of the trade. They were used for different purposes: hers to prevent from death, theirs to preserve in death.

Nathan caught up with Jayne. Emily was behind him.

"What *is* this room? I don't think I want to even think about happens here," exclaimed Emily. "What's that terrible smell?"

"Embalming fluid," said Jayne. "I couldn't resist examining the working area. I was starting to see what tools they use." She saw a leather case with its instruments laid in regimental order: surgical knife handles and various types of blades, including her favored, practical crescent shaped blade. Jayne also noticed the several choices of aneurysm needles in another case. "Here's one I've never used. This is a tool for guiding arterial and drain tubes into the openings made in the body's arteries and veins. This aspirating pump is also an interesting part of the embalming equipment. I'm not sure about some of this other equipment."

Echoing Jayne's enthusiasm for the room, Nathan's investigative mind was also active. He looked at a container.

"This one says its cream. The directions on the side say it's to be massaged liberally over the skin of the face and hands."

Nathan opened the jar. "Okay, ladies, come and indulge yourselves. This cream will make you look years younger."

Outraged, Emily hit her brother in fun as she reprimanded him, "Nathan, how uncouth. Don't you have any respect?"

Jayne was tempted to try the cream, but quickly reconsidered, "Nathan, we wouldn't want to contaminate the cream. We'd better not."

Jayne moved to better read the shelves of bottles, and agreed. "These without a doubt, contain the actual embalming fluids. Are you ready to investigate another room down here?"

Emily started out of the room. "Come on, follow me," she suggested. "Let's go over to the cosmetology department. I think you'll find the room far less depressing."

As he opened the next room, Nathan quickly assessed the inhabitants and opted to return to the salesroom. He told Emily he was going to look for their dad, and quickly departed.

Rosie and her tour were already in the room as Emily and Jayne entered. "Come over and join us ladies. I was about to show these stands the person's neck fits in to hold the head steady so I can work better. I do the makeup first, and then do the hair."

Dottie shuttered as she asked, "Do you dress them, too?"

"No. I'm the cosmetic specialist, not the dresser. They don't have anything on but a sheet when I do my work. I wouldn't like to dress them. Nevertheless, I ask to see what clothes they'll wear so I can plan their make-up accordingly. If I do their nails, I have to take their hand out from under the sheet. Since I know most of the deceased, I know who does and who doesn't usually wear polish. Some ladies would just die if their nails didn't match." Realizing her *faux pas* when her audience gasped, Rosie amended her statement, "Well, you know what I mean."

"What do you do with their hair, Rosie? Are there any special problems?" enquired one of the other women.

"Sometimes I have to do a quick dye job. Just like the nails, you know. Women and men want to look their best. Usually their hair is still damp when I get here because the body has been hosed down, so I only need to dry and style the hair. I put on a lot of gel to make it stay in place well."

"How do you get the back to look good? Isn't that hard to do?"

"Would be, if I did it, but I don't. Everybody gets the same back treatment-flat! Nobody will ever see that side again, so I don't even mess with it"

Disturbed by the responses, several ladies began primping the backs of their hair and examining their nails.

"Sometimes I have trouble with hair on an autopsied body. There can be all kinds of stitches making it difficult, not only to cover up, but to comb around."

A little spooked by the whole conversation, Emily tentatively questioned, "Does the body ever move when you're working on it?"

"Naw, that's never happened. I did have a scare one time though. While I was busy concentrating, I heard a mysterious noise. Before I could look around, a low-flying bat hit me in the head. Boy, did I ever jump and yell. I guess I spooked it, too, because it flew out a high open window. Did you know the Indiana brown bat could end up on the endangered species list? Bats are quite helpful by keeping the mosquito population at bay. Some people even keep bat houses to entice bats to live near their homes."

Everyone listening was now bending down and looking around for any unexpected air raids.

"Oh, don't worry," Rosie assured everyone. "I'm sure this crowd will keep those pesky bats away. Hey, since we're down here, would anyone like to lay on the table and allow me to give a demonstration?"

Sounds of booming thunder, strong winds, and hail caused the beautician to continue to raise her voice as she delivered her message.

Madelyn entered the small room, "Oh, Emily, I'm so relieved to see you. Where's Nathan? Did he make it down okay?"

"Don't worry, Mother. He was with me but he went to find Dad. He saw this was a hen party and wanted no part of it. I'm sure he'll entertain himself, safely."

As Emily answered her mother's question, the intensity of the storm increased measurably again, even causing the lights to flitter for the first time.

The effects of the storm startled Madelyn. She continued to talk to Jayne and Emily. "Jayne, I'm so glad to have the opportunity to tell you about Nathan." Madelyn was happy to have a moment to tout the virtues of her son to a doctor, even if she was an animal doctor. *Such an attractive and polite young woman, in such a laborious specialty. I wonder if she would consider different life choices once she's married.* Madelyn didn't approve of her children's choices in dating and was always looking for better matches for them.

Madelyn continued talking through the thunder of the storm, "I'm sure the two of you would get along very well. He's so handsome and educated. He's working on an advanced degree at Notre Dame right now. I'm sure you would love his cat, too. What's its name, Emily, I can never remember?" Madelyn was almost yelling as the storm reached a louder sound of violence.

Being on the receiving end of her mother's matchmaking antics, Emily attempted to apologize to Jayne with her facial expressions. Emily screamed her answer through the clatter of the storm. "Soho, Mother."

Emily turned toward Jayne, she commented, "You'd think she'd keep better attention to her grand-pets than she does." She gave her mother some disappointing news. "Patrick is here with Jayne. Nathan wouldn't steal his best friend's girl."

Disappointed, Madelyn acquiesced, "Oh, Patrick is a fine young man, too. You are very fortunate to be seeing him, but if that doesn't work out."

"Please, Mother, you're embarrassing Jayne. Let's change the subject."

Jayne smiled and responded, "That's alright, Emily, I can take care of myself.

However, I did want to tell you, Mrs. Monroe, how much I enjoyed meeting your brother. He was a gentle hearted man in many ways, but especially with his dog, Buddy. Buddy had so many health issues and Gussy wanted to give him the best care to prolong his life in a comfortable way. I hope you can find some comfort knowing we were able to follow Gussy's final wishes. Since Buddy died a couple of days after Gussy, we were able to cremate him in time to honor Gussy's request. His friend's ashes are going to be with Gussy forever. Gussy carved a little wooden box for his ashes. It was such a touching way to acknowledge his love for Buddy.

Buddy is with Gussy in the casket ..."

A deafening roar covered up the rest of Jayne's words.

Emily attempted to gain control of her group by asking Jayne to continue her story about Gussy. "I was so touched to see Buddy's cremated body was in the intricately carved box in Gussy's hands."

Madelyn's astonished reaction coincided perfectly with the extinction of all lights in the basement. "What? You can't be serious. Gussy's dead dog is in that box with him? I can't believe it! I hope no one else knows! What will they think?" Suddenly aware that she was yelling into darkness with lots of ears, Madelyn immediately lowered her voice. "I can't believe Gussy would do this to his family. How humiliating!"

Her mother's reaction didn't shock Emily. However, Jayne was. She apologized, "I'm sorry, Mrs. Monroe. I didn't mean to upset you. I assumed everyone in the family knew of Gussy's decision for Buddy. I certainly didn't mean to shock you this way. Personally, I think it was a gracious act of love on Gussy's part."

Simon had begun distributing flashlights apologizing for the inconvenience, and the basement slowly became lighter again thanks to the flashlights.

Jayne excused herself as she received a call on her cell phone. "Hi, Patrick. Are you still with Permelia?"

"Yeah, it's been pretty bad out here. The worst seems to be over. We lost electricity a few minutes ago. How about you?"

"It's dark here, too, but they brought some flashlights around, so it's not too bad. Are you going to come back here, or do you want me to catch a ride with someone?"

"You stay there. I'm going to help Permelia light a few more candles and oil lamps, and then I'll head back to the funeral home. The rain was heavy, but the lightning has moved on. I'll see you in a little bit."

Everyone hastily expressed his or her condolences again before going out into the waning storm. Soon the only mourners left were the immediate family, Raymond, Jayne, and Pastor Todd. The family was ready to leave for the night.

There were no tornado touchdowns.

20

The storm came to its conclusion, and the poker friends gathered in the back room of the Legion. Everyone, except the twins, was relieved to report they found no damage to their properties from the storm. The twins hoped their trailers would be damaged or blown away. They wanted insurance proceeds for any damage.

Donnie sniffed his misfortune. "Now if my trailer blew away, I would have insurance money to show a gal a real good time in Louisville line dancing. I'd look sharp in my crocodile boots. We could have even stayed at a classy hotel. Oh well!"

Jake corrected him. "Don't think you would have the time for such luxuries anyway, Donnie. We've too much important stuff on our plates right now. Let's get down to business. Glenn, what did you and Richard find?"

"We didn't have any luck finding copies of the letter," Glenn said. "There were a bunch of papers, but nothin' looked important. We tried to leave things like we found them. I don't think anyone saw us. We went in the unlocked back doors to both buildings. Gussy didn't feel it necessary to lock up." Richard nodded his head in agreement with Glenn.

"Did you find any money?" Billy Bob interrupted.

"Yeah, he had some hundred dollar bills in some of his drawers, but we left them so it wouldn't be obvious anyone had been snooping around," Richard said.

"Oops, we took all the money we found," Billy Bob snickered. "We thought Gussy wouldn't miss it. Everybody knew he had stashes all over. He didn't trust no bank to keep all his money. What the cops don't find they won't know about."

Feeling generous, Donnie added, "We could share the loot with the rest of you. Don't want you to think we'd cheat you guys."

Solomon cut in. "Thanks, but no thanks. Just be smart and don't throw the wad around. Keep it under your hat 'til all this blows over. We found nothing of interest."

The twins quickly agreed to keep a low profile, even though they each already spent quite a bit of some of what they took.

Jake continued the meeting. "We now have the money situation in hand, what about the letter? Donnie, did you find any copies around the hotel?"

Donnie answered, "Nope. Lots of papers, but didn't find no letter. His office was a mess. I'm sure our rummagin' won't be noticed. After we found that first money, you can bet we didn't leave any drawer or shelf untouched. Just notes and papers about his properties, but nothin' 'bout any of our dealin's."

Jake knew the prospect of free money would have all his boys doing a thorough search. He doubted Donnie and Billy Bob were the only ones who kept the cash they found. "Okay, sounds like you took care of the business we needed. Were you careful to show you had business in the hotel?" asked Jake.

"Of course. We both had girls upstairs. We took turns going down stairs to rummage so one of us was always with a girl."

"Good. Just keep your stories simple and don't spout off about the money."

Anxious to finish the business of the evening so he could get home, Solomon began his report. "Jake and I had some success. We didn't find a letter, but we found the old typewriter. We didn't find a computer; I don't think he knew anything about the new technology. And in a pile close by we noticed carbon paper. We found that the ribbon was well used. Some of the words match the recently typed letter. You know, the letter he wrote us.

"I hope that he didn't keep a copy for himself. He used the carbon paper more than once. The text was nearly unreadable. We burned it and took the ribbon anyway.

"We also found old phone records. We did away with those, too. We weren't sure they were important," Solomon continued, "But who knows if they might tie us to Gussy. Better safe than sorry."

All gave high-fives. They were relieved their missions seemed to be over.

Sensing the business was finished for the night, Jake dismissed everyone saying, "Let's all go home and get a good night's rest. I think we did good."

21

Following the ferocious Friday night storm, Saturday dawned with a refreshing feeling of cleanliness and hope.

Emily slept as long as possible. She needed to compose herself after last night. She stayed up late reading her Bible. Then she quickly dressed in her navy linen suit dress. She accessorized with gold jewelry, navy leather sling-back pumps, a matching shoulder bag, and donned her white straw hat with navy ribbons. With little time left before her mother's designated time of departure, she rushed to the B&B's dining room for her required morning cup of coffee. She said a quick prayer of thanks and a request for strength.

Madelyn and Stuart came down the hall.

Madelyn said, "Emily, are you still eating? We're ready to leave. You should have eaten earlier with us if you wanted a leisurely breakfast. Now finish your coffee and let's get moving."

Emily popped the last bite of a jelly donut into her mouth. Her mother continued. "Dear, you know you must be careful what you eat. You don't want to get like that friend of yours, oh, you know whom I mean. She's downright dowdy and overweight. You don't think I've kept myself in such good shape by eating just anything. Keeping thin and fit takes sacrifice. Now, let's go before you eat anything else."

Madelyn turned and moved to the front door. Emily grabbed a blueberry muffin, wrapped it in a napkin, and deposited it in her purse. She thought, *Well, so much for getting "dowdy." I'd rather be full and content.*

Over at Raymond's home, Raymond and Nathan ate waffles for breakfast. Nathan looked at the Thursday edition of *The Grovetown Tribune*. Nathan wanted to acquaint himself with the paper, as well as read the short article about Gussy.

They both looked quite smart in suit and tie. Nathan knew his mother would check him for socks, so he would defer to her wishes for this day. She need not know, even though he intended to pack a pair, he inadvertently forgot. He would have been "shamefully stockless" without the ones she had so "thoughtfully" brought for him.

A few friends were already inside Dyers when father and son arrived. Several more mourners preceded the arrival of Madelyn's entourage. She didn't mind. She enjoyed a grand entrance, even if it were only in Grovetown's funeral parlor. She knew how stunning she looked in her black silk attire. The multi-tiered handkerchief skirt displayed her shapely legs well. A matching short jacket with soft lapels completed her outfit. She chose 18k gold earrings, necklace, and bangle bracelets for her jewelry. Her high sling-back heels further added to the commanding entrance she made with her husband, in his black Armani suit.

Another well-dressed woman walked into the room.

"Sally, I can't believe it. I never expected to see you here. How in the world did you find out?" Madelyn yelled with surprise greeting an old friend.

Sally, pleased her unexpected appearance was welcome, explained, "I saw the obit in an Indy newspaper. Trinkle is not a common name, as you know. I skimmed the piece to see if I wanted to come last night, but I had a previous engagement. I decided to make the trip down today."

"I'm thrilled. Last night's weather was too bad for you to travel anyway—a real zoo here. There were tornado warnings forcing people to hurry home or flee to the basement here for protection. Please tell me you can stay for lunch. There'll be plenty of food and time for us to catch up. Christmas cards don't do it, do they? Please say you'll stay!"

"If you're sure it's no bother, I'd love to stay for lunch. I do want to get home tonight. Samuel is golfing. He won't be expecting me home before six. They always do a late supper at the club before going home. Isn't that Raymond over there? Do you think he would mind if I sit with him. I really don't know anyone else."

The proposed arrangement didn't thrill Madelyn. She suggested, "Why don't you sit with me and my husband, Stuart? Raymond will probably sit with his children, Nathan and Emily. Come, you must meet Stuart!"

Sally realized her friend was still the same take-charge person, and she obediently followed to Stuart's assigned spot. Simon Dyers advised the mourners it was time to take their seats for the service to begin.

When Pastor Todd walked up to the podium, a hush came over the room. He began by asking all to bow their heads in prayer. After the prayer, he graciously thanked everyone on behalf of the family for all their expressions of sympathy.

Todd introduced Nathan. Nathan read Psalm 23. Singing "Great Is Thy Faithfulness" followed it. Many mourners remembered not only Gussy, but also the loved ones they'd lost. You could hear sniffles.

The pastor next introduced Jake. Jake, self-assured in front of an audience, seemed humble. He remembered some of his memories of Gussy. They included a few school stunts, as well as some business ventures through the years, and he mentioned how much Gussy was already missed at the poker games.

"Each of our group will miss Gussy's dry wit and astute card playing. He fooled us many-a-time with his classic poker face. We often wondered if it was a wooden mask he carved and wore to fool us." This comment caused several chuckles. He finished his remarks on a serious note.

"I speak for all of our Tuesday night players when I say we consider it an honor to be part of this tribute to our great friend. He'll never be forgotten."

Raymond was the next speaker. "Although Gussy and I knew each other all my life, it was in the last few months we developed a true feeling of brotherhood."

Madelyn was relieved when Raymond avoided mentioning he and Gussy were brothers-in-law.

"He was a sensitive man, perhaps exemplified most through his beautiful carvings. He was a wise businessman, although keeping silent on details of his financial situation. In reality, he was a wealthy man but he never portrayed himself as anything but a poor and humble guy. He inherited much wealth from his parents. He used his abilities to expand his holdings. His 'uniform' may have varied with the color of his flannel shirt, but nothing else seemed to change. Who knows how many pairs of bibs he owned? They were all the same."

Many chuckles and nods showed the crowd's agreement. Madelyn's grimace bore her opinion of her brother's lack of style.

"As I said, Gussy had a change of heart these last few months. Pastor Todd is going to go into more detail, but I want to share a few personal moments Gussy told me. He was determined to rectify some mistakes he made. He wanted to personally apologize to those he harmed in some way. I know he began to take care of some of those issues before he passed."

Raymond paused and slowly scanned the room before continuing.

"Gussy may have talked to some of you, asking your forgiveness for a wrong he felt he did against you."

As he again paused, Raymond saw and heard restlessness in many parts of the room.

Raymond turned to look at his dead friend's body before he continued. Tears were in his eyes as he made a final touching revelation. "I'm sure my dear friend wouldn't mind me sharing this well-guarded secret from his life. Just last week, as he and I studied First Corinthians 13 together, Gussy opened up a little. This chapter is the 'Great Love' chapter of the Bible. Gussy was so touched by the words 'and the greatest of these is love'.

"He tearfully told me how much God's love meant to him. He was so sorry he hadn't acknowledged it until this late point in his life. He then looked down at his hand and showed me a scar I'd often noticed, but never knew how he'd gotten it. I assumed it was from his carving or his time in the military, but I didn't know. He said it was a remembrance of a lost love, the only woman he ever really loved. To demonstrate his love, he said he carved her a heart shaped box. In the process, he cut his hand. He simply bound it up to stop the bleeding and didn't get stitches. All these years the scar sorrowfully reminded him of the love he found but lost. You see she died before he gave it to her. He knew her when he was in basic training."

Gasps, especially from the women, filled Raymond's silent pause. Madelyn and Henrietta were stunned as they heard the revelation. Neither realized their brother was involved in a romantic relationship. Madelyn could hardly restrain herself from jumping up and asking the woman's name.

Again, Raymond wiped his eyes.

"Gussy said the scar meant so much to him, but in the last few weeks it has come to mean something even more important. Now when he looked at it, it reminded him of the pain and scars Jesus bore for him. He was looking forward to sharing this testimony with his friends, so

I'm sure he wouldn't be upset I shared it. He was so humbled by Jesus' sacrifice for his sins and wanted each of you to know Jesus as he did in his final weeks."

Emily and Nathan both rose to hug their dad as he returned to his seat. You could hear more sniffles. Pastor Todd returned to the podium.

"Thank you both for sharing with us about Gussy's life. I'd like to concentrate on my relationship with him in the few months I've lived in Grovetown. We met mid-December, ice fishing at Tucker's Bridge. We fished a few times, knowing only first names. We discovered more about each other. Gussy wasn't turned off by the fact I was a minister. In fact, since we already had a good rapport, he seemed glad to have me on hand to answer some questions. When he inquired why I fished, I told him my grandfather took me almost year round until he was too feeble. I told him when I read in the Bible Jesus told us to be fishers of men, I decided to follow Him and do just that.

We developed a fishing camaraderie."

"Gussy was very open to having me share from the Bible and explain God's Word. By the time the ice thawed, we were meeting regularly on Monday mornings to fish and chat. He wanted to know what I preached about on Sunday, and our conversation would continue from there. I was able to explain the plan of salvation to him in our favorite fishing spot, right there at Tucker's Bridge.

"I explained how the Bible says in Romans 3:23 'All have sinned and fall short of the glory of God.' I asked Gussy if he realized he was a sinner separated from God. He said he certainly knew he had sinned many, many times in his life. He said he knew he deserved severe punishment from God. He was afraid he was going to hell. I told him, yes, our sin does deserve punishment, but God loves us so much He has given us a way to avoid punishment and be accepted by Him in heaven. The only way is by believing in and accepting Jesus as our Savior, recognizing Jesus died in our place and offers us forgiveness for our sins." Pastor Todd paused and looked around the room before he continued.

"Gussy thought that sounded too easy for him. After all, he said he had done many bad things in his whole life. He said there must be something else he'd have to do. I told Gussy to look at Tucker's Bridge as a bridge that allows us to cross over from one side of Deer Fly Creek to the other side. I told him Jesus was the bridge God made for sinful man to be able to cross over from the shore of sin and death to the shore of forgiveness and eternal life through Jesus. John 1:12 says, 'To all who received Him, to those who believed in His name, He gave the right to become the children of God."

"I asked Gussy if he wanted to cross that bridge from death to life, and he tearfully said he did. We prayed together, and he accepted Jesus as his very own. The spring water was still too cold to baptize him that day. We went back to Tucker's Bridge in late March. I baptized him there in the same spot where he accepted Jesus. Tomorrow was to be the day he would make his profession of faith in front of the entire church. I'm sorry he didn't get to do that but am thankful the Holy Spirit led him to Jesus and salvation. My dear friend is already in heaven with his Savior. He is rejoicing with the saints and angels.

"None of us knows when our last day on earth will be. If there is any here today who haven't accepted Jesus as Savior, you can certainly do it now. As Gussy did, please tell me. I'll talk and pray with you. What a tribute it would be, to have others follow his example of faith on this day as we celebrate his life."

Pastor Todd bowed his head and prayed for the comfort of the family and friends gathered. He thanked God for His great love in sending Jesus as the perfect sacrifice for all those who believed and accepted Him, especially Gussy. He ended by praying for the moving of the Holy Spirit in the hearts of those who didn't know Jesus as Savior.

The mourners sang "Amazing Grace" to end the service.

The family had a short time of private goodbyes before the funeral director closed the casket. As the family moved to their assigned vehicles, the pallbearers performed their duties.

The service at Sinking Springs Cemetery was uneventful.

22

The funeral ended and the family headed to Henrietta's for lunch. The ladies of the church's funeral committee honored Henrietta's request to bring the covered dishes for buffet style lunch at the Trinkle family home on Persimmon Lane."This dining room is perfect to serve a buffet meal," said the chairperson of the group. "The antique dining set, with all the side pieces, makes such a pleasant setting. Henrietta's linens, family silver, glassware, and china are so elegant."

"Even our ordinary food looks classy in Henri's Havilland serving bowls and platters. I really admire her silverware. Sure wouldn't want the job of keeping them polished, though."

"Looks like we finished just in time. I see the family cars arriving," announced one of the women.

"Thank you again for all of your help. The room looks lovely and the food smells delicious," Henrietta said.

The chairperson said, "Remember, Henri, don't worry about cleaning up. Another group of ladies will be here later to take care of that for you. You move to the parlor and enjoy your time together." The doorbell rang, allowing a natural end to the conversation. The women from the church each expressed their sympathies and quickly exited to allow the family privacy and the opportunity to eat the meal.

The bell announced the delivery of the many flower arrangements and plants from the funeral home by Melissa, the florist. As part of her service, she tastefully placed them throughout the parlor, dining room, and hallways.

Pastor Todd blessed the food. Everyone proceeded to the buffet.

"I'm going straight to the hot items," Nathan proclaimed. "The mashed potatoes, chicken and dumplings, and hot rolls are calling me. I sure need those carbs for my running."

Madelyn snidely remarked. "Well, dear, I hope you'll eat some of the healthier dishes, also. You know large waistlines run in your father's side of the family."

Nathan rolled his eyes at his dad. Raymond unsuccessfully covered his snicker. Emily laughed out loud. They knew Madelyn too well.

While the family ate, they conversed about the touching service led by Pastor Todd. Emily and Nathan asked their dad and aunt more questions about Gussy's life. They enjoyed some of the childhood stories, both new and old. They discussed Gussy's secret life. There were many questions. Who was the woman? How did she die? Why didn't anyone know? They were all mystified.

Madelyn and Sally told Stuart about some of their college antics. Each went to different colleges. Madelyn studied at Northwestern University; Sally at Indiana University. Still the two kept in touch and spent time together whenever possible. The stories caused animated laughter.

"Mom, may I get some dessert for you?" inquired Nathan.

"I couldn't. There's nothing here my personal trainer would allow. Please bring me a cup of decaf." Nathan dutifully filled his mother's cup, along with taking drink orders from others.

Emily made a sampler plate of small servings of the desserts for her aunt. "Sally, may I do the same for you?"

"That would be nice, Emily. Just small pieces, please. I have a sweet tooth, but like your mother, I do want to watch my weight. We're no longer young. Used to be able to eat whatever I wanted without any problem, but not anymore."

Emily then filled her plate. "I may pay for it, but this homemade cherry cobbler is too tempting." Emily began eating with gusto. She was on her second bite when she let out a loud, "Ahhh. My tooth! I think I broke it!" Everyone recognized Emily's plight, Raymond was the first to ask to see inside Emily's mouth. She was looking at the cherry she removed from her mouth. "Sure enough, here's a cherry pit *and* a piece of my tooth." She allowed her father to look into her mouth and locate the problem.

"Does it hurt, Emily?" her concerned dad asked.

"I really don't think so."

"Well, thank heavens Sally's here. Her husband, Samuel, is a dentist. They live in Indianapolis. You look and give your opinion," ordered

Madelyn.

"I'm sorry, I'm not trained to diagnose, I'm merely the wife and mother of dentists," apologized Sally. "I could call Samuel and ask his opinion, but it's difficult to discover how serious over the phone."

"Of course, how silly of me," Madelyn responded. "Emily, are you sure you're not in pain?"

"No, just my pride. I'm not hurting, so don't think this is an emergency at all."

"Even if it doesn't hurt, you must see a dentist as soon as possible. Sally, could you get her in to see your husband next week?" Madelyn suggested. "Didn't you say his office is close to Emily's school?"

"I'd be glad to do that, Emily. I'll tell Samuel to make sure he can work you in next week. Let me give you his card from my purse. Call the office on Monday. Samuel always tries to leave a couple of spots open every week for such emergencies."

Emily gratefully took the card. "I appreciate this, Sally. I've never established myself with an Indy dentist. Been meaning to do that all year, but I never took the time. Fortunately, I inherited good teeth from Mom and Dad, so haven't needed any special dental care. I'll be sure to call early Monday morning. Thanks."

Madelyn added, "Maybe if Sally's husband can't fit you in see if her son can instead,"

Emily carefully inspected some more of the cherries before taking another bite.

"Surely you're not going to continue eating cobbler are you," exclaimed Madelyn. "I don't think anyone should have anymore. Besides the calories, it's too dangerous."

"Oh, Mother, don't be ridiculous. This stuff is too delicious not to eat. Who hasn't gotten a cherry pit sometime or other?"

"Emily's right, Mom. I often get one, but it's well worth the risk," chimed in Nathan.

Eager to change the focus of the conversation, Henri said, "Sally, I'm pleased you could come today. Madelyn always speaks so highly of you. I think it's great how Purdue's 4-H program brings people together. I remember when Madelyn sang in the 4-H chorus at the Indiana State Fair. I know you both stayed at the Deaf School outside the fairgrounds. Madelyn said you guys had a blast at the fair. Weren't you here for the

Persimmon Festival?"

Sally replied, "Yes, I was. I visited a little before my sophomore year at I.U. Madelyn was Persimmon Queen."

"I don't think the house has changed much since then. I try to keep the house like it was when my parents' died. I have a housekeeper keep the rooms clean. I have my own bungalow. Someday I may move back in. Madelyn, why don't you give her a quick tour?"

"Of course, Henrietta, I'm sure Sally would enjoy seeing the house again."

The friends proceeded to the stairway. "Well, you saw the double parlors, dining room, solarium, dining room, and kitchen. I don't think I ever told you about the summer kitchen. These old houses had summer kitchens because the stove in the indoor kitchen would make the house too warm in the hot weather. Then there was always a possibility of fire. When you were here, it was a bachelor apartment for Gussy. When he returned from Vietnam in 1968, they added a small bathroom with a shower. After my parents died, Gussy turned the summer kitchen into his workshop. He spent a lot of time whittling and woodworking. He found his life rewarding. Did you meet my brother when you stayed with me for the Persimmon Festival?"

Sally said, "No, I don't think so. When I wasn't with you, I pretty much stayed in your room. I also roamed the town and went down to the river."

Sally continued to comment on the old house, "I love the elaborate marble fireplaces with the mirrors above.

"Madelyn, do you have a fireplace. I think a crackling fire makes the atmosphere of a room cozy."

"Our house has a modern fireplace in our family room."

Madelyn replied, "Ours is too."

Sally glanced around. She commented, "I think the matching chandeliers in these double parlors are stunning. The many crystal prisms reflect the sunlight with colors of a rainbow. How did the family keep them clean?"

"The maids cleaned the chandeliers in the Victorian heyday. When the older generation passed, my father and mother did it together. Dad on the ladder and Mom washing them in soap and water with a touch of vinegar. They sparkled."

Sally asked, "When was this house built?"

"The house was built in 1877, during the Victorian Age. Clutter and more clutter were in vogue. Notice the red-flocked wallpaper. You know the ceilings are fourteen feet tall. Note the transoms above the doors. They opened to allow a breeze in the house. Before Gussy died, he lived in the back of the house only. He said he only needed a galley kitchen, bed for him and Buddy, and a TV. He wouldn't take care of the plants in the solarium, so Henrietta hired a housekeeper who tends to the needs of all the vegetation."

"I wish we had a solarium. You have some rare plants. I love the openness. What fun to sit in there with a book and some coffee."

They headed upstairs.

Sally commented, "This beautiful curved staircase is striking. The walnut woodwork is so well made. Do you still have a second staircase?"

"It's still the narrowest and steepest stairs I've ever seen. I never liked climbing them. When my grandmother lived here, she had a maid. Those stairs went to her room above the kitchen."

Sally followed her friend to a suite of rooms. "These rooms belonged to my parents. Not much has changed."

Madelyn continued to describe the room and point out what she felt were highlights. A walnut bedroom suite sported a wedding ring quilt. The dressing table had a matching bench. Attached to the dresser was a tri-hinged tall mirror. An old blue tinted mirror on which antique perfume bottles sat adorned the low front shelf. The mirror complimented the blue wallpaper and pieces in the suite. The small attached sitting room has a comfortable reading chair and a vintage Tiffany lamp. Loaded bookshelves were on all the walls.

Madelyn continued across the hall to Henri's old room. She said, "Henrietta used this room until she moved to her little bungalow after my parent's death. My grandmother made the cheery yellow flower garden quilt. See this small cherry secretary desk in place of a dressing table. The cherry factory in Homer, Indiana, made it. Henrietta always exhibited more interest in inward grooming than outer appearance. She wrote at this desk. Come on. Let's go to my old room. "

Madelyn opened the door to her old room with a flourish and stepped aside to let Sally enter. "Well, here it is. My room hasn't changed much."

"Oh, Madelyn, I never saw such a fancy bed until I stayed with you.

I envied all these yards of fabric flowing from your canopy, all the way to the floor. I thought your childhood was the dream of every little girl. How fun it would be to close yourself inside the curtains, in a world of your own. How neat to sleep under a canopy. I felt like a princess." sighed Sally.

"Henri and I pretended we were in a castle. Since it was my bed, I would be the queen. Of course, if we played Cinderella, I would be her, and Henri was the nasty stepmother or stepsister." Madelyn and Sally lingered in the attached summer sun porch, each lost in thoughts of her own.

23

The Grovetown Red Hat luncheon met, as it did every month. You had to be fifty-years-old to be a Red Hatter. Younger women could join, but they were required to wear a pink hat and lavender dress while the older women wore red and purple. This month the women chose Sunday, after church to be their day. Sunday was an unusual day to meet. However, there were a few widows, and wives whose husbands could entertain themselves with golfing or naps. Today was also Mother's Day. Members' families said they would pay for their mother's lunches for the expensive cuisine at the Falls Restaurant.

Realizing the luncheon would be during Madelyn's stay in Grovetown, Rosie McCorkle, the hairdresser, invited Madelyn to the gathering. She asked Henrietta for her phone number so she could invite her, before she arrived in Grovetown.

Madelyn Trinkle Starks Monroe dressed to the hilt in full Red Hat regalia sauntered in a tad late. Because of the advance notice, Madelyn packed appropriate apparel for the luncheon. Her dress was an eggplant colored silk frock. On her slender feet, she wore red leather five-inch high slings. Of course, her red leather purse matched perfectly. She accessorized with a gorgeous Issenberg Red Hat pin. She wore a felt hat covered in red feathers. She wore Boucheron brand perfume. Expensive, but lovely smelling.

Madelyn ensured she obtained the attention of most of the regular diners in the room. She ignored the seating by the hostess and proceeded to her sister "Red Hatters" table. Rosie introduced her as Madelyn Starks.

Madelyn smiled, but quickly interjected, "No, Rosie, I'm Mrs. Monroe now and have been since 1989."

Feeling chagrined, Rosie corrected herself. After the usual introductions and formalities, she said, "We're all so sorry to hear about

Gussy. Do the police know who did it?"

Madelyn replied, "The whole case is under investigation, but it's pretty clear he *was* murdered."

Madelyn looked around the table and made a mental note of the woman at the table while judging their choice of clothing. She saw Dottie the cook and Carol, the waitress from the Donut Shop. There were several other women. Madelyn quickly went through the Rolodex of her mind noting all the scandals she knew about these women.

While everyone was deciding what to order, the group continued to exchange compliments on each other's dress, hat, jewelry, and accessories.

A club member dressed in a long sequined purple outfit asked, "Carol, where did you find that dress and cute little red sequined bag? I've looked everywhere for sequined items."

She answered, "At the little Red Hat Boutique over in Peony. I don't think we can find hats like this in Grovetown, even though the secondhand shop out on the highway has some Red Hat items. Why, I found a nicely molded straw hat for summer there a few weeks ago. We should all go to Peony to shop together. A road trip would be such fun. We could eat someplace there."

Rosie said, "Well my red hat today is a discount store special I spiced up with a purple ostrich plume and blue and lavender flowers. Why I saw one similar for $25 in a catalog. Of course, I wouldn't pay any more than twenty."

The waitress came for their drink orders. Most of the women ordered one of the specialties of raspberry iced tea and water with lemon. Madelyn requested water with lemon and a glass of chardonnay to everyone's chagrin. Carol thought, *It's Sunday morning and way too early in the day for respectable citizens of this town to order alcohol."* Carol overheard Madelyn telling the ladies her hat cost $100.

"Our Chicago group attended the musical *Menopause.* What a hoot! You really should try to get tickets, although I'm sure you wouldn't be able to now," Madelyn said.

Another member said, "We heard about it on the radio and wanted to go, but it seemed too far to drive to Indianapolis. I think that was the closest location. So, was it really worth the cost of tickets? I heard they were quite expensive."

Before Madelyn could answer, the waitress arrived with their drinks and asked if they were ready to order their soup and salad.

The waitress said, "Our lunch special includes soup, salad, and half a sandwich or quiche. Today's soup du jour is French onion soup. We also have cream of baked potato with cheese. The specials today are tomatoes stuffed with tuna or chicken salad. We also have a broiled chicken breast with our house mustard sauce, or you can substitute the bacon, spinach, and cheese quiche if you prefer. What will it be, and what kind of dressing on your salad?"

Except for Madelyn, the usual dressings seemed satisfactory. When it came time for her to order, she said, "I'll have raspberry vinaigrette."

The waitress said, "I'm sorry. We don't carry that."

"Then bring me French Tarragon."

"Oh dear, we don't have that either. I can offer you oil and vinegar or balsamic vinegar."

Madelyn snapped back," Well, I *guess* balsamic vinegar and oil will just have do. Would you put it on the side? Also a glass of Chardonnay."

The soups and salads arrived. Rosie led the group in a prayer of thanksgiving. The women discussed clothing, gossip, and husbands before the conversation turned serious. One member said, "Oh Madelyn, we're so sorry about your brother." All the women nodded in agreement.

Dottie asked, "Do the police know how he was killed?"

Madelyn, not wanting to discuss this, replied succinctly, "The police know he was stabbed. However, they didn't find the murder weapon. They say they don't know much else."

Rosie queried, "What are they doing in the investigation, if I might ask?"

Again, Madelyn was short in her reply, "It seems the police aren't doing much at all. They did talk to witnesses, neighbors, and business employees."

"Do they have any suspects?"

Another member chimed in, "How terrible! Why would someone stab him?"

Dottie couldn't wait to brag on Ron Green's, behalf. "Well, as you might not know, Madelyn, my boyfriend, Deputy Ron Green, will soon be in charge of the investigation. Chief Petty is leaving on vacation. I'm sure the case will be safe while the Chief is away. Jake Achsworth is going to help Ron, too. Between all of them, the case is bound to be solved soon."

Carol interjected, "While serving breakfast yesterday, I overheard someone say Raymond and your son are going to be investigating too. Are they? How interesting to see if they have any more luck than the police do. What do you think Madelyn? Who do you think will solve the mystery first?"

Madelyn woefully responded, "I asked Nathan to become actively involved in the case. He hasn't decided. I guess we'll have to wait and see who succeeds. Don't you all think it's in poor taste to speculate about the death of my brother, Gussy?"

Rosie recognized Madelyn's reluctance to continue discussing the murder and turned her attention to the conversation on the other side of her. "What did you say about your grandchildren being in a ballet recital?"

The woman sitting next to her responded, "Yes, I was saying the recital was really well directed. Both my granddaughters were in it. Their teacher, Permelia, is eccentric. However, she seems to be able to work with children and teach them too. And she certainly knows how to put on a good show."

Rosie stated, "Yeah, I know. I live next door to her. I saw some strange doings at Permelia's house the other night. She was in her garden dancing around and chanting some strange song. She was dressed in a long white robe. I thought she acted as if she was in a trance at times. I think she was performing some kind of ritual. Does anyone know anything about this?"

No one responded.

Rosie continued, "Well, I think it's odd. I wonder if she's involved in some kind of cult. I heard she attends the Catholic Church, but not on a regular basis. I guess she's a Christian. Her teaching yoga and belly dancing along with ballet and tap seems out of the norm. She does have several adult students, I understand. Most of them are new residents living in the Forest Estates subdivision. Some of her students look like hippies or yuppies to me. But I don't think she'd intentionally cause any harm."

The ladies finished their soups and salads, Henrietta and three more red hatters appeared to join the group. Rosie leaned toward Madelyn to remind her who the women were. "These are our members who always join us late if our gathering is on Sunday. They go to church first. There's Alice Achsworth, Jake's wife, in the purple pantsuit, her sister-in-law, Margaret, Glenn's wife, with the red boa. Of course, you know Melissa. She did the beautiful flower arrangements for the funeral."

Rosie announced loudly to everyone, "Let's all scoot our chairs to make room for our 'goody-two-shoes' Red Hatters."

Everyone obliged, laughed, and made adjustments at the table.

Madelyn was quick to begin a conversation with Melissa. "I'm so glad to meet you. Rosie told me you were the person responsible for the lovely flower arrangements. I was surprised Grovetown has such an accomplished florist. I'm certain your talent is overlooked in this environment. If you ever consider moving to Chicago, I can guarantee your abilities would be well-compensated."

"I certainly appreciate your high praise, Madelyn. I feel very blessed God has bestowed the ability upon me to do my job. As for Chicago or any large town, I'm very happy in Grovetown. I plan to live my life here."

Someone down the table began to talk to Melissa; Rosie leaned toward Madelyn and whispered conspiratorially, "Well, I know why Melissa is happy here in Grovetown, Raymond! After Melissa's husband died two years ago from cancer, she and Raymond have become quite the item."

Madelyn grimaced. Nobody told her anything about her ex-husband's love life.

The main course arrived. Most of the Red Hatters ordered chicken or tuna salad. Madelyn ordered the spinach quiche, or as she called it, *quiche aux epinarde*, in French. She also ordered another glass of white wine. The conversation drifted to mundane talk of children and grandchildren while they ate their delicious lunch. Madelyn wanted to talk about her husband, Stuart, his great job, and how they met.

She broke into another conversation with an exclamation, "Oh, you have to hear about how Stuart and I met. I wanted to go to the beach that winter." Turning toward Melissa, Madelyn continued. "Raymond was always too busy with the newspaper. I decided to travel alone to Haiti and its newly opened beaches. The plane landed in Chicago on the international leg of my vacation. This most luscious looking man got on in Chicago. He sat next to me on the plane. We talked over martinis. He impressed me. I fell head over heels in love with him. Stuart was on a business trip to Haiti. He was opening a baseball factory. You know, the wages are much lower there. His last name was 'Monroe'. I've always wanted to have the initials 'MM' like Marilyn Monroe, and I thought now I could. Isn't that exciting?"

Most people nodded or grimaced, while Rosie said, "How nice for you." She knew talk of affairs wouldn't make most of the woman at the table pleased.

Alice was quick to change the subject away from relationships. She was the hostess for the next meeting, so she took the opportunity to ask Madelyn, "Where do you hold your Red Hat meetings?"

Madelyn arrogantly responded, "Well, the *Rouge Chapeaus* certainly have more sophisticated places to choose from than your group does. We often meet in a private dining room of a downtown hotel or country club. We've taken a cruise on the lake or flown to a unique spot out of town. We're toying with the idea of a long weekend in Paris to shop. We haven't finalized anything yet. Our busy schedules make it difficult in deciding on an agreeable date."

Slightly intimidated by Madelyn's report, Alice proposed to the entire group, "How about us trying that new French-style cafe out west of Peony. I don't think it will be Paris, but it would be a bit daring for our group."

Not so sure about the menu choices there, Melissa rued, "I don't know. I've heard it's one of those vegetarian places. I can't imagine not having meat on the menu."

Carol, added, "I've heard they have funny breads, too. Something called Panini bread that looks like it's been run over by a tire. I think it has a bunch of strange cheeses with avocado and tomato. I guess it's supposed to be tasty. I can imagine what our customers at the café would say if we served sandwiches looking like they were run over by tractors."

Rosie, the Queen of the chapter, didn't want her group to look like hicks. "I think we should go. A French restaurant could certainly add to our experiences as a group although a bit out of our comfort zone."

They all agreed, although there was no real vote. No one ever voted. This chapter's motto was "If I don't wanna, I ain't gonna!"

The dessert was a small bowl of rainbow sherbet. Even Madelyn accepted the Sunday special dessert.

Rosie asked Madelyn another question, "What is your Red Hat group's name again? I didn't catch it?"

"We're the *Rouge Chapeaus*. What's your group's name?"

Carol answered for them all. "No, we don't have one . Do we need one? Girls think about a possible name and bring it for consideration at the next meeting." The ladies immediately started whispering and giggling. They shared some suggestions. Madelyn made her own list in her mind. She was sure they wouldn't appreciate her impossible names: *Barefoot Broads, Straw Hatters, Sassy Sycamore Sisters, Grovetown Mad Hatters*, and *Hokey-Pokeys*.

The party broke up with each lady taking the favor Rosie brought them—a bottle of purple nail polish with cute little red hat decals for each nail. Excited by the favor, the Grovetown ladies each vowed to have their nails decorated for the next outing.

Madelyn received her favor. She snidely thought to herself, *How tacky!*

24

Sunday after church service and a quick lunch, Patrick and Nathan formulated a plan for the day, to go canoeing on Deer Fly Creek.

Patrick said, "It's a seven-mile trip down the river. Let's drop your car off at the sewage plant. Then we'll ride together to the boat dock north of the falls. Patrick's Chesapeake Retriever, Dexter, sat in the back seat staring out the window. That way we'll have a car at the end as well. Okay with you?"

"Sure. No problem. I've really missed our canoe trips. Remember when we went down Blue River south of Grovetown?" Nate replied.

"Yes, I also remember swamping the *Gypsy Girl* at least twice. I try to go canoeing a couple times a year with a local group, Deer Fly Creek Kanu Klub. Besides canoeing, the Klub spends a lot of time clearing the creek after big storms. Before the death of my sister Permelia's husband in Afghanistan, he and I used to canoe the creek whenever we both were in town."

On the way to the launching area, the men talked about Patrick's medical practice and listened to the radio. Nathan liked to listen to NPR radio, particularly jazz. Patrick, however, listened to a Christian station. Dexter, Patrick's big dog just hung out with them.

Patrick kept the Moody station on. Nathan enjoyed the gospel music He asked for the call numbers so he could set the station on his car radio.

Patrick said, "Does your mother still want you to delve into the mystery of your uncle's death? Are you going to get involved? I'll help if you like. I'm sure your father will."

"I don't know. I'm going to be busy with my thesis and working at the paper too. I'm not positive I can dedicate as much time to this as Gussy deserves. Mum is putting a lot of pressure on me. Dad says he'll help if nobody finds the killer by the time I come back. Guess I'll pray some more before making a final decision. Sometimes God has a plan for you."

They carried the silver aluminum canoe down to the banks of the creek. The pair hated wearing life jackets, but kept the required flotation devices nearby with a large ice-filled cooler of Cokes, bologna and cheese sandwiches, and bottles of water. Black rubber bungee cords secured the cooler. Of course, they carried a mandatory container of bug spray for the ever-likely Deer Fly attack. The insect was responsible for the name, Deer Fly Creek.

Patrick, faced the bow, grabbed the gunwale, the support structures running along the canoe hull, on one side and shifted his weight to the middle of the canoe. He then grabbed the far rim with his hand and steadied the craft, sitting in the stern. Nathan followed in the same way into the bow. The techniques for using the paddles were different for each. Patrick steered the canoe with one paddle, while Nathan kept the momentum with the other. They operated in tandem. Dexter sat on the cooler in the middle. Being a Chesapeake Retriever he loved water. His self-appointed job was to watch for wildlife. The creek was teeming with fish, animals, and birds. The threesome settled into a silent pattern as they rounded the first bend.

The water level was up due to the spring rains making the run an easy ride. The current was fast. Still, this small river wasn't quite "white-water" so the men easily canoed under the first major landmark, Tucker's Bridge. The old bridge reminded them of Pastor Todd's funeral message.

Nathan commented, "I was so touched to learn Uncle Gussy accepted Jesus and was baptized right along this spot. I'm sure all at the funeral would think of Gussy when they see the bridge. Others might follow Gussy's example and accept Jesus there."

Patrick agreed. Both were silent again for a while, as they carefully maneuvered through some unexpected debris in the creek.

Nathan said, "I couldn't run in the Mini-Marathon. However, there's a run Saturday, June 4 in South Bend ending on the fifty-yard line in the Notre Dame Stadium. Doesn't the run sound exciting? Let's do it!"

They passed a lounging turtle on a fallen tree. Patrick replied, "It sounds like fun, but tell me more."

Nathan proceeded to give various details. He also mentioned another upcoming run at Muscatatuck State Park near Grovetown, Saturday,

July 2nd, of the Fourth of July weekend. "I thought we could camp Friday and Saturday nights in the park. Get up at dawn Sunday morning and make it back in time for church.

Patrick responded, "Sure if I recover from the 10K at South Bend. I understand 10 kilometers are about the length of this canoe trip. This canoe trip is about seven miles while the run would be six miles. I guess we can try to do both runs. That is if you and I practice and prepare. I'm out of shape, big time." The two friends agreed to the adventure.

The guys reached the falls. They steered the canoe carefully through the rocks. They followed the rhythm of the water over and down the falls. Amateur canoers often swamped if they didn't get the proper angle through the rocks. There was an unusual amount of trash collected on the rocks; but the boys were able to maneuver the falls without capsizing. The sights and sounds on the rippling waters of the river promised the peaceful calmness of a pleasant day on Deer Fly Creek. They heard singing birds, an occasional jumping fish, frogs plopping into the water, and saw turtles sunning on rocks,

The conversation reopened on family matters. The men discussed their sisters, Emily, and Permelia.

Patrick said, "Permelia's life with her small son seems to be okay, I guess. She loves her garden. She teaches some dance and yoga classes in our grandparent's house, using it for a good financial supplemental income. Loneliness is a major concern since her husband's death. How's Emily?"

"Emily's quite well, thank you. She enjoys her teaching job, but she seems to be a loner, just her and her cat, Mr. Whiskers. Did you know she's staying for the summer to help my aunt computerize the library? The library found grant money to hire a computer assistant. Aunt Henri immediately thought of Emily. Emily was thrilled. She didn't have a summer job lined up, so this was perfect."

After another bend, they were startled to see more trees and limbs down, forming a logjam. The guys were required to portage the canoe around and over the jam. They first pulled the canoe onto the bank. Each one carried their oars and flotation devices in one hand, and a cooler handle in the other to bank. They carried the canoe upside down on their shoulders; accompanied by Dexter proudly carrying his coffee used for a water bowl. Nathan said, "That trick is magic! Did you teach him?"

"He figured it out by himself. He's most happy when he has something in his mouth. He often greets me with a surprise of some sort. Retrieving goes with his breed. Let's eat a bologna sandwich before we start again," said Patrick.

Nathan's praise of the obedient dog was short-lived. Dexter dropped the coffee can, bound into the water, soaking Nathan. He spotted some wild geese on the other side and was off to retrieve one. Of course, the feathered creatures flew off before he could claim one. After much persuading from Patrick, Dexter swam back across the creek. He climbed the bank and shook off his wet and dirty coat.

Patrick said, "Look at this gook on his fur. Why's there so much scum? That storm did a number to the trees. I bet it's good fishing here, except for the debris. Guess the canoe club members will have to clean up this mess. I'll notify their president as soon as we get back to town."

Nathan agreed.

After a short rest, they put the *Gypsy Gal* back in the water and continued to the landing.

25

Emily, Henrietta, and Nathan enjoyed their biscuits and gravy at the Grovetown Café the following day.

Henrietta stated, "I love coming here. The café reminds me of Garrison Keller's mythical 'Chatterbox Café'. Emily, do you remember when we would listen to him on Saturday night?"

"I enjoyed the stories about the Lutheran church. He always ended the program with *That's the news from Lake Woebegone, where all the women are strong, all the men are good looking, and all the children are above average.*" The three laughed.

Nathan said, "I'm always impressed with the biscuits and gravy here. I love how you can come in, eat a filling breakfast, and have coffee for less than $6. I always leave a $2 tip." *This place seems the same as the last time I was here.*

Henrietta said, "This is one of the more pleasant places to eat in Grovetown. The breakfast is always great. Moreover, the giant tenderloins are packed with extras for lunch. On Friday nights, they have all the catfish and shrimp you can eat. We'll have to make a point of coming back during the summer." They left the café.

They walked to the attorney's office. Emily changed the subject, "I'm going to the dentist in Indy to fix this tooth."

"Oh, Emily. I'm sorry. I forgot your tooth. I've been distracted with everything going on. I love you and can only imagine how much pain you're in."

Emily said, "Thankfully, it doesn't hurt too badly. It does make me self-conscious of everything I put in my mouth. I won't have to worry about it much longer.

The entire family arrived at Dabney Shrewsbury's attorney's office above the Citizens Bank on Sycamore Street within minutes of each other.

Madelyn scrutinized Emily's choice of clothes. She looked at Emily dressed in a pink cotton suit with her black pumps. "Your suit goes well with your long blonde hair."

Madelyn wore a smart blue and gray striped skirt, matching gray silk blouse, and a blue jacket. Of course, Madelyn looked stunning and she knew it.

"Mother, you look lovely as always," said Nathan.

The receptionist greeted the group's arrival. Madelyn noted she was an average looking woman; dressed in a black skirt, black low-heel shoes, and a drab brown blouse. Madelyn thought, *She definitely has no taste in her choice of clothes.*

The attorney, Dabney Shrewsbury, had salt and pepper hair. He was dressed in a pin-striped suit, blue shirt, and dark blue bow tie. Madelyn thought, *Oh my goodness. A bow tie. I would expect nothing less from an attorney from this town.*

"Henrietta, I'm so sorry to hear about Gussy," the attorney said. "I do hope you've been able to take care of yourself through this time."

"Thank you for the condolences. I'm holding up well, but only by the grace of God."

Henrietta turned to introduce Madelyn, Stuart, Emily, and Nathan. "Mr. Shrewsbury, do you remember my sister and her children, Emily and Nathan? This is Madelyn's husband, Stuart."

"I barely recognize Emily and Nathan. I haven't seen them in quite some time since they were small kids."

He added, "May I have my secretary bring some coffee?"

Nathan replied, "No thank you."

Dabney said, "Have a seat. We'll get right to the subject at hand. I've already made each of you a copy of the will. The will provisions are standard. I'll summarize the major provisions."

"Gussy's will was written the 10th of January 1983. Gussy thought it best to have a supervised estate instead of non-supervised. This means the Executrix, Henrietta, will file a detailed inventory with the court, post a bond, and obtain the court's permission for any major decisions. As you can see, Madelyn and Henrietta share the majority of the estate after payment of debts, taxes, and my fee, an hourly rate of $150. Henrietta is entitled to an Executrix's fee. Emily and Nathan have smaller bequests. Each will receive $20,000."

Henrietta proclaimed, "I don't want to be paid anything."

Madelyn was pleased.

Dabney further described the probate process. "It's all pretty well cut and dried. I'll call an appraiser, who will assess the total value of Gussy's estate. You'll have time to decide what you want to do with the assets."

They spent a few minutes discussing Gussy's holdings. They were amazed at the extent and value of the estate.

"I think Uncle Gussy was quite frugal." Emily proclaimed.

Madelyn, anxiously, with some force in her voice, said, "How long is it going to take? I'd like to start thinking about investment opportunities. The money will earn much more the sooner the better."

The attorney replied, "According to Indiana law, the estate can't be settled before a minimum of six months. With the size of Gussy's estate, there may be Federal estate taxes, as well as Indiana inheritance taxes. I'd say it'd be between nine months to a year."

Madelyn exclaimed, "That long!"

26

She left her apartment for the dentist for her broken tooth. Emily moved at a crawl on 82nd Street in Indianapolis. She couldn't remember such a traffic jam in the Castleton area, except for the hectic Christmas rush. It was always crowded on 82nd Street at Christmas time. Then police are needed to direct traffic in a New York-style traffic jam. Emily thought, *How commercial Jesus' birthday has become.* Today's stop and go traffic was definitely out of the ordinary for May. Apparently, a thunderstorm knocked out the electricity. The stoplights were out of order. Emily was a stickler for promptness, and hated being late.

She was going to be late for her dentist appointment with Dr. Samuel Jacobs; husband of her mother's friend, Sally. She picked up her blue cell phone and called her neighbor. Both teachers were off school for a teacher's work at home day.

"Why, hello, Emily." Evelyn answered She recognized Emily's voice immediately.

"I need an important favor," requested Emily.

Without hesitating, Evelyn agreed, "Of course. What do you need?"

"Could you please look up the phone number of Dr. Samuel Jacobs? I'm stuck in the most horrible traffic on 82nd Street. The traffic lights are out. I've sat for nearly twenty minutes without moving. I have an appointment at Dr. Jacob's office. I know I'll be late; I hate being late."

"I'm glad our electricity isn't off. Give me a second."

"No problem, Evelyn, take all the time you need. I'm not going anywhere."

Emily rang the dentist's office. She said she'd be late.

She arrived thirty minutes late. Emily thought *This is not the way to start a doctor-patient relationship.* Fortunately, the next patient arrived early and replaced Emily's scheduled appointment time. After x-rays, Emily tried to relax while she waited for Dr. Jacobs to finish with the other patient.

A short time later, Dr. Jacobs entered the room, with a cheery introduction of himself. "Hello, I'm Dr. Jacobs." He shook her hand. She thought he was very polite and handsome. But she thought, *Did Sally marry a younger man? Oh, he must be her son.*

Dr. Drew Jacobs said, "I'm sorry my father couldn't fit you into his schedule. I'm Drew Jacobs, his son. I had cancellations so it worked out fine. In the event you need more than a filling, you'll be my father's patient. I'm helping out."

Emily was quick to thank the dentist for seeing her on such short notice. "I want you to know how much I appreciate you working me into your busy schedule. I don't have a regular dentist. I've never had an emergency dental problem before. You're certainly the answer to my prayers. I've been a bit negligent with my teeth since high school. I need to start having regular cleanings and check-ups again."

Dr. Jacobs did an initial exam. Emily asked, "What do you think? Can you save my tooth?"

"Well, Emily, I'll have to look at your x-rays before making a final diagnosis, but I certainly want to do everything to save the tooth. Let me read the x-rays."

A few minutes later, he informed Emily of his findings. "It looks like we can try a filling first. I hope it will do the job. If the filling doesn't hold, you'll need a crown. My father does them. I always like to try the least expensive and less aggressive action first. Often that takes care of the problem and makes my patients happy."

Emily nervously quipped, "Will it be very expensive? I'm not sure any of those solutions will make me happy, but you are the authority. I'm at your disposal. Let the drilling begin!"

Dr. Jacobs said, "I understand the cost of dental care can be expensive. I'll try to keep your costs down. If I see it will be more than you can afford there are some options for paying over time. However I won't cut the services and treatments to your mouth."

Before the Novocaine took effect, Emily said, "Thank you!"

Dr. Jacobs, like other dentists, started a discussion while he worked on Emily's tooth. "My mother, Sally, was pleased to meet you and your brother at your uncle's funeral. I'm sorry to hear of your loss. Gussy must have been an interesting person from what my mother says. She was pleased to reconnect with your mother. They had a close relationship from activities in 4-H. She said how it was so nice to see her after a very long time. She speaks highly of Grovetown and its residents."

Drew Jacobs was conscious of his patient's inability to talk. He formed any question to accommodate a head response.

The dentist asked, "I heard your uncle was stabbed. Is it true?"

Emily silently shook her head, "Yes."

"Are there any leads? I would think in such a small town as Grovetown everybody knows everybody's business."

She shook her head, "No."

"Well I hope you and the rest of your family have closure soon."

He called in his assistant to finish the tasks of filling the tooth. She asked, "Do I need to come back?"

"Not unless you have any trouble. If you do, please call the office. We'll be sure to work you in as soon as possible. Meeting you has been a pleasure. Unfortunately, it took a cherry pit to break your tooth to meet me. He thought, *Emily is lovely. I don't remember seeing a woman as cute as she is in some time. I think I'll ask her out since she's actually Dad's patient. Guess I'll wait a few days and call her. Eye candy, but it won't rot your teeth*

*****

Emily found herself thinking about Dr. Drew Jacobs. *Wow! I could make going to the dentist a habit. Dr. Drew Jacobs is quite good-looking.*

At home, she slowly ate her supper of a bowl of Campbell's Chicken Noodle Soup, her favorite with a glass of milk. Dr. Jacobs suggested only soft food for the evening.

She fed Mr. Whiskers and played with him awhile. He loved chasing a peacock feather. The large cat craved attention even only after her short time away from him. Next, Emily called Nathan to learn more about the police investigation.

Nathan answered, He had "caller ID" so he knew who was calling. "Why, hi, Em. What's up? Are you okay? How did the trip to the dentist go?"

"Yeth, I whent to the denthist and I'm okay, ethept for having twable thawlking." She burst into giggles at her vocally challenged state.

Nathan joined her in her laughter. "As a journalist, I would have trouble committing your last statement to print. I've never been the greatest at writing dialects. Are you really still doped up?"

"Yes, the Novocain hafsn't worn off completely, but I may have exaggerated a little bit though. Oh, I keep thinking about Uncle Gussy. Dr. Jacobs asked about the investigation. Have you learned anymore?"

"Nar a thing, I'm sorry to report," he Irishly replied to her query.

"Do you think the police are actively searching for the killer?"

Nathan answered, "I think so. I understand they've been talking to business people, friends, and neighbors. However, they don't have any solid leads. I did hear there were a couple of strangers in town that day."

"Why don't *you* help, like Mother wants?"

Nathan pushed his glasses up. "I think I'm going to get involved. I've been talking to Dad about it. I hope I don't upset you, but I'm thinking about including Uncle Gussy's investigation in my thesis."

"Nathan, It's sounds luvlaly. I certainly understand your hesitation, but you know Uncle Gussy loved a good mystery. I think he would feel honored to have you include him in your work. Would it be published?"

"Thanks, Sis. I appreciate your support. My thesis would be available to read in the Notre Dame Library, I think. I doubt it would appear in any commercial publications. You know what? I did hear through the grapevine Chief Petty's leaving for California soon after I get back there. He and his wife are going to their son's graduation from UCLA. They are vacationing at the same time. They're touring the Southwest for about a month or so. A search for a viable suspect will most likely be put on a back burner."

"Well, there you go. You *must* help!" Emily commanded. When are you returning to Grovetown? I can't leave until the 28th.

Nathan answered, "May 18, ten days before you."

"Great!" she fervently declared. "Hopefully you'd have the whole case settled by the time I arrive. I hate to say it, but the murderer has to be someone in town. There aren't many outsiders roaming around."

"I need to learn how real investigative journalists work. So working on the murder investigation may give me the edge I need for my paper."

"Exactly! 'Investigative work', key phrase. You must help investigate Uncle Gussy's murder."

"I agree," Nathan said. Since my time in Grovetown is also my summer vacation, I want to take some time for canoe trips and a run or two with Patrick."

"Those should be fun diversions. I know you'll need some time off. I will, too. We might find it feasible for me to go canoeing and watch the runs. I know it would be fun and would give us some time together. Also, those activities might make it feel I'm having a real summer vacation."

Nathan said, "The Notre Dame Race is in early June, while the Muscatatuk Run is during the Fourth of July weekend. Patrick and I would like to do both, if we can get our training up to par."

"This sounds great!" announced Emily. The subject changed again, this time by Emily. "How is Mother? Have you talked to her? I talked to Aunt Henri and she seems to be adjusting. She's so worried about handling the estate. She seems a bit overwhelmed."

"Mother seems fine to me. Besides pressing me to get involved, her other major project is figuring out how best she can invest her inherited money. And how quickly she can have the money in her hands."

Emily answered, "Really? She shouldn't be counting her chickens before they hatch. I hope, for her sake, everything goes smoothly."

27

Drew Jacobs looked for Emily's phone number in her file. Her information said she was a teacher. He was going to ask her out for a date. He saw no ethical conflict since his father was her dentist of record.

On Thursday evening, the day after she was at the dentist office, he dialed her cell phone. He noted, *I'm glad her number was on the info sheet. What with cell phones and no land phone, I see huge problems and difficulties in finding someone's phone number or address. I wonder how the system could change to make the information transparent.*

Emily didn't recognize the caller's number a 317 area code. The prefix was the same as hers. She never answered unknown callers especially from unfamiliar numbers. She thought, *I might as well answer. My intuition says the caller's okay.*

"This is Emily. May I ask who's calling?"

"It's Drew Jacobs. I wanted to check in to see how your tooth is doing. How are you?"

"I'm fine, thank you. Once the Novocaine wore off, I felt no different than before I ate the cherry."

"Good. Now we need the filling to stay. I explained your situation to my father. He said you could call him anytime if a problem offers its ugly head. And I have another reason for calling you. Please call me Drew. May I take you out to dinner Saturday night? We could also catch a movie. *Walk the Line* is playing. Johnny Cash's story. *King Kong* is a remake of the old classic. *Memoirs of a Geisha* has excellent reviews. Is it too little notice?"

Emily was pleasantly surprised. She instantly blushed. *At least he can't see my scarlet face over the phone.*

She said, "I don't have any plans for Saturday night. I'd like to go to dinner with you. I've heard good reviews of all three movies. I enjoy good country music and would find Johnny Cash's story informative. I accept your offer."

"I think we'll have fun. Do you have a favorite restaurant?"

"I like all sorts of dining: Italian, Hoosier cooking, Chinese. You choose. I'm not familiar with many restaurants."

Drew asked, "Have you ever been to the Kopper Kettle Inn in Morristown? You can sit in the garden and tour the old house. The restaurant is well known for country-style dining. The specialty of the house—fried chicken, mashed potatoes, gravy, corn, and green beans. And of course fried biscuits. Definitely my favorite—comfort food. How does the Kopper Kettle sound?"

"I've heard about it, but I've never been there. The menu sounds tasty."

"Super, it's a date. I'll make reservations for dinner. Please give me directions to your home. I'll pick you up at six."

*****

On Sunday, Drew again picked Emily up. This time after church. They had a fast lunch at a small café in Broad Ripple. Next stop was a trip to the Indianapolis Museum of Art. Nothing new to Emily. She saw the remarkable exhibits differently from when she took her students.

And so the whirlwind continued. Daily conversations. Dinner Friday night, Saturday in Brown County, window-shopping. Sunday sail boating and swimming at Geist, and talking every day for the next week.

Emily thought, *Wow! I've never had a man give me this much attention. This dating Drew is like running a marathon. What do I do? Emily, slow it down.*

Emily's last day of school, was Friday, May 27. She would be in Grovetown Saturday. She was nearly packed. She took time for another date with Drew Friday night.

Drew knew the time was coming for her move to Grovetown. She would be almost three hours away. He thought, *At least we have cell phones. I want to be with her all the time. I think I'm falling in love with this tall, green-eyed girl. I never believed in love at first sight. I do now. Why I haven't even kissed her. Of course, we've always been in public places. I don't have the nerve to ask her to come to my place. I've never known a girl like her. I know I'll have to court her. When will I see her next? Maybe tonight she'll let me kiss her tonight. Dare I? Drew, you have to take it slow man. Take it slow.*

Drew stopped by a florist when he was able to take a break. He ordered two dozen pink long stem roses. Not in a vase. He wanted a long box for loose roses tied with a red ribbon. On the card was a message: "Your students will miss you but I'll miss you more. With love and friendship, Drew." His instructions to the florist were to deliver to the school before noon.

Drew arranged for a private table, at the Columbia Club on the Circle downtown. He was a member of the exclusive Columbia Club. *This is an evening to impress.*

28

Nathan and Soho returned to Grovetown from South Bend late Wednesday night May 18. On the drive he thought about his last date with Judy. *I hope and pray I can determine where I want my relationship to be with Judy. Do I want to spend a lifetime with her?* He quickly unloaded his car at his father's house. Nathan reacquainted Soho with his new litter box, food, and water locations. He fell into bed and was instantly asleep.

Nathan awoke excited and refreshed, ready to attack the day. Raymond was already up when Nathan appeared in the kitchen. Raymond poured out the remainder of his coffee into a travel cup.

Newspaper offices open early. In Grovetown, it was promptly at seven am Thursday when the paper came out. The *Grovetown Tribune* office was in an old two-story building owned by Nathan's father. The frame building was painted yellow with forest green shutters. There were flowers in outside pots. Raymond liked it cheerful and welcoming. Inside it was all business.

He fiddled with his keys and unlocked the front door; Raymond said to Nathan, "Let me show you around. I've changed it a lot since the last time you were here. You'll notice I don't have the old presses. I sold them on commission in an auction. Now we computerize the newspaper and send the files by computer to an offset printer in Peony. My assistant, Larry, picks the papers up quite early on Thursdays. The printing is a bit more expensive but worth it."

Nathan listened and readjusted his glasses.

Raymond continued, "This is the same reception office where the public brings articles and ads for submission."

The reception area had large window boxes filled with violets, a potted lemon tree, and some green plants. There were ecru mini-blinds on the windows. They open for southern exposure. The heavy utilitarian carpet was the same forest green as the outside shutters. On the counter were silk sunflowers in a crystal vase. Behind the counter was a large antique walnut desk with a desktop computer. Personal pictures and knick-knacks adorned the desk where the receptionist/accountant, worked daily from eight to four.

On the walls were matching framed front pages from memorable historical events: An English newspaper's rendition of the sinking of the *Titanic*, a Dallas paper's story of Kennedy's assassination, An Indianapolis newspaper's coverage of "The Day of Death" on the Trade Towers 9-11, and a poster depicting D-Day stories from around the world. Visitors to the office enjoyed perusing pages of the news. They talked about their personal memories of applicable events.

Nathan was impressed with his dad's flair for creating a homey but business atmosphere. "I see you chose to use the Indy coverage for 9-11. Very astute of you. Certainly shows folks here they too were affected by the catastrophe."

Raymond led Nathan to the adjoining conference room. "We meet in here to layout the pages and assign stories for the next edition. We need plenty of room to spread it out."

"I like your use of Indiana art in here. I remember seeing these paintings at home," said Raymond.

"You're right. These used to hang at home. The artist's name is Trover. He's dead and renowned for his oil paintings of Brown County. A friend of your grandfather bought them from some guy selling paintings downtown Indianapolis on the circle in the fifties. Turned out the guy was Trover. "

"Let me show you my personal office. It's where the old workroom and presses used to be. I have a lot more space than I had before."

When entering the office located behind the conference room. The first thing a visitor noticed was a framed copy of the First Amendment, a necessity for any serious newsman to have on display. Nathan liked the framed colored photographs. "I assume you shot all of these photos. I'm impressed. You have an eclectic collection of your work. I especially like the one of the Tucker Bridge over Deer Fly Creek. I have good memories of times we spent fishing."

Raymond was fond of his grandfather's antique roll-top desk. The oak desk seemed to be an anachronism. Everything else in the room, including Raymond's wireless laptop computer, were the most advanced available.

Built-in walnut bookcases covered one wall from floor to ceiling. A sliding library ladder provided easy access to the wide assortment of books: reference books, dictionaries, atlases, encyclopedias, and some favorite non-fiction books. Kerouac's tattered *On the Road* was propped open on the desk, one of Raymond's current books he was re-reading. Nathan remembered Grisham's *The Last Juror* hanging open over the arm of his dad's favorite chair at home. Raymond was notorious for reading several books at a time. He passed the habit on to his son.

Raymond then took Nathan across the hallway and showed him his old office, which was now his assistant's room. Raymond was somewhat embarrassed to let anyone see it. Larry kept his previous cubbyhole so crammed and in such disarray. His new larger office was as messy. A big area provided him more space to clutter. Even the desk appeared lost in the piles of newspapers and other stuff.

He glanced at the clock. "Ottinger is picking up the paper in Peony. Any other day he's late. Promptness is not his forte, but he's such a good writer. I'm willing to overlook the flaw. He writes most of the local news stories, especially on the politics of the town and school board. I have him edit the submitted articles first. I then do the final editing and title the ones I intend to print."

Nathan commented, "I don't remember you ever being kind to me about my tardiness for getting out of or in bed, dinner, school, church, or anyplace we were going. You were hard on me about the way I kept my room. I was satisfied, but you didn't approve of my decorating. I thought my clothes looked okay, wherever they landed. Have you changed much in your old age?" he asked as he pushed his glasses up on his nose.

"Not as far as you're concerned. Look how well you've turned out. Perhaps if I were tougher on him, Larry would be wiser in his political and religious beliefs. I certainly don't agree with many of his views. He proclaims to be an anarchist and atheist. Nevertheless, he seems to be a good person, considerate, and caring. I respect his freedom of thought. We've both learned to tread lightly on those subjects of major disagreement. As you see from his poster, he is a Hunter Thompson fan. He even has a framed cover of *The Rolling Stone Magazine* in memory of Hunter's death. His favorite book is Hunter's *Fear and Loathing in*

Las Vegas. He says it's a great example of Gonzo journalism."

Nathan asked, "Did you ever read the book?"

"Well, yes. I didn't like it. There were too many references to drugs and foul language. Surely you studied 'gonzo journalism' at university?"

His son responded, "I read the book too and expressed similar views as you in a paper. The professor explained Hunter's technique was to make a statement about an issue by mixing fact and fiction. I suppose he was trying to make a point about the drug culture and laid-back attitudes of the 70s."

Raymond continued, "The sports editor and some of the other columnists work from home. They send their articles to the office as attachments to e-mail messages. This seems to work well for all concerned.

"This is Larry's old cubbyhole I offer you for the summer. Sorry it's so tiny, but I know you'll put every inch to good use. I left it white. The space looks larger that way. You have a blank canvas to do with as you wish. I'm sure you'll come up with some clever ideas. The walls are yours."

Raymond showed Nathan the stairs to the second floor and the storage room. Back downstairs, Raymond proceeded to the back area of the building. The last room was the busy workroom. A large utility table used for the mail copies distribution was center stage. One section was a break area. A small table and chairs offered a place for refreshment. On the counter were a coffee pot and microwave. A small refrigerator sat at its side. Raymond proceeded to make a pot of coffee.

He commented, "We keep Coke, Diet Coke, bottled water, and some small containers of milk and juice. When we're getting out the paper, my receptionist makes sure to keep sandwiches, yogurt, and snacks on hand. We often work late into the evening. Let me familiarize you with the various equipment in this room."

Raymond showed Nathan the computer, printers, and copy machine along with other necessary items.

Nathan interrupted, "Dad, I'll use my own laptop. I bought a new one. My old one was acting up, and I didn't want to take a chance with my thesis being botched."

Raymond continued, "All the equipment in the building is networked. Won't be difficult to add you to the network. All articles are sent to the main computer as they are readied for press. Submissions to the paper are digitized. I take many of the photos, but I have the sports editor take those needed for the sports news. Contributors may also submit pertinent pictures with their articles. I decide what pictures are used. It's at my discretion whether to use them according to quality, interest, and space. Digital cameras have certainly made a dramatic change in the newspaper business. Seems almost everyone in town proudly owns a digital camera. Sometimes I really miss using my old faithful 35mm SLR, Konica. We shared many memorable events, and some horrific ones I'd rather forget. I still shoot with it to obtain special effects. You can buy 35mm film, but you have to send the film off to be developed. "

"I remember many conversations you had with Mom about your camera. Konni's cost disturbed her. I really didn't understand why she was so upset."

Raymond responded with chagrin, "Yes, your mother always complained, 'I'm tired of this other woman in your life. Seems like you and Konni have more memories together than we do.' She couldn't adjust to being married to a newspaperman. I know I neglected her more than I should have. I tried to give her time and you kids, too. Oh, well, that's the life of a journalist."

Surprised by Raymond's lament, Nathan expressed his own feelings. "I know you weren't always able to be there when we were young, but you did make it to the most important events. You certainly tried to make it up to us in our teen years. I'm sorry if you feel you were so remiss. I know you've been there for Emily and me through both good and bad times. I hope I never seemed to judge you. In fact, I pray I'll be the kind of father you've always been to me."

Before Raymond could comment further, the phone rang. Ottinger hurried in with the newly printed newspapers for distribution. There was barely time for Raymond to introduce the two young men before the business of the day was underway. A couple of people dropped in to place ads. Julie hadn't arrived yet, so Nathan assessed the situation and took charge of the reception desk in time to process the ads.

The delicious aroma of Raymond's coffee, cooling in its mug, reached his nose, but not his mouth. Nathan realized summer vacation was over and summer obligations have begun. He hurriedly ran towards the coffee.

29

Chief Petty arranged to meet Jake at the café. The Chief was leaving on vacation in a few days. He needed to settle details regarding Gussy's murder investigation. The two ordered the famous breaded tenderloin deluxe sandwiches. Jake said, "Why can't they make a bun big enough?"

They discussed the ongoing investigation into Gussy's death. Petty was leery about leaving Deputy Green in charge. The Chief had a proposition. "Jake, I'd like for you to help oversee the progress of the case, while I'm out west." Jake eagerly agreed to the request, grateful for the opportunity to stay on top of the developments, and possibly sidetrack the investigation if needed.

*****

A few days after Petty left for California, Raymond and Nathan made an afternoon appointment with Green. They met in the newspaper conference room. The two were not aware Jake was involved in the investigation. They surmised Green would be more open than Petty with information.

"Glad we've put this week's paper to bed. We need to get ready for Green. I'll go start some coffee," offered Nathan.

"Great! Be sure to use Costa Rican coffee. I bet Green won't be impressed. However, we'll appreciate it. I always like to celebrate going to press with a special brew," announced Raymond. "I asked the baker at the donut shop for Green's favorite doughnuts. He said all the officers preferred jelly-filled but I also got my favorite chocolate doughnut holes. I hope that suits you."

"They both sound yummy. I do prefer tiger-tails. I'll treat us another day with them, perhaps for next week's printing celebration."

"This could be a fattening summer!" exclaimed Raymond. "You know I'm glad Green agreed to a private meeting here. This town has too many curious ears to talk in any public place."

Father and son heard the front door open and close. They went to meet their guest.

Ron's eyes gleamed at the sight of the pile of doughnuts. Raymond provided a steaming cup of the delicious coffee to the officer.

"This is great! These are my favorites," Ron declared as he automatically dunked a strawberry-filled pastry in his coffee. He devoured it. As expected, he made no comment about the specialty coffee. He quickly chose another doughnut; pleased to see it was blackberry-filled.

Raymond began, "Deputy Green, I'm so glad you agreed to meet us today. We're anxious to hear about the case. You understand we're speaking off the record. If there is something, we can report to the public, we'll be glad to do so. However, right now we're more interested as family members than as reporters. Have there been any new developments or suspects in Gussy's murder?"

Not waiting to swallow, Green mumbled with a full mouth, "Nope! Nuttin'! Seems to be a cold case already, you know, like on TV?" Green laughed at his own brilliance and dunked another donut.Disappointed with Green's statement, Nathan delved further. "Who have you interviewed as possible suspects?"

"We interviewed the neighbor, Lawson, Gussy's tenants, some business people, including Joe at the filling station, and, of course, Gussy's poker buddies. Everybody had an alibi and no motive. Joe mentioned a couple of strangers who came into the station that afternoon. He described them as a hippie hobo and a snobby broad. Haven't found any leads on who they were, just passin' through, I guess. I even talked to the Budweiser truck driver seen at the gas station in town. He said the kid went with him to Peony. He dropped him off at the park

"What about the poker guys' alibis? Did you check them out?" Raymond asked.

"Nah. They're Gussy's best friends. Why would they want to kill him?"

"It does happen. Best friends often share secrets they don't want anyone else to know. What kind of alibis did they have, anyway?" Nathan persisted.

"Well the guys had verified alibis. However, the chief did wonder about the twins' fishin' stories. They had some teensy-weensy differences. Heck, I didn't even notice 'em myself. But, we just never found nuttin' to hang your hat on."

Nathan made a note to check with the twins about their stories. "I'm not even sure who played poker with Uncle Gussy. Who were they?"

"All the Achsworth brothers. Jake and Glenn were paintin' at Glenn's house; Solomon and Richard were checkin' on liquor prices for their businesses. Just know those fellers ain't lien'. And the twins were fishing, as always. Heck, if you think they're all suspects, why anybody in town could be, even you guys." He chuckled at his ridiculous conclusion.

Convinced the discussion of suspects was going nowhere, Nathan asked, "Have you received any new forensic evidence?"

"Well, you already know the autopsy report said Gussy was stabbed. It's also got some other information didn't mean much to me. I got it right here. Ya wanna see it?"

Suppressing his investigative juices, Raymond calmly replied, "Surely I can find something you missed. Mind if I make a copy and look at it later?"

"Sure, don't see why not."

Nathan asked, "Have you had any luck finding the murder weapon?"

"Nah, nothin' with blood on it, anyway. The State cops used stuff with lights, like on TV, to check Gussy's tools for blood but didn't find nuttin'. Besides, none of the things they found seemed to fit the holes in Gussy."

They were anxious for Green to leave so they would have the opportunity to delve into the autopsy report. Nathan asked, "What's going to be your next move, Ron?"

"Well, thought I'd take a couple more of these doughnuts and mosey on down to the bank. They're having a party for their 100th year celebration. I wanna get there before all the good food's gone. You guys interested in joining me?"

"Not right now. Nathan will go later to get the story for next week's paper. Thanks for coming today, Ron. We appreciate this report. Hope we'll find something for you to investigate. Might see you later at the bank."

"That'd be great. I'll probably be there awhile. Good place to visit with everybody. Helps keep me up on the town's gossip. So long," he mumbled as he stuffed another doughnut in his mouth and left, lighting a cigarette. Nathan turned to his father, "Wow. He's not like any police officer I've ever met. I can't believe he let you make a copy of the report."

"Chief Petty would never have let us take such liberties. Let's see what we can find out, shall we?"

They made duplicates so they each could have a copy and a clean copy as well. They each silently scanned the report. They found the report included the weights of organs, the state of tissues, and other technical details of the body. That part meant nothing significant to the men.

The most important results were facts establishing the multiple stab wounds evident in the chest and abdominal area. The forensic specialists took measurements of their depth. The depths ranged from two to twelve centimeters. The most severe was a puncture of the aorta. The technical people said, "He bled out." They believe a sharp instrument caused the wounds. The technicians ruled out a common knife. The weapon was cylindrical in nature. Identifying the exact type of murder weapon is not the medical examiner's responsibility. The forensic team used a new method. They made plaster casts of the puncture wounds. Their report showed a tool similar to a large screwdriver could be the weapon used in the murder.

After reading the report, Nathan turned to his dad, "Well, Dad. What do you think?"

"Looks like a viable possibility one of Gussy's tools was used to kill him. I'd like to rule out premeditation on the part of the killer. Something traumatic must have happened in the workshop to cause someone to violently attack him."

Nathan said, "Do you note what he ate before he died?"

"Yeah, I saw. His last meal was macaroni and cheese. Wonder if it were the café's special that day."

Nathan said, "Well, the Chief said the killer could be anyone. We're no closer to finding out who did it."

"I tend to agree with you. I hate to admit it, but I think I disagree with Green. Anyone could have killed Gussy."

"Hey, Dad, what's your alibi?" Nathan laughed.

"I'll tell if you tell," quipped Raymond. Their light bantering seemed to lessen the gravity of the matter for the moment.

30

On Memorial Day, Nathan and Patrick decided to go on another canoe trip. This time the young men thought it would be fun to take their fathers, Raymond Trinkle and Paul Mattox. They rented a second canoe for their fathers at the landing. Dexter would ride with Nathan and Patrick in the *Gypsy Gal*. They needed two cars to transport the canoes and supplies. For an additional fee, the canoers could leave the rented canoe at the end of the trip. The company transported it back to the landing.

The foursome picked up subs from the local café. They stuffed the coolers, one for each canoe. Paul, Patrick's father said, "I think we'll have enough to fill us up with these Cokes, water, chips, and subs. Maybe we can drift for a while, talk, and eat."

The fathers said in unison, "Sounds good to me." All their paraphernalia was loaded into their designated canoes and they set off.

The day was beautiful for canoeing the shimmering waters of Deer Fly Creek. No storms in a week. Therefore, the creek's water was low and slow.

Patrick questioned Nathan about the investigation. "Do you know if any progress is being made? I sure haven't heard much in the way of rumors."

Nathan watched a jumping fish. He said, "The police aren't talking much, but Dad and I unofficially met with Deputy Green at the newspaper."

"What did he share?"

"We saw the autopsy report. Gussy suffered at the end of his life. How Awful! Green actually let us make a copy of the autopsy report. I'm sure it's second nature to you to hear about the wounds someone reports on paper, but for me, it makes me shiver to think about it. The report even said what Gussy ate for his last meal. He may have partaken of the daily special at the café. Patrick, would you please obtain the lunch menu for that day."

Patrick said, "Death is never easy, especially if the deceased was someone you loved and cared for. I can't believe he actually gave you a copy of the report but I've heard tales of Deputy Green's incompetence before. I'm glad all of my dealings with the police have been through the chief. What else did the autopsy report say?"

"Well, I made a copy for you. There were multiple stab wounds. Dad and I have various theories, but I keep coming back to one. I think it could have been a crime of passion." Nathan sniffed, took off his glasses, and rubbed his eyes.

Patrick said, "Many murderers will overkill, like more wounds than needed. Often those are committed in moments of passion."

Nathan was getting upset. Patrick thought he should change the subject. "How's Henrietta doing managing the estate?"

"I guess ok. She wants to do everything right. Cleaning out his buildings has been a lot of work; she's trying to get appraisals of his property. Uncle Gussy had quite a bit of money set aside. Of course, he did little in the way of repairs to his real estate. He paid little in taxes—just hoarded. He hardly ever spent money on himself. I know my mother will be pleased to inherit her portion. She constantly calls Henrietta and the attorney. She wants her money yesterday.

"The inheritance will certainly help Henrietta financially. Town librarians aren't high on the pay scale. Emily can sure use her money since she makes so little teaching. She still has some school loans. Of course, the gift he left me will help me pay off my school loans. His personal items aren't worth much. I'd like to have some of the wooden figures or boxes he made. He had such a way with wood and produced some lovely things. Oh, did Jayne tell you how aghast my mother was when she found out Buddy was buried with him, in the same casket?"

"Yes, she did. I'm sure Jayne wouldn't have spoken so freely to your mom if she'd known your mother was unaware. I'd love to have seen and heard her response."

Nathan concurred. "The same goes for me."

Paul and Raymond, in the other canoe, were silent most of the time, relishing the nice weather and the gentle flow of the creek in all its naturalness. Neither of them canoed much anymore, so they had to keep their minds on the business at hand. They didn't want to swamp the canoe. Capsizing would be embarrassing.

When the canoes reached the falls, the boys proceeded down them first. The fathers followed at a safe distance, successfully. The slow current was beneficial for their victorious descents.

They progressed toward the place where the trees were down the last trip; Patrick knew the Kanu Klub cleared the debris. He spoke to them about the hours they spent doing the job right after their last trip. The boys' canoe reached the area before their fathers' arrival. The area looked as if the club hadn't been through. He would have to call them again.

New trees down everywhere. A logjam caused pools of stinky, stagnant water in several areas. Patrick exclaimed, "I can't believe it. This creek is worse than the last time we were here. And I know they cleared most of the problems a few weeks ago."

Nathan said, "Look over here! I agree with you. I can't tell if there's water in some of these pools or scum."

Patrick, a doctor, was very concerned about the situation. What was causing the scum? He knew it wasn't normal. He pulled the canoe with Nathan's help up to the tree blockage.

He said, "Nathan, it looks like we'll have to portage, again. When Dad and your father catch up with us, make sure they know what they have to do. I'm going to empty a water bottle and take a scum sample to the hospital lab in Peony when we return to Grovetown. We can't have this situation in our river. It's bad for the health of the community."

Nathan agreed. The two paddled to the side of the creek. The fathers soon appeared around the bend. Nathan yelled explanations and instructions how to portage.

Raymond said, "I'm starved and thirsty. Our fathers must be too. Why don't we eat our sandwiches while we're grounded?" Everyone agreed with Raymond. Patrick collected his water samples while the dads helped Nathan get lunch together.

Patrick's concern with the stagnant water dominated the lunch discussion. He pressed his comrades for a quick departure. "If you don't mind, I want to hurry down the creek to our vehicles. I'd like to get these samples to the Peony hospital lab as early today as possible. Since today is a holiday, I'll have to wait to call the Health Department Office in the morning. At least the tests will start ASAP."

"This logjam would make a great special interest picture," Raymond commented. "I think I'll get my camera. I'll drive back here later and take one. The local canoers need to be alerted. If your results turn up any problems, it would be a natural follow-up report to the picture. I hope there won't be any health issues."

Everyone concurred to eat and get to the end. They packed up their lunch remains, launched their canoes, and paddled on down the creek. The water was swifter now they passed the logjam. Nathan agreed to go with Patrick to the hospital, and the fathers went their separate ways.

31

Henrietta began her day as usual. She dressed in a light blue top and skirt, with a navy blazer. Her wardrobe was filled with such mix and match pieces. She felt her position as head librarian necessitated a professional appearance. She never wore pantsuits at work or church. She ate her usual breakfast. She preferred flavored hot tea, buttered toast, and fresh fruit. She read *The Peony Daily.* She checked to see if there were any new reports on Gussy's death. As usual there was nothing new reported. *I sure do miss my brother. Why can't the police find his killer? Dear God, I know You are Sovereign. Please help me to understand why no one has located a suspect. I trust in knowing everything is in your hands. Thank you for being with me. In Jesus' name. Amen.*

Emily woke up to her clock radio, tuned to the local Christian radio station. She was glad to find out the Moody station was available in this area. The station was her favorite at home. Henrietta said it was fine for Emily to wear jeans at the library. She quickly dressed in comfortable blue jeans, a chartreuse knit top, and denim blazer. Her chartreuse slingbacks added an extra flair to her outfit. She fixed her breakfast of a bagel with cream cheese, low-fat yogurt, and an orange. She joined Henrietta in the dining room. She missed her usual coffee, but her aunt did make a fine cup of Joe.

Henrietta finished the highlights of the paper; Henrietta began the crossword puzzle of the day. *Having Emily here for breakfast is pleasant.* She often carried on a one-way conversation with her yellow male canary, Bookworm. Now she had Emily with her.

She said to Emily, "I scanned most of the highlights in the paper today. The writers in the county seat don't know any more about Gussy's death than we do." She started the crossword puzzle. "What is a four-letter word for 'being in charge beginning with the letter ''R'?"

Emily smiled because she knew her aunt threw her an easy one. "Rule."

Henrietta asked for some help on some of some more difficult puzzle words. Emily wasn't much help, but she tried.

Emily's newest puzzle passion was Sudoku number puzzles. They were unknown to her aunt. Emily brought some Sudoku books with her; *I'll teach her later.*

It was time to set off for their first day of work together at the library.

*****

Emily said, "Henrietta. Mr. Whiskers' has a problem jumping up on the furniture, table, and such. Most other cats are always on the table or kitchen cabinets. Maine Coons are quite large in stature and weight. I suspect the poor baby has a weight problem. The breed doesn't even reach full size until they are five or six years old. He's three. His six-inch whiskers gave me his name, Mr. Whiskers."

Henrietta exclaimed, "Why, I've never seen nor heard of such whiskers."

They walked the short way to the old brick Carnegie Library. The pair enjoyed the spring sights, especially all the brightly colored peonies. This season in Southern Indiana was Henrietta's favorite time.

She commented on the flowers, "Peonies bloom here before Memorial Day. Did you know why the blooms have so many ants?"

"No, Why?"

"The botanists say ants help the flowers open by walking in the pods. Aren't the colors of the peonies vivid? I like the pink rather than the white. You missed April's daffodils, violets, and tulips. The flowers were even prettier this year than last. We had some early flowers in March, but a late ice storm destroyed them."

Emily responded, "The managers landscaped my apartment complex. The area consists mainly of a little lake with geese and ducks. They keep the lawns mowed. No weeds in sight. The hired gardener does an excellent job. The management landscaped around the lake, pool, entertainment center, and entrance. The authorities encourage each tenant to maintain their areas. Everyone is supposed to be green. I have some potted plants on the balcony. Gerber Daisies in orange and yellow. Of course, they are annuals. I hang a large Boston fern out there too. I bring him in during the winter. I also summer my lemon tree so it can have sun. My lemon tree bloomed, and there are small lemons. "

Henrietta said, "I would think the geese and ducks are interesting to watch. Is the lake stocked with fish?"

"There are fish and a few fishermen besides the hungry geese and ducks. We have a geese population problem. Geese are very messy. Kids are reluctant to be at the lake much. The honking fowl can also be mean. The apartment managers want to reduce the population. One idea is to place a large plastic coyote nearby the lake. When motion detectors activate the wild animal, his head moves back and forth and howls."

Henrietta remarked, "Do you think it'll work?"

"They hope so. Apparently, a church used this method, and a bunch of wild geese took off in V formation."

The couple continued their walk in silence inhaling the nice morning. They arrived at the library and opened it up. Henrietta retrieved the books from the outside book drop. She noted how rusted it became over the winter.

She commented to Emily, "This drop box could sure use a paint job, don't you think? What color would you recommend?"

"Why, red, of course," Emily responded. "It's for returning books read. I'm sure we can talk Nathan into doing the job for us. He'll need some breaks from helping Dad."

Henrietta took Emily down the old, wood, rickety stairs to the children's section. The area was bright and cheerful. Many of the books were old. Henrietta remarked, "We're trying to obtain some grants to update our children's selections. A patron painted the lovely murals on the walls. She was so talented. She drew the cartoon characters by hand, and then painted them. They're of characters from books. There are Snow White, Harry Potter, Charlie Brown, and an asparagus from *Veggie Tales*. She wanted to do another wall. Unfortunately, she became quite ill. She was ill for several years. None knew she received bad blood from a transfusion when she was treated for a severe nosebleed. The blood carried Hepatitis C that killed her liver. She died from cancer, after a liver transplant. She was a faithful Christian. She wouldn't even let us pay for the paint. She said, 'I did God's work to honor our Lord Jesus.' It was so sad. Before she passed, she told everyone she saw, 'I love you, but Jesus loves you more.' She was a collector of hats, old and new. She not only collected hats but also wore them everywhere. Her daughter counted over three hundred in her collection. In her honor, attendees at her showing received a hat. Her best friend bought us the new set of young adult research books as a memorial."

The singsong ring of Emily's cell phone broke the quiet of the library. Emily tried to answer it quickly. On Caller ID, the caller was Madelyn Monroe. "Hello, Mom, What's up?"

"I hear you're in Grovetown. Why didn't you call me when you arrived? You worried your poor mother."

"I'd only call if there's a problem or if I wasn't in touch with you for a while. I think I'm settled in."

"What have you learned about Gussy's death?"

"Nothing."

"Well, that's what your brother said yesterday. I need to go. A friend of mine wants to shop for clothes for her cruise to Alaska. Taking a cruise to Alaska is all the rage right now. Tell your aunt I'll call her tonight about ten. Bye."

Emily hung up, apologized to her aunt. She said, "I'm sorry to interrupt our conversation. If I didn't answer her call, she would call again and again every ten minutes."

"I fear you're correct."

"Mother is going to call you tonight at ten. I think that's too late, but you know her."

"We need to update our handicap accessibility. You have to climb those steep outside steps to enter the library. The inside stairs are too narrow and steep to put in a lift. There's no room for an elevator anyplace."

Emily asked, "What can you do? Can't the library get funding to expand?"

"We tried but there was so much outcry about the tax situation. The tax increase was quite nominal, less than a dollar for each property. The town council pulled their support because of the public outcry. Many of the protesters have never been in our library. We lost a large grant to remodel the Carnegie Library. Citizens were upset about the terrible rise in taxes due to the reassessment. The tax increase caused by building the new high school you saw the other day. People have commented the new high school looks like a prison. I think so too. The Carnegie is the loser."

Emily asked more questions, "What can you do now? What about the parking situation? There's little parking, except on the street."

Henrietta responded, "We were able to demolish an old empty house on library property and put in a stone parking area. Four vehicles will be able to park there. Patrons can come in the back door and climb fewer steps."

"That's a start," said Emily.

Henrietta continued talking about the library setup. She said, "Now we keep old Grovetown newspapers in this room off the children's section. The other cubbyhole is a limited genealogical area. Well, we better go upstairs and officially open the library. Then I'll show you the computers and other equipment you'll be using."

Emily learned the basic operations. Her principal position was working on the computerization of the stacks. She would also be helping patrons check out books, answer inquiries, and provide help to anyone with the computers. Henrietta had two part-time helpers along with a cleaning person. Library volunteers, Friends of the Library, give their time. They handle fund-raising, book sales, and the children's summer program.

One of the aides handled business at the desk. Henrietta and Emily took a quick lunch at the café. Henrietta bragged about the giant deluxe tenderloin. They didn't disappoint. The ladies split the Indiana's specialty with homemade coleslaw and fries. They discussed the upcoming preparations for the annual book sale. Henrietta explained, "The Friends of the Library use the money raised for prizes for the summer reading program. I'm thankful to have such dedicated community support. Our little library is kept alive because of their involvement."

The two women returned to the library. Henrietta explained how she began to prepare for the book sale. "I've weeded out all the old books. I've pulled those outdated, too worn to keep, or fiction not circulated in seven to ten years."

Henrietta continued, "This has kept me busy for a few weeks. You can help by pulling cards of the books I've already removed. I want to do the weeding myself since I know my patrons. Then we'll get down to the nitty-gritty of computerizing, so we can become automated."

The women walked by the circulation desk; Henrietta remembered she hadn't fed her blue beta fish, Shakespeare. She fed him first thing in the morning. He lived in a glass vase with a calla lily growing in the water. Multi-colored marbles covered the bottom of his vase. His home sat upon the circulation desk for everyone to enjoy. He came to the top of the vase when he saw her coming, knowing it was feeding time. He was especially agitated today because he missed his regular feeding time.

Emily worked pulling and discarding cards of the culled books. The day went quickly. Henri was going to prepare a simple supper of cubed steak, green beans, and boiled new potatoes. The library was open until eight. The aide would handle the rest of the evening and close up.

On the way home for supper, Henrietta and Emily discussed Gussy's death investigation.

Henrietta said to her niece, "Emily, the police are accomplishing nothing."

Emily replied, "Yes, I know. I'm so glad Nathan has agreed to help. Why, I'd help, if I could. Surely, there are some leads or clues. Maybe Father would get involved."

"I think it's great Nathan's getting involved. He likes to do investigative reporting."

Emily giggled, "I suppose after this story, he'll be a professional investigator. He'll become insufferable."

*****

The land phone rang. "Good evening, Henrietta speaking. May I help you?"

Madelyn answered, "It's me! I want an update on progress of the estate. I called the County Clerk's in Peony. What use was my calling? A waste of my time. The court's docket only shows two items: the filing of the will to probate and bond certification. So, what's going on?"

Henrietta answered, "It's so thoughtful you called. I pray you're well. We're still doing the inventory and appraisals. The estate tax forms will take time. I wish the government would pass inheritance relief on big estates. I know the country needs taxes, but the taxes on this estate will be substantial. I hate to see such a financial loss to the family. We'll have to pay a lot of state taxes, too. To save money, I won't take an administrator's fee."

Madelyn exclaimed, "Good! Of course, you won't. The management of an estate is an easy job. What do you mean a lot of taxes? I thought the government raised the minimum for Federal taxes."

"Yes, the IRS changed the rule. Nevertheless, appraisals are coming in pretty high. There's still a lot to appraise. His half of the farm is worth much more than I imagined. Of course, I'll retain my half. The income from cash rent allows me save money and buys some extras. Gussy was quite frugal, and he took advantage of tax laws."

"Wasn't it cheating?"

"No. That's not what I said. Let me give an example. Mr. Shrewsbury, the estate's tax attorney, explained Gussy took depreciation through the years. Recaptured depreciation adds to the appraisal value making a greater amount for taxes. There also may be income he didn't report to the IRS. I think it's called 'keeping a double set of books' or maybe 'cooking the books'. The tax subjects are way beyond mental comprehension.

Madelyn said, "I'm sure it's all over my head. Are you making any headway?"

Henrietta said, "We're working as fast as we can. The attorney said after we conclude inventory and appraisals in the estate, I can petition the court for an order allowing me to make a partial distribution. Luckily, there's no debt."

"Well hurry up. Good. That saves some money. Can I speak to my daughter?"

Emily said, "Hello, Mother. How are you? Well, I hope.'

Madelyn answered, "I'm fine, I guess. This estate situation is driving me crazy. Oh well, are you having any problem with your tooth?"

"Not yet. Dr. Jacobs says he hopes it will work. Otherwise, I may have to have a crown, which is costly. I have no dental insurance. I'm a bit worried."

"I'm sure you'll figure out something. Did you meet Sally's son? He's a dentist and works with his father. I hear he's quite handsome. You need a young man with promise. You don't have anyone yet, do you?"

"Oh, Mother! I'm happy like I am. Moreover, I like who I am. I have plenty of time to wait for Mr. Right."

"Did you meet Sally's son at the dental office?"

"Yes, I did. Samuel couldn't fit me in. Dr. Drew had a cancellation. He filled my tooth."

"Yes, a man with promise. Is he handsome? Sally says he's single and not involved with anyone Someday he'll take over the practice. Definitely a man of promise."

Emily commented. "He's nice and handsome too."

"When do you have to go back for another dentist appointment?"

"I don't have another appointment. If the filling falls out, I'm supposed to make an appointment with his father. Drew can't handle complicated tooth matters yet."

"Don't you need a cleaning? You could see him again. You have to seize the day. Carpe Diem!"

"Mother, please let me do my own thing. I can do my own dating. You know I'*m* a big girl. But I love you anyway. Bye, Mother."

Emily returned to her discussion with her aunt. "You know there's a lot of work with this estate stuff. I think you should keep track of your time. I wouldn't blame you for needing to cover your time and expenses. You still have a big job ahead. Gussy must have really trusted you. I'm sure you're trusting in God to help you with all these legal matters. I know He has been helping me with my grief."

Henrietta replied, "God's been guiding me. I don't want or need a fee. I'm fine. God provides."

They made chamomile tea. Each relaxed with a book. They sipped the calming tea then were silent for about ten-fifteen minutes.Emily interrupted the quiet. She asked, "What books are you reading these days? I'm reading a unique story, *The Shadow of the Wind,* by a Spanish writer, Carlos Ruiz Zafon. The novel isn't a murder mystery but a mystery anyway. I think the book is a very good read. I've also read a couple of books by Dan Brown, *Angels and Demons,* and *The Da Vinci Code.* You know *The Da Vinci Code* is controversial. I suppose that if you take it as fiction, it's so-so. Some people believe it to be true, but I don't. I hear Ron Howard is making a movie based on the book. I enjoyed the mystery in *Angels and Demons,* though. However, I like the *Cat Who* books by Lillian Jackson Brown and the *Mrs. Murphy* books by Rita Mae Brown. I'm reading the *Harry Potter* series. Some students in my class are reading them. I want to understand what they read."

Henrietta replied, "I'm reading Beverly Lewis' new Amish series. She is such a good Christian writer. Did you know she was born in Amish country? I'm sure that's why she writes and knows so much about the Amish practices. You should start this series."

"I've heard of her books. Sounds like some good summer reading. I think I will."

Henrietta and Emily were home and enjoyed the rest of the evening despite Madelyn's call.

Emily said to her aunt, "I'm so happy you allowed Mr. Whiskers to stay with you too. He's well-behaved but mischievous. You have to hear his story. I found him in a shelter. He was probably five months old. I took him to a vet to be neutered. The veterinarian clinic was over two miles away. Somehow after the surgery he escaped from the clinic. The clinic employees were devastated about him running away, but not as much as I was. Well, a few days later, I was leaving for work and there he was outside my apartment building. He had some burrs in his fur, but otherwise appeared unhurt. Amazingly he found his was back to my place. Apparently there are some, but not all, cats and dogs who have the homing ability to return to a certain place. There are woods and a stream between the clinic and my apartment. I like to say Mr. Whiskers came home 'over the river and through the woods'. Isn't that remarkable?"

Henrietta replied, "Why I've heard of that happening in the news and movies but I've never had first-hand knowledge. He's been a good cat so far. He hasn't even tried to eat Bookworm. "

Henrietta covered Bookworm's cage and she, Emily, and Mr. Whiskers retired for the evening after a busy day.

32

Permelia, dressed in a peasant blouse and a long gypsy style skirt, picked up her land phone. She didn't have a cell phone, only a Tracfone for emergencies. She wanted to reconnect with her old high school friend, Emily. Today is Wednesday. Businesses in town closed on Wednesdays. The library closed on Wednesday, too.

She rang Henrietta's house and asked to speak with Emily.

"Hello," Emily answered.

"Hi, Emily. This is Permelia. I thought since you are off from the library today, you might want to come over and see my gardens."

"Oh," answered Emily, "What a great idea! I'll be over in a few minutes. Let me get changed."

"Super!" exclaimed Permelia. "We'll have lemon mint tea, or would you prefer chamomile?"

"Either will be fine, but I've never had lemon mint before. I drink chamomile to calm myself after a hard day at school," replied Emily.

Permelia decided, "Well, it's lemon mint for sure. I'll go out and pick some before you get here. There's nothing as tasty as fresh lemon mint tea with local honey. I get mine a little south of town from a nearby bee handler. Did you know local honey is a natural preventative for many allergies? I gave Robbie this local honey daily this spring.

His allergies have been so much better. I guess it's similar to allergy shots."Emily was ten minutes late to Permelia's house. Drew Jacobs called. He said, "You're off this afternoon aren't you? I took the afternoon off. Some of the guys are hitting the links. I'd rather be with you than golfing. Would you want to meet in Bloomington and go on an afternoon picnic and an early movie?"

"Oh, Drew. Your plans sound like fun, but I'm spending the afternoon with a classmate from high school We're going to look at her herb garden, have tea, and talk. I'm sorry. However, I have a dental appointment Friday with your father. That filling seems loose. I might see you briefly. My brother and a couple of others are going to Notre Dame for a run."

Drew said, "Okay, we'll talk and figure something out. Enjoy yourself. Talk to you Friday." He hung up disappointed.

Emily arrived; Permelia showed her to the parlor and excused herself to check on the tea. Numerous papers and books scattered on the coffee table drew Emily's attention. On closer examination, she saw the papers were recipes for herbal vinegars and herbal creams. The books had the following titles: *Garden Witchery, The Magical & Ritual Use of Herbs, Complete Vegetable & Herb Gardner, The Pleasure of Herbs, Brother Cadfael's Herb Garden,* and *The New Age Herbalist.* She wondered about the book selection. She knew Henrietta wouldn't have most of them in the library. They were surely Permelia's private collection.

Permelia returned. "While the tea finishes steeping, let's go outside and see my gardens. I'll show you where I picked the lemon mint for our tea."

She showed her the vegetable garden: zucchini, tomatoes, cayenne peppers, green peppers, spinach, green onions, and lettuce. Everything was coming up on schedule, and it would be ready for picking at their appropriate times.

The rock garden plants were only getting started. Sunflowers had already sprouted. Emily saw several plants she didn't know anything about. She had plenty of questions.

Permelia pointed out the parsley, chives, basil, rosemary, thyme, comfrey, lemon mint, spearmint, tansy, catnip, tarragon, dill, oregano, marjoram, and sage. Permelia knew all their botanical names and uses. Each garden section was marked with appropriate copper signs. Emily was impressed with the markers. "Where did you find such unique labels?"

"We have a coppersmith near town. He has many interesting things for sale. We'll have to make a stop in his shop one day soon. His handmade copper articles are very tempting. Be sure to take plenty of money with you. I never go in without buying something."

Puzzling over one of the markers, Emily asked, "What do you do with comfrey? I don't think I've ever heard of it before."

Permelia answered, "Comfrey is hard to find. One of the earliest herb experts, Culpepper, said it's good for many things. You can use both the leaves and roots of comfrey. Externally, you make a poultice of the leaves to use on bruises, wounds, and sprains. You take moistened, pulped root and apply it around a broken bone, and it sets like plaster. Comfrey helps bones heal quickly. 'Bone-knit' is another name. Today it's thought to be carcinogenic if consumed orally. People used the herb to alleviate the symptoms of colds, bronchitis, and stomach ulcers in medieval times. They used to eat the tender leaves in salads. Sometimes they cooked the leaves. That practice is discouraged now."

Emily was impressed with her friend's knowledge. She looked at another sign, Emily commented, "I've heard of tansy. What is it used for?"

Permelia replied as they studied the herb, "Tansy leaves are often put in cookies. They taste marvelous. I made some cookies we'll have with our tea. Tansy expels worms, aids indigestion, relieves flatulence, treats gout, and promotes menstruation. Their leaves are bitter and aromatic. I stew it with rhubarb. I also add it to sauces, cakes, creams, omelets, and custards. In medieval England, people made tansy pancakes to eat in celebration of the end of Lent. Tansy also is used to repel insects like fleas and moths."

"Why, I never knew you could use herbs in so many ways," expressed Emily.

"Most herbs can be used both medicinally and for culinary purposes," said Permelia. "When my son was a baby, I made catnip tea to ease his colic. The potion worked most of the time. Let's go back inside. I'm sure the tea is ready by now."

"I'm hungry. I was getting up when you called. I slept in. It's my day off. I didn't even take time for a cup of coffee. I'm ready for tea and those interesting sounding cookies."

Permelia placed the tansy cookies on a Japanese Geisha plate. The mint tea was steeping in a Geisha teapot. Permelia poured the tea into matching handle-less Geisha Girl cups. She added spoons, honey, and napkins.

She led her guest into the Victorian parlor.

"I forgot how lovely your grandmother's house is."

Emily's comments pleased Permelia. She said, "This burl walnut set was hers. I have memories of Granddad sitting in the man's chair with the arms. Grandmother sat in the armless lady's chair. Guests sat on the loveseat. The style of the antique parlor set is Eastlake. I don't use it very often. When my brother, Patrick, and I visited my grandparents. They allowed us to sit on this loveseat together. My grandparents shared stories."

Emily noticed the antique upright walnut piano. "I remember you took piano lessons? Do you still play?"

"Yes. That old relic upright piano served its musical purpose in life. Now I amuse myself playing the out of tune relic. The tuner comes routinely, but it's impossible to keep an old piano tuned. I don't want to trade it for something new before I know if Robbie may become serious about music. I don't want to buy a keyboard. I'd love to put the piano in my dance studio so I could accompany my ballet students. However, it's quite heavy and cumbersome. Very difficult to move."

"Where is your studio?" queried Emily.

"It's across the hall in the second parlor. Those sliding large wooden doors are perfect for privacy. I removed all the furniture from in there. I mounted mirrors and practice bars on the interior walls. I've hung Turkish tapestries of belly and sword dancers on the exterior walls. I also have ballet posters framed. My favorite is the three-foot by five-foot picture of ballet legs and shoes. The tights have huge holes. The dancer is on pointe with pink toe shoes duct taped together. I sanded and varnished the parquet floor. We can go in before you leave if you wish."

"If not today, then sometime soon. How many pupils do you have in your classes?"

"For my ballet classes, I have ten beginners, seven intermediates, and five on-point. You missed this year's ballet and tap recital. We were so fortunate to have it in the auditorium of the new high school. The stage is beautiful with velvet drapes. There's plenty of comfortable seating for family and friends."

"Is there also a recital for your belly dancing classes?"

Permelia laughed. "My four students aren't brave enough yet. I encourage them to make costumes to wear to class. Wearing the long skirts on the hip, a bra type top, scarves, veils, bangles, and beads makes the dance a lot more fun and authentic than sweats. The skirts made of semi-shear material often have more than six yards of fabric"

"How did you ever get into belly dancing?"

"At I.U. I took an elective class, 'Experiences in Middle Eastern Dance Orientale' that introduced me to a fascinating culture. I fell in love with the music."

Emily wanted to know more about the dance and culture.

"Why is the music different?"

"The rhythms are quite different than European-based music. Mid-Eastern music is hypnotic. Finger cymbals make certain rhythmic sounds. Men normally play the music. A drum, a dumbek, play other beats: Dum tek, dum tek, dum tek a tek. You feel the beat within your body."

"Do only women dance? I've only heard of female belly dancing, like the one at the Chicago World's Fair way back in the early twentieth century."

Permelia answered, "Both men and women dance. A sword dance is two men dancing with swords. I can dance balancing a sword or cane on my head. Dance Orientale is also called Belly Dancing. The historic art goes back to Biblical days."

"Wow. Dance Orientale sounds difficult."

"Once you know the moves and how to isolate body parts, your body learns to move with music. The music tells you what to do."

Emily asked another question, "How can you listen to Middle Eastern music and learn about the culture? Aren't all Muslims heathens and terrorists? Didn't pagans kill your husband?"

"Yes, Islamic terrorists killed my husband. However, I realized not all Moslems are evil. Most of those who follow the true tenets of Islam are not violent. We have people like the KKK who pretend to be religious but don't follow the teachings of Jesus. I don't blame all Moslems for Steve's death. I know Islamic students at I.U. who condemn actions of other Muslims in their home countries."

Emily responded, "With the present international situation I would be reluctant to talk about the Middle East with my young students. I know a few Islamaphobes."

"I know how many Americans and Christians feel, but Christians read the *Old Testament*. Many books of the Bible support violence and some Christians do evil actions in the name of God. Why don't we discuss my feelings about Muslims when we have more time?"

Emily replied, "Okay. I wondered if I you would like to go to Bible

Study with me tonight?"

"We could make a trade-off. I'll go to the class with you if you take belly dancing. Or perhaps you'd rather study yoga?"

"I think I'd prefer the dance classes. I don't understand yoga but I don't think I'd feel comfortable. My church leaders have warned me that yoga teaches heresy. Many say the practice is sacrilegious. I'll come to your belly dancing class tomorrow, and you go to church with me tonight."

Permelia said, "I'd like to discuss yoga sometime with you. So many people misunderstand the way yoga works. I guess I could go to church with you. I have no excuse; I don't have a class tonight. Sure. I'll go as long as Jenny can sit for me. We have a trade-off deal; she sits for me and I give her kids ballet classes."

Following Bible Study, Nathan, Patrick, Emily, and Permelia went to the Dairy Queen for sundaes. Emily mentioned their plans for the weekend. "I'm going home on Friday for a dentist appointment. The guys are coming up later. We're going on to Nathan's for a run at Notre Dame on Saturday. We'll come back to my apartment to spend the night. We'll go to my church Sunday morning. We'll be back in Grovetown Sunday afternoon. Come with us, it would be fun."

"It does sound fun. Let me check first with Mom and Dad. If they can keep Robbie, I'd love to go. I'll call them right now."

Permelia talked with her parents about the proposed plans. They agreed to watch Robbie for the weekend. She had great expectations of a fun weekend. She thought, *I need to be out with other people. I like Emily, Nathan, and Patrick. I need friends.*

33

A ppointments started promptly at nine am; Patrick knew his day was going to be busy after the weekend. Patrick planned to use his morning enjoying a cup of coffee, and praying for the day to be one of healing and correct decisions. He started reading chapter five in Brendan Manning's *Ragamuffin Gospel*. The phone rang. His receptionist nurse, Becky, would arrive in about 10 minutes. He decided to let the answering machine take the call.

"Hi, Dr. Mattox. This is Ralph Pugh from the Peony County Health Department. I'm calling to let you know the—" Patrick caught Pugh mid-sentence.

Patrick heard all he needed to hear when he answered. "Well, hello, Ralph. This is Dr. Mattox speaking." Without the usual amenities Patrick said, "You sound like you're calling on official business. Are you?"

Ralph replied, "I'm afraid so. Grovetown has a serious problem. The sample you sent us shows Deer Fly Creek definitely contaminated with raw sewage. We'll make an order. No one is allowed in or near the river until the mess is cleaned up. The cleanup will be a huge operation."

"Oh my."

"As you probably are aware, the state has a standard operating procedure for situations like this. We've already started the process on our end."

"What is the SOP? I'm sure contacting the local authorities, and the community, but what else needs to be done?"

"All is in process as we speak. We were compelled to notify the state and federal authorities, who started the ball rolling. The higher ups are dealing with most of the details." Ralph sighed before he continued. "Dr. Mattox, I've never encountered such widespread contamination. The problem is catastrophic. Notifying the medical community was next on my list. That's why you're getting this call. I wanted to alert you personally since you are the only doctor in the immediate area."

"This is terrible! When I saw scum on the creek, I knew we had to find out what was going on."

Ralph said, "You certainly stumbled on something major, Doc. We'll have the *Grovetown Tribune* alert the community. We'll also publish the warning in the Peony newspaper and on the radio."

"This story is going to cause a big stir."

"I need to meet with you ASAP to figure out some details."

"Of course. I'll help in any way I can."

"We need to alert the public as soon as possible. I know it will be difficult to keep the public out of the creek. They definitely can't eat any fish in the river or swim in it. Would you be available for a lunchtime meeting at your office today? It's necessary to get on this right away. This is an emergency!"

"Fine. I'll have Becky rearrange my appointments and order lunch in for us. Why don't you and I meet first at noon, and then I can have the newspaper editor meet us this afternoon. I'll make the calls."

Pugh had a few final words. "I have one more request before our meeting. Would you be able to have the last five years of available medical records checked for cases of hepatitis, and dysentery? Can it be accomplished in such a short amount of time?"

Patrick answered, "I don't think that'll be a problem. In the couple of years, I've been here, I've seen about three cases of hepatitis, and four cases of dysentery. Dr. Strong left his old records. I'll have Becky check them over."

The health officer and the doctor talked about the gravity of the situation for a few additional minutes. The phone conversation ended. There was a lot to accomplish before noon.

*****

Ralph and Dr. Mattox made a plan of action at lunch and reviewed their notes. Ralph changed the subject. "Do the police know anything more about Gussy Trinkle's death? The last I heard they had the autopsy results. The report indicated stab wounds were the cause of death. I assume they're still investigating."

"Oh yes, but it appears the investigation may become a dead case file if there isn't a break soon. I heard everyone's alibis have panned out. I don't know where it will go next."

Patrick continued, "Raymond and Nathan are looking into the police actions. However, there's a catch. Chief Petty's gone on vacation."

Ralph sighed.

"Well, I need the community warned. Signs are up along the creek to stay out, no fishing, no swimming, and the like."

Patrick asked, "What more can I do? What's your next action with this messy situation?"

Obviously, we need the newspaper to alert the public as well. The paper needs to do all they can to tell everybody to stay clear of the area. I know you can understand. Would you have time to contact the newspaper and coordinate the warnings to the readers?"

Patrick responded, "No problem. The editor of the *Grovetown Tribune,* Raymond Starks, is a good friend. I'm positive he'll help. Anything else?"

"Spread the word! Patients, family, friends, and anybody else you can tell. I have a lot going on. Well, I best leave. I still need to go to the Works Department and talk to the Manager. He might as well be told he needs to discover the genesis of the problem."

*****

Patrick turned to his own first assignment. He was relieved Raymond answered his phone on the second ring. "Good morning, Raymond. There may be an important news story for you. Probably not be a Pulitzer, but it's certainly that caliber for Peony County. Have I piqued your interest?"

"You betcha! Is it about Gussy's murder?"

"Unfortunately not, but it *will* be a paper seller. It'll be a scoop."

He filled him in on the problem and the need for newspaper involvement.

Raymond turned to his son, "Nathan, I think your thesis is practically writing itself. Looks like you have some real-life investigation ahead of you to add to the thesis material."

Nathan responded, "I heard some of your conversation, I was thinking the same thing. This development could add an interesting angle to my thesis. Off the top of my head, I was thinking the agencies involved will investigate the matter, but I'd like to find out what I can. Agencies can act so slowly. It's like assigning something to a committee where things can die."

Nathan continued, "I'd like to do some investigative legwork. You know like find out who were involved in the original sewer installation, including the construction company, town workers, the private installers, the attorney, and other details."

Raymond smiled. "It seems the investigation gene didn't skip a generation. As I recall, there were rumors of sewer problems some time ago. Nevertheless, the town's Work Manager quelled them when he produced the map of the sewage installations. He certified all the connections were completed as required, According to the State agencies, everything was kosher."

"But, Dad, something apparently went wrong. Raw sewage doesn't fall from the sky. We need to get a leg up in this mess. Who was the Works Manager?"

His father said, "I believe it was Glenn Achsworth."

"We need copies of the town's public records on the matter."

"Well, son, I'm interested in going back through my newspapers. I'll go back and see what I can dig up myself."

They strategized awhile longer. Nathan felt he had a lot of work ahead. He knew he could do this research much easier than solving Gussy's murder.

"So, son, what do you think?"

"I'm in!"

34

Promptly at eight am, Emily arrived at Permelia's house. The girls were headed to Emily's dentist appointment. They planned to meet up with their brothers. The girls were going to watch the boys run in the Notre Dame marathon. Emily popped open the trunk of her PT Cruiser. Before Emily could get out of her car, Permelia came bounding out. She threw her backpack into the trunk.

"I can tell you're not the one who's headed to a dental appointment. Looks like you're rarin' to go!" laughed Emily.

"Sure am. I'm ready for some adult time with friends. Don't get me wrong, I adore being a mom. But it's been ages since I've had a weekend to spend with only adults." Permelia looked at Emily and smiled.

Emily couldn't help but grin back. "I look forward to the rest of the weekend after my dentist appointment. Let's go. The sooner we get done at the dentist, the sooner the weekend can begin."

"I love this car, Emily. She says 'fun'! What do they call this color?"

"It's eggplant, so I've named the car *Veggie*. My kids in Sunday school like the name because it reminds them of some of their favorite videos, *The Veggie Tales*. I bought it gently used, so the payments are affordable. Sometimes when I really feel whimsical, I spruce it up with some magnets."

"What kind? Where are they? Can we put them on now?" begged Permelia.

Before she could answer, Emily's cell phone rang. She hesitated to answer. She looked to see who called. The person calling was her mother. She let the call go to voice mail.

Emily said, "I'm sorry Permelia for the interruption. My mother called. I'll call her back later. Now, back to magnets. Yes, let's do them. I have *Veggie Tale* characters, polka dots, and flowers. Which do you feel like?"

"Flowers, of course. Can I help put them on?"

"Yes, you *may.*" Corrected the teacher. Emily got the packet from her trunk and the girls giggled as they found the perfect spot for each blossom. "Don't forget to remind me to take them off when we get there. I've learned the hard way: if you leave them on after you parked your car, you may not have a full bouquet when you return."

"I promise on my tippy tip toes to remember," Permelia swore as she raised her arms and spun around on her toes. She added, "I've heard in the sixties and seventies Hippies painted flowers on their vehicles. People said Hippies were somewhat wild. Free love, sex, and drugs. Marijuana and something called LSD."

Emily said, "That's the impression I got too. We had a course in sociology about changes in cultural attitudes and their relationship to political movements. Very informative. We'll use flowers but we're not Hippies. I wonder if our parents were."

They were finally on the road and heading north. The girls were eager to talk. So many years passed from when they were in high school.

"If it's not too difficult a subject for you, may I ask about your husband?

Permelia said, "I don't mind. Some memories are easy to relive."

"How did you meet your husband?" Emily asked her friend.

"We had a French language class together at I.U. The class spent a week in France, not only in Paris. We traveled to the south of France. The purpose of the venture was to hear the various dialects of French. Parisians speak with a different accent from those in the south of France. I especially enjoyed the side trip to Languedoc in South Eastern France. Toulouse-Lautrec was born in the area in the small town of Albi. Steve and I were in the same study group. We became fast friends and were soon dating. Our relationship accelerated in the City of Love during 'April in Paris.' We were madly in love, and we married soon after returning to the States. We stayed in school, lived in married housing, and graduated. Robbie was born in Bloomington. After graduation, Steve joined the Marines a few months before 9-11. Of course, with the war his squadron was deployed to Afghanistan soon after graduation."

"Why did he enlist?"

"He was from a military family. He was in ROTC at I.U. The military program helped finance school. Of course, we had no idea a war would be in our future. He proudly fulfilled his obligations to our country."

"No one thought we'd have to fight. Many of the students—both men and women joined the armed forces. Those military men and women who serve were certainly brave. We owe them all so much for their courage. Where was Steve from?" Emily asked.

"He was born in Wichita Falls, Texas while his father was stationed at the Air Force Base. Later His dad transferred to be an Air Force boot camp trainer at Lackland Air Force Base."

"His mother?"

"She was of Spanish/Indian origin from Mexico City. She met Steve's father when he vacationed with his family in Mexico. She eventually became a United States citizen."

"What about his father?"

"He was born in Brownsville, Texas. His father was of Spanish extraction. I've been in touch with some of the Barcelona cousins."

"Did he go to high school in Texas?"

"Steve graduated from Keystone, a private school for students with science and mathematical skills. He studied Russian and Classical Latin. Languages were one of his strong points. His French was better than mine. Of course, he was fluent in Spanish, living in South Texas. He studied Mid-Eastern languages, Arabic, and Turkish, at Indiana University. The Marines placed him in a unit working in translating."

"Where did you and Steve live before he was deployed?"

"In base housing in San Diego. We made friends and socialized with several other couples from Steve's own squadron. We had pitch-ins and learned many regional dishes. We taught each other card games popular from our various home states. I taught everyone how to play euchre, as my cultural contribution. No one ever heard of the game. The kids loved the gatherings, too. We were all close friends, kinda like a family."

"Sounds like you had fun."

"Yeah, we did, but the parties became more somber. We were all in a state of shock as the impact of the news of the 9-11 attack started to sink in. We held our breath as we waited for our loved ones orders. When his squadron finally received their orders to the Middle East, we wives formed a support group. We were all scared of what might happen."

"Did you hear from him often?"

"I maintained my schedule of writing to him every day. When we could, we were in contact by e-mail. He couldn't tell me much about what was going on there, but he usually wrote four times a week. We didn't have Skype on our Dell, so I kept him supplied with photos. I wanted him to see Robbie grow up."

"I'm sure Steve loved your mail and pictures."

"He assured me he would see his son grow up and enjoyed seeing the early photos. I was so glad Robbie could call Steve. 'Dada' before he died. I had several pictures of him around the house for Robbie to see."

Emily said, "I notice you still have lots of those pictures around. I'm sure it helps both of you to remember those good times."

"Oh, yes. Suddenly our lives changed significantly when the Marines came to my door with the news at five o'clock in the morning. When I heard the doorbell ring so early in the morning, I knew something bad happened."

Emily gasped and looked quickly at her friend. "Oh, my. I can only imagine. How devastating to you and Robbie."

"We took his body to San Antonio to bury in his family's plot. The Roman Catholic Mass and the playing of taps at the graveside were very moving."

"I noticed a flag at your house. Is it the one they presented to you at the service?"

"Yes, it is. We stayed with his parents a short while, but I wanted to be back home in Indiana to be with my family. I'm sorry. We need to change subjects. I'm getting too emotional to continue to discuss Steve. I miss him so much, sometimes more than I can handle."

"That's okay. I don't want to upset you. I'm sorry you had to go through that experience. I'll pray for you and Robbie."

The girl's discussion was lighter. They continued their trip to Indianapolis. Emily discussed her college years at Northwestern University and the antics of the children in her classroom. The girls' friendship grew. Time passed by quickly.

Emily said, "I wish it weren't necessary to go back to the dentist. The filling's loose. I'm to see Dr. Samuel Jacobs today."

Emily's cell rang.

"My dear, where are you? I haven't heard from you recently. Are you okay?"

"I'm fine Mother I'm in the city on my way to Dr. Jacob's office.

The filling's loose."

Her mother said, "Oh my. Will you see Dr. Drew Jacobs?"

"No, his father is to handle any problem now."

"Oh. I do hope Drew will ask you out. Maybe you could request to talk to him. You two would make an attractive couple, don't you think?"

"Oh Mother. I know how you like to make matches for me, but please let me handle my dating." She thought, *Of course I'll see Drew. He wanted to go out tonight. Moreover, I do want to, but obligations to see my brother run takes precedence. Wouldn't Mother think otherwise? This relationship is for my eyes only. Otherwise, she'll have me married with children.*

Dr. Jacobs said, "You were right to come in. I fear you'll lose the filling any day. I'm afraid to drill your broken tooth. I don't think it could hold another filling. You'll need a crown."

"Will it be expensive?"

"It's not cheap. However, we can work with you. We can do all the papers for you to obtain a loan if needed. The loan would have no interest for two years. I know this is an unexpected expense. I don't want you to worry about the cost."

Emily replied, "Thank you for your help. I have some savings."

"Well, I'm glad to hear that. Here's what we do. I'll anesthetize the area, clean it, and make an impression. I can do that today. We'll set up an appointment for the permanent crown. Now, let's get that tooth fixed."

Drew poked his head in the room. "Hi! Em. I'm sorry you have plans for the weekend. Please think of me. I'll be thinking of you. Please save next Friday for the Strawberry Festival."

Emily smiled a teasing smile.

35

The girls arrived at Emily's Indianapolis apartment to find Nathan and Patrick waiting for them in their car. Emily said, "I hope you haven't waited too long."

They both shook their heads and Nathan said, "No problem."

Without much delay, the foursome set off in Sham, heading North on Highway 31 to South Bend for Notre Dame's "Finish on the Fifty" 10K run. Registration was from noon until eight pm.

Patrick said, "We'll make it there, but it's going to be close."

Nathan said, "We'll have to have a late supper tonight. If we could have gotten there sooner, we could have eaten pasta at the College Football Hall of Fame. We need plenty of carbs before our run. Since I figured we'd be late, I've made nine o'clock reservations at Bruno's, a fantastic Italian restaurant."

"Great!" exclaimed Emily. "We have a Bruno's in Broad Ripple. I love to go there if I'm celebrating something special. I have so many favorite dishes. I especially like salads, minestrone, and pasta with garlic sticks."

"Well, don't keep the menu to yourselves! Let us in on some choices," begged Patrick.

Nathan laughed at his hungry friend's question. "They have about anything Italian you'd want: veal and chicken parmesan, chicken and shrimp fettuccine, lasagna, chicken cacciatore, pizza, and of course spaghetti and meatballs. Good salads, soups, and breads are included. Now you're making me hungry, too. Emily, what do you have in here to snack on?"

"What every health conscious woman would have: string cheese, granola bars, water, and almond M&M's. They won't melt in your hands, but sometimes they do melt in your car."

"I'm the scientist to test those out," volunteered Patrick.

Nathan said, "If we arrive late there's no guarantee we'll receive an official T-shirt. They're first come, first served. There are usually a lot of unregistered show-ups, especially if it's going to be a pretty day."

"Who cares about a T-shirt?" Patrick commented. "We want to run."

Emily piped up, "I feel a shopping trip in our near future, Permelia. After the men finish, we'll go back to the apartment to shower and freshen up. We can leisurely check out the bookstore T-shirts and stuff. I'd like to buy a Notre Dame sweatshirt."

Great," agreed Permelia. "I'm sure Robbie would love to have a Notre Dame shirt."

The group was very congenial and talkative on the two and a half hour trip. They exited the car and began stretching, Patrick said, "That was a tiring ride up here."

"I know, but I've driven it so many times. The drive to Notre Dame is old hat for me."

They all were excited as they saw the registration table and rushed over to beat the deadline time. As feared, they were too late for a T-shirt. They registered and received their run numbers. They hurried back to the car and their sisters so they wouldn't be late for their reservations at Bruno's.

Nathan's apartment only had one bedroom and the office. The girls slept in the bedroom. Patrick slept on the office couch. Nathan took his comfy chair. The arrangements weren't the optimum. Still the men slept well. So did the girls. All were up early. They chowed down protein shakes and coffee.

Patrick said, "Let's go run. I'm hyped."

*****

The boys felt their finish on the Notre Dame fifty yard line was presentable. They showered and hunger attacked them. Lunchtime. They ordered pizzas. The girls wanted vegetarian with extra cheese.

Nathan said, "I need a super deluxe with everything but anchovies and with double cheese."

Patrick ordered the same but with anchovies.

The gang of four leisurely toured the Notre Dame campus, they returned to Nathan's apartment to relax before picking up a bucket of Kentucky Fried Chicken.

The foursome stayed a second night at Nathan's apartment.

They planned to watch old movies, Indiana Jones in *The Raiders of the Lost Ark* and *The Temple of Doom*.

Emily said, "You know, it's been a long day. I'm too tired to stay up and watch a movie."

Permelia agreed.

Nathan said, "You party poopers! Why I'm getting a second wind. I'll read until I'm sleepy."

Patrick joined the girls' choice of turning in.

Everyone but Nathan took to their rooms. Emily said her nightly prayers while Permelia took a shower. Patrick quickly said a short prayer to thank God for giving him strength to run as well as he did. Nathan read his novel for an hour or so. He devoted another half hour to his daily Bible reading. He was nearly asleep when he hit his chair. Both girls read for a while.

Emily also wrote in her journal about the busy day. She quietly said her prayers. Both slept well.

*****

It was a beautiful Sunday. The parishioners of the First Baptist Church enthusiastically greeted the group of young people. This was a large church. The parishioners and the public fondly called it the "Wal-Mart church" because it was a recycled store. The pastor welcomed the members of the church and visitors. The service began with a favorite hymn everyone knew, "Just a Closer Walk with Thee." The pastor read a Psalm and then a pastoral prayer. He asked for prayer requests. Another prayer and song. He prayed before and after the collection. Before his sermon, he asked if there were any testimonies. One person stood and praised God for providing help in her hour of need. The service continued with another song. The Pastor asked for help in delivering his message. There were more prayers and hymns. One hymn was "This Is My Father's World ", along with some newer ones. Permelia recognized some hymns her grandmother sang as she hung out clothes.

Emily thought the pastor gave a marvelous message. He spoke of Amos and his desire to see all peoples, rich and poor, taken care of. Many of the congregations were unfamiliar with the book. Emily recently completed a study of Minor Prophets in her Bible study. The book of Amos was one her lessons.

The minister began, "I'm going to talk about a small chapter of the

Old Testament, The Book of Amos. It's rarely discussed in our day and age."

Permelia never heard of this book. *I'll have to read Amos when I get home.*

The pastor said, "The author of this book is the Prophet Amos written about the time of 760-750 B.C. Although Amos was from Judah, he prophesied in a neighboring land, Israel, after the split in the two countries at a time when Israel enjoyed a good life economically and politically. Israel wasn't following God's path. Amos told the people God stood in judgment of Israel for its self-righteousness. He condemned the way they were acting. The greedy people practiced slavery, immorality, idolatry, and other corrupt activities. He tells the people God is unhappy with them and they will suffer future consequences."

Permelia was surprised to learn Amos talked about women of the corrupt society of Israel. He called the women who oppressed the poor and needy as "cows." The pastor said, "Amos considered the women fat and indulgent." She heard in Chapter 7, "Amos tells the arrogant men their wives would become prostitutes." The minister continued with more dire predictions including telling them their sons and daughters would die by swords, their land would be divided, and they would die as pagans in a foreign country. There would be locusts in swarms ruining the crops. Sanctuaries would fall into ruin. Chapter 8, Verse 2, Amos says, "Then the Lord said to me. The time is ripe for my people Israel. I will spare them no longer."

Permelia thought, *God could and would punish his people if needed to keep them faithful.*

Continuing with the sermon, he said, "One of the key passages of Amos, Amos 5:14, says, 'Seek good, not evil, that you may live. Then the Lord God Almighty will be with you, just as you say he is'. This is a warning to all of you; you must do good works in your life or suffer the consequences of being out of favor with the Almighty. However, remember it isn't the good works you perform that allows you to be saved. You only need faith alone."

Permelia heard this statement bringing back some teachings of the Catholic Church. *Steve told me in the Book of Peter; it says "Faith without works is dead." What's the truth? I'll need to talk to Emily. How can both statements be reconciled?*

The Pastor summed up the comments of his sermon. He brought the sayings in the book of Amos to a present day application.

"The Prophet, Amos, tells us emphatically to change our ways. We must stifle our greed and materialism. We have to speak up when we see our lives driving in ways conflicting with God's direction. We need to be watchdogs for our society. We'll find hope and encouragement in the Lord's teachings. We must end our worldly ways with the knowledge. The Almighty will find honor by walking with Him in righteousness. Let us pray."

The service ended with the Doxology.

Emily shook Pastor Butcher's hand. She told him how inspiring she found the sermon. Emily was surprised and pleased Permelia seemed to understand the message, listened intently, and even sang the songs with the others

Nathan thought, *It would be nice if they took communion every Sunday. I'm sure communion would show another positive attribute to Permelia.* He accepted his church's way. Communion services were only once a month. Today wasn't the day.

*****

The four enjoyed brunch at a buffet near the church. Permelia was quiet as they ate. She was intent on thinking. She pondered; *I felt more relaxed at their church today than I have in any of my Wiccan rituals or at Mass at St. Elizabeth. Strange. It's remarkable how content, I feel.*

The breakfast buffet was tasty, especially the scrambled eggs along with French toast and plenty of raspberry syrup. Over coffee, the subject again turned to a discussion of Gussy's death. There were no new clues. The police still knew no motive.

Permelia asked about any progress in Gussy's investigation.

"Really nothing new. I wish I had more confidence in the Grovetown. Police. I don't think the police are really doing their work," Nathan said. "I know they've talked to friends and neighbors. You know I've researched murders, and I've learned suspects are often close to the victim. Gussy was so well liked by everyone. Those distinctive flannel shirts and overalls were an amusement when he walked down the street with his mangy dog, Buddy."

Permelia laughed. "Gussy loved his dog so much."

Emily agreed with Nathan. "Nobody in Grovetown could have

killed him. He had too many friends. I bet it was a stranger, but who."

Before they left the restaurant, a phone rang. Permelia recognized her emergency pre-paid phone. Surprised, she saw the call was from her father. "What's up, Dad?"

In reply, "You need to come right to St. Francis Hospital in Beech Grove."

Permelia, "Why? Is someone ill or hurt?"

"Robbie fell and broke his arm."

He has a compound fracture."

"What? Is he in serious condition?"

Her father responded, "This kind can be serious but I think he'll be fine. However, the doctor in Peony thought he should see an orthopedic surgeon. He might need surgery."

"Are you at St. Francis?"

"No. We're about two hours out. We'll meet you there. Remember you are going to the old hospital in Beech Grove."

Permelia said, "We're on our way"

Her father said, "Be careful. I don't want you in the hospital too."

*****

She explained the situation to the others. All immediately headed to the car, stopped at the apartment and packed hurriedly.

Emily drove Emily's vehicle. Permelia rode with her. Emily knew the city. Nathan and Patrick followed Emily. It would take at least three hours to Beech Grove. They would have to go through Indianapolis. Nathan faithfully obeyed the speed limits. He told Patrick, "I want to go faster, but I know I shouldn't. I remember God's rule. I must obey the government's laws."

The drive seemed to never end. Everyone was tense.

To Permelia, the drive took forever.

She said to Emily, "I shouldn't have been away this weekend. I feel so guilty. My poor little boy. I'm sure Robbie must be in pain and so scared."

"Oh, Permelia, I know you're upset. May I suggest you and I pray while we're driving?"

Permelia didn't object to praying. In fact, she was pleased her friends would ask their God to help. She was surprised however. The Baptist religion was still foreign to her. She felt ill at ease.

Emily prayed to God asking Him to help the doctors know what they needed to do. She also asked God to grant Permelia the strength to handle the situation.

Permelia thanked Emily. *Thank God!* She then thought, *Did I just thank God? Is it Goddess?* They finally arrived. St. Francis Hospital was established as a Catholic Hospital more than sixty years ago.

Emily immediately noticed the crucifix with Jesus hanging in agony on the cross. There were statues of Mary and Joseph everywhere. The hospital was a maze of corridors and rooms. When they entered the reception area, a nun directed them to the emergency room. Were it not for the Sister's reliable instructions Emily and Permelia might never have found the room.

The nurse in the emergency room said, "Your son is in an examination room with his grandfather. We have documents you need to fill out before we can do surgery. However, I'm sure you'd like to see him first. He's been asking for you."

Nathan, Emily, and Patrick waited in the sitting area while Permelia was led to her son in the ER. When she entered his curtained area, she could tell he was in pain, and frightened. Robbie was quite relieved to see her.

Permelia greeted him. "Oh, my, Robbie, are you okay? I hope it doesn't hurt too much." She tried to calm Robbie's fears. The nurse quickly gave him a shot preparing him for surgery. He tried to speak, but the shot was already making him woozy. The nurse said, "We've checked your son in room 308. If you'd like you can invite your party to wait with you in that room until Robbie returns from surgery in a little while."

They met the orthopedic surgeon outside the door to the ER. He explained the surgical process and when to expect Robbie to be out of the recovery room.

He said, "If you don't mind, I'd like to say a prayer before I perform the operation. I always want God's guidance in my work. If it's okay with you, please join hands. In the name of the Father, Son, and Holy Spirit." He made the sign of the cross. "Dear God in Your graciousness, please guide my hands as I enter the surgical theater. I always need your help to allow me to successfully do my job. Be with me, Jesus, as I treat this young man. Be with his family and friends as they wait while we're in surgery. I ask all this in the name of Our Lord, Jesus Christ. In the name of the Father, Son, and Holy Spirit, Amen"

Permelia accompanied her son to the operating room. The doctor allowed her to go until the area was secure. She asked Emily, Nathan, and Patrick to go with her to Robbie's hospital room. She turned to her friends and said, "I'm so glad you all are with me today. I appreciate your support so much. Thank you for staying with me."

Emily suggested they pray. All held hands while Emily led them in prayer.

The friends settled in to drink coffee and talk.

Emily asked Permelia. "Our cross doesn't have Jesus still on the cross. Why do you? Don't Catholics believe Christ is risen?"

"Of course we do. Our Crucifix has Jesus on the cross to remind us of his crucifixion."

After several hours of waiting with coffee and hospital food, the doctor came back into the room. He announced the surgery was a success. "He'll have to stay in the recovery room until he wakes. We'll administer pain relief, as he needs. We want to keep him overnight at least. He may have pain. I don't expect any problems. Do you have any questions?"

Permelia asked, "May I stay here with him? My father will pick us up tomorrow."

The surgeon said, "Why of course. Your presence will help him relax. I'll have the nurse arrange your sleeping area."

Nathan led them in a prayer of thanks.

37

K en Lawson prepared to leave his yellow frame two-story house in Grovetown. Late spring rain pelted the window at a heavy rate. The weatherman predicted at least two inches of the torrential rain. The heavy rain wouldn't have damaging winds.

I suppose I'd best take my large Purdue umbrella. Ken graduated from Purdue's School of Mechanical Engineering many years before. He was retired from the Ford plant in Peony. His wife tragically died from liver cancer two years ago. He lived alone in their home. He spent much of his time reading, watching sports, and working on his genealogy. Ken looked out the window at Gussy's house. He remembered how he felt finding Gussy in his shop behind the house. Ken was still upset about Gussy death. *I'm going to light some prayer candles after Mass. I want to ask the Virgin Mary to intercede on Gussy's behalf.*

Ken collected his umbrella. He walked swiftly to his little red Ford Tempo. He knew it was old. *I should give it to Goodwill. Nevertheless, he loved his compact vehicle. I know Ford doesn't make that model, not even parts anymore. My front windows won't roll down. I sure like cruise control but I guess I can watch my odometer and obey the speed limit. I do miss the air conditioner. The back doors don't lock. I don't need the back door to lock. I'll keep valuables in the trunk.*

Lawson told everyone who commented on his vehicle, "Why it's barely broken in. The car only has 152,000 miles and may look bad, but it runs."

Ken was on his way to Sunday Mass at St. Elizabeth's Church, located on Elm Street. St. Elizabeth's was built with limestone from Bedford, Indiana. Today's Mass would conclude with the blessing of new construction within the church. The church recently remodeled the cry room to include a handicapped accessible bathroom and confessional. Today was the first day to be in service. The blessing of the facilities was today. The Knights of Columbus were in attendance in full regalia, with plumes, capes, and swords to show the importance of the blessing.

St. Elizabeth's was small with a peaked roof, hanging chandeliers, and beautiful stained glass windows. One of the most striking stained glass features was a blue rose window above the Crucifix. Below the Crucifix stood the brass Tabernacle, where the Blessed Sacrament was kept. The large stone altar dominated the center front of the church, between the statue of the Virgin Mary carrying the babe Jesus, adorned in blue with a white trimmed veil and the statue of Joseph. The Baptismal Font sat on the right side of the altar. During the Church's Ordinary time between Easter and Advent, the backdrops surrounding the cross and the priest's robes were green. Other times of the year, they were white or purple depending on the seasons of the church calendar.

Father Daren sat on the right side of the altar. Since Vatican II, the altar and priest faced the congregation. Vatican II also changed the Mass from Latin to the common language of the people. In the seventies, the congregation was encouraged to sing the prayer songs along with the priest and choir. Prior to Vatican II, a Cantor or choir sang the songs. The Stations of the Cross were etched in the stonewalls. The red votive candles were located at the back of the church by the organ. Ken would light these candles for Gussy. Holy Water fonts were located at all of the doors. Everyone entering could put the holy water on their fingers and make the sign of the cross, saying "In the name of the Father, Son, and Holy Spirit."

Guests were welcome to attend Mass but couldn't take Communion.

Ken arrived about ten minutes before the service started. He entered the front door of the church and placed his umbrella in the vestibule. Adam Lebrowski, the greeter this week, welcomed him. Ken said, "What rain we've had today! This has surely been a rainy spring!"

Adam answered, "I heard a few minutes ago there are flash flood warnings. Looks like we're likely to get plenty more rain. Thank goodness, most people already have their gardens out."

"Luckily, the few farmers who grow corn managed to get them planted before these rains," Ken replied.

"'Knee high by the Fourth of July', or so the saying goes," said Adam. "Wish we had some of the fertile Rush County farmland. Our hills aren't conducive for corn and soybeans. Fields in the northern part of the state near West Lafayette and most of Indiana are more fertile than ours."

"At least we can put out our truck gardens and raise hogs, beef, and chickens. I hear the turkey farm out north of town is doing well," Ken replied.

"Yeah! I've heard the same. We have more Amish moving into Peony County because the land is so much cheaper here. Even though our county isn't financially dependent on agriculture as it was in the past. You know my daughter raised a hog in 4-H. Then she became a vegetarian because of it. Finally, she came to her senses at Ball State. She craved a hamburger."

Adam chuckled as he listened to Ken's story. "My kids are in 4-H now. You wouldn't believe the variety of projects they offer nowadays. My kids have taken recycling, genealogy, photography, video production; microwave cooking, and my daughter's favorite, consumer clothing. Some of those projects are more expensive than we had in 4-H."

Ken nodded as Adam continued, "Our worst fiasco was the year my daughter took cake decorating. The cake looked beautiful at home. They thought it was good enough to be the grand champion exhibit. Unfortunately, the air conditioner in our van stopped working, and the trip to Peony took too long for the icing. By the time we arrived at the fairgrounds, the icing had turned into a lava flow. My wife and daughter were hysterical. It was a three-tiered cake. My daughter had enough *tears* to convince the judge to give her a red ribbon for effort."

The men enjoyed their stories so much they neglected to notice the pews were filling up with parishioners. The chiming of the church bells brought the men's attention back to their reason for being there. Ken exclaimed, "Well, sounds like it's time for me to find my pew."

"Me, too," exclaimed Adam. "My other girl is one of the servers today. My wife will be angry if I'm not here to watch the procession. My wife has an allergy attack today. This is my daughter's last time because she graduates from high school." Adam hurried off and left Ken to himself.

Ken seated himself in his usual pew. He passed a woman lighting votive candles and putting her donation in the tin. Most people were already kneeling and praying. He genuflected, did the sign of the cross, and kneeled to pray. Soon the cantor led the congregation in the anticipation song. Then came the processional. The white-robed altar servers were Adam's daughter, carrying the cross, and a young boy, who looked barely eight. Before Vatican II, altar servers were always boys. Girls in this role caused much controversy in the Church for a while but the church pretty well accepted them as the norm now. The lector carried the book of scriptures above his head, and lastly, came Father Daren in his green robes worn during Ordinary Time. The service proceeded normally through the prayers, readings, and homily. Next followed a special ritual planned for the day, the blessing of the recently completed renovations. The remodeled area previously was a soundproof cry room used for disruptive children, nursing babies, or other issues with children demanding privacy. Now the room was partitioned into three areas: a confessional, a small cry room, and the much-needed handicapped accessible bathroom. The priest gave a few words of dedication and sprinkled Holy Water around the room. Many children were up and down, anxious to try out the new facilities. The renovated area was in the front of the sanctuary. People could see who were coming and going to the room. The parade of children continued during the general prayers, collection, and the beginning of the Eucharistic service.

Communion was ready to commence. The congregation heard a child yell, "Mama!" the voice of the child came from the now popular room. Water poured from underneath the door.

Due to the messy interruption, no one moved from his seat to take communion. All waited to find the cause of the child's outburst. The little girl screamed. Her mother ran to comfort her daughter. She yelled, "Everything is flooded." Water poured out of the bathroom. The priest motioned to Sister Mary Margaret. He told her to quickly assess the bathroom situation. Anxious to join her on the quest, Father Daren made a quick decision to end the Mass without observing Communion and the usual closing rituals. He abruptly proclaimed, "Mass is ended!" He haphazardly made the sign of the cross as he hurried to see he ruckus. As he left to enter the cry room, he remembered to turn around and pronounce, "Go in Peace to Love and Serve the Lord."

The congregation filed out. Father Daren grabbed the attention of the plumber-carpenter, George Waterman. He was the plumber who installed the bathroom. He seldom attended Mass. George elected to be present today for the dedication of his remodeling project.

"I'm relieved you chose to attend today. With your expertise, I'm sure you did an excellent job. But what do you think could have caused today's catastrophe?"

George was encouraged by the priest. No one could blame George Waterman for the problem. George offered an alternative answer. "I haven't had an opportunity to inspect the damage, but I believe the excessive rainfall we've been having could have been more than the plumbing capabilities are able to handle. Would you like me to get my snaking equipment? I can come back to check out the problem this afternoon?"

"I'd never ask you to work on Sunday. However, I would be forever grateful. I'll try to have the mess cleaned up before you return." He was already on the phone making the call as George left.

38

The plumber ate a leisurely lunch before returning to the church. He didn't believe there was a serious problem. He enjoyed the construction part of his job, but was more than willing to let someone else do the "clean-up" duties. He was glad to see the bathroom floor cleaned up. A dry surface was ready for his attention.

The water level in the toilet was still high. George decided to try the simplest solution first. He used his trusty plunger several times to no avail. The obstruction seemed to be something immune to the common cure.

George decided to check the old bathrooms in the basement. He was surprised when he saw they were also overflowed. The water covered the floor. He went to the kitchen to use the phone. Fortunately, the rectory number was above the phone.

"Father Daren, our problem is *much deeper* than we thought. I'm in the basement. The toilets also overflowed. Was there much use of them today?"

"I'm sure there wasn't. Even if someone chose to use the downstairs restrooms instead of the new one, they couldn't. During the service, I locked the door to the stairs so that no one could go down there today. The janitor unlocked the door when he came to clean up."

"Well, our problem is much more serious than we first thought. I'll use my snake equipment through the floor drain in the basement. Hopefully, I can dislodge whatever is causing the backlog."

Again, reassuring George of his confidence in him, Father said, "I'm sure you'll find the solution. Give me a call if you have any more questions and when you find the causes."

Undaunted by the challenge, George gathered his tools. He began the process of running the line through the pipes. His repeated efforts were still unsuccessful. The roto-rooter found no obstacles but the water refused to recede. He wasn't pleased to consider the most drastic alternative: using a backhoe to dig up and expose the sewer line.

Back to the phone, he again called Father Daren. "Hate to tell you this, but we got a real serious problem here. This is beyond my usual Band-Aid remedies. We're talkin' real work here. I'm gonna have to bring in my backhoe and dig up the lines. I think somethin' big might be cloggin' the pipes. I've seen a dead groundhog stuck in pipes before. I'll bring the backhoe first thing in the morning. Luckily enough I don't have any jobs on the books for tomorrow. I'll plan to start first thing in the morning."

Unfortunately, George was wrong about the seriousness of the situation. When he returned home, his business phone's answering machine was flooded with calls. The church's toilets weren't the only backed-up ones. There was an epidemic of back-ups in Grovetown. The cause of which had yet to be discovered.

39

Madelyn received a phone call about nine Friday morning. Her sister, Henrietta, said, "Hello, Madelyn. I hate to bother you at this time of the morning, but you didn't return my call yesterday. Something urgent has come up."

Madelyn responded, "Oh, have the police solved Gussy's murder?"

"No, I'm afraid not."

Madelyn bluntly inquired, "So what's so pressing you had to call this early? I don't usually start my day for another hour. Is the estate ready to close?"

Henrietta calmly proceeded to inform her, "Sorry, no. There's a wrinkle in Gussy's estate. Beth Basford, the new attorney in Grovetown, returned from an elongated vacation in southern France. She wasn't in contact with anyone in town, for several weeks. When she came home she heard Gussy died. She called me to see if we found his will. When I explained we were already in probate with a will written in the eighties, she expressed surprise. She said she wasn't aware an old one was still in existence. She told me Gussy wrote a will earlier this year. Madelyn, you must come down here again, I fear. I'm not sure what this new will entails, but we need to meet with Ms. Basford on this coming Monday afternoon at two. I've already checked with Emily and Nathan about the time. No problem with them. I hope it isn't too short of notice for you."

Madelyn responded, "I'm afraid it's not convenient. I have several appointments scheduled this coming week. Stuart will in all likelihood have to work. Are you sure we have to do this now?"

"Yes. I know you have a busy schedule. The sooner we can deal with this, the better. Monday is the best for Ms. Basford. If you need to have a different day, I'll give you her number and you can set up an appointment. I'm available anytime. I think Emily and Nathan can adjust their schedules."

"Well, I'll have to come down Sunday, by myself. I guess I'll have to make my excuses and work it out. Do you have any idea what's going on?"

Henrietta replied, "The only thing I know is there's a second will. I'll call Emily and Nathan and confirm the schedule with Ms. Basford. Madelyn, Please stay with me? I have plenty of room in this small house. There are three bedrooms. What fun!"

"On no," Madelyn said. "I'll make my own plans. I'll probably stay at the bed and breakfast. You know how I like my privacy."

Henrietta responded, "I understand. How nice it will be to see you again. Goodbye." Henrietta was disappointed, but it was Madelyn.

Madelyn knew Stuart would be working this week when she returned to Grovetown. She hated to drive alone for such a long trip. Madelyn called her old friend, Sally. "Sally, I need to be in Grovetown early this coming Monday. Apparently, unbeknownst to anyone, Gussy wrote a new will with a different attorney."

"Oh, sounds like an interesting enigma. Do you know why he had a different will drawn up?"

"It's mysterious." Madelyn replied, "We have no idea. Would you go with me?"

Sally thought, *This could be a valuable trip.* She asked, "What do you propose?"

"I thought if you were available, I could fly to Indianapolis Sunday. I'll rent a car at the airport, pick you up, and then drive to Grovetown. We'll stay at the Goodnight Bed and Breakfast where I stayed during the funeral."

Sally answered, "I do happen to have a fairly free schedule next week. What do you think about this idea? After your meeting, we could spend Monday night also in Grovetown. We'll leave the next morning for a pampered trip to the French Lick Spa. We could even stay a night there so we could see other local sights, like West Baden and the local wineries. What do you think?"

Madelyn replied, "Sounds like a great adventure. Hang on just a minute while I find my calendar. I think I can rearrange my affairs for the extra days." I enjoyed seeing you at the funeral. I hoped we could spend some time getting reacquainted. *What's this about a new will? I wonder what's going on.*

Madelyn came back to the phone, "Sally, I think I can work it all out. We'll have so much time to talk." Let's plan our trip. I know there are spa packages. I'll check on the Internet. I'll arrange my flight from Chicago. When I call you back, we can decide what spa packages we want."

The women ended their conversation. Both looked forward to their upcoming exciting fling.

*****

Madelyn picked Sally up Sunday afternoon in Indianapolis. They checked into the B&B. They ate at the inn. The women talked about old times in glee club and other activities in 4-H. Next morning at breakfast, the women discussed their plans for the day. Sally planned to shop on Main Street while Madelyn was at the attorney's office.

*****

Madelyn wore a new red Neiman Marcus outfit to the reading of the will. She was immediately impressed with the pretty, young attorney. Madelyn noted Beth Basford was tastefully dressed in an attractive coral-colored suit. Madelyn thought, as her matchmaking mind went into gear, *How attractive this attorney is, well dressed too. She might be the answer to finding Nathan a suitable wife. I think she may be perfect. Now how can I encourage him to consider the notion?*

Ms. Basford offered her condolences. As Dabney Shrewsbury did, she passed out copies of the newly discovered will. "Before we begin, I'm sure you have questions about the ramifications of another will. I understand your concerns and take such matters quite seriously. I've been in communication with Dabney Shrewsbury. He and I have discussed the details of the two wills. I've confirmed the will you have in front of you replaces the recently probated will. Mr. Shrewsbury agrees with me. This new will takes precedent over the previous one."

Henrietta responded, "Yes, I spoke with him as soon as I received your call. He stated the will you have is the valid will. I'm glad you returned from your vacation when you did."

Madelyn cut in, "Beth, I loved traveling through the south of France six years ago with my husband, Stuart. We ate in such novel, quaint cafes. Did you go to Carcassonne? I loved the ancient walled city. Where did you stay?" Madelyn was anxious to show how travel savvy she was.

Beth replied, "Why, yes, my friend and I went to the castle in the medieval walled city. We were very impressed. I'd be pleased to compare travels at another time. However, we must talk of the matters at hand. Gussy's current will is very different from the one you read previously. We must explore the various consequences."

Madelyn, with disappointment at not being able to discuss her travels in France, reluctantly silenced.

Beth Basford said, "Prepare yourselves. What you learn today may shock you. This will is quite different from the old will in almost every way."

The group looked at each other. They nervously settled into their chairs for the reading. She continued, "I'm surprised Gussy's copy of the will wasn't found. I have the original, but there should have been two other copies, one for Henrietta, as the Executrix, and one for himself. Since I returned home and learned of Gussy's sudden death, I can at least rectify the problem at hand. Look at your copy of the original. Please turn to the page at the end showing he signed the will on February 8, 2005. He revoked all previous wills and codicils." The group all turned to the last page. They nodded to each other.

"Now return to the first page, where you may find the news mystifying. Here Gussy acknowledges he has a child."

All audibly gasped in surprise.

Basford continued, "Unfortunately, all he knew was the approximate date of birth, June 1971, believed to be in Indiana. He knew the first name of the mother was Suze, surname unknown. Finding the mother and child will be quite a challenge. He wasn't sure if he had a son or daughter."

She stopped to allow this information to sink in with the surprised family.

The attorney said, "Were you aware of his child?"

They all shook their heads, "No."

"Do any of you know of any woman named Suze?"

Again, everyone shook his or her heads, "No."

"I didn't think so. I know this is difficult to comprehend, but let me go on. Please notice the next provisions, beginning with the appointment of Henrietta, as the Executrix. This is the same provision as in the old will."

She explained the provision for the distribution of the estate varied from the outdated will. She recited Gussy's words, "I devise and bequeath all of my real estate in the city of Grovetown and all of the contents therein to the town of Grovetown in reparation for my wrongdoings. I desire all my other real estate including my farmland and personal property be sold and added to my cash assets. After all estate costs are paid, including Federal Estate taxes, state taxes, costs, attorney fees, and Executrix's fees the balance of my estate is to be distributed as follows: to my sister, Henrietta Trinkle, I devise the sum of $10,000.00; and to my sister, Madelyn Trinkle Starks Monroe, the sum of $10,000.00; to my nephew, Nathan Starks, the sum of $5,000.00; and to my niece, Emily Starks, $5,000.00. All the rest of my estate is bequeathed to my child, born to a woman, called Suze, in June, or July 1971. Her last name is unknown to me. I direct the child be found. Any costs incurred in finding my heir shall be an allocated expense of my estate."

Again, the family gasped. Madelyn was especially upset. She had plans for a large investment of her portion under the old will.

Ms. Basford said, "Gussy wanted the estate to be unsupervised without the consent of heirs. This means Henrietta can administer the estate without the probate court approving her every move. She also explained there would be no need for an inventory.

Henrietta was relieved. At least this new will removed some technicalities. However, the new complication, finding this child, was beyond her comprehension.

The attorney expectantly, asked the heirs, "I'm sure you are all surprised, and may need some time to absorb this information. Are there any questions immediately coming to your mind? "

Madelyn piped up, "Why did he leave his town real estate to the town? How does he expect us to find an unnamed child if he couldn't? Do we even know for sure he had a child? Why didn't he tell us, his family? Was he out of his mind? Can we contest his sanity? Who's Suze anyway?"

Beth replied, "I felt he was sane when we talked. He told me what he wanted without reservation. He said he was starting a new life. For the rest, I'm in the dark as well as all of you are. There also is a clause stating if anyone contests the will, that person is completely excluded from the will, and that person forfeits their inheritance to the unnamed child." Ms. Basford paused to allow her statements to sink in before she continued. "I would be hesitant to dispute it. Referring to the notes I always keep, Gussy was quite clear and adamant about the way he wanted things to go."

Madelyn heard enough. "I don't believe my brother knew what he was doing." Then, she got up and left the meeting.

40

The family gathered at Henrietta's for supper. Emily and Nathan left a message for Madelyn at the B&B to say they were having a family dinner. Madelyn wasn't in attendance. She was too upset. The subject of the evening's conversation was obvious.

Pastor Todd was very surprised at the news. He said, "Gussy never even hinted about a child. Gussy complained lately his single life meant years of loneliness. He seemed upbeat about his future. I assumed it was because of his many friends and his newfound faith in Jesus. Perhaps he was praying for a relationship with his child."

Henrietta said, "I don't know of anyone named Suze. All of you said you didn't either. What about the name being a nickname. Anyone?"

Silence.

Todd said, "I haven't a clue who she might be. If I did have information on a matter such as this, I would be forthright in helping to resolve the situation. Unfortunately, I'm at a complete loss. As I related at the memorial service, he told me there was one lost love of his life, but he didn't go into any details. I'll certainly pray about the matter to see if the Lord brings any relevant info to my mind. Perhaps he gave me clues proving helpful. I know Gussy was dealing with several issues from his past. He wanted to resolve any conflicts. Would he have some important papers stashed somewhere?"

Henrietta added, "Gussy had a couple of places where he worked, besides his workshop and home. Hopefully he's left something somewhere."

Nathan added his thoughts to the discussion. "I would be willing to help in any way. Perhaps Dad and I will unearth some clues in our search for Gussy's murderer. We'll go through his papers, looking for possible suspects and motives. There must be a way to locate the child. How many women have the name of Suze?"

Henrietta interjected, "I'm very baffled by this revelation of a long-lost niece or nephew."

"I've always wished we had an extended family," said Emily. "Of course, dear. We'll put our capable heads together to accomplish the task, or tasks, at hand. Pastor Todd, would you please pray for our protection and success?"

Pastor Todd nodded. Everyone bowed his or her heads. "Dear Father, we humbly come to you, acknowledging you as Lord and recognizing your omniscience and Sovereignty. You know the answers to all these questions we're facing. We ask the guidance of the Holy Spirit to solve these mysteries. We know you are God. If it were your will, guide us in bringing Gussy's murderer to justice. Lead our thoughts and actions to accomplish this. We're thankful you know the location of Gussy's child. We wish to welcome this child into a relationship with the family. Prepare this child's heart to be open to the shocking news of a new family who desires to meet and love this child. Father, we also come to you as our Shield and Defender. Protect this family as they delve into the search for Gussy's murderer. May your angels surround and protect these dear ones as they battle to unravel these secrets. Our prayer is to bring these situations to a successful resolution, but we pray all will be according to your good and perfect will, through Jesus Christ, our Savior. Amen."

41

Without any greeting, Madelyn burst into the room at the inn exclaiming, "What an afternoon!"

In response to Madelyn's sudden appearance, Sally questioned, "What do you mean? Why are you so upset?"

"Sally, you won't believe what irresponsible act my brother did and revealed in this new will. He had an illegitimate child. What a crisis? I don't understand. How could he?"

Sally, in an apparent state of disbelief, whispered, "Oh, my!"

"I forgot, you didn't know my brother, and apparently we didn't know him at all. There has never been such a scandal in the Trinkle family! I'm glad my parents aren't alive to hear about it. I'm so embarrassed. Soon everybody in town will know."

Sally said, "I'm sure Gussy's confession was a blow to your family's reputation. How did he announce it? How did Henrietta respond?"

"Of course she was appalled as we all were. What a development!" Madelyn emphatically exclaimed. "This exasperating revelation certainly makes unexpected changes in our lives. This unknown child, if there even is a child, is getting the bulk of the estate. Gussy also mysteriously gave his Grovetown real estate to the town. We have no idea why. I will get substantially less money. Actually, I'm only bequeathed a pittance. My investment plans are null. Gussy could have told us he had a child. How inconsiderate. And to top it all off, we don't have no clue who or where this child is."

Sally sympathetically agreed with her friend. "This must be very frustrating to all of you. How could there have been a second will written without anyone's knowledge? Why wasn't the family notified about it sooner?"

"Well, it seems unbeknownst to everyone concerned, Gussy went to a new attorney to write a new will. When he died, the new lawyer, Beth

Basford, was on an extended trip to southern France. When she returned, she learned of Gussy's death, produced the new will, and notified us to meet for the reading."

Sally further inquired, "How are you ever going to find this missing, mysterious child? Do you have *any* leads?"

Dejectedly Madelyn responded, "None at all! With no more information than we have, I don't know how we'll find him or her. I suppose Henrietta, as Executrix, will try to follow Gussy's footsteps some nine months before the estimated date. She will see if they can find any clues from what Gussy did, where he was, and with whom. Nathan now has more duties than investigating Gussy's murder."

"Both tasks sound extremely difficult. It's kind of like looking for the proverbial *needle in the haystack*," Sally commented.

Madelyn acknowledged this observation with a quiet, "Yes. This all adds to the mystery surrounding Gussy's death. I can't believe this is happening. I don't know what to believe about my brother."

42

Sally and Madelyn headed for their girls' outing at the French Lick Spa and Resort in southern Indiana. The scenery was pleasant as they traveled on the hilly, crooked roads canopied by the foliage of late spring.

"I remember how I would gripe at my parents for making me sit in the backseat on our frequent trips to Paoli They knew I was going to get carsick on these curvy roads. I *always* got sick on these roads. My Father would make me take a bucket along. Of course, I wouldn't want to throw up in the bucket. Too gross. It didn't help to have Gussy making fun of me, either. He would dare me to vomit, and I would get so mad, of course, I wouldn't, no matter how sick I felt. As soon as Father would stop, I had to make a beeline to the nearest bathroom. My brother became even more obnoxious. During the family visit, he'd follow me around with the bucket, gagging and spitting into it. So disgusting."

"What did your father do? Didn't he chastise Gussy for his grossness?"

Madelyn shook her head and replied, "Of course not. Gussy was too sly. He wouldn't do it in front of Father, only when we were away from the adults. He was always clever and hid his teasing well."

Sally continued her questioning, "Didn't Henrietta stand up for you? Surely she'd tell your parents what Gussy was doing."

"She was usually with the adults. Henri knew my stories were true, but she was seldom an eyewitness. She'd stay out of the discussions. She was, and still is, a peacemaker."

Madelyn carefully maneuvered the tricky roads and commented on the challenge the winding roads created for an unacquainted driver.

"Madelyn, I'm always surprised by the difference between the terrain of the Indianapolis area and southern Indiana." Sally continued her comparisons. "I believe it has something to do with glaciers. I remember from geology class the ice floes stopped around these areas and made silt deposits."

"Oh, I see. So that's what happened." Madelyn responded. They followed the curves, indicated by the many "S" signs on the roadside. "I wasn't interested in studying such things in school. Of course, I've always been *aware* of the hills of Brown County. I wasn't particularly interested in how they got there. I've heard Paoli Peaks is still operating during the season, but often has to manufacture their snow."

Sally said, "Yes, I know. My son, Drew, has skied there. He prefers the Michigan slopes because they are more challenging than Paoli is. In Michigan, the snow is natural. Do you get to Brown County often? Nashville has become a lucrative tourist trap in the fall with the many quaint Nashville shops and artisan wares. An old classmate of mine from college has a weaving shop in. Nashville. I heard a midwife delivered her first child in Wisconsin. Can you imagine? I needed drugs. She nursed. What a way to lose a figure!"

They continued driving. The girls noticed the presence of livestock, but very few large crop areas. Sally commented, "These corn fields look small and the crops are way behind those up north. Surely, it won't be the traditional 'knee-high by the Fourth of July.' This land is quite poor. Why, I haven't even seen any soybean fields."

Madelyn agreed, "Amish are moving into this area even though the land is poor. But the land is cheap. Look for farmhouses with white curtains on the windows, no elective wires, and white and grayish clothes hung outside on a clothesline. We might even see a buggy or two."

She pointed to limestone quarries between Bloomington and Bedford. Indiana has very good limestone for building. "One of my great uncles worked in the quarries. Did you ever see the 1979 movie, *Breaking Away?*"

Sally said, "I don't remember seeing it, but I could have. I did see *Hoosiers.*"

"Well the movie is set in the Bloomington/Bedford area. The old limestone quarry workers, 'cutters', cut the limestone used for construction of many Indiana buildings including much of Indiana University. Oh, did you know the I.U. campus has been lauded for its beauty?"

Sally interjected, "Of course my Alma Mater was acclaimed as beautiful. So I can brag."

"Sally, I know how nice the campus is. Once I dated an I.U. frat boy. Anyway, the movie's about a relationship between local working class kids and the fanciful world of wealthy kids. You know, like the students at the university. Anyway, the quarries are the backdrops. But tell me about you."

Sally said, "Samuel's a very successful dentist. His practice has proven to be lucrative. He established his practice in the Glendale area, which was *the* place to live and work when we were first married."

Madelyn reminisced, "Your wedding was a total surprise! I couldn't believe you decided to leave, and get married. I was so envious of you finding a husband at school. Remember there was such pressure to get a MRS degree. I wasn't going to Northwestern to find a husband. I knew Raymond and I would marry as soon as we finished college."

Sally shrugged as she answered, "I guess the good life came too easy for me. I lost interest in classes. I never told you then, but I was already pregnant when we got married. Samuel was happy with the news of a child. Therefore, we just did it. I knew he would always have a good job, so anything I might add to our income would be immaterial. I decided to devote my whole life to raising our son and making a stylish home for my husband, and I knew I didn't need to finish my degree."

"It does surprise me, Sally. I had no idea you were pregnant at your wedding. Such an impressive ceremony. I was positively thrilled to be included as one of your bridesmaids. Why did we lose contact?"

"I can't remember why, can you?"

"I think life got in the way. I was graduating from Northwestern, getting married, and starting a marriage with Raymond. Life was so busy when the kids came along."

Sally said, "I was happy for your marriage to Raymond, your childhood sweetheart. I was shocked to learn your marriage lost its fairytale ending."

"Yes, it was a bad time for us. I think you've met your expectations, perfect husband, perfect child, and perfect home. Have your romantic dreams been fulfilled?" Madelyn inquired.

Sally pondered for a while before she answered. A narrow escape with a semi on one of the close curves quickly brought her back to reality. "Yes, but there were some surprises and disappointments along the way. Probably the most disappointing was not having any more children. Maybe it wasn't meant to be."

"Oh, I'm so sorry."

"But, we started our lives in a stately old two-story brick in the elite section of Glendale, close to Samuel's office. Drew attended the best private school, Park Tudor. He excelled in everything—academic studies, athletics, and the social graces. All of this prepared him well for the exclusive Wabash College, then I.U. Dental School. Drew's professional career flourished. His fraternity brothers are all in successful fields. The fraternity was a great way to make lasting friendships and business contacts. The Glendale area lost prestige."

"Is that where you live now?"

Sally replied, "No. We moved to a more affluent section of Indy, Geist. We built a showplace by the water not too far for Samuel to commute, close to the best shopping in town at Castleton and Keystone at the Crossing. Drew comes visit when he can. We're members of the yacht club. We do enjoy our social life in Geist. I became involved in charity fund-raising. This year our benefits brought in $300,000 for improvement to the children's wing of an Indianapolis Hospital. I'm often in need of fancy attire for the benefits. I go to Chicago bi-yearly to shop so I don't see myself coming and going. Maybe we can shop together in August for our fall wardrobe."

Sally gave a quick sideways glance at her friend and continued, "I know there is no comparison to my Indy shopping venues with those offered in Chicago. Your attire surely came from a designer boutique. I'm green with envy."

Obviously enjoying the overdue compliment, Madelyn was more than willing to share some of her shopping expertise. She knew she looked stunning in her fully lined yellow sateen lawn dress. The khaki silk spaghetti straps, neckline ruffle, and sequin-studded sash accented the box-pleated skirt. Her accessories included matching heels and a big buckle bag.

Madelyn "humbly" addressed the admiring Sally, "Oh, and yes. The sophisticated shopping opportunities in Chicago are a definite benefit to living there. I picked this outfit up the other day on a quick run through Neiman's. I thought it would be very practical for a couple of events this summer. I wear it out of town, allowing me one more place to wear it before passing the item on to a benefit auction. Our busy social life requires lots of different outfits. I like to avoid any social embarrassment by being seen too often in the same thing during a season. I often keep a journal of my ensembles with guest lists to avoid attending a function in the wrong outfit."

Madelyn brought Sally up to date on her own life. "Did I ever tell you about Stuart and me meeting on an airplane heading down to the Caribbean? We were both traveling to Haiti. We ended up staying at a quaint famous hotel, Hotel Oloffson, a very trendy place to stay at the time. One of its claims to fame is that the author, Graham Greene, stayed there while he wrote some of his books. He wrote *The Comedians* set in Port au Prince there. We didn't get to see his room, but the lobby, bar areas, and grounds were much the same as when Greene was there. Haiti's Mardi Grass Festival was taking place with daily parades, steel drums, and colorful costumes.

"Tell me about the people. I've heard Haiti is one of the poorest countries in the world."

Madelyn said, "Yes the country is so poor. I detested the constant pleading by the local, filthy beggars. The decent homes of the wealthy protected themselves with cement walls embedded with broken glass strategically placed to deter the unwanted rabble."

Sally interrupted, "I knew you met on your trip to Haiti, but I don't know many details. Why on earth did either of you decide to go to Haiti?"

"Well, Stuart was heading to Haiti on business," Madelyn informed Sally. "He planned to set up a baseball factory. The wages were so low there. He knew it would be an excellent investment."

"I wanted to get away to some exotic place," replied Madelyn. "I was so bored in Grovetown, and sick of Raymond working at the newspaper all the time. He never wanted to go anywhere, not even Louisville. He refused to go on this trip with me, so I decided we needed some time apart, and he agreed. I immediately decided on Haiti. I knew nothing about the island. I wanted a tropical location, and quick!"

Sally interjected, "I know how it goes. Samuel and I've had a few stale periods, ourselves."

Madelyn replied with emphasis, "This was more than staleness! I wasn't sure I even loved Raymond anymore. I really hoped my getting away would help rekindle the fire. Instead I fell in love with Stuart. He is intriguing, traveled, well-read, handsome, suave and rich, to boot. His last name was Monroe, and I could become Madelyn Monroe. My initials would become "MM," like my heroine, Marilyn Monroe. Our relationship blossomed quickly. Our newfound love took its own course: I divorced Raymond, left the kids in Grovetown with their father and their familiar school. I thought it best not to disrupt the kids' lives. Stuart and I wanted a life free without baggage."

"Tell me about your wedding." Sally asked.

"When Stuart and I got married, it was a simple ceremony performed by a judge friend of Stuart's. The wedding was in the Presidential Suite at the Downtown Marriott, where we stayed our wedding night before flying to Paris for our honeymoon. We stayed in Paris for a week and another week touring all of France."

"Wow! What an adventure. Was anyone else at the ceremony?"

"Oh, yes. Emily and Nathan, of course, along with 40 of Stuart's close friends. Henrietta didn't want to come. She was terribly upset by the whole situation."

"Does Stuart have any children?" Sally asked.

"No, he and his first wife were never able to have any children. They apparently discussed adoption, but never got around to it. His wife died young. It was best they hadn't adopted. I would had a difficult decision to make if children would have been involved in the marriage."

Sally agreed. "I've heard step-children can make second marriages difficult. Did Emily and Nathan pose disruptive?"

"Not at all. They lived with their father."

"What did you wear for this wedding, white or off-white? Finding an appropriate ensemble is always such a quandary?"

"I wanted to make sure I followed the correct etiquette of Chicago society. Stuart and I decided ecru was the best choice." Sally shook her head in agreement with their decision. "I found a little shop in Chicago where I could have a dress made perfectly to my desires. I wore a floor-length, long-sleeved, shimmering beaded lace overlay, on top of an ecru satin under dress. The seeded beads were cultured pearls. I chose it because Stuart bought me real pearl earrings in Haiti. He was extravagant and bought me such an expensive gift at that stage of our relationship. He surprised me with a wedding gift, a matching necklace he had purchased unbeknownst to me, on the Haitian trip. He felt so sure I was the woman he'd waited for so long, so he bought them with great expectations for our future together. They complimented the dress perfectly."

"Oh, Madelyn, it's so romantic! Samuel is very generous with me, but he has never done anything so sentimental or spontaneous. He wants my input before he makes any purchase. I think I would fall over in a faint if he ever gave me such an unexpected gift. Did you wear a veil?"

"I chose to wear my hair up, adorned with an arrangement of freesia. I carried a bouquet of calla lilies and freesia. Our wedding day was memorable, the beginning of a wonderful life together."

Sally sighed as she responded, "It certainly sounds like life has been good to you."

42

Madelyn and Sally approached the West Baden Springs Resort. The Springs Hotel, closed for renovation, charged a fee to tour the central area of the magnificent building sporting a lavishly restored atrium. The hotel with its cream-colored towers and red dome ascends one hundred feet and boasts a circumference of 200 feet. It was the largest domed structure in the world until the construction of the Houston Astrodome. The West Baden Springs Hotel was once called the "Eighth Wonder of the World." It boasted a beautiful sunken garden on the grounds. The women would wait until the next day to take the tour and see the plans to build a casino between the hotel in West Baden and the French Lick Resort.

Madelyn exclaimed at seeing the grandiose sight, "Isn't it marvelous!"

Sally agreed.

The girls were booked at the nearby French Lick Hotel, in the town of French Lick, Indiana. The porter took their bags. Madelyn's luggage consisted of a mutely colored tapestry-rolling bag with a matching carrying case and dress bag. Sally had chosen a country style quilted dress bag and duffle, handmade from quilted material. She'd found the set in Zionsville, a small town filled with quaint boutiques. They parked the rented Lincoln.

The French Lick Resort was also in the process of renovation. Both West Baden and French Lick were excitedly waiting for the revival of the resorts and for the construction of a massive casino. The luxurious double Resort/Casino would have high prices to match.

They proceeded through the torn-up lobby area to the restored antique check in desk.

Their shared room overlooked the outside domed pool and hot tub spa. The outside architecture of the enormous meandering hotel was in their sight through their window. The decorative details included wrought iron fire escapes. Lack of visitors for years now caused the hotel to close many rooms in the massive facility. The hotel was a tribute to a time now gone when it played a large part in society. The closed ballroom, once the place to dance and quiet meandering corridors reminded Sally of the decrepit hotel featured in the movie, *The Shining*. She looked around with caution expecting to see Jack Nicholson pop up around the corner. The halls were wide, echoing, empty, and creepy. The carpet and wallpaper were terribly mismatched. The majestic grand hotel's heyday of the 1920s had passed. The construction work signaled a hope for a renewal of the resort's appeal. The hotel's regal-standing would be reborn.

They arrived in late afternoon in time to relax before the spa experience. Their deluxe spa package included a stone massage, Pluto mineral water bath, body scrub, reflexology, and a pedicure. The Pluto water bath was the start of their adventure into an old world society of the very rich.

Madelyn said, "After the massage, let's walk in the gardens. Then we should eat at the hotel restaurant. You know the Pluto water bath was so relaxing but I wouldn't want to drink the smelly stuff. During the 1920s, it was all the rage to 'take the waters'. You could buy bottles of the mineral water. Did you know Pluto water comes from the springs on the grounds of the hotel? In the past, Pluto water was used as a strong laxative. I guess it was effective within one hour from ingestion. Did you know carloads of the Companies shipped Pluto water by rail all over the states? A few people still drink the disgusting water."

Sally said, "Why, I wouldn't drink that rank stuff! Smelling it while bathing in it was bad enough."

Madelyn continued with the brief history lesson, "President Franklin Roosevelt 'took the waters' here. He received treatments for polio at this very hotel. I wonder if he had a bath in the same tub we used. The attendant said the big bathing tubs were original. Oh, this must have been quite the place to be. There were trains coming into town all the time with tourists. The trains would then leave with the bottled water. Now the trains are part of a rail museum. If I'd lived back then, this is where I would come, just to be seen."

Sally responded, "I know this resort was popular in the early 20th Century, but I didn't know why."

Suddenly, Sally changed the subject back to Gussy's will. She asked, "Madelyn, I've been thinking. Do you know how Henrietta plans to find your brother's child?"

Madelyn still annoyed by the afternoon's meeting at the attorney's office, said, "I don't have any idea how anyone could find this child. The family had no idea Gussy even dated anyone, let alone sired a child. I guess the romance must have been a quick one; you know even a one-night stand. We never saw him with a woman. He was, though, somewhat wild as a young man. He quit high school and never graduated. Gussy said, 'I don't need to.' He was correct. A high school diploma or none wasn't important in deciding if you were to be sent to Vietnam. A warm body fulfilled the requirement to be a bullet stopper."

Sally said, "I don't remember meeting Gussy when I came to Grovetown for the Persimmon Festival."

"It's possible you met Gussy, but he didn't live in the house then. The family made the summer kitchen behind the house into a bachelor apartment, now his workshop after his return from Nam. You may have run into him."

"I can't recall. I spent most of my time looking at crafts and such. I may have even studied a little. My classes were already in session. If I remember, I didn't get to stay long. How one forgets even important events as we age." Sally shrugged. "Oh, by the way, I was a little jealous of you. You looked so lovely as Queen."

"Why thank you," said Madelyn. "It was fun, but hectic. I didn't even have time to finish a term paper for my World History class. No wonder I had trouble keeping my grades up," she laughed.

After supper, the girls walked around the gardens on the manicured grounds. They roamed the hotel interior and visited the numerous gift shops. Madelyn bought Stuart a very expensive shirt. Sally bought a hot pink hat with an ostrich feather. The hat cost three times more than the shirt.

Sally said, "Let's go to the pool. I looked out our window. I saw only a few people; I bet we can sit in the hot tub all by ourselves."

"Yes, let's do it."

The two women acting like adolescent girls returned to their room about eleven thirty. The pool was still open, but all guests had gone to bed.

Back in the room, Madelyn opened a bottle of Oliver's Soft Red wine, from the local winery. They enjoyed the wine along with some cheddar cheese and crackers.

Sally said, "Why, Madelyn you think of everything. You even brought crystal wine glasses."

"I can't drink wine from plastic glasses."

They talked way into the night. Madelyn talked about her children,

"My son, Nathan, you met him, is finishing his Ph.D. in some kind of journalistic studies. Why would he waste his life in journalism like his father? Moreover, he has a Notre Dame master's degree to boot. Newspaper work is not a career. To work at a newspaper is less like a job and more like a hobby. I don't know what he owes for student loans, but I bet it's a pretty penny for a useless diploma."

Sally interrupted, "I'm so pleased Drew decided to follow his father into dentistry."

He's doing so well. He doesn't have a girlfriend. This generation of, I think they're called 'Millennials', doesn't make marital decisions until they are in their late twenties or even thirties."

"I know. At least they aren't rushing into early marriages. I hope Emily finds a suitable husband, one worthy of her and who will support her in all ways." Madelyn thought, *Drew is unattached. Emily thinks Drew is handsome, and he's a dentist to boot. Why Emily could quit her lowly job, as a teacher. Maybe Sally will help them get together. 'Match maker, match maker, make me a match.'"*

They finished the first bottle of wine and opened the second.

Madelyn continued, "Sally wouldn't it be nice if Drew would date Emily? He filled her broken tooth. Your husband couldn't fit her into his schedule. Why don't you and I promote their seeing each other? Perhaps we all, including our children, could get together for dinner."

Sally took a glass of wine and slurped it quickly down.

We should encourage them to spend some time together. I don't think I'm meddling. A little helpful push. Don't you agree? They would make a lovely couple I know. Wouldn't it be fun to have the same grandchildren?"

Sally poured another glass of wine. This time, she gulped it down.

44

The morning after the reading of the new will, Henrietta addressed her niece at breakfast. "Emily, do you have the article ready to put into the papers?"

Emily opened a leather folder. She showed her work to Henrietta. "I hope this will be okay. I want to get Dad's opinion on the wording too."

Henrietta added, "I've noticed there are a lot of ads nowadays for families. Some looking for children to adopt. Others looking for lost family members. Children looking for natural parents. Parents searching for children they put up for adoption. There must be more people cut off from their loved ones than I ever imagined."

"I know there are people estranged and searching for loved ones. There are many couples searching to adopt a child. Aunt Henri. I think this is a reasonable first step. Once we get the wording right, I want to send it to newspapers in Peony, Bloomington, and surrounding counties. I thought we could place it in some local town papers. Dad may have more suggestions. Want me to read the draft to you?"

"Thanks, but I'll leave the editing to the experts. Between you and your father, I'm sure the ad will be fine. I'll go on to the library. You go to your father's office. I'm anxious to begin our library search, too."

"I agree," said Emily. "Now I left out any mention of the name. As soon as the article is ready and off to the various papers, I can begin to search the library's archives of *The Tribune* for birth announcements listed around the possible birth date. I know starting there is a long shot, but we don't want to leave any stone unturned. We can expand the search as needed."

"Without Gussy's suggested date, June 1971, in his will, we would be totally lost. We have a lot of work ahead of us."

They cleared the breakfast table. Each quickly left for their respective duties.

Emily arrived at the newspaper office. "Dad, I printed my rough draft. Will you please check it over?"

"Certainly. Let me see it."

"The Estate of Gustafason (Gussy) Trinkle of Grovetown, Peony County, IN is searching for a missing heir. An illegitimate child of Gustafason Trinkle born about June 1971. Mother's name unknown; and birth place unknown. Please submit name, date and city of birth, and other details to prove your claim. Appropriate interviews may be arranged. Please contact the Executrix of the Estate of Gustafeson Trinkle, Henrietta Trinkle, 204 W. Mulberry, Grovetown, IN."

"Sounds good. I would make a couple of changes however. I think we should use the paper's P. O. Box number for responses. We don't want to make Henri's address available to outsiders. In addition, we may want to remove her name from the ad. Who knows what kind of people may respond. I think offering a reward would help."

"Oh, my, you're right Dad. I certainly wouldn't want to put Aunt Henri in harm's way." Emily took her pencil and made the appropriate changes. "I'm not sure the estate can offer a reward. I'll have Aunt Henri to ask Ms. Basford, the attorney. Besides your paper, I thought we would notify Peony, Bloomington, Indy, and the other county papers around. Do you think we should send the ad to papers in Louisville and Cincinnati? Do you have others to suggest?"

"Why don't you let Nathan and I take care of getting your ad published? We'll make sure you receive all the responses, of course."

"Great!" exclaimed Emily. "I'll gladly leave the chore in your capable hands. I'll go to the library. I'm going to start searching the archives for birth notices. Thanks, see you later."

Emily entered the library. Henri was feeding her fish, Shakespeare.

"I'd like to get on the web and see if I can find information on methods and hints to find birth announcements. If I can find sources on the net, it'll be easier than driving to Indianapolis or other places."

Henrietta responded, "I think so too. Well, I'm glad you're here. I need to restack the books turned in overnight. You do the search. Please watch the desk too. See what you can find."

Emily was on the computer for over an hour. She found several sources where one could type in the limited information available."

Henrietta returned from stacking books. Emily said, "Gosh,

I'm already feeling like I'm trying to escape from a quicksand hole. Overwhelmed! I need to figure out a way to keep track of all this information."

Henrietta looked over her niece's shoulder at all of the information Emily already accumulated. "You know what, dear; I bet we can make a spreadsheet to track it all. Surely, we can sort the information easily. Here, let me help you."

"You know, Aunt Henri, this is going to be time consuming. I brought my laptop. I can do this after work and from home. During the day, I can dig into the computerization of the books. I don't want to take up the time from my task of working in the library."

"I think it's a great idea."

45

Nathan, Patrick, Emily, and Jayne found themselves in canoes on Deer Fly Creek. They believe the creek is navigable now after the clean-up. The pairs decided to have a male/female challenge for the day trip. Of course, Dexter, Patrick's black lab would be in the canoe with the boys, while Jayne's Corgi, Queen E, would ride with the girls.

Before they jumped into their respective canoes, Nathan said, "I'll sit in front. Patrick, you steer. We can change later if you wish."

"No problem. I'm sure Dexter will help."

Emily exclaimed, "I love it out here on the river. The beautiful scenery and animals. I'm okay with turtles and such, but please God, no snakes!"

Patrick replied, "Of all the times I've been on the river, I've never seen snakes. Deer Flies are in abundance, however. You girls did put on DEET didn't you, and a high SPF sunscreen?"

"Yes, dear, you needn't remind us," Jayne responded. "See, I even have on a ball cap like yours. Well, not *exactly* like yours. Mine has Purdue on it. At least your Colt's hat is more tolerable than Nathan's old torn and worn Notre Dame hat."

"Well, thank you, Jayne," Nathan sarcastically retorted. "This hat *is* perfect and fits my head just right. Perhaps Emily's Chicago Cubs will be neutral ground for us all. I think we all like the Chicago Cubs, don't we?" Nathan addressed Emily and Patrick, He continued, "I know our fathers are Cincinnati Reds fans. The Cubs are doing well. They beat the Reds. Perhaps the curse is finally over, thank goodness!"

Patrick answered, "I didn't get to watch that game. There was an emergency."

"You're right, you missed it," said Jayne. "I still have it taped if you want to watch it."

Patrick explained, "I always hope to see the Cubs games on ESPN.

If I know ahead of time, I tape them. Jayne helps too. She's become such a Cubs fan."

Jayne smiled and added, "We try to watch them together."

Patrick continued, "We're planning to take a weekend to see them play in Chicago. Jayne has friends there."

"We can save a lot of money if we stay with them," Jayne explained. "They have a huge house in Wrigleyville. I think they have like five bedrooms. Plenty of room to keep us. Both of you could come, too—a *real* road-trip with a *real* destination."

Nathan was interested. He responded, "Sounds like fun." When do you plan to go? I would drive from South Bend and meet you there. I would want to include my girlfriend, Judy. Of course, we would stay at a hotel. Two rooms won't be cheap, but we'll manage. We can surely save the money."

"I thought we'd go in August, after you start back to school," Patrick answered.

Emily, the worrier of the group, asked, "What would you do about your patients, Patrick? You don't have a partner, do you?"

"No, I don't currently, but I try to answer only emergency calls on weekends. I'd have to change my office message to tell callers to contact the emergency room in Peony. Not often have I, so I wouldn't feel too guilty going to Chicago."

Realizing Emily hadn't joined in the planning, Jayne added, "You should come, too, Emily. You wouldn't want to miss out on all the fun."

They agreed to work out the details soon.

They canoed toward Tucker's Bridge. They saw several lazy turtles basking in the sun on the banks. There were some smaller ones in the creek. The great blue heron was catching fish.

The water was smoother than their last excursion. The two canoes stayed close enough for conversation. The subject turned to Gussy's murder.

Jayne asked, "Have the police found anything? Chief Petty is out of town. I suppose not much will be discovered."

Nathan replied, "Yes, Petty's still in California. So not much is happening. My father and I are doing a little investigation into the murder. We've read the police reports and autopsy results. The other evidence and interviews may not be available until the chief returns."

Emily said, "And Aunt Henri and I have started looking for the child mentioned in Uncle Gussy's new will. I'm afraid it won't be easy for any of us. So far, we don't have any good leads. We've only started."

Nathan continued, "Well I don't have much confidence anything will be settled until Chief Petty returns. Deputy Green is handling the case now. He's doing ok, but he's low on detective expertise. I hear Jake Achsworth is helping him. But I don't think it's going anywhere."

Jayne quickly said, "I hope this doesn't become a cold case."

Nathan said, "Surely, all of us together can find the murderer. I hope that the girls will discover the identity of the child. I still can't believe my uncle had any serious relationship with anyone. How could he have a meaningful relationship without someone knowing? In addition, a child. Sounds impossible! Of course, the period of free love after the Vietnam era. You know about those Hippie Flower Children. I can't imagine Gussy involved in a sexual affair without love. Maybe he did. Still it doesn't sound like my Uncle Gussy."

"It seems odd to me he didn't marry the mother. That fact will help lead to the child in some way."

"It appears strange. Could it be the mother didn't want him to have any contact," Emily added.

Nathan responded, "Well, could be. We sure have a lot of unanswered questions."

Jayne's corgi pawed at the side of the canoe, showing she was ready for a potty break. The boys floated ahead and left the girls behind to handle Queen E's needs. As the boys came round a blind bend in the river, Patrick practically screamed, "There's a large log jam up ahead! See it?"

Nathan responded. "Yikes! Do you think we can avoid hitting it? Luckily, the girls are trailing behind us. I hope we can figure out how to help them."

"If you steer well, we'll be okay. We could portage around the logs if we have to."

Their minds were on the difficult task. As they got closer to the jam, they were startled.

Nathan exclaimed, "Look at all the disgusting scum around the logs. I know you'll want to get another sample to test."

Patrick had little time to respond as the canoe rammed into a fallen tree underwater. The canoe swamped, throwing all, including Dexter, into the water. Dexter swam to the bank near Tucker's Bridge. The two men righted the swamped canoe and pulled it to the bank to get to the wet dog. They tried not to swallow the rancid water.

Patrick exclaimed, "Why, there seems to be something metal down here. I about stepped on it. I'll try to pick it up." He reached down and pulled the object out of the water. The men were speechless for a few seconds, and then he said, "Why, it's a giant screwdriver. Look the wooden handle is really old."

"The screwdriver must be over a foot long. You know, I think I've seen something like it in Gussy's workshop. The tip looked about like a regular screwdriver, but three inches down the metal shank, it changed shape, looking like an angular tube."

"It looks like it could be dangerous." Patrick replied. "The handle looks hand hewed. Man, this heavy screwdriver looks ominous, don't you think?"

Nathan said, "I bet it's an antique. What a fine weapon it would make. Do you think someone could kill with it?"

"Oh, yes!" answered Patrick. "I wonder if it could have been used to kill Gussy?"

They saw the girls' canoe. The guys helped them portage their canoe and made sure they were all in the canoe including the corgi.

Patrick explained he needed to take a sample of the scum. He finished the small task and said, "We shouldn't dilly-dally. We found this monstrous old screwdriver. Look."

Jayne said, "Wow! Do you think it's important?"

Nathan answered, "We don't know, but we're taking it to the police station."

46

Nathan and Patrick arrived at the police station with the strange-looking screwdriver. They found Deputy Ron Green and Jake sitting outside in the sunshine and drinking strong coffee.

Jake said, "Why hello, boys. May we help you?"

"Wow, Jake, you sure sounded real official-like!" replied Patrick.

"He's been practicing," quipped Ron. "I sure hope you boys ain't here to report a crime. We have 'nuf to do trying to find Gussy's killer. Are you here to help, too?"

Nathan came forward chuckling, "Well kind of. We found a vicious looking tool down near Tucker's Bridge while we were canoeing. We thought, since the autopsy said Gussy was stabbed, you might want to see it."

Deputy looked over at the long screwdriver. He exclaimed. "Wow, I wouldn't want to meet someone with this big screwdriver in an alley some dark night. What a weapon it might make!"

Nathan let the deputy examine it.

He noted, "It doesn't seem rusty or have much water damage on the wooden handle. I would say it wasn't in the water long. Wouldn't you agree, Jake?"

"Uh huh, I agree with you. Why, I don't believe I've ever seen a screwdriver that long. I wonder what it could be used for," Jake responded.

The others except for Nathan, chimed in, "We haven't either."

Nathan said, "I think it looks like a screwdriver I once saw in Gussy's workshop. I asked my uncle about it and he said it's quite old."

Green said, "I should take photos of it. Could you call your father? I'd like photos taken before I send it to the city for examination and comparison with the autopsy report. I've heard forensic experts are so smart that scientists can even find out if there's human blood evidence even after weeks. They say it doesn't even matter if it's been washed off."

Jake said, "I always watch CSI. Never can figure out which of the towns they're in. How confusing—Las Vegas, Miami, or New York. How can anybody know which is which?"

Green agreed, laughing at Jake.

Jake thought, *I'm glad I was here. I'll need to come by more often for chitchat with the police; you never know what you'll learn.*

Raymond arrived to take pictures.

Green said, "I want you to sign this paper to show when you took possession of the object, boys. I'll have to make sure a forensics agent signs for it. We have to protect the chain of custody. We wouldn't want some shifty-eyed defense attorney keeping this out of evidence if we find out it's the probable weapon."

Green asked Patrick, Nathan, and Raymond, to go with him to the site near Tucker's Bridge. Green said to Raymond, "Where did you find it? You'll have to take me there. How am I going to know how to mark off and tape this crime scene? I wish Chief Petty was here."

Raymond answered, "I do too. This could be a break in the case."

Green said, "I may call the Chief. He'll be back day after tomorrow, but I bet he'd want to know right away. If this is the murder weapon, I don't want to mess anything up."

They headed to the bridge.

Green asked Patrick and Nathan to point out the location where they found the screwdriver.

"Right about here. See on the right of the bridge downstream. I remember because it was right near the logjam about ten feet from shore and about six feet from the other bank."

Green exclaimed, "This will be a very difficult task. I'm going to need time to examine the scene."

He then radioed the county sheriff's office explaining the situation and asked them to send their detectives ASAP to seal off the area.

Green said, "Time is of the essence. We can't have the bridge closed down very long."

He put up orange traffic cones blocking both sides of the bridge and got to work.

47

Nathan found his way to the office of Henry Bridges, the current City Works Manager. Mr. Bridges took office seven years ago. He replaced a temporary fill in when Glenn, the previous Work Manager, retired from office.

Bridges sat at his desk. Nathan entered. Bridges said, "What can I do for you? I don't receive many social calls."

Nathan got right to the point.

"Mr. Bridges, my name is Nathan Starks. I'm working with my father, Raymond Starks, at the newspaper for the summer. I'm sure you've heard by now about the recent report from the Peony County Health Department. The town has a serious problem. Raw sewage is flowing into Deer Fly Creek. I understand the governmental agencies are investigating. I'll be honest. I have my own agenda. I'm researching to develop the story for the paper. May I see the public records dating back to the installation of the main sewer line? I understand the entire town's documents fall under Indiana's Open Door Policy. I also have lots of questions."

"Yes, Pugh came by and talked to me." Henry thought, *Oh yes, he came by all right! Just in time to make my already bad day worse. Now you're here.* "He explained the problems with the sewer. There will be investigations." *Oh yes, there'll be investigations, many investigations!* "So I can give you documents but no opinions. I certainly understand why the paper would be interested in such a story." *Wouldn't the press like to know the rest of the story!* "But, you need to realize I'll be able to answer questions within a very limited scope. Remember I didn't work in this capacity when they installed the sewers. I may not be able to be of much assistance than what the records can tell you."

Bridges and Nathan discussed what documents were located in the back office. Bridges continued, "I'll see if I can locate the master plans showing the sewer routes and hook-ups. The locations of the laterals are also shown on this diagram." *However, it won't tell you if there are missing laterals.*

"Mr. Bridges, please excuse my ignorance. Can you educate me? What are laterals?"

"Laterals are the hookups to the sewer from the sewage line of the properties with the main line. They bridge the main line to those of the buildings. Every property has its own lateral to connect to the main sewer. Just a minute and I'll get the map from its file." Bridges thought, *Why are laterals missing and not shown on the blueprints?*

He returned with the oversized blueprints displaying them on a table. "This shows the layout of Grovetown. Look here. This line is the main line to the sewage plant. This other line is the storm sewer flowing to Deerfly Creek. You can see they are separate. The rule is 'Never the twain shall meet'. These lines are the laterals. They connect the property owners' personal sewer line to the city's main." *Except when they don't.*

Nathan commented, "Boy, looks complicated to me. May I have a copy?"

"Of course, it's a public document. I'll need to take it to the copier at the town office. I think as large as it is it will have to be pieced. I think they charge a dollar per page. I can have it done by tomorrow morning. Okay?"

"Fine. How were the completed sewer connections documented?"

Bridges answered, "Well, the works manager certified his inspection and approval of the connection." *But someone lied.*

"I have those records also. Do you need the inspection certifications?"

"Yes, please. I'll have Dad send a check, or do I need cash?"

"The town clerk usually won't accept checks, but I know the newspaper's check will be fine. Are there any other documents you need?"

"Yes. I require a copy of the construction contracts, change orders, town board minutes, payment records, and any other applicable papers to the construction. All you have in regards to the sewer, from beginning to end."

"Some of those documents are at the clerk's office. You'll have to see her. I fear a significant amount of time will be required to find it all, but I'm sure we'll cooperate as best we can." Bridges surmised, *I don't want to be involved in a sewer blowout causing quite a stir. Good luck is all I can say.*

Nathan said, "Thanks. I'll check with you in the next day or two."

Nathan went to the town clerk's office. He finally arrived back at the newspaper office to report his findings.

"Dad, let's go to dinner at the café. I'll explain my discoveries."

Raymond said, "Let me finish this article on the summer baseball teams. You update your notes while they are still fresh in your mind."

*****

The café was crowded. They found seats near the town big shot's communal table. Today, Glenn Achsworth, Deputy Green, and the town board President were sitting there.

Raymond ordered the Special of the Day: lasagna, bread sticks, salad, and applesauce.

Nathan opted for the giant breaded deluxe tenderloin and French fried onion rings. He knew this violated any good nutritional guide he knew. He exclaimed, "This giant tenderloin is what puts Indiana on the map."

Both ordered sweet tea.

Nathan noted, "Henry Bridges was receptive to my requests. He was quite congenial and said we'll have his paperwork copied by tomorrow. The town's material will take a little longer. The clerk needs time to locate the records."

His father looked pleased. "Lookin' good. I'm sure we'll be busy analyzing a lot of materials. I think we have a head start on the investigations ahead of the other agencies."

Unnoticed by the duo, Glenn, the former Works Manager, eavesdropped on the pair. His ears pricked when he heard them talk about the sewer. In the past, he'd always squashed any rumors and innuendoes. Of course, he knew there was contamination in the creek and the source. He thought, *Why are Raymond and Nathan sticking their noses in it?*

Raymond continued, "We need to read all the old newspapers for some other insights. Surely there are a lot of newsworthy tidbits on the subject."

Eventually, the talk shifted to the never-ending subject of Gussy's murder and the lack of progress by the police. The former Chief of

Police, Jack, listened to every word.

Back at the Works Office, Henry Bridges ruminated on his morning. *What a day! I can't believe this morning. And it's only Wednesday. What's going on? I hate talking to plumbers who find problems with back-ups. How could anyone know the Catholic Church backup would be a result of no hook-up to the sanitary sewer line? Then all those other houses and buildings. No laterals? They just don't disappear. I know all this rain could cause me to turn gray. Of course, extreme rains plug up the storm sewers, but this. Ralph Pugh from the Health tells me sewage is running into Deer Fly Creek. And who shows up next? Why it's the nosy newspaper!*

48

Henry Bridges knew all the upcoming work would prove some of what he already knew or suspected. Grovetown was going to a plumber's heaven—thousands of dollars in fees in their pockets. He called all employees of the Works Department in for a meeting Thursday morning. "Okay, guys, I know the next few days are going to be busy. You know about sewage going into Deer Fly Creek. We need to know why. We're going to smoke the sewer lines. Let me explain what we'll have to do."

"To smoke test the sewer line we put a non-toxic, harmless, odorless, and non-fire hazard 'smoke' down the sanitary waste sewer lines. This test will help us find problems with the sewer, such as obstructions or defects in the system. I don't believe we'll have any rain or winds tomorrow to prevent the test. I made up some flyers last night. Today, you guys will go all over town hanging this notice at each building or residence. The cards give the resident or owner info on what to expect, and a phone number if they need help or answers to additional questions."

One worker piped up, "How will we know if there's a problem or defect?"

"Well if you see smoke, we know there's a problem. I'll explain all that when we start the actual process. You'll have a chart of addresses and buildings to record if smoke comes out the roof downspouts, driveway drains, foundations, and defective service pipes. Well, go distribute. Try not to take too long a lunch. I'm authorizing overtime pay if needed."

His crew left.

Bridges got out the materials for the chart along with a cup of strong coffee. *There may be a few defects, but the main sewer line isn't the problem. Some buildings have laterals, but they aren't hooked up. Why? What was going on? The whole mess smells bad. At least it's not my fault.*

*****

The smoke test revealed no inter-connection between the storm sewer and the sanitary. All attendees at the meeting showed relief to know they wouldn't have to dig up the sewer lines.

The group decided to use ping-pong balls on a sampling of buildings. They flushed ping-pong balls down the toilets to see where they went. The ping-pong balls would show if a specific building was connected to the sanitary sewer. If the ping-pong balls ended up floating in the sanitary sewer, all was well. That building was connected correctly. A different test was to see whose waste was going into the river by way of the storm sewer.

Bridges called all the plumbers in the area to a meeting. He asked for information from the plumbers about the back-ups on their job schedules. Clogged pipes only caused a few backups from the buildings themselves. Another group of sewer problem stemmed from the owners failing to connect to their lateral. They kept the old system of emptying into the storm sewer and down to the river. This situation was easy to rectify but not cheaply. The solution was expensive for the owner. The plumber would put in new pipes from the building to the sanitary line. Often times, expense was the reason they chose not but to connect in the beginning. Bridges thought, *Who inspected the non-connections and certified they were in compliance? I knew something was wrong but not the extent. Where will this end?*

The independent plumbers discovered, but didn't report at first a major omission. A three-block area of town didn't have laterals for hook-ups. The plumbers, who discovered this serious fact, fixed the problems as best they could. Their plan of action for the problem with no laterals was to join as a group and report the perplexing situation to the Works Manager. George Waterman, the plumber who discovered the problem at the church, volunteered to tell Bridges.

Bridges now aware thought, *What should I do? Ay. Ay. Ay!*

He immediately asked for verification from the plumbers. Next, he told his workers to find a bright red liquid dye.

*****

The workers flushed red dye down every toilet in the three-block area. The test found all but one building's toilet water with red dye going straight into the storm sewer and down to Deer Fly Creek.

The building where dye didn't show up in either sewer line was a different problem. That building wasn't connected to either sewer line. The waste of that structure goes straight under the floor of that specific building. The sewage emptied into a cellar.

49

Henrietta locked up the library at noon. She and Emily walked home. They enjoyed the beautiful sunny afternoon. Emily asked, "Why do you close the library at noon on Wednesday?"

Henrietta replied, "Our Carnegie Library began closing on Wednesday afternoons decades ago. This allowed the businesses to have open hours on Saturday mornings. The Kiwanis Club took advantage of the Wednesday closings to meet at Cook's Restaurant, now demolished. There was a back room set aside for meetings and parties. Did you know even back in the seventies and part of the eighties, women couldn't join the Kiwanis Club?"

Emily responded, "Why, I didn't know. Wasn't it sex discrimination!"

"Of course it was! There were complaints throughout the nation. The feminist movement helped make some changes, but we couldn't get the 28th Amendment—Equal Rights for Women—passed," replied the librarian. She thought, *And we surely couldn't now.*

Emily then said, "I know. I took a women's history course. I guess we've tried to get equal right's laws passed since 1923. Even now, I hear women at church gossiping about other women, with young kids, who worked. They say, 'Women belong in the home.' Others feel the mother working deprives the children of a nurturing family life."

Henrietta said, "I know. Since I don't have children of my own, it's difficult to know what the right environment is for healthy children. When both parents work the children may get less attention than if only one parent works. Now, some parents decide one will work and the other one stays home. Recently I see many where the stay at home parent homeschool. I can see both negatives and positives of homeschooling. I worry about the lack of socialization, although many are incorporating 4-H and scouts as part of the child's class work. I don't know the answer but having Jesus in the home is the important thing."

Henrietta changed the subject.

Henrietta asked, "Emily, would you please go to the mailbox at the post office after we reach home. I'll start our lunch. Thought we'd have bacon, lettuce, and tomato sandwiches."

Emily said, "Our ad started running a week ago. I'd like to see if we've had any responses to our search for Gussy's child."

"I hope so. I'd like to get right on it. Your mother calls several times a week to see if we've had any new info. She wants the estate closed quickly. I think we all want it closed, but we also want to know the truth. Madelyn is so anxious. We need an answer. Let's say a prayer for guidance. Dear God, We praise You and know You'll guide us in your search. Amen."

Emily said, "Yes, I know my mother is anxious. However, Aunt Henri, you can only do so much. I know the mystery of Gussy's child is heavy on everybody's mind. I'll go to the post office. Would it be okay if I go exercise before I bring the responses home to you. I promise I won't get too chatty while I'm there. Besides, they close at one. I barely have time to get my clothes changed, get there, and do my thirty minute workout before they close for their afternoon break. However, I know we're both anxious to see what kind of results we may find in the mail. I promise to hurry home."

After the requisite half hour of exercise. Emily hurriedly walked to the post office for the mail from the rented box. She thought about what she would find. *Please God; I want to receive as many responses as we can.. However, may they be the right responses. Please help us be effective in our search for Gussy's heir."*

She opened the mailbox to find several letters. Glancing at the envelopes, she saw a variety of postmarks and return addresses. One really caught her attention had a local postmark and address. There were two from Bloomington, several from Peony, and a few from Indianapolis. With great expectations, she excitedly walked briskly back to her aunt's.

Emily opened the door. Henrietta was anxiously waiting. She greeted her niece with a question, "Did we receive any responses?"

"Oh, yes. I can hardly wait to see what they all say."

Henrietta led her to the 1920s style maple library table, an heirloom from her mother. Henrietta located lined paper and her old Mont Blanc fountain pen filled with emerald green ink. Emily knew her aunt didn't allow anyone else to use this special fountain pen. Henrietta claimed the nib was worn to her unique writing style. That idiosyncrasy was standard among fountain pen writers. She knew her grandmother would be happy that she was using her pen.

Emily was satisfied with her job of reading the letters. She would have much preferred using a computer transcribing the results but she reached for her Mont Blanc pen from its velvet bag.

"You tell me where they're from, Emily. I'll use one sheet of paper for each letter."

Emily agreed, exclaiming, "Okay, I'll open the local one first."

She said, "This letter is from a woman in Grovetown. Henrietta, do you recognize the name?"

Henrietta said, "No."

Emily wrote the info down, with address and phone number.

Emily scanned the letter, "The handwriting isn't very legible. There are numerous spelling and grammar mistakes."

Next Emily opened the envelopes with Bloomington addresses. One said he was a male African -American professor at I.U. Another was from a female admissions clerk at the University. The third was from a fast-food restaurant manager near the I.U. campus.

Emily said, "Here's one with a Peony address. He says he lived at a campground near Peony. Was the campground the old gypsy camp?"

"I've heard there were some gypsies in the county. Nevertheless, other travelers camp there too. Some locals like to have camper trailers there by the lake as a getaway."

Emily said, "Let the process begin!"

50

She called Emily, "Please give me your opinion. I want to look good tonight. I thought I'd wear my light green and beige pleated dress, beige open toe shoes, and matching Guess purse. Doesn't it sound appropriate?" *I'm so glad I bought this even if it was a bit above my budget.*

Emily answered, "Permelia, you'll look quite fine. A green dress should bring out the green in your eyes."

"Should I wear my beige Derby-style hat? Will I stand out too much? The hat has an orange flower. I know I'm flamboyant, but I don't want to appear too ostentatious." *I hope Emily says it's ok. I think the look is classy.*

"Sounds like a nice outfit. I'll wear a hat, too. Don't you wish they would come back- in-style? Of course, I don't think you nor I care so much about *being in style.* As long as we're comfortable with ourselves." *Mom wouldn't agree.*

"Yes, I'd like hats to come back, but I'll wear them anyway even if no one else does. Thanks! I'd better finish dressing. See you in a while." *I'll be OK. I won't try to be somebody I'm not. I needed some reassurance. I'll feel more comfortable being myself. I wonder what Nathan likes in a date. I would rather scare him off as myself than someone I was pretending to be.*

She remembered the quivering sensation she felt when Nathan called to ask her out. After she agreed, she felt guilty. *Am I cheating on Steve? I wonder is a date with Nathan an injustice to his memory.*

Permelia finished dressing, and she put on a string of pearls and pearl earrings, her first wedding anniversary present Steve gave her. She loved the warm feeling of pearls and she remembered his warm touch.

Oh, Steve, I love you so and always will. These pearls will be my support tonight. I know you'd want me go out and try to make a new life for Robbie and me. I'll make you proud! Remember, I love you.

She brushed the tears out of her eyes as her son walked into the room.

Robbie said, "Why are you crying, Mommy? Do you need a hug?"

Permelia pulled herself together. She hugged her young child.

She pointed at her neck. "Robbie, I'm ok. See my pearls. Your father gave them to me before you were born. I was thinking about him. Let me take the pearls off so you can feel how soft and warm they are."

Robbie held them in his palm. "Momma, why are they so warm?"

His mother explained, "They're warm because they were on my warm neck. They get warmth from me. Aren't they pretty?"

"Why did Daddy give them to you?"

"Why, Robbie, he gave them to me because he loved me. Let's get you dressed in these jeans and your green and blue T-shirt. I'll help you put the shirt on over the cast. I like this red cast you picked. I know red is your favorite color. You'll be staying overnight, so I packed your jammies. You can stay up until nine tonight instead of eight. I know you'll have fun. Now, go find a book to take grandfather to read to you. I think you might get to watch DVDs, too. You'll probably want to take your stuffed bear. Yogi will be happy to take a ride and see a movie at Grandma's."

She hoped his cast would be off soon. Robbie so enjoyed being outside in the nice weather. He was unhappy because he couldn't be in junior Little League or ride his little red tricycle. *This Christmas I think Santa will bring him a blue bicycle with training wheels. I hope that he can go swimming later this summer. I know he's miserable, however, he hardly complains at all.*

Her father arrived on time. Permelia said, "I've packed a change of clothes. Now, don't spoil him too much. I know he'll have fun."

Her father told his grandson, Robbie, "Oh, we'll have a great time. Your grandmother is making spaghetti and meatballs for supper. I'm fixing popcorn with sliced apples. We'll eat them with cinnamon. Grandma's making lemonade. We'll watch the *Shrek* DVD I've rented. You'll like it, I know."

To his daughter he said, "These movies are supposed to be fun and teach a lesson. All people are the same inside. I don't think he's too young to watch them."

"Dad, I trust your judgment. I'm sure you checked the rating and it's PG."

Her father and son enthusiastically left. Permelia laughed at their great expectations for the evening. She wasn't surprised her goodbye kisses were barely noticed.

She expected Nathan soon. She straightened up the living room. Permelia wanted him to see what a good housekeeper she was. There wasn't much mess--some toys and papers. She stowed away her Wiccan books though. She thought, *I wouldn't bring out these books. Oh how I hope my home shows I'm neat and organized. Why am I so worried? I want Nathan to like me for myself.*

Again her mind was actively processing the visuals Nathan would see when he first entered her living room. She checked the bathroom to make sure all was in order. She took one last quick survey of her home.

I wonder what Nathan will think about my Virgin Mary. Oh my, I know many Protestants believe Catholics worship the statues of Saints. We don't. Why won't Protestants understand that? We ask Mary and the Saints to intercede for us with Jesus. However, what if Nathan thinks I do?

Steve's grandmother gave Permelia the two-foot-high statue of the Virgin holding the baby Jesus. A blue glass rosary accentuates her blue robes. When an old church was demolished her husband's grandmother received the statue. The rosary was his grandmother's and now belonged to Permelia.

She was ready when Nathan arrived to pick her up promptly at five forty-five. Their reservations at the restaurant at Deer Fly Creek Inn were for six. They were going to have an early supper before heading to Peony for a movie.

Permelia opened the door. Nathan stood there. *Doesn't he look debonair? I could swoon, but it would be a terrible faux pas.*

When getting in the car, she noticed Emily and Pastor Todd were already sitting in the backseat. He opened the car door for her. She said, "Thank you. *It's been a long time since someone opened the door to me.*"

Arriving at the restaurant, Nathan opened her car door again and when she went into the restaurant. Permelia thought, *What a gentleman!*

The hostess seated them in a cozy corner of the room. He then pulled her chair out for her. *I think he is trying to impress. Well, he is.*

When the waitress arrived, Nathan ordered an appetizer for them all, a sampler plate of little tacos, fried cheese, and jalapeno poppers. Emily ordered raspberry tea and water with lemon. Permelia followed with the same. Pastor Todd wanted coffee while Nathan ordered a Classic Coke. They chatted about little insignificant items while their drinks came. For supper, Permelia ordered chicken cacciatore, a salad, and green lima beans. Emily decided on baked cod, baked potato, and a salad. Nathan ordered a medium-rare sirloin steak with baked potato and lots of sour cream, salad, and steamed asparagus. Pastor Todd ordered a medium-well T-bone, fried potatoes, and broccoli.

The conversation continued with the mundane and a discussion of each of their jobs and education. Emily asked Permelia about her belly dancing classes, Nathan and Pastor Todd were a bit surprised, but neither laughed or even said a word. They listened intently.

Permelia continued. "Did you know Dance Orientale or belly dancing is one of the most ancient dances in the Middle East? Some say it goes back to Biblical days. Remember the story in the Bible about John the Baptist and Salome. Belly dancing received its bad reputation from Little Egypt at the World's Fair in Chicago, in the early 20th century. Burlesque shows didn't help, either. The dance serves many purposes in the Middle East. I could go on and on, but I would take up the whole evening. Many of my students take belly dancing for exercise and will only dance for their husbands."

Permelia laughed.

"I'll quit by saying it's quite an art form, really kind of like the more accepted form of classical ballet."

Emily broke in, "I'm taking the belly dance class, too. Permelia has agreed to go to Bible Study with me, in return for my classes. I like Curves, but this exercise uses different muscles. Would you like us to demonstrate Egyptian head slides?"

The ladies did whether they wanted them to or not. The men chuckled, unable to contain themselves any longer.

After the delightful supper, the conversation drifted into chitchat. The waitress came by with a tray of desserts. They all looked delicious. The men ordered coffee, but the girls ordered hot tea with lemon. Emily craved the lemon meringue pie while Permelia wanted strawberry shortcake; Nathan would have fresh rhubarb pie, as did the Pastor.

After dinner, the couples arrived in Peony. The four discussed the movie options at the small old-fashioned theater decorated with duplicates of vintage movie posters: *Ben Hur, Giant, Casablanca, and Gone with the Wind.* Tonight there were only two new ones to choose from, *Are We There Yet?* Alternatively, *Diary of a Mad Black Woman.*

The guys said they thought they would like to see *Are We There Yet?* Emily disagreed. She said, "The women from church say *Diary of a Mad Black Women* is both hilarious and morally good."

The men replied, almost simultaneously, "OK."

Pastor Todd said, "Well, you girls get to pick this one. We'll choose the next time."

Both Emily and Permelia thought his comments were quite promising for future dates. During the movie, Permelia wished Nathan would put his arms around her. The closest she got was sharing his popcorn.

During the movie, Nathan thought, *I'm not thinking guilty because I'm here with Permelia instead of Judy. I thought I might. Strange.*

Permelia was impressed with the movie's message: infidelity, and breaking trust could result in forgiveness, consequences of sex outside marriage versus chastity until marriage could lead to a strong, loving relationship. She imagined religious people wouldn't approve. However, her companions seemed quite at ease with the movie's messages. She looked into her friends' faces. She wondered if their state of mind had anything to do with their faith in Jesus.

Permelia thought, *Could I find mental peace from Jesus? I certainly enjoy being with my friends. I wonder if I could ever be as comfortable living a life like the one they profess in Jesus. Would belief in Jesus help me with my emotions of feeling as if I'm betraying Steve? Am I? Where is God in the scheme of my life?*

Emily also was thinking, *This is my first date with Todd O'Neil, and I hope there will be more. I enjoy dating Drew, too. Dear God, am I being too vain by having two men wanting to date me? The situation does make me feel special. I don't want a serious relationship with anyone yet, but I do like going out and enjoying myself. I pray it's okay to be dating two men. I like the attention. Dear God, am I being vain?*

She felt confused. She saw Drew or talked to him almost every day for the last month. She thought, *I enjoy being with Drew but something's wrong. I know Drew is in love with me, but am I in love with him? I don't feel that zing I expect to feel when I fall in love like all the girls in college said you would. They said if you couldn't say you are in love then you aren't. Drew isn't a bad man. He hasn't pushed himself on me. I know Drew wants to kiss me, but he honors my feelings. I have no idea what Pastor Todd's feelings are for me. I know Pastor Todd shares my values. Does Drew? Will one of these two men be the love of my life? I'm so confused, Oh, Dear God please direct me as I continue to see both of these attractive men. Let me know your will as I serve you.*

51

At eight o'clock Sunday morning, Permelia got out of bed to start her day. She planned to go to the Baptist morning worship service with her son and Emily but first she prepared breakfast. Robbie likes a bowl of Cheerios, half a banana, and a glass of milk. She prefers a bagel with strawberries and cream cheese. She didn't drink coffee. She prepared a cup of Jasmine hot tea with a slice of lemon.

Robbie didn't own a suit. She dressed him in a short sleeve green shirt and a pair of khaki trousers. He wore brown dress shoes.

Now, turning her attention to herself, she wanted a demure outfit.

Looking through her closet, she found the right ensemble. She chose a simple black skirt with a white short-sleeved silk blouse, adding her 14-carat gold medallion on a gold chain. The medallion was two inches in diameter. Christ was on one side and Mary on the other. The twelve disciples formed a circular frame around the main figures. It was a present from her husband Steve, on their wedding day at St. Luke's Catholic Church. She wore low-heeled black patent-leather sandals. She liked to go stocking-less, but realized it wasn't quite the correct thing to do today. She felt insecure.

As she started into the living room, she said to Robbie, "I hope I look good enough. I wouldn't want to embarrass my friends." Permelia attended a non-denominational protestant church growing up. Her attendance was at the insistence of her parents. Nevertheless, she never made a personal commitment to Christ. Her most recent church experience was her irregular attendance at St. Elizabeth's Catholic Church in Grovetown since she moved back home. Her involvement was only a smoke screen for the local society to see. Visible attendance also hid her Wiccan practices. Permelia thought taking Robbie to religious classes would help him socialize with other children and give him a beginning knowledge of a religion.

Now, she and Robbie were going to Sunday school at the First Baptist Church. Permelia was deep in thought while she finished doing her make-up. *I wonder if I'll learn more about the Bible in Sunday School. I wonder why adults go to Sunday School. I thought Sunday School is for children like CCD is in the Catholic Church. The Baptists have Bible Study, Sunday School, and church services? I understand much more about the Bible now—lots more than when I took that course at I.U. in Bible as Literature. Why do they need Sunday School in addition to the studies and church? I'll ask Emily.*

She remembered the peace she witnessed in the others at the hospital. *Everything is so positive with my friends. Emily told me she credits her inner peace to her faith in Jesus Christ. They all have such faith that permeates their lives. Would I find peace if Jesus saved me?*

She and Robbie waited on the gingerbread wrap-a-round porch on her Queen Anne home. Emily picked them up promptly at nine. They traveled the short distance to the small church.

Emily said, "Are you both ready? At Bible school, we'll be studying the Book of John. Do you have a Bible?"

Permelia answered, "Unfortunately, I don't have one with me. Do I really need a Bible today?

"You'll be able to understand better if you have the scriptures in front of you."

Emily replied, "Don't worry. Extra Bibles at the church are available to use. I'll get you one for today. We're starting on Chapter Three, a very important chapter in the Book of John."

Emily turned to Robbie, "My, don't you look handsome! I'm glad to see you're managing with that arm of yours."

Robbie was slightly embarrassed, yet pleased with the attention. He politely responded, "Thanks, Miss Emily."

Emily said, "Let's go everybody. I'm so glad you are going with me today. " They entered the church. Sunday School was about to start. Emily and Permelia helped Robbie to his room. His mother encouraged him to go in. When he saw some friendly smiles, he smiled back and sat down.

In their room, Emily found a loaner Bible. She told Permelia, "We have small classes. There are seven or eight participating. We sit in a circle." Emily introduced the teacher who gladly gave Permelia the study guide. Permelia was happy to see three familiar faces: Patrick, Nathan, and a mother of one of her ballet students. The other members of the class introduced themselves.

The instructor welcomed Permelia. Class opened with a group prayer.

"Shall we all join hands? If any of you have particular prayers please speak when I indicate to do so."

Permelia was impressed the members all participated. Everyone but she spoke up with specific intentions.

Nathan said, "I'd like prayers for my Uncle Gussy to find his being in God's presence a restful conclusion to his life on earth."

She felt God was actually in the room listening to each prayer. Permelia was surprised by the number of times someone included her in conversations. Emily expressed thanks to God for Robbie's healing, as well as others in their families or community who were facing problems. There were requests for the presence of the Holy Spirit to help each to receive understanding of the Word. Permelia didn't speak aloud, but she felt compelled to quietly add her agreement to what she heard.

The study began. Permelia remembered hearing of Nicodemus, but she was amazed at the knowledge of most of the class members. They spoke of Jesus' capability to perform miracles. She couldn't keep her thoughts from turning to Robbie's recent accident and the good medical care he received, as well as the prayers of her friends on Robbie's behalf. *Could God have been concerned about her son's needs enough to be a part of his healing?*

She pulled herself back to the present when the teacher pointed out the importance of the statement of Jesus, "I tell you the truth...."

Recently Permelia was searching for truth in her life. She always thought the truth was in Wicca, but she now seriously doubted the tenets of Wicca as a religion. She saw the results of a different experience with her Christian friends and their beliefs.

Class members spent part of the class time talking about the many times the Bible's truths were revealed in their personal lives. Their stories made an impact on Permelia's thinking. She didn't share but thought, *Will I ever be sure of the truth?*

Permelia was shocked the class was over so soon. Mrs. Ratliff previewed the next week's lesson on the subject of being born again.

Permelia's interest was piqued. She'd heard the term before, but really didn't know what it meant. She vowed to read the lesson and Bible references before next week so she wouldn't feel so inadequate in her knowledge. She hoped to have time to catch-up by also studying the first two chapters she missed. She hoped her friends would help her with questions she was bound to have. She left class in anticipation of opening her Bible and reading about the truth it presented. Nathan, Emily, and Patrick escorted Permelia and Robbie into the sanctuary.

They sat in a pew halfway down the aisle. Jayne, Patrick's girlfriend, was already there with her Bible ready. Pastor Todd opened the service with a greeting and prayer. Emily felt very welcome. Besides the congregation, he greeted and included visitors in his prayer.

"Today is Father's Day. Would all the fathers please stand." Pastor Todd said. Applause honored Raymond and some others.

Permelia, with tears in her eyes, thought about Steve. How proud he would have been to stand as a father. She thought, *My father doesn't practice a religion. Would this church be a good place for him and my mother to attend?*

He asked Jesus to direct his sermon and for it to honor Jesus and God. He prayed for certain people and families by name in need of special prayers.

Permelia thought, *Why, he sounds like he's having a personal talk with Jesus.*

After the prayer, Pastor Todd made some announcements.

Permelia was surprised there were so many activities like the upcoming pitch -in and the plans for the youth, children's plays, women's quilting groups, and study groups.

Permelia contributed what she could for the offering.

There was a small choir, after the prayer with several beautiful and meaningful hymns sung.

Why, I can join the choir. Some of the songs included one she knew: "Amazing Grace." Another, "In the Garden", Permelia remembered her Grandmother singing. There were other beautiful songs new to her, like "Wonderful Grace of Jesus" and "It is Well With my Soul." She sang along following the hymnal. She saw many of the members singing without looking at the words. She realized those hymns were familiar to them. Young adults accompanied by guitars performed some upbeat songs. The presence of drums surprised her.

The service progressed with what she thought was routine until it was time for the sermon.

Pastor Todd's sermon was on Elijah. "The Angel of God was sent to Elijah to make a great journey of forty days and forty nights. The Angel told him to take nourishment for sustenance on his journey. He was reluctant to but finally did take sustenance. However, Elijah had a bigger battle. King Ahab and his wife Jezebel believed in the pagan god, Baal. Elijah was going to show that Baal was not God. The people gave sacrifices to Jehovah and the pagan god Baal. The test was fire. Would there be fire to burn the sacrifices, both or only one? The worshippers of both prepared and slaughtered their sacrificial animals. Baal worshippers started first. They danced and sang to Baal and nothing happened. Elijah encouraged them to do more. They did but no fire. Elijah encouraged more fervent singing and dancing to no avail. After the pagans were through, Elijah soaked his sacrifice to the God of Jehovah three times with water, and called on God to send fire. Fire came from the true God."

Pastor Todd completed his sermon. He did something Permelia had never seen.

Pastor Todd invited any of the congregation who wished to make a testimony, to approach the altar to ask for prayers or to receive Jesus as their Savior. This was a new experience for Permelia.

A man in his sixties approached the altar. Permelia knew him from around town. She didn't know him personally. He introduced himself. He began his statement with "Praise be to God." He first talked about his now deceased wife whom he helped walk a couple of years ago down to this same altar for her testimony before she died. Now he said it was his turn to request prayers and to testify to his own faith. He explained the terminal medical conditions affecting his life. He asked for prayers. Nevertheless, what he did next would forever change Permelia and her future.

He began, "To God for His great glory. I give grace to God thanking Him for the great life He has given me. I have seen death and I don't fear it. I just don't like the indignities that go along with it. As a Christian, I'll walk through this life knowing with confidence that I have been healed. I leave behind only a broken shell. Years ago, I accepted Christ as my Savior, accepting His sacrifices for my sins, my imperfections made perfect through Him.

"I may live to be a hundred. Nevertheless, James says, 'We're just a mist soon to vanish.' Therefore, we need a different concept of time. We have now and we have eternity. Now is this fleeting sliver of time. Now is the only time we can influence eternity. And now is *now*. If you have not yet accepted Christ, you can do it *now*. Tomorrow is not guaranteed. You need to decide *now*. We have preachers, elders, deacons, and teachers, aching to pray with you. You have to do it now! I thank all of you for your concerns and prayers for my family and me. To God be all the glory."

The silence was palatable broken only by the sniffles of the entire congregation. Permelia pulled out her lace handkerchief and wiped her eyes. *I must think about what he said. I know I must.*

52

The first day of summer, June 22, approached. Permelia faced many questions. Where were she and Robbie's lives headed? The Wiccan High Festival of Mid-Summer's Eve was imminent. She was outside catching the warming sun rays of the season.

She said to her black cat, "You know, Magic, after Steve's death I sometimes have no idea where my life is going. You're a good confidant and friend. I don't know what to do. Something's missing."

Magic mewed as if understanding everything she said.

She continued, "At least Robbie's arm's healing. However, I really need answers. I feel like I'm beginning to adjust, but where am I going? Will I find calm or will I keep meandering? I read my Tarot cards. The Hanging Man card came up. You know there's significant changes are a'coming. What changes? Will they be good or bad? "

Magic listened, but didn't answer.

"You know how comforting Emily, Nathan, and Pastor Todd were at the hospital. They gave me strength. I don't remember ever having that feeling before."

To Permelia, the teachings were about Jesus Christ as Savior and how faith in Him would bring eternal life.

"Could there be something to faith in Jesus Christ bringing me peace, Magic? You know the Goddess religion of Wicca teaches the chant, *We all come from the Goddess and to her we shall return, like a drop of rain flowing to the ocean.* Many of the beliefs of Wicca are similar to some of the teachings I'm learning in Bible study. The Wiccans believe, 'Do what Ye Want, But Harm none.' The phrase seems so similar to *Do unto others as you want them to do unto you.*" The testimony of the man at church was still on her mind. She found it difficult not to think about his haunting word, NOW. *What do I do? Whom should I talk to? Moreover, when? NOW!*

She knew about Jesus, the Bible, and Biblical stories, like the tale of Adam and Eve, the great flood with Noah, David and Goliath, Moses and the Egyptians, and the miraculous birth of Christ.

Magic sat still, looking like he understood all as she continued, "Surely, the stories are creations of imagination. They sound like make-believe yarns to me. My new friends and the people at church say those stories are true and the Word of God. They say everything in the Bible is true. I don't know. Is it possible a whale swallowed Jonah? Nathan and even Patrick seem so secure in their beliefs. Patrick and I attended the same church as a kid, so when did he change? He told me he was a 'born again Christian' and saved by Jesus Christ. Magic, how can it be? I think I'm missing something, and the something is beyond my grasp. Where do I go? Whom do I talk to? I love you, but I don't think you can explain the mystery of faith. The Catholic Church hasn't given me the answers and Wicca certainly hasn't. How can the Bible be true? The stories make no sense to me. They are too outlandish. A whale swallowed Jonah and he survived. Sure. What do I believe? How will I know what is true?"

She found herself reciting her mantra, "Sa Ta Na Ma," for the circle of life from birth to death. She chanted it repeatedly.

"Magic, I know I'm boring you. You could go catch a mouse."

The cat yawned a wide open-mouth yawn but stayed by her side out in the garden.

"Okay, even though some of the basic tenants of both religions are similar, Christianity has the presence of Jesus. I do the sign of the cross at St. Elizabeth's, but do I believe in the ephemeral Holy Spirit? I'm going to meditate on this and try to sort out my feelings and beliefs."

She took a coffee break. She walked back into the house, made coffee in her French Press, and picked her Bible up from the kitchen table. Permelia turned to the Book of John. She realized Sunday's study could help her analyze the matter. She reread John 6:35, the section she studied on Sunday. She read from The Green Bible, an edition emphasizing nature with parts in green designating terms of nature. She saw little difference in the wording from the NIV version she used in Church.

She read to her attentive cat, "Jesus said to them, 'I'm the bread of life. Whoever comes to me will never be hungry, and whoever believes in me will never be thirsty.' *What does this mean? How can this be possible?*

She continued reading aloud, "Very truly, I tell you, and whoever believes has eternal life."

What does it mean "eternal life"? I think I need to talk to Emily or Pastor Todd.

In the meantime, she decided not to celebrate the Solstice of Mid-Summer. She told Magic, "Well, I should probably pack all my Wiccan paraphernalia away while I study this mystery of faith, as they call it. The athame, tarot cards, books, my Book of Shadows, ritual manuals, and pentagrams, will all go in a box up in the closet."

I need to do something about "NOW"

53

Everyone throughout the small town heard the stringent sounds of the fire, police, and EMT vehicles. The members, both male and female, of the volunteer fire department, half-dressed, hurriedly left their homes. Fortunately, at this hour the streets were relatively traffic-free. The firefighters' reputation was driving haphazardly.

One fireperson, a woman expressed her excitement. "My goodness, a real fire. What's more boring than washing fire engines every week?"

A little boy yelled to his mother, "See the blue lights! I'd like to ride the fire engine fast, fast, fast! I want the sirens loud, loud, loud, Mom!"

His mother tried to silence the boy. "Jimmy. This is serious. Someone might get hurt."

Lights from many of the houses interrupted the darkness of the hour. Phones were ringing to stir family, friends, and neighbors. No one in town was immune to a noisy awakening. Few knew the details of the cause of the ruckus, but everyone speculated. You could hear from the crowd, What's happening? Anybody know? There's the ambulance. Was anyone hurt? Is there a fire? Where?

It didn't take long for answers to some questions. The destination for the emergency personnel was the office of *The Grovetown Tribune*. The building's alarm system initiated the excitement of the night. The alarm, programmed to ring not only in the police station, also rang at Raymond's residence. The Chief arrived first at the burning building. He quickly assessed the situation.

Raymond appeared on the scene and approached the Fire Chief, "Oh my! How bad is it?"

He answered the worried editor, "Well, Raymond, it looks like the fire is located in the upstairs rear of the premises. Hopefully, as soon as the team organizes a plan of action, the blaze can be contained."

Raymond wasn't willing to wait for the trained personnel to take charge. He didn't join the growing crowd. Instead, he unlocked the front door and entered the reception area of his newspaper building. He grabbed the fire extinguisher, and flashlight mounted on the wall inside the door. He kept the flashlight there in case of electrical failure. Ice and thunderstorms often interrupted the town's electrical service.

Cautiously heading towards the back of the building, his progress was slow due to the amount of heavy black smoke. Reaching into his pocket for his ever-present hanky, he instantly realized he was clad in his plaid pajama bottoms. He didn't have his handkerchief. The heat grew more intense as he proceeded down the hallway past the open office doors. Hoping to help contain the fire, he closed the doors before continuing up the stairs to the second floor.

The thickening smoke affecting his ability to see, his flashlight revealed the source of the billowing smoke. The smoke was coming from the closed storage room door at the top of the stairs. Unfortunately, Raymond realized too late that he was wheezing. He collapsed on the floor from the smoke.

Nathan arrived at the fire to see Raymond talking to the fire chief.

"What's happening?" Nathan yelled to the chief.

"We're about ready to enter the building to find out. We think the fire is in the back part of the building. We won't know for sure 'til we get in there."

"Where's Dad? I don't see him anywhere!"

"He was right here. Don't see him now," responded the chief.

Nathan scanned the area and said, "I bet I know where he is. Looks like his keys are in the open door lock. He's probably inside. Get someone in there fast. Alert the EMTs. I'm calling Doc Mattox."

Nathan knew his father was a man of action. He wouldn't stand around if he thought he could do something.

Nathan let the professionals rush inside to find his father. They returned shortly with a semi-conscious Raymond. The editor attempted to explain the location of the hottest fire, but his coughing prohibited a coherent response. By the time Patrick arrived, the EMTs were successfully treating Raymond in the ambulance for his smoke inhalation. Nathan stayed at his father's side.

Outside the ambulance, Pastor Todd, Chaplain for the fire department, ministered to Henrietta and Emily. Pastor Todd called the women as soon as he heard where the fire was located.

At the site of the parked medical vehicle, Patrick gave the patient a quick examination. He found Raymond conscious and shook up, but unharmed. He allowed Raymond to return to the fire scene. Henrietta and Emily were relieved when Raymond and Nathan exited the emergency vehicle.

"Are you sure you're okay, Dad?" questioned his worried daughter.

"I feel fine now. Looks like the entire town has come for the show. Where's the Fire Chief? I want to see how things are going."

Nathan pointed his finger in the right direction. The Chief was in conversation with Jake. Raymond quickly joined them.

Restored to his normal state of mind he said, "Did you find where the fire did the most damage?"

The Chief answered, "Yes, the fire was confined to the storage room upstairs, but there's smoke everywhere. We're letting things cool down before we look for the cause. We won't know for sure 'til later this morning. We suspect arson. We found a broken window to the storage room. I hope we'll be able to find some clues inside. What do you store there?"

"The only things in there are issues of the paper and miscellaneous office supplies so we left the door open and the window cracked a tad because it's musty in there. The door is hard to open. Nathan and I were working in there yesterday. We're planning to run a series on the current sewage problems and a possible link to the installation of a few years ago. We have been going through old issues of the paper to research events at the time of the original installation about ten years ago. We worked late, 'til about ten."

The Chief said, "Too bad the door was open. If closed it would have helped prevent fire damage to the downstairs offices. There's plenty of smoke damage clean up to tackle, but the rest of the building and equipment seem to be intact. I'm afraid most of the content was totally destroyed."

Nathan walked up in time to hear the Chief's comment. "How awful! We spent so much time on our research. We left the papers and our notes on the small worktable in there. Oh, why didn't we take the papers out of the room with us? What'll we do now, Dad?"

"Guess we'll start again," Raymond lamented. "Fortunately the library keeps bound copies of the old newspaper issues. We at least know which years to search now. Emily will surely have some time to help us."

Nathan said, "Hopefully we'll soon have answers to the question of arson."

After the fire was totally extinguished, the crowd dispersed, returning home for a short night's sleep. Emily, Henrietta, Patrick, and Pastor Todd said good night to Raymond and Nathan.

"I want to make sure you're okay, Dad. Nathan, take him home so you can both get some rest. I'm sure you'll be back early in the morning to inspect the damage," Emily said. She hugged her dad and left with the others in her group.

Father and son thanked the volunteers and EMTs for their hard work. They were both exhausted. They got in their cars and headed home.

Jake was the last observer to leave. He heard the conversation about the newspapers. Unbeknownst to everyone but Jake, another alarm was going off in Jake's head. The twins' mission wasn't finished. Who knew there were duplicate papers at the library?

54

Henrietta and Emily worked the evening shift. The library assistant was off at dinner time. Before she left she asked, "Are you planning to work after eight like you did a few days ago? I don't know how you stay so busy. I thought Emily had the computerization right on schedule. Do you need me to stay?"

Henrietta answered, "I believe we have it under control. Thanks for asking. Emily is doing a super job. I had no idea my niece was so disciplined and effective. I remember her as a little girl, trying every excuse possible to escape from practicing her piano lessons. I imagine she can't even play a song."

Emily interrupted, "Why, Aunt, I can too play the piano. I'm able to pick out a simple melody as long as I play without chords. Those are the lessons I tried to avoid. Of course, I can play 'Chop Sticks'. I can even play hymns, the ones I like the best, like 'In the Garden', my favorite, 'The Old Rugged Cross', and certainly 'Amazing Grace'. I always cry when singing 'Amazing Grace'. Doesn't everyone?"

"Oh yes, my dear. I'm happy you learned those songs. I never mastered the piano. My father stuck me with the flute."

The library closed at eight p.m. The computer users, many young students who didn't have their own computer at home, college students, and visitors checking their e-mails, were winding up their work, and hurriedly copying any applicable papers, before the library doors closed.

Henrietta said, "Let's lock both doors. We'll keep the lights lit on this floor. Turn off all the other lights. Also, please lock the basement door. We wouldn't have to have all this security, but when school is out the teenagers hang out in the front of the library, Most of the time they are well behaved. However, some vandals came in the library and trashed it. The perpetrators used a fire extinguisher and sprayed all the stacks of the books. The cost to the library was over a thousand dollars to restore the area. Thank goodness, we had insurance. My Beta fish, Shakespeare, lived although they knocked over his fishbowl/vase. There was enough water to keep him alive through the night. Rectifying the damage took days and days. Now, we lock the doors no matter what. The library is the guardian of all these precious books and I'm the servant."

"Oh my, no wonder you take precautions."

Henri reacted, "Emily, we mustn't dwell on the past. We have the mystery of Gussy to deal with. Let's get going on the computer to see if we can find Gussy's mysterious heir. We have most of the birth announcement records for several newspapers on computer."

Emily's cell phone rang. "Hello, Mother."

Her mother said, "I'm just checking on you and the estate status. What's going on?"

"Well, tonight Aunt Henrietta and I are working at the library."

"What are you doing?"

Emily replied, "We're still working on the search for Gussy's child."

"Do you really think there's a real-honest-to-goodness child?"

"Mom, no matter what, Henrietta has an obligation."

Madelyn asserted, "Let me speak with your aunt."

Henrietta said, "Madelyn, it's nice of you to call. Are you well?"

"I'm well. However, this estate hassle is bearing on my soul. When is this farce going to end? I don't believe a child exists."

Henrietta replied to her sister, "I know it must seem to you that we're doing nothing to bring the estate to a close. We're doing what we have to. We're investigating into the missing child. We have a duty."

"Well, can't we speed it up? How long do you have to look before everyone will know there is no child?"

"I'm not sure. Soon I'll let the Attorney know where we are. Madelyn, we're doing our very best. In fact, we're researching late tonight at the library."

"Okay. I'll call again."

Henrietta said, "Good night, Madelyn."

Emily said, "Did my mother calm down? I hope so. I don't think getting so upset is good for her."

"Your mother is so anxious to see the estate closed. She called again this morning after breakfast. You were in the shower. She complained about how long this business was taking and wanted to know why we couldn't close the estate now. I told her we were doing the best we can."

Emily responded, "I know, I spoke to her a couple of days ago and assured her we were working diligently on the matter. She seemed quite upset. I too tried to calm her. But you know my mother."

Her aunt replied, "Yes, I do. Let's get to work. Why don't we do the newspaper vital records first? We need to make some headway. I think I'll start on the Peony County newspaper announcement notices in the short time period involved. And we need to set up the interviews soon."

Henrietta said, "I think I can tackle the Bloomington records."

It was about ten pm. The women felt more and more discouraged as the minutes speeded along. The pair quietly concentrated on the task ahead; each worked as fast as they could. They found nothing relevant to the child.

Emily said, "I feel very depressed."

Henrietta said, "I agree. This is going nowhere."

Suddenly, Emily, felt uneasy. She said, "I think I heard a sound of breaking glass somewhere outside."

Henrietta expounded, "It's probably a teenager out on the sidewalk hanging out. They hang out a lot when the weather is nice. They might have broken a bottle. I'm sure we're okay. The kids outside probably broke something."

Emily said, "OK. Maybe I'm imagining sounds."

"You know if we were superstitious, we might think it's the ghost of Carnegie. He might be lurking around until we can persuade the town to restore his library. Wasn't it great Carnegie had such a philanthropic spirit? These Carnegie libraries are throughout the U.S. in small towns like ours. Let's finish our work here and go home to enjoy a cup of chamomile tea and some coconut macaroons. I made them last night while you were engrossed in your researching."

Emily said, "I think mild tea and cookies would be relaxing. Our searches haven't accomplished much. Let's pack up now and walk home. I'd like to live in this small town. I like that one is able to walk most places. I feel safe. Of course, Gussy's murder is a bit disturbing. I know his death was caused by outsiders."

Emily then whispered, "I'm a bit scared. Tonight is spooky. I think I hear men talking down stairs. I don't know who they are. We'd better call 911."

Suddenly they heard another loud sound. The frightened girls turned off the lights and hid in the small office behind the antique oak circulation desk. No longer did they feel safe.

Henrietta quickly dialed the emergency number. She whispered, "This is Henrietta, the librarian. I think there are at least two men in the children's section downstairs. Emily and I are hiding behind the circulation desk. I don't think they know we're here."

The dispatcher said, "Stay where you are. I'm sending the police now."

Henrietta said a hasty prayer.

The burglars in the basement heard the sirens.

One said to the other, "The police are coming. Let's scram!"

The two men dropped the tools they were going to use to start the fire. They ran up the short staircase out the back door and into the street. They hid behind the American Legion across the street.

When Emily heard the police coming up the front library stairs she ran and opened the door for Deputy Green. He hurried down the basement stairs. He discovered an overturned leaking gas can. Books were askew on the floor. Bookcases were on their side. A high broken window was noted. He searched all over in and out to see if the burglars left.

He yelled to the girls, "They're gone. You're ok. Looks like a botched break-in."

He went outback where he saw one of the small high windows broken. He thought to himself. *The intruders must have been skinny to get through that window. Were they going to start a fire with the gasoline? Any connection to last night's fire?*

He called the Chief. Jake was at the Legion drinking when he noted the police cars. He ran over to the library to see what was happening.

The Chief took over. He saw Jake. "Jake, glad you're here. You can help. I'm going outside to see if there are any footprints in the mud. Hold this flashlight while I measure any prints. Ron, you call Raymond. Get the crime scene tape from the car. Then go to the station and bring the fingerprint kit, some gloves, evidence bags, and the plaster of Paris kit I keep to make molds of shoes and things."

He said, "It looks like there are two sets of prints, one larger than the other. I think the threads look like a tennis shoe and the other looks like a cowboy boot to me. We'll make plastic casts."

Jake agreed. *I'm so glad I was at the Legion. I don't what any questions. Gotta stay on top of this. I need to have Donnie get rid of his boots. Several people in town wear cowboy boots, but better be cautious on this one.*

55

She only ate two of the miniature hamburgers, and then with her ever-handy toothbrush, she tried to eradicate White Castles' famous smell. She realized going to the dentist wasn't such a good idea after White Castles. She cleaned her teeth and tongue. She felt sure no one could smell the tasty little items. She still had an hour to kill so she stopped by Macy's to walk through and see some new dresses. Last night was nagging at her. *Why was the library broken in? Who? Who killed my uncle? Why was there a fire at the newspaper office, and now the library had a break in? What's going on? Is it all connected?*

Emily told the receptionist, "I'm Emily Starks to see Dr. Jacobs."

"He'll be with you in a few minutes. Please have a seat. You might want to look at Martha Stewart's magazine, *Living."*

She barely started reading, when the receptionist ushered her into the Dr.'s office.

Dr. Jacobs asked about her health.

Emily said, "I'm fine now, but last night my aunt and I were working late at the library. Someone broke in the downstairs while we were upstairs. I'm still a little upset. The night was scary."

"I imagine so. Did they catch the intruder or intruders?"

"No. The police said there were two."

"I hope no one was hurt."

"No, we're fine. Oh, Dr. Jacobs, I hope my breath doesn't smell too bad. I ate at White Castles. It's been some time since I've had any. I felt compelled. I'm sorry. I know I'm silly. I should have waited 'til another day."

"Please don't apologize. I know the craving for White Castles. When I was little, my family would take us kids to the zoo, near Fountain Square on the south side. We always stopped for White Castles afterward. The zoo was the old one. There weren't many animals and all were caged.

Now we have the super zoo complex with dolphins and a butterfly enclosure. The big cats can roam. There are no cages. Indianapolis has become an enlightened community, no longer *Indy No Place.*"

"I'm sorry. Now open your mouth. Let's do your tooth. You won't need Novocaine. I'll pop the temporary cap out, clean the area, and then I glue on the new cap. You shouldn't have any pain."

"Great, don't relish being numbed."

All went quiet as he popped out the temporary cap. She hardly felt a thing. The assistant came in and cleaned out the hole. Dr. Jacobs came in to finish the crown.

Drew peeked in the treatment room. He smiled at Emily. "I'll pick you up at your apartment at six. Okay?"

Emily replied, "I'll be ready. See ya."

*****

Emily went to her apartment. It seemed empty with Mr. Whiskers down in Grovetown. She planned to stay the night in Indianapolis, go out with Drew, and spend some time Saturday shopping at Keystone at the Crossing before driving back to Grovetown. Drew wanted to see her Saturday night too. Even though she tried to always, tell the truth. She told him she had previously arranged plans. She told the truth, but she didn't reveal she was going to dinner and a movie with Pastor Todd, Permelia, Nathan, Patrick, and Jayne.

Dear *God, I'm trying to be honest. Am I sinning by not telling Drew about Todd and vice versa? I like them both, but I'm not in love with either. Drew is serious, but he respects me. If I should fall in love, I promise to tell the other. Please, dear Jesus, help me to make clear and cogent decisions in this matter.*

Her cell phone rang. Caller ID recognized her mother's phone number.

"Hello, Mom. How are you?"

Madelyn said, "Em, I haven't spoken to you when we could talk. I was too upset about the estate last night. Where are you?"

"I'm in Indy. I went to the dentist today. The filling didn't work out on the broken tooth. I had to get a crown."

"Did you see Dr. Drew Jacobs?"

"I did. Today Dr. Jacobs, Drew's father, finished work on the crown. I have a new tooth, or so it seems. Oh, Mother, after we talked last night, we had a break-in at the library. Henrietta and I were scared. The police said there were two intruders, probably men. But they got away."

"Oh my! Are you both okay?"

"Yes, we're both fine now. We were quite frightened. The incident was awful."

Madelyn said, "I'm glad. You said you saw Drew. Tell me about it. Is he as handsome as his mother says?"

"He is." *I'll have to tell her that we've been dating. However, not now. I want to see where my dating leads.*

"Good! I hope you made a good impression. I'm sure you did. You are such an attractive young woman. Did you talk?"

"A little bit." *Should I tell her the truth? No. We're not serious. She'll be on me all the time if I do. No, not unless we become an item.*

"I'm going to call Sally and see if she'll talk to her son. Maybe Drew will call you soon."

*****

Drew picked Emily up at her apartment exactly at six. He said, "I have a surprise for this evening. I have two lawn chairs, a blanket, ice tea, two glasses, and tickets to Marsh Symphony on the Prairie at Conner Prairie."

Emily replied, "Oh, I've always wanted to go. A couple of teachers at school have attended. They say it's so much fun. I hear there are fireworks at the end."

"I'm pleased you're excited. I want Kentucky Fried Chicken. We'll run in and purchase two meals to take to the Prairie. What do you think?"

Emily said, "Sounds super! Am I dressed appropriately?"

"Your sundress is ok. You would probably do better with sandals instead of heels. And you might want a sweater."

"Please sit while I change shoes and grab a cotton shawl."

In the car, Drew said. I know you can't see me tomorrow. I heard my Dad talking about the zoo. Would you like to go to the zoo? I can pick you up in Grovetown Sunday morning and take you home Sunday night."

Emily said, "That would be great, but I want to go to church first. I can be ready around noon. Would that give us time to see much?"

"It's normally open 'til five but sometime until seven. We would have at least a couple of hours. I would very much like to see you.

Didn't you tell me you're going to Muskatatuk State Park on the Fourth of July weekend?"

"Yes I'll be gone that long weekend. Nathan's going to run."

"Emily please reserve Friday evening, July ninth for my birthday. I'll take off work early and pick you up about three."

"Sounds like fun."

"Oh, there's a KFC."

Emily thought, *Is this summer a whirlwind or a tornado? I have never been as busy since college.*

56

Henrietta made cinnamon toast and brewed French roast coffee. Emily, dressed in jeans and a T-shirt, said, "We need a plan of action to contact all those who responded to the ad."

Henrietta replied, "I think we should each contact half of the replies. I'll use my phone. Is it true they call my phone a 'land phone'? You use your cell phone."

Emily answered, "You're right on. Yeah that's a land phone for sure. I've been saving minutes on my phone all month, so I should have enough. I wonder what advances will be made in cell phones. When more and more cell phones are in use, will you be able to find someone in a phone book?"

Henrietta said, "I'm not the one to ask. I don't even know how to answer a cell phone. Let's start after we finish breakfast. I'll find the letters, paper, and pen. I'll use my favorite pen, my Mont Blanc."

"I'll use mine too. Do you use a slim nib, a medium, or a broad nib? I use the broad. The writing looks like it flows. I like using turquoise ink. The color makes me happy."

Henrietta answered, "I like the slim point. Everything looks neat and succinct. I need some black ink. Do you have to order ink from Amazon? Or is there a local shop in Indy carrying pen supplies?"

"There's a shop in town, but I order on the net anyway."

She finished her second cup of coffee, Emily's aunt found all the needed materials in the antique walnut secretary.

Henrietta said, "I think working together at the kitchen table will be the easiest."

Emily agreed, "I think what you propose is an organized method. Why, we can even share thoughts on the prospects. Let me get my materials. Why don't you turn the radio on the Moody station for background music? The sound might keep us calm and focused."

Henrietta said, "Okay, when you return, I'm going to say a prayer for God's guidance."

"Praying seems like an excellent idea. I think we'll need God's guidance. I'll be back in a few."

After a short prayer, Emily, and her aunt made lists dividing the responses between them. Each wrote the name, address, and phone number on separate sheets of paper. They wanted space to make notes on each person after their interview.

The first call Emily made went to an answering machine. She left her name, a short message, and her phone number. The next—no answer, no answering machine.

She said to Henrietta after she was off the phone, "What a way to start—an answering machine. Are you having any better luck than me?"

"Well, I've only called one person, Maria Fernando. She told me she was a migrant worker. She said she worked in the tomato fields near Grovetown at the time she conceived a child. She says she was with a couple of men and was pregnant when the crew moved on to other work. Nine months later, she gave birth to a baby girl, named Blanche. She says, in broken English, she has no money for even a blood test let alone a DNA test."

"Oh! I hadn't thought about the DNA costs being a problem. I said, I'd let her know if the estate would pay. Aunt Henri, shouldn't the estate pay?" Emily asked.

Henrietta replied, "I'll ask the attorney, but I think it would be part of the search expenses. We can't skip any possibility leading to the heir."

Emily and Henrietta both received some mail from respondents in hopes they wouldn't require a DNA test. They said they were the heirs. They wouldn't offer proof, not even a blood test. There also were several unlikely prospects—too old, too young.

She returned to her task. She dialed a number and said, "Is Esther Beatty available?"

A man responded, "Just a second. I'll get her."

When Esther answered, she said, "Hello, who is calling?"

Emily said. "This is Emily Starks. I'm following up on your letter where you say your daughter is heir in the Estate of Gustafeson Trinkle."

Esther replied to her statement, "Yes, I answered your ad. I think my daughter may be the child you are seeking. You see, I had her in late

May 1971, about nine months, after being in Grovetown for a farm tour. I had a brief affair with a young farmer, but I don't remember learning his name. We went to his farmhouse."

Emily asked, "Are you willing to take and pay for a DNA test? Where do you live?"

The woman replied, "Of course. You'll need my daughter's permission and blood sample too. I teach agriculture at Purdue. I'd rather not travel to Grovetown. However, I have a doctor in West Lafayette who could draw the blood, and send the sample to whatever lab you wish."

Emily said, "I'll call you back when I've set up with a lab at I.U. Medical Center in Indianapolis."

The next few calls were again either no answer or disconnected numbers. Henrietta had a couple of answering machines. She left a message on each machine.

Emily asked, "Henri, are you having any luck? Have found anyone named Suze?"

"No Suze. I left some messages. I talked to two people who wouldn't take a DNA test or wouldn't pay for one. This task is more difficult than I thought. Let's take a break and eat lunch. I thought we would have a spring salad and a bacon, lettuce, and tomato sandwich. We can have lemonade. I bought some fresh tomatoes at the Farmer's Market. I picked up some fresh asparagus too. I thought a cheese sauce would go well for supper."

Emily thought, *I hope we get to eat in peace with no phone calls. My ear hurts.*

A phone rang. A call on Henri's land phone interrupted their delightful lunch. She answered and discovered the caller was her sister, Madelyn.

Henrietta whispered, "It's your mother."

Madelyn came right to the point, as she frequently did. She avoided the amenities, "Why is this estate taking so long? I need to make my investments while the market is low. Can't you speed it up?"

Her sister explained, "We're still trying to find the unknown child."

"Do we really have to look for this mythical child? Why, it's already been a long time? Why aren't you finished with the research?"

Henrietta, trying to be calm said, "Madelyn, We must keep looking and the estate can't be closed for at least another three months. We've published the required notice to unknown heirs in several newspapers. We're receiving responses. We've started the interviews. Finding the heir may take time. I feel a duty to Gussy find his child. Emily and I have been talking to several people. Some seem a possibility, but others are quite improbable. We're setting up appointments for DNA testing. However DNA results may take at least a week or so."

Madelyn disturbed asked, "When will this search stop? I need to know so I can invest the money. I told you my financial advisor says now is the time to buy. I needed it yesterday. I don't think a child exists. How much longer will you search?"

Henri more upset with the noticeable greed of her sister, said, "Madelyn, I'll call the attorney and get back with you."

Madelyn curtly replied, "Well, okay!" She hung up abruptly.

Henrietta shook her head. "I can't believe my sister is so impatient," she exclaimed to Emily.

"I know, but we should forgive her and pray for her. I pray for her often."

They quickly finished their interrupted lunch. Soon both resumed their tedious task. A young man claimed his mother, now deceased, told him she met his father at the Persimmon Festival in a small town in southern Indiana. He agreed to take and pay for the required test."

Emily talked to a young woman who claimed her mother told her about this farmer in southern Indiana. She said she'd have to get back with Emily if she decided to take the DNA test.

Emily told her, "Well, I need an answer within in 10 days."

One young woman only knew she shared the same birth month. However, she had no money for the test.

The pair were tired after a few more calls. Emily wanted to go to exercise her stiff back from the entire intense session. Nevertheless, she decided to make another call or so.

She talked to a former waitress and bartender from Peony, who admitted she was somewhat promiscuous when she got pregnant. Her child was born about the time indicated. She would pay and take the test.

Henrietta called her last person.

A young woman answered on the first ring. When she found out who called, she said, "I thought you'd never call. My mother was a runaway teenager. She repeatedly talked about a young man she spent the night with in Grovetown. She never told me who he was, but I was born the month indicated in the notice."

"Would you be willing to pay and take a DNA test?"

The girl responded, "Sure, I'll be quite willing to take the test, but I'll need to know how much it will cost. I hope I can afford it. I really, really want to know who my father is."

Henri assured her she would work with her and set her a time to call tomorrow.

Emily answered her phone, "Hello, Emily Starks here. What can I do for you?"

"My name is Eugene Simmons. I hope I can help you and me too. I got your message about the notice. I'm sure I'm the unknown child and heir you've been looking for. I was born in June 1971. My mother was quite the 1960s hippie, totally against the war in Vietnam. She married a fellow student at I.U. soon after I was born. I thought he was my father. I called him, Dad. When he died, my mother told me he wasn't my real father. She told me she traveled with some other kids in a VW bus. They camped at a park near Peony, Indiana. They all smoked marijuana. She was quite stoned. She says she had a one-night stand with some local who called himself 'Gus'. She's dead now."

Emily responded, "Your story is very interesting." She asked a few more questions. Her last question was a request for him to have a DNA test.

Eugene said immediately, "I can pay for and will take a test anytime you want."

I feel hopeful about this man.

Emily finished the phone call. She related the conversation to her aunt.

Both women thought Eugene was a strong possibility.

"Let's quit for the day. I'm out of ink. I'll call the attorney. I'll catch her up to date with details and find out how to answer Madelyn."

Emily replied, "Then I'm off."

57

The Muscatatuk Run was on the Fourth of July weekend at Muscatatuk State Park. Nathan, his sister Emily, Pastor Todd, Patrick, Patrick's sister, Permelia, and Patrick's girlfriend, Jayne, headed to the park Friday night. They stopped for lunch on the way at a quaint diner. The tables sported gingham tablecloths. Ruffled white cotton café curtains were on the windows. Rustic paintings adorned the walls. The cafe served lunch country style. The special today, a Friday, was all-you-can-eat fried catfish. All decided on the fried favorite. German Catholics settled this area of southern Indiana in the19th century. Fish was the standard meal on Fridays. The waitress served salad, fresh corn-on-the-cob, green beans, cottage cheese, slaw, and biscuits on the circular table in large bowls and platters. Real butter along with apple butter for the biscuits accompanied them. The entire party ordered sweet tea with a slice of lemon. She brought a large pitcher of tea to the table.

Pastor Todd said, "Let's give thanks for this bountiful meal." They all ended in a joint, "Amen."

The waitress offered fresh cherry cobbler.

Jayne said, "I don't think I can eat another morsel."

Patrick said, "Jayne, we need the extra nourishment. I also know how much you relish cherries. Emily, you too. But don't break another tooth."

Jayne said, "I love cherries. Why, yes, I do prefer a cherry pie to cake for my birthday. I thought you like me slim. But, okay."

She told the waitress, "I guess. However, Emily, you, and Permelia must too. I'm not going to gain a pound if you don't also."

They acquiesced. Patrick, Nathan, and Pastor Todd needed no extra encouragement.

During lunch and the drive, the conversation touched many subjects, including Gussy's murder. The investigation was stagnant causing

Emily and Nathan concern. They left stuffed from their lunch. They found a nearby general store on the curvy country road on the way to the park where they bought necessary supplies for two nights under the stars. The basic provisions included a healthy supply of energy bars for the two runners, Patrick, and Nathan.

They all traveled in Mr. Stark's large newspaper van, carrying tents, sleeping bags, and provisions, a tight fit. Reserved at the park were two campsites. The guide steered them in the direction of the campsite. As requested, the park officials, provided a grill, fire pit, and chopped wood. The showers and bathroom facilities were nearby. The girls would sleep in one tent and the men in the other.

The weatherman indicated the weather would continue to be nice through Monday the Fourth.

The subject of conversation took a serious note. Nathan said to Emily, "Boy, I hope and pray Gussy's death won't become a 'cold case'."

Emily said, "Nathan, you and I, with father, are going to have to step up our efforts to solve the murder. Hopefully, finding the screwdriver is a good omen."

Another one of the subjects of interest was a conversation on the differences in religious practices and beliefs.

Emily said to Pastor Todd, "I have a fellow teacher friend joined a different church instead of the Catholic Church, where she'd attended since birth. She became an Unitarian. She goes to a church near Butler University in Indianapolis. The minister said that everyone needed to realize each flower was different from another, yet all together, the flowers made a beautiful bouquet. Each attendee was to bring a flower for the next service. I've never heard anything like this."

"Yes, the Unitarian Church is quite a bit different from Christian churches. As you know, there are many differences amongst the various denominations."

Emily understood, "I know that, but even Catholics honor the Trinity. The Catholic's basic beliefs are Bible-based, but what about Unitarians? My friend said they have a pagan group within their congregation. How is that?"

Permelia was listening to the conversation. *She thought I best not mention my Wicca practices.* She felt uncomfortable at this turn in the discussion. She looked down at her lap.

Patrick looked on at Pastor Todd, listening to his explanations.

Pastor Todd continued. "I think it's important for you to know that the Unitarians accept all beliefs, even ours. However, there is no continuity of one belief for all amongst their congregation."

Emily became quiet while she pondered his statements.

Nathan asked, "Well, what do they believe?"

"It's quite complicated. There are probably as many varieties under the umbrella of the Unitarian Church as there are under Christian denominations," explained Pastor Todd.

Emily then asked, "Can you tell us some of their tenets?"

"I can't give you all their beliefs. To fully explain them would require hours. I would probably have to refer to my books of theological writings. However, I can try to give you a quick overview."

Nathan exclaimed, "This is interesting. Please go on."

Emily concurred. Permelia didn't join in the conversation.

"I'll try to touch on some central ideas, but remember there are differences, so don't take any of it as written in stone."

They all giggled at his little quip.

"Well, I'm not sure where to start, but here goes. They contend their church started during the Reformation. One of their concepts is the rejection of the traditional view of Jesus. To them, He is a deity and to be worshipped. I won't go into the reasons, it would be too lengthy."

"How could that be?" asked Emily." I thought all Christians believed Jesus is one and the same with God and the Holy Spirit."

Pastor Todd continued, "I'm afraid not. Unitarians practice a form of pantheism. You know about the recent New Age trend among some younger non-believers. They say God exists in all things, like nature, animals, humans, and even plants. So do members of the Unitarian Church. Nevertheless, remember some also accept varied Christian teachings. They combine all beliefs of the major religions."

Nathan proclaimed, "How odd!"

Jayne chimed in, "And confusing!"

"They also say that the Devil, Heaven, and Hell don't exist. Most consider those terms all in your mind. They see the Bible as allegorical. They believe Jesus existed, but is not a god. His story is the pattern for perfect living. Some even believe in reincarnation because of some Biblical statements, i.e. John the Baptist was the reincarnation of Elijah.

Thank goodness Unitarians have no missionaries."

Emily spoke first, "Is there more?"

Pastor Todd replied, "There's quite a bit more, but I'll only mention a few. At college, we spent almost three weeks learning some of the information. Some call it a liberal sect. I would call it a cult. They don't accept the Trinity or many of the truths of the Bible, as we know them. They say the Biblical authors, although inspired by God, were subject to error. I think that is enough for now. I could lend you some books on the subject, if you wish."

Emily and Nathan said as if one, "Absolutely not! It's blasphemy!"

Permelia, still quiet, was thinking of her training in Wicca. *How similar.*

Stopping by a pizza place before entering the park, they bought several pizzas, pepperoni with mushrooms and onions, a deluxe with everything but anchovies, and a vegetarian pizza. The men built a fire even though it wasn't cold in the woods; however, it was damp. The warming fire took the wet chill off. They sat on old aluminum chairs. They devoured the pizza and cokes. They saved some for a snack later. The runners needed all the carbs they could eat so they would be ready early in the morning.

All told a camp story or two, except for Jayne. She never had been camping. To cook and sleep outside was a novel experience for her. The sun would set in about an hour. The couples needed to go to sleep early for the run in the morning.

But, Patrick said, "Let's explore these woods. I saw some trails."

All agreed. They were excited about what might be seen and heard. Patrick and Jayne led the way. The others followed in pairs, keeping together.

Permelia noted, "You know it's quiet out here. Of course, we can hear the birds and a rustle or two. I wonder if there are squirrels in these trees."

"I see mushrooms. Pastor Todd, are they edible?" asked Emily.

Pastor Todd replied, "I don't know, but I surely wouldn't want to try."

Patrick yelled, "See the red tail hawk. He's soaring. Did you know hawks soar while turkey vultures circle?"

Nathan queried, "Do you think he'll find any prey?"

"Oh!" Emily said, "I hope not. I know he has to eat and they are both God's creatures. Of course, God didn't give us them to worship. I still can't believe my friend, Eleanor, believes everyone should worship flowers, plants, and animals."

Pastor Todd agreed, he said, "I'm happy you realize there is but one God, and we must worship Him." He lightly touched her bare-skinned shoulder.

Emily felt a strange tingling sensation when he touched her.

Talking loud enough, Permelia, with laughter in her voice said, "Oh, how I wish we could take some of these lovely wildflowers back to the camp. I know it's illegal to pick plants in state parks. I can wish, though."

Nathan, excitedly, whispered, "Shh, I think I hear a woodpecker. Don't move."

Jayne, also whispered, "I see something red on the side of that big oak tree." She pointed towards the tree.

Patrick exclaimed, "Why, that's a rare pileated woodpecker. I haven't seen one in a long time. They're about a foot tall."

"My goodness!" they all exclaimed almost in unison.

Pastor Todd remarked, "What a beautiful and majestic creature God has given us to admire."

Nathan, taking Permelia's hand, whispered, "Let's get away from the rest and walk on the rocks over there by that little stream."

He walked with her, still holding her hand, towards the rocks. He thought, *Permelia didn't pull away. How nice. We've dated awhile. I hope I'm not too forward. I think its okay.*

Arriving by the rocks, he suggested they sit down by the bubbling flowing water.

Turning and looking her in the eyes, he exclaimed, "Permelia, you have no idea how I've wanted to talk to you alone. We're always with other people. I didn't want to discuss some subjects in front of anyone but you. I remember when you were a little girl and tried to follow your brother and me. We thought you were such a bother, but now you've become a beautiful woman and no bother at all."

She blushed, averting her eyes.

He said, "We need to talk about some things before we get too involved."

Nathan came right to the point, "Permelia, I want us to date more often. I want to spend more time with you. Tonight is a perfect start. Would you like to see more of me? I pray you might think the same. I think Robbie would enjoy having a male around. I don't want to interfere in your life nor am I trying to replace Robbie's father. I do want to spend time with both of you. Do you want to be involved with me?"

Before she could answer, Nathan slowly put his arms around her and tentatively cupped her face and kissed her cheek. "May I kiss you?"

"Please."

Nathan kissed her lightly on the mouth. He was noticeably surprised when Permelia grasped his neck and pulled him closer. She kissed him back. She replied in a low voice, "Oh, Nathan, I find you so attractive. Yes. I'd like to see a lot more of you."

Permelia thought, *I haven't felt this way in a long time. I want him to kiss me more.*

She wanted his kisses to continue. Instead, Nathan took her hand and motioned to Permelia to sit on the largest flat rock across from him.

He bent low and kissed her again. He sat up straight. "Permelia, I have a girlfriend in South Bend. I needed time to understand God's intentions for my relationship with Judy. I know I want you in my life, not Judy. Please don't take offense about what I say. I want more than just to be friends."

Permelia said, "I'd like to get to know you better too. I don't consider it offensive that you'd like to spend time with my son. A male influence would be good."

She gave Nathan a big smile.

Nathan smiled back. "Permelia, I must make something clear I want to have a Christian woman in any serious relationship. I could never love someone who is not at least studying Christianity. Patrick told me of your dabbling in the occult. I've been watching you at church and Bible study. I think you're having doubts about your beliefs in Wicca. Am I wrong? You are ready to accept Christ as your Savior, aren't you? I could never have a real relationship with someone who worships a Pagan god. Are you considering becoming a Christian?"

"I believe I'm questioning my old beliefs. Yes, I'm ready to change, I think. I haven't practiced any of the craft for a while. The service and the prayers have given me the calmest of times. I've never found any religion that teaches about Jesus as your church does. I already want to study the Bible and learn more about Jesus Christ. Please pray with me. I'm not sure how to pray. Please help me."

Not knowing what he would say, she looked at him with questioning eyes, wondering if her studying Christianity would let her pass a first test with Nathan.

Nathan answered, "Yes, Permelia, I think you are open to finding Christ. I'll help you as you come to know Him through the Holy Spirit. I also want to become involved with you. I think I love you. No, I DO love you. He took her hand. Let us pray, 'Dear God, please help this lost soul discover you. Let her accept Jesus as her Lord and Savior. Amen.'" She joined him in saying Amen.

He drew her lips toward him again and gave her another passionate kiss. She responded back, quivering from the warm feeling.

Nathan then said, "We must get back. Everyone will wonder where we are." They walked hand in hand.

Later, that evening, after dark, the three men sat next to their dates with their arms around their shoulders, pretending they were keeping warm on a very cold night. Soon each of them knew they should go to their respective tents to sleep. Morning would soon be upon them. They slept until they smelled Emily's coffee. They would only have enough time to drink their coffee and eat their energy bars. Soon they were off to the starting line. Nathan and Patrick ran. The others cheered them on.

Tired after the run, Patrick's and Nathan's bodies demanded food. They went back to the campsite so the two runners could clean up. They'd seen a Burger King on the road to the park. Everyone craved a Whopper and some French fries.

Sitting in the restaurant, Jayne uttered a big sigh as she bit into the Deluxe Jr. Whopper. She said, "I know this isn't the most nutritional lunch, but it's a holiday weekend and we should splurge. We also need to celebrate the good showing of Patrick and Nathan in the run."

All agreed, as they devoured the junk food.

Pastor Todd suggested, "Tonight we men will grill those little steaks, along with some asparagus, onions, and charcoal-baked potatoes. We also need to buy some bacon, OJ, and a dozen eggs for breakfast tomorrow, too. You girls may cook breakfast."

Permelia exclaimed, "Sure! But we better buy some dried jerky, onion dip, and a pack of potato chips just in case of a catastrophe for tonight."

The girls laughed at Permelia's comment. The guys looked away.

Returning to camp, naps were in order. Emily and Jayne immediately fell asleep. However, Permelia thought about the prayer. Her mind was racing. She kept thinking about the sweet kisses and the passion of last night. She thought, *I hope Nathan doesn't think I was too forward. I want to be with him. I know I can give up Wicca, and even burn all those books, and my Book of Shadows. I feel that Jesus is with me, but I need to know Him better.*

She was finally calming down and thought she could rest dreaming of being in Nathan's arms.

The men did a fine job grilling the steaks and vegetables. They enjoyed s'mores like six-year-old children. The three couples sat in a circle around the fire. Soon, Patrick, Nathan, and Pastor Todd put their arms around their girls again. This was normal for Jayne and Patrick with their long relationship. Permelia welcomed Nathan's attention. She cuddled into Nathan's waiting arms. She thought, *We feel like a perfect fit.*

Pastor Todd wasn't too sure about Emily's reaction. However, he thought, *Emily, please don't slap my face.* She didn't and he felt pleased with his daring.

They were all silent, listening to the sounds of the hissing fire. Soon each pair were holding private conversations. There was a waning moon, soon to be a dark new moon in a day or so. Letting the fire go out made the woods sleep in silence, except for an eerie howling of a coyote. The couples were quite comfortable sitting in the dark. Emily somehow knew that Patrick and Jayne were in a passionate embrace and kissing. She could faintly see Nathan and Permelia cuddled together and looked like they too were kissing. Just then, Pastor Todd leaned over and kissed her tenderly first on the forehead, nose, cheeks, and finally fully on the mouth.

58

Judy, Nathan's girlfriend, was oblivious to what was happening at Muscatatuk State Park this Fourth of July weekend. She drove from South Bend, traveling on SR 31, through the center of Indianapolis. She headed to Grovetown. She was very excited she was going to see Nathan for the first time in two months.

She thought, *I hope he'll be surprised since I traveled all this way to see him. How nice to be with him again. Surely, he'll be happy to see me too. I hope he's more serious than on our last date. Why didn't he call more than four times? Not even every week. He was always busy when I called him. He sounded somewhat distant the last time we talked. I'm sure he's been working steadily, but still. I pray everything's fine between us. I wish I didn't feel a sense of doom.*

She planned this surprise visit since he left in May.

She stopped for lunch and coffee near Greenwood.She imagined her evening; *I hope Nathan will be excited to see me too. I won't call until I reach the Deer Fly Creek Inn. I want my visit to be a complete surprise. I can stay until the sixth. I know it's a short time but I hope the visit will be a quality one. I'll do my best to make it so. This drive is taking forever. I didn't realize Grovetown was so far.*

She continued down the road. She Googled the map to the inn and info about the area of Grovetown. She discovered several country roads off the Interstate. She said to herself, *I don't want to get lost. The description of the Inn says you can see the falls from the dining room window. It sounds romantic. Maybe we can take a walk along the river, called Deer Fly Creek. I wonder why they named it that funny name. Well, I'll ask at the inn. I wish I were closer to Grovetown. I'll invite Nathan in for a late coffee. Maybe? What will I do after I check in? I guess I'll shower and change out of these jeans and T-shirt. I know I shouldn't have spent so much on the silk sundress. Nevertheless, tonight will certainly be worth the cost. I love these high heel beige shoes and purse. They go so well with the lavender and beige dress. I want him to like the way I look and smell. I'll wear my favorite perfume, Yves Saint Laurent's Poison. As expensive as it is I save it for special events. And this is one! I think I'll also spray some on the bed. I can wish. I'm ready. Is he?*

She checked into the Inn and immediately noticed how country it looked. Before changing, she called Nathan on his cell phone. The call went straight to voice mail. *No, I'll not leave a message. I want to tell him I'm here personally.*

Judy didn't change into the cute sundress after her shower. She thought, *I'll put on my Capri jeans and a shocking pink tank top. I like how they fit. I think the look makes my body appear shapely and a little sexy. I'd better wear the pink sun hat. The pink sandals with princess heels complete my ensemble. I feel so pretty in pink.*

She asked the hotel clerk, "Why is the river called Deer Fly Creek. That's a unique name?"

The girl at the desk said, "Deer Fly Creek was named by the locals after the abundance of deer flies along the bank. These insects are annoying biting flies. They are bloodsuckers. We call them little monsters. If one of them bites you, it's a true bite, not a sting. Likely, it will become an itching open sore with a hole in the skin. And it will probably become infected."

Judy said, "Oh my! Are people allergic to them? Are they on the banks of the river too? I wanted to take a walk."

"Oh, I think you'll be okay if you walk before dark. If you go on the river, kayaking, or canoeing you are bound to see them. Yes, some people are quite allergic. Some bites swell up to five inches in diameter and turn bright red. The bite is painful. Some people get big bruises too."

She decided to take a short walk before calling Nathan again. The sun was shining, no rain and the temperature was 90 degrees. She muttered to herself, *Isn't this a romantic place?* She saw a few of the infamous flying insects, which she slapped away. "Ye gad!" she said aloud.

She returned to her nicely decorated room; she noted the cute chintz curtains, antique furniture, and primitive paintings on the wall. The pictures looked like oil paintings by local town artists. Judy tried to call

Nathan again close to four in the afternoon. Still voice mail. She was getting quite anxious. She hoped they could go to supper together. She finished unpacking. She turned on the television for the noise value.

After a while, Judy called again. This time, she decided to leave her name and asked Nathan to call her back on her cell phone. As time went by, she thought, *I might as well get dressed for supper. I'll wear a simple sundress and sandals.* The inn served supper from five to nine. *Surely, I can get in touch with him before eight. I hope I don't have to eat alone. Where is he?"*

Judy started to believe his cell might be out of battery power, or he'd left it somewhere. She thought, "I know he'll call back soon."

More time went by. She tried to get interested in the book she was reading, but she couldn't concentrate. She tried his cell phone again. By this time, she was nearly in tears and wondering if she should have come here without calling Nathan beforehand. Where could he be?

She said to herself, *I'll call one more time before I call Nathan's father. He told me his father's name was Raymond. I think the name of the newspaper is The Grovetown Tribune. I may have his father's number somewhere. Didn't Nathan give it to me before the funeral?*

She called. This time, when her call again went to voice mail, she left a message: "Nathan, please call me. I'm in Grovetown. I'm staying at the Deer Fly Creek Inn. I'm at the Inn now. I hope you'll be here soon. I love you."

She waited about ten more minutes. She looked for his father's number. She couldn't find it, so she looked up the number for Nathan's father, Raymond Starks. He answered on the third ring.

"Hello, this is Raymond Starks speaking. May I help you?"

Judy responded, "I'm Judy Darcy, Nathan's friend from South Bend. May I please speak to him?"

Replying, Raymond said, "Oh. I've heard so much about you. I'm sorry, but Nathan's not here this evening. Can you call him tomorrow?"

"Well, I need to talk to him tonight."

Raymond explained, "He's out of town. He participated in the Muskatatuck Run and is camping in the state park overnight. He plans to be home about ten tomorrow morning."

"Oh," said Judy, a sunken feeling in her gut. "Well, can I reach him on his cell?"

"Unfortunately, no, he left his cell here. His cell has been ringing all afternoon. He didn't want to have any distraction at the run while he relaxed in the woods. He's been working very hard on his doctorate thesis and worrying about finding his uncle's murderer. You knew someone killed his uncle don't you?"

"Yes, the murder. It's probably been me calling." She continued, "I'm sorry to have bothered you. If you speak to him tonight, please have him call my cell no matter how late. He has the number. Otherwise, please have him call me as soon as he comes home. Thank you, Mr. Starks."

She was despondent. She thought, *My coming to Grovetown unannounced might have been a very bad mistake. I wish I'd called during the week. I could be having a very romantic camping trip. Oh well, I'll go down to supper. I'm not even going to change into something dressier. I hate eating alone. Might as well take my book.*

Judy wasn't hungry. She was nearly in tears. She ordered some comforting red potato soup with cheddar cheese and a Caesar salad. She didn't drink very often, but tonight, she ordered a half-bottle of the house red wine. The half-bottle was two glasses. She ordered a large chocolate sundae with a cup of black coffee. Chocolate always made her feel better.

She finished the wine, her sundae, and coffee. *Was the Inn restaurant always this empty? Is everybody in town camping or cooking out this Fourth of July weekend? Is that man sitting by himself looking at me? He must know I'm alone. I wonder why he's by himself too. I think he's good looking. He looks a lot older than I do. Look at his jet-black hair. It's the kind of hair women want to put their fingers through.*

The wine affected her thinking. She felt tipsy. She thought, *I don't think I've ever felt so relaxed. The wine must be affecting my mind. I've had one glass with a meal before—not two. I wish Nathan were here. I probably would let myself melt in his arms. Oh, what could happen? Whatever he wants. But where is he?*

The attractive man, sitting at a table nearby, stopped at her table.

"Hi, my name is Peter McIntosh. I noticed you reading a huge book. Please tell me about it. You seem enthralled. However, you look sad. Is it a tear-jerker?"

Judy, more than a little tipsy, started telling him, "Not a tear jerker." She said, "My name is Judy. Would you like to join me? I was waiting for someone, but he doesn't seem to be coming. I've been stood up, I think. My eyes are red from allergies," she lied.

The man seated himself across from her at the table. He thought the red eyes were from crying.

"I saw you and thought, *My, she looks inviting.* I noticed you had wine with your dinner. I'd like to buy you an after-dinner drink. May I?"

She didn't hesitate. She thought his suggestion sounded okay and innocent enough.

"Yes, you may. What is an after-dinner drink? I don't think I've ever had one."

He said, "Brandy is the one I like. There are others too. You've seen movies, haven't you where dinner concludes with a brandy."

Judy nodded and replied, "I think so."

The man ordered two brandies. He offered a toast, "To a pleasant evening."

They chitchatted about the novel she was reading. Then he asked the general questions. "Where are you from?" "What do you do for a living?" "Why are you in Grovetown?" "Where did you go to college?"

The conversation stayed cordial from both sides.

Judy said, "My, this drink makes my throat feel warm and burns a little when I swallow. Is it a strong drink?"

"Somewhat. Sip it slowly. Brandy is a liqueur, best savored."

Judy smiled. She thought, *He seems like a gentleman. Talking to him is good for me. Keeps me from crying.*

Her new companion called the waitress over. Judy charged her meal to her room tab. Peter ordered two more brandies on his tab. He suggested, "Judy, shall we sit on the swing on the front porch. The evening is lovely. It's cooled down a bit."

He pulled out her chair from the table and escorted her to the porch, a brandy in each hand.

59

The couples broke camp early. Breakfast, cooked by the girls was most tasty. The coffee strong and awakening. They talked about their trip. Each twosome could only think about their newly found relationships. Patrick and Jayne played a little tootsie/wootsie under the table.

Once in town each went their separate way to shower and dress for church at eleven.

Nathan entered his father's house. Raymond explained about Judy's call and handed him the phone. Nathan didn't know what to think. He called the stored number for Judy. She answered on the first ring.

*****

A ringing phone woke Judy. She was naked in bed at nine-thirty in the morning. She usually wore a T-shirt and panties to bed. She thought, *Why are all my clothes in a pile by the couch? I always hang up my clothes before going to bed. What happened last night?*

She didn't remember anything except eating at the restaurant and the giant, yummy sundae. She looked in the bathroom mirror. Her eyes were red. *Did I cry all night? Why does my head hurt? I never have headaches. Nathan didn't come to the Inn. Why? I remember there was this nice looking man I talked to. Who was he? I think I drank too much. Why are some funny looking glasses on the table? Was someone in my room? Well, I'll worry about that later.*

She started to dress. Her cell phone rang. She answered and heard Nathan's voice. She masked her voice hoping Nathan wouldn't be able to know she had been crying.

She said, "Oh, Nathan, I'm so glad to finally hear your voice. Guess what? I'm in Grovetown. I arrived last night and tried to reach you, but your father told me you were out of town."

Nathan said, "Yes, I ran in the race at Muskatatuck State Park, and we decided to camp a second night. Why are you here?"

Wondering who "we" were, and "why", she said, "I wanted to surprise you, so I came down for the Fourth of July weekend. When might I see you? Can you come to the Inn for breakfast, or should I come to your house?"

"Oh my! I'm sorry I didn't know you were coming. You should have called. Church is at eleven. Would you like to go with us? You're welcome to. I've already eaten and can't talk long because we arrived home only a while ago. I need to shower and freshen up. You can't imagine how dirty one can get while camping."

Judy replied, "I forgot it's Sunday. Yes, I'll go to church with you then we can have a late lunch." *However, who is "we?"*

Nathan said, "I'll pick you up at eleven. Bye, Judy."

He picked her up for church.

It was weeks since they had seen each other. Judy reached forward for a kiss. Instead, he gave her a big hug.

He said, "We'll miss Sunday School—no time with us coming home so late." He introduced Judy to Emily, Permelia, Patrick, and Jayne. The church service was calming for Nathan. Judy didn't feel comfortable. She was Episcopalian. She always felt out of place in any other church. She was used to the rituals at St. Mark's, and Nathan felt uncomfortable at her church. He didn't feel God's presence.

After church, he introduced her to Pastor Todd. He said, "I'm so happy you could join us for worship today,"

Judy thought, *Nathan introduced me as his friend from South Bend not his girlfriend.*

*****

Judy and Nathan sat at the Inn's restaurant. He said a little prayer. She was used to his praying aloud in public, but it always made her feel a bit self-conscious. She thought people were staring at her. The conversation during the meal was mundane and of no consequence. They talked about their activities since they parted, and other generic subjects. He explained the murder investigation was going slowly. He said, "My thesis leaves me little time. I have no free time to speak of."

Then, Nathan changed the subject.

"I hate to tell you this, but I have to go to the newspaper office. There was a burglary at the gas station last night. Dad and I need to work this afternoon. Why don't we have a light supper here at six and see a movie." Nathan thought, *She drove all this way. I feel obligated to show her a good time. She was my girlfriend. What will she say when I tell her about my feelings for Permelia?*

Judy tried not to show her disappointment. "I'd like to spend all afternoon with you, but I understand."

He asked, "Do you have a book to read this afternoon while I'm away?"

"Yes, I do.

"Good. There are also some trails along Deer Fly Creek. Watch out for Deer Flies! Bye, I'll see you at six."

Judy noted to herself, *He didn't try to kiss me. I wonder what is wrong. Well, he's probably worried about the article for the paper.*

Nathan drove back to the office. *I wish she hadn't come, but I'll make the best of it. She'll enjoy the Fourth of July celebration tomorrow. I'll have a conversation afterward about the change in my feelings. Dear God, please help me to have the right words. I don't want to hurt her. She's a nice girl. I can't keep her thinking our relationship can continue. Dear God, please help me In Jesus' name. Amen.*

*****

Judy saw the man she met last night sitting by himself across the room. He turned to look at her with a big smile, left his table and came over to her table.

"Hi, did you sleep well? I so enjoyed our evening. Did you happen to find my glasses? Would you spend the afternoon with me? We could even take in a movie and supper. You still look so sad. Is everything OK? I saw a man eating lunch with you. Did he bother you?"

"No. He's a friend from South Bend. I came to see him for the Fourth. He's a journalist. He's required to work this afternoon at his father's newspaper. Yes, I would love to spend the afternoon with you. However, he's coming here for supper at six, so I can't do dinner and a movie."

The afternoon with Peter McIntosh went by so quickly. Judy found herself so comfortable with him. They talked and talked. She didn't even mind him putting his arm around her. When she needed to get ready to meet Nathan, he suddenly pulled her close and kissed her. She didn't pull away but kissed him back. Judy couldn't help but think of her handsome Nathan. However, he never aroused such passion in her.

*****

Nathan and Judy ate a pleasant dinner at the inn. The conversation was a lot about nothing.

They drove to Peony to see an old Meg Ryan movie, *Sleepless in Seattle*, a favorite of Judy's. She'd watched it at least four times. Judy never tired of seeing the romantic film. She owned the DVD. She wondered why Nathan didn't hold her hand or put his arm around her during the film. He drove her back to the Inn.

"Judy, my friends and I'll come by at noon to pick you up for the town's picnic. Don't worry about it being a pitch-in. Permelia, Emily, and Jayne are bringing fried chicken and lots of fixings." He dropped her off giving her a little peck on the cheek.

*****

Permelia also brought a broccoli asparagus salad, with ingredients from the garden. Everyone was surprised she was still picking asparagus this late in the season. Emily was famous for her grape salad. She never took any back home. Jayne made fried chicken. The food was plentiful with lots of different varieties of fried chicken, of course everyone were there to eat all they could. Nathan's Aunt Henrietta made her usual, tasty cherry pies. The fireworks weren't being set off until dusk. All the parents made bedtime exceptions for the expectant children. The parents loved to see their kids' wide eyes as the sky show proceeded.

There were no speeches or bands playing like a century ago. Nevertheless, there was an old-fashioned three-legged race, potato sack race, and tug-of-war. Grovetown residents thought you couldn't have Fourth of July without these traditional activities. Donnie and Billy Bob never failed to win the three-legged race. A bunch of teenage boys formed teams for the tug-of-war over a man-made river of mud. The Chief of Police won the sack race with little competition. The weather was a cool eighty-three degrees with a breeze. Excitement for the fireworks filled the air.

Judy thought, *These aren't the fireworks I planned to have with Nathan.*

The afternoon passed by with the pleasantries of a party. All stomachs were full.

Judy found herself in a dither. She noticed Nathan acting distant, avoiding eye contact. *What was going on? Something isn't right. Why was he paying so much* attention *to Permelia? Maybe I should have stayed home.*

As time went on, Judy knew something was wrong. There was some chemistry between Nathan and Permelia. She was catching on. She said to herself, *I'll watch them awhile.*

Fireworks were imminent. She walked over to where Nathan and Patrick were talking. She approached them and said, "I'm sorry to interrupt but, Nathan, may I speak to you alone? Will you walk with me over by that tree?"

He agreed.

Judy blurted out, "What's the matter? Don't we have a special relationship? I thought we did. I feel like you don't want me here."

Nathan didn't want to hurt his old girlfriend. He didn't know what to say. He hoped to have this discussion another time when they were alone.

However, he replied, "Judy, you're a special friend to me. We've enjoyed fun times together. I don't know how to tell you about our relationship. I wanted to talk to you after the fireworks back at the inn. However, maybe it's time now. I can't continue to lead you to believe there's a future for us. I once thought so. We now can only be friends. I plan to have a different life. I'm sorry."

Judy started crying. She couldn't stop. She knew people were watching. She wanted to run. Peter watched her from several yards away. He noticed that the man talking to her was the same person he saw with her at lunch. He walked over. Judy ran into his arms.

There was a cheer as red, white, and blue explosions covered the sky.

60

The group of people most concerned with the sewer problem held an important pow-wow around the large mahogany conference table at the newspaper office. Present were Henry Bridges, the current works manager, Nathan, Raymond, Patrick, a representative of the EPA, the Peony County Health Inspector, Ralph Pugh, and the Chief of Police.

Bridges spoke first, "What a terrible situation we have on our hands. Raymond, thank you for the article warning the populace to stay out of Deer Fly Creek. Of course, we found a couple of teenagers who wouldn't listen. Also, it was good of you to let us use your conference table. As all of you know, the water results showed heavy contamination. Now we may have some idea why. We wanted the Health Department Officer to be in on our conversation to help discover how we ended up in such a mess."

He spread the blueprints and other papers on the table for all to see. "I'll try to simplify the complicated. I hope you'll see the extent of our conundrum. Nathan, would you please give us a summary of your findings from the newspapers and Town minutes?"

Nathan looked around the room. "I hope I don't leave any important facts out. They found raw sewage in Deer Fly Creek in 1995 contrary to all regulations. The health department and other State and Federal officials made the decision Grovetown would be required to put in a new sewer system. The new system was to have separate lines. The storm sewer would remain flowing into Deer Fly Creek. A second line would be for waste products. And neither the twain shall meet. A town bond issue was to pay for the new central sewage construction. The residents would pay an additional fee based on the amount of water they used for a sewer charge, through their utility bill, to pay for the bond issue. The amount of that fee has gone up drastically each year,"

Patrick interrupted, "It sure has. I can attest to that." The others nodded in agreement.

Nathan resumed his explanation. "The law required each property owner to connect to the laterals of the new sewer. Mr. Bridges will explain about laterals when I finish. This hook-up required the hiring of a licensed trained plumber. The normal charge was expensive and if the house was old, it could cost much more. As you know, there are many buildings in town over 150 years old. The town required a license and bond for the private contractor/plumber. A private construction company would construct the new sewer lines and laterals. That bond issue I previously mentioned financed the cost. There was a rumor that the town didn't take required bids."

"Many of the property owners were very upset because of the initial and future costs. Utility bills increased substantially. The connection for all structures was also expensive. Most property owners raised rents to offset their costs. I know I've simplified, but you should have the general idea. Let's hold any questions until Henry Bridges briefs us."

Continuing to the more complicated and technical part of the subject, Bridges took over and pointed to the blueprint, "You'll notice this is a copy of the original. I've marked the storm sewer lines in red. The new waste sewer is in blue. Both sewers are supposed to run parallel. The storm sewer goes to the river. The waste sewer line empties into the sewage plant. The properties are marked in black, while the laterals are in green. Are you able to follow me so far?"

The County Health Department agent replied, "I think so, but what are 'laterals'?"

Nathan asked Bridges to explain about the laterals. "Laterals connect to the property line as a bridge from the building's property line to the new sewer. It was the owners responsibility to pay for the line from their building to the lateral to connect to the new sewer for waste from the building. That line goes to the new sewer plant, where it's processed and purified. Questions?"

The Health Officer asked, "Is there any chance the two lines are interconnected? That could be a source of the waste in the river."

Henry replied, "There should be no way that could happen. We tested for cross-contamination. We found nothing. Unfortunately, it appears that some properties, contrary to law, didn't connect properly to the main waste line. Also in some areas, a structure couldn't connect because the construction company didn't put in a lateral for connection.

All were at attention. Jake became alert. Bridges said, "Let me explain. Again, each property would connect to the new sewer by the use of laterals. The storm sewer didn't change. How did this all come to be? There must have been big problems and oversight. I hate to think it was fraud but fraud can't be ruled out."

The EPA representative broke into the discussion, "If we suspect fraud, I'll have to call in the White Collar Crime Section of the Indiana State Police."

Raymond asked, "Does anyone know where the sewer construction company is and how to contact them? We need to talk with them to sort this out, but it doesn't seem we'll be able to. I found their name, on the engineering documents. Raymond and I looked into the matter and discovered the company's names. The owners are from Ft. Wayne. The Secretary of State's office said there was no filing of annual reports for over five years. The addresses and phone numbers got us nowhere."

Raymond checked the court records. He discovered some of the parties were divorced, but found no leads on anyone's present address. Checking Federal Bankruptcy papers, he didn't find any record of filing.

"I fear we're at a dead end without hiring a private detective. They seem to have disappeared. We can't find any current addresses or phone numbers. We ferreted out all info available from the archived newspapers at the library. The fire destroyed our copies. That brings up another question. Is there a reason for the destruction of our archived newspapers? Was there an attempt to destroy the other set at the library? Could there be a connection between the arson and this investigation?"

Frowning, the Health Department representative inquired, "Do you think there's a relationship?"

Nathan answered, "We don't know? Do we?"

The others nodded with questioning faces.

Bridges said, "Let's pass around the contracts, town papers, engineering documents, bond documents, and reports on Grovetown's property connections, and repairs. Examine them well. Eat lunch and return with pen and paper with your thinking caps on. See you about one."

*****

Bridges returned to the conference room after lunch. He made some fresh coffee. He noticed a large easel with paper and markers now in the room. He exclaimed, "This will be perfect to help organize our thoughts.

Everybody slowly trekked in. After all settled, Bridges uttered, "I hope you all had a good lunch."

Patrick nodded, "The café's ham and beans are always the best."

Bridges continued, "Let's see if we can spend more time pouring over all the documents for an hour or so. I made a fresh pot of coffee. I think we may need it. Then we'll brainstorm."

The members each took another stack of documents to examine. The room became very quiet except for the shuffling of papers.

*****

Bridges stood, grabbed a red marker and stepped over to the easel. Bridges started the discussion, "I think we can assume certain facts. I'll outline them. There are only two main issues. First, we now know in some locations no laterals were constructed. Therefore no one could connect. Secondly, we see some properties didn't connect properly, therefore their sewage went into the storm sewer water and into Deer Fly Creek. The inspector certified both those with no lateral and those with a lateral who didn't connect. Why did this all happen? How could that be? Did the EPA sign off on the job?"

Someone from the EPA said, "Yes, we were led to believe the project was complete, and all was in order. We approved the documentation, terminated the project. And released the bond. I think we're going to need expert help in this matter. I imagine an investigation is in order. I'm only a lowly administrator. Why don't I take all the papers and the notes to my office and hand it all over to my engineers and their people to investigate?"

Bridges agreed. "Petty, will you call the Sheriff? There may be fraud. There are too many questions and few answers. The officials may want to coordinate with you people and bring in the State Police. Also, of course, the Attorney General's office. This town's problems run deep. There needs to be a thorough investigation. I fear there may have been extensive fraud."

Bridges looked around the room. He could see the relief on the faces of the men. The matter was out of their hands. "I believe we all agree to that approach."

All nodded and said their good-byes.

61

The door wasn't locked. The door is never locked. She opened the metal, windowless front door to his green 1970 trailer, Carol thought to herself; *This door doesn't need to be locked. Who would want any of Billy Bob's stuff? Well, they might want to use his old fishing poles and such, but I doubt those would even interest anyone. The paint on his trailer is the most disgusting color of green. Not hunter green nor bright green. But more of a drab green. They called that color of green institutional green. At least that's what my older brother said, after serving in the Vietnam War. He said, "If it doesn't move, paint it." It's too bad he came back with Vietnamese Syndrome. Now they call it Post Traumatic Stress Disorder. He's still messed up.*

She entered the front room. The room felt closed in with the combined kitchen dining room. She gasped. *Whoa! How can he make such a mess? Why, the mess is even worse than last week. I hope he appreciates my cleaning up after him.*

Carol walked down the short hall to the tiny bedroom. She picked up trash and dirty clothes. She carried a big black trash bag for trash and a smaller white one for clothes. She found Coke cans, half-filled beer bottles, pizza boxes, and fast food bags. She thought, *How does he live like this?* She thought, *Has anyone made this bed since last week?* She stripped off the soiled sheets, pillowcases, and bedspread. She hunted around the minuscule room. She found one set of clean bed linens, made up the bed, and headed to the bathroom/shower. As always, she washed down the floors, commode, sink, and walls with bleach. Carol threw all the towels, washcloths, and a rug into the appropriate bag. She expressed her thoughts to herself, *He's such a slob! If I didn't love him so much I'd be so outta here. But I do wonder who* else *may have been in this bed.* She knew he saw other girls. Christ wouldn't approve of her digressions from his teachings, but Jesus might forgive her for being with Billy Bob. She prayed to Christ to forgive her, like the prostitute in the Bible. She remembered the words of Pastor Todd, "God loves you, even though you only attend Church Easter and Christmas. I know you believe, and He believes you do too." Still Carol felt she had to sleep with Billy. He is all she knew. She realized Billy Bob would never marry her or anyone.

She observed the kitchen/dining area. She uttered in consternation, *It's a wonder he doesn't have cockroaches. Well, he might. I'm not here overnight so who knows what critters fly about after dark. I've heard that if all life on Earth died, cockroaches would survive. The nasty little varmints! But they are God's little varmints.*

Her phone rang with one of those designated rings. She recognized the ring as Billy Bob's.

"Hi, big boy. I'm at your place. Where are you?"

Her boyfriend said, "I ain't gonna get home for at least a couple of hours. I'm still on a job. We should plan to hook up another day. Okay?"

Carol said, "Well, I guess." Disappointed, she said, "I can finish up cleaning and go by Rosie's to see if she has time to trim my hair. Why don't you call me when you get home? We might be able to have some time together?"

Billy Bob, trying to be sincere, said, "Oh, honey, I hope so."

Carol said, "Love ya!"

Billy replied, "Bye. See ya!"

Billy Bob felt smug. He said to himself, *I have Carol at my beck and call. And she cleans my house and does my laundry too. Why would I ever want to marry?*

He sauntered back to his rendezvous with Carol's best friend, Jeannie.

She scraped dried eggs and grease off the plates, and cleaned the stained coffee cups. She decided to wash the dishes, and let them dry by themselves.

Now, she muttered, *I'll straighten up the couch, coffee table, and such, and get out of here.*

She said aloud, "You have to make a mess to clean up a mess."

Therefore, Carol threw everything off the couch onto the floor. She stashed the horribly stained and smelly couch cover and pillows into the dirty clothes sack. She took all the newspapers, magazines and such putting them all into a huge pile on the filthy carpet. *I'll bring a machine* next time. Carol noted, *This carpet needs a super cleaning, but it would be better if it were replaced.*

She separated the newspapers from the magazines. She found a molding bologna and cheese sandwich with mustard and pickle. "Yuck! Gross!" she exclaimed as she pitched it in the bag. Billy Bob's reading material included an NRA magazine, the *Sports Illustrated* swimsuit edition, *Playboy*, and three more explicit "dirty" ones. Then Carol found some assorted unpaid bills with no envelopes. One was a notice. His electricity was to be turned off tomorrow before noon. *Oh well. At least I don't live here. I'll leave him a note attached to one of his Budweiser bottles in the fridge. He'll surely see it there. I know he should have money. He doesn't spend any on me. He's so irresponsible. Why do I even put up with him?* Carol continued cleaning. She put all the newspapers in a bag by themselves. She said, "Might as well recycle. I think the Boy Scouts are collecting papers."

She had been working steadily. She stopped suddenly when she saw a folded paper stuffed inside the *Playboy* magazine. The paper looked like an important letter:

April 20, 2005

Dear Jake, Glenn, Donnie, Billy Bob, Solomon, and Richard,

We did an awful thing to this town and its people. You all know it was wrong. I no longer can keep my part in the matter secret. Jesus does not approve of our actions. I must ask him for forgiveness and become right with Christ. You may not understand, but I must.

I want to give you a heads-up about my plans. I'm going to the next Town Board meeting in May. I intend to tell them what we did. I'm also going to pay back my share of the money we made.

I think you should join me in this matter. I'll pray about it. Think about it. I'm sorry if my actions cause you trouble, but I can't live with this guilt any longer.

Sincerely,
Gussy

She stashed the letter in her pocket. She questioned, *This is quite a mystery. What did they do?*

She drove to the library and made a copy of the letter. *I'll hurry and put it back before Billy Bob gets home.* She ran in the trailer and stuck it back in the *Playboy* magazine where she found it.

*****

Carol completed her task. She drove her old Ford to the beauty shop. She wanted to discuss the letter with Rosie, her best friend.

Rosie saw Carol and hung the phone up. "Hi," she said, "are you here for a haircut?"

Carol replied, "Yes and no. I need to tell you something in private. Do you have time?"

"Sure, once I put Mrs. Moore under the dryer. We'll go to the break room and have some coffee."

Carol nervously walked back to the crowded break room/storage area. When Rosie walked in, she handed her the letter. "Read."

62

Grovetown's Chief of Police, Mike Petty read the letter. He immediately knew the letter was a serious clue into Gussy's life and possibly his death. The police made a copy for Carol. She went back to Rosie's shop.

Petty, raised his cup of coffee, with a favorite saying on it, "We Do Not Serve Doctors, Lawyers or Indian Chiefs." to his lips. He yelled at his Deputy, "Come in here Ron. You need to read this and brainstorm with me. Grab some coffee."

The Chief had his feet up on the desk. *Okay, with this clue I'll solve this murder. This is a good day. I can feel it. This letter is a red flag.*

Ron sat down across from Petty at the Chief's massive walnut office desk, with his mug of hot, black coffee. He liked his coffee straight like his booze. He could think well with it strong and black.

He said to the Chief, "None of that sugar and cream for a real man." He thought it expressed the same meaning, as "Real men don't eat quiche." He read the letter and said, "Well, well, well. What have we here? What luck. So Chief, what's our plan of action?"

Chief Mike Petty picked up the Gussy Murder Book. He felt he was like the police officers in the city who had murder books for each murder. He pulled out the alibi statements of all the poker players named in the letter, along with all the other case notes. He looked at his deputy, "Ron, you need to set up meetings with all these guys. I don't want Jake to know what we're doing since he's named. Sure do wonder what this is all about."

Ron grabbed the phone book and the calendar, he asked, "When do you want to see these guys?"

"ASAP. However, you set the time. Don't let them choose. We want to be in control. Tell Billy Bob we're coming to his trailer. And make that appointment with him within the next hour or two."

"What am I to tell him? What do I say if he asks why?"

The Chief answered, "Tell Billy Bob and Donnie it's about fishing. We want their interviews separate. Tell the others it's about the murder case. We want Billy Bob to tell us what the letter means and the 'who, what, when, where, and why?' of all this."

Ron, excitedly, replied, "Will do. Are we going to do that 'good cop/bad cop' thingy?"

Petty answered, "We could with the ones we'll question at the station, but at Billy Bob's place we'll play it by ear."

Ron set up the times. Mike went into his cubbyhole private office. He opened the big black safe where he kept evidence, in this case, the giant screwdriver. He lifted out the large plastic see-thru bag; He noted on the attached sheet his name, the date, and time. He knew he always had to be careful to protect the chain of custody. He thought fingering the murder weapon might inspire him. He returned to his large crowded desk. Ron told him they were to see Billy Bob at three. He put the big tool on the top of the desk in front of himself .

The Chief said, "I wonder if the letter is connected to the murder or some other matter. I think we should put this screwdriver on the desk as a good-luck charm. This wicked looking object could be instrumental in keeping us on point and might even provide us insight. We'll put the letter here too. OK. Screwdriver talk to me! Is there any connection between these guys and Gussy's demise? Gussy was going to say something involving his poker pals."

Ron queried, "Chief, do you think you can solve Gussy's murder?"

"Well, Ron, I hope so. This summer has been a mysterious one. You know it's not just the murder to solve; it's the arson at the newspaper, the break-in, and attempted arson at the library. The rumors around town allege a possible fraud in the sewer mess. Don't know what's happening to Grovetown."

Ron interrupted him, "What? Do you think they might be connected?"

Then Petty replied, "I'm beginning to wonder. Lots of coincidences."

They finished some other business quickly. The two headed to Billy Bob's trailer. Billy Bob was waiting. He mumbled, "Why do they want to talk about fishin'? Could the Chief want to talk about the fishin' contest in August? They might want some tips. They know how good I am at catchin' fish and big ones too. That's it. That's why the Chief wants to talk to me."

He decided to pick up the new pizza box covered with flies along with at least a six-pack of empty beer bottles. He muttered, "Can't let them police think I'm an alki, can I?" He closed the door to his bedroom. He noticed a crawling cockroach. He crushed it with a dirty towel. He thought, *Good thing Carol cleaned up. Wouldn't have liked them seeing my housekeeping skills.*

He flopped down on the broken down sofa only to get up again when he heard the knock on the door. He yelled, "Come in. Come on in, the locks broken." He thought to himself, *Ought to get that fixed 'fore someone comes in and steals everything.*

Chief Petty entered first followed by his deputy. Deputy Ron was to take notes. Petty immediately said, "Hi. Billy, let's talk. I'll get right to the point. Let's talk about fishing. I need for you to retell me what you were doing the day Gussy was murdered."

Averting his eyes from looking at the Chief and stammering, he replied, "That's been a long time ago. Don't know ifn' I can recall."

"Well try."

The trailer resident continued, "Oh yeah! I went fishin' with Donnie, as I told you before."

"Did you two ride together?"

"No, we met there."

"Where were you fishing?"

"We were down at Tucker's Bridge."

"Anyone else there."

"No, we was alone. Didn't see nar another person."

"Did you catch anything?"

"No, the fish just wasn't biting. We stayed there awhile. Went on down the Creek and tried there too. We caught a couple 'throw-back' catfish. Nothing else. Stayed there until about two. We headed to the Legion for a few beers and a burger and fries. We was really hungry havin' had nuttin' to eat since breakfast. Then I went home to clean up for our poker game. Game started about eight. Watched some TV too."

Chief Petty told Billy Bob, "Why, that's strange. Your brother told us bluegills were really biting. He even said some were big enough for supper. He fibbed. So who's telling the truth, you or Donnie?"

"Well, I am! They was too small. That's why I didn't remember them."

"OK, you told us before that you rode with Donnie. Now you say you met at the bridge. So which is it?"

Looking confused, Billy Bob said, "You know I really can't remember. Oh, yeah, that's right I did ride with Donnie, so he could brag about his new CD player."

The Chief pushed on, "You said you didn't have anything to eat so you went to the Legion. Donnie said you guys had sandwiches to eat while you fished. You know Billy, somebody is not telling the truth. Let's have it."

"Don't know what you mean. Chief, you know I wouldn't lie to you. Don't you believe me?"

Chief Petty smiled with a big grin. Ron stood by not smiling or frowning as if he didn't care. Then Billy said, "Ron you also know I'd never lie to the police. Guess I'm confused."

"Let's talk about something else," said Petty. "We heard you received a letter from Gussy before he died. Tell us about it."

"Don't know about no letter."

"We heard you even used the letter as a bookmark in a magazine."

Billy, needing a break, said, "Guys I need a Bud. He headed for the refrigerator. Want some too?"

The two shook their heads and in unison, replied, "We're here on police business, not a social call."

Billy Bob walked back to the dirty couch with holes all over the upholstery. He sat down and sipped his beer.

Petty repeated, "Again, tell me about the letter you got from Gussy."

"I told ya, I don't know about no letter."

Petty said to his deputy, "You have Judge Miller's phone number don't you? Guess we'll have to get a search warrant. Billy Bob seems to be hiding something."

"I'll ask you one more time. Tell me about that letter!"

Stammering and meekly he said, "I can't tell you anything. I promised Jake."

"You promised Jake what?"

"I can't tell you. He'll get mad at me."

"Why?"

"He told all of us to get rid of the letter. But I didn't 'cause I couldn't find it."

"Did you ever find it?"

"I shouldn't tell you. We promised."

"Who are we?"

"I'm not 'sposed to. Really I can't tell nobody."

He looked Billy in the eye, he said, "Now, Billy, I'm getting tired of this garbage. Either you tell me what is going on or we're taking you down to the police station! You are hiding something. I want to see the letter. We think your 'secret' might implicate you in Gussy's murder. Ron, go get that info to call the judge. We'll tear this place up until we find the letter. So, let's get to it."

Hardly able to speak, he realized how scared he was. He thought, *This ain't goin' so good. What do I do? I ain't goin' to jail for no one.* He put his beer down. He lit a Winston and started to talk. He pulled out the letter hidden in the centerfold of his "Playboy" magazine. "OK, here it is." He explained about the poker game the night of Gussy's murder, and how they all established alibis and agreed to destroy the letters. He couldn't shut up and even explained what the letter meant, down to the details of the sewer fraud.

Petty interrupted, "Were you involved in the fire at the newspaper office?"

Billy admitted his and Donnie's involvement and why they had to destroy the papers. He thought, *What does I got to loose?* He even volunteered the details of the break-in at the library. He talked, talked, and talked.

Feeling better after the confessions, he asked, "So what are you going to do to me? I didn't have nuttin' to do with Gussy's death, but we figgered one of us did. You believe me don'tcha? I'm sure tellin' you both the truth now. You gotta believe me. One of the other guys killed Gussy."

Petty replied, "Well, you're coming to the office with us. You need to write all this down. We'll drive you. You are not to tell any of the others that you've talked to us. I'm not going to arrest you on the arson and burglary charges now. No handcuffs. However, you are a major suspect in Gussy's murder. So are your poker buddies. You're looking at First Degree Murder. Then we'll interview Jake, Donnie, and the others."

63

B ridges drank his black coffee. He sat in front of the computer. He saw an e-mail from the EPA. Copies went to the State Department of Health, the Attorney General's Office, Sheriff of Peony County, State Police, Peony Health Department, and the Grovetown Police Department. He was quite surprised with the speed of the results to come from the EPA. Only a few days had passed before a report came.

He said to himself, *My goodness they must have worked day and night.*

Bridges read the preliminary conclusions. He realized the enormity of the situation. He picked up the phone, called Ralph Pugh, Peony County Health Official, Chief Petty, Beth Basford, the town attorney, and the President of the Town Council. He told each one. "We need to meet today. I have the EPA report. There are some very disturbing implications. As you'll see, the results are very damaging and accusatory. I've invited Raymond and Nathan from the *Grovetown Tribune* because they've been digging into the sewer construction. I know it seems irregular, but they've promised not to publish, and our talks are off the record. Besides the disclosures, help the town with transparency. Let's meet before lunch, say ten thirty."

*****

Promptly at ten thirty, all parties sat around the conference table.

Works Manager, Henry Bridges, informed them, "I'll pass out copies of the printed e-mail report from the EPA. You may have already read it. Please read it carefully."

All finished reading the document. You could hear the audible gasps breaking the silence.

Henry Bridges began, "As you may gather the investigators allege fraud, kickbacks, and favoritism to say the least. No waste sewer line exists down the middle of several blocks of Tulip Drive. No line was constructed. All property owners in those sections did not and could not connect to the sewer."

The mayor said, "Why?"

Bridges said, "We can only surmise the reason, Let me continue— money!

"Property owners benefited. They escaped paying to hook up. The construction company benefited. They were paid for work not done. They made out like bandits. Other lines had sewer lines but no laterals. Again, who benefits? Property owners and the construction companies."

The Mayor of Grovetown interrupted, "Beth, as town attorney, please look into the town's legal situation in this upsetting matter."

The Works Manager continued, "A certain plumbing company, Davis and Sons, worked around town on early connections to the new sewer. The Works Manager and the Town decided plumbing companies were required to have a license to do the work to connect the properties. Davis and Sons and other companies were denied licenses for various reasons. The Davis Company went out of business."

Chief Petty asked, "Well who were licensed?"

Nathan, pushing up his glasses, interjected, "I can tell you. I researched the newspaper articles and the town council minutes. They only granted licenses to Gussy and Glenn's brothers, Jake, Billy Bob, and Donnie Achsworth. Convenient, wasn't it? You know they made money. We don't how know how much the twins inflated the cost to the townspeople."

Raymond yelled, "Nepotism, big time!"

Bridges took back the conversation, "There are some other concerns. Apparently, many seniors live on limited incomes. Some had to take out loans to cover the connection bills. Those costs often were several thousand dollars. Who benefited? Why who else, the banks, and financial organizations."

Chief Petty said, "A lot of people made loads of money."

Bridges answered, "Well the Works Manger signed off on inspections of non-connections. Did he get a kick back? Who else? You could look at the bond attorney from Peony. The Town Board had to know. Fraud and kickbacks abound. This investigation will continue, and I expect some indictments along the line."

64

Drew picked Emily up at three on his birthday, July 9.

Emily immediately said, "Happy Birthday, Drew. She handed him a gift bag with two wrapped gifts." *Finding a gift for Drew was quite a feat. I've never been in his apartment. I don't know his reading preferences. I wouldn't buy him something like cologne. A gift of cologne is too personal. Therefore, I chose something Nathan would like. A fountain pen and black ink. I wish it were a fancy one. I couldn't afford a Pelican, a Parker, or a Mont Blanc. I hope he likes it. The price was within my budget. I bought a nice black enameled one and, of course, black ink from Levenger. How am I going to tell him about Todd? And hurt him on his birthday. This is awkward. Nevertheless, it has to be. Dear God, be with me, help me. Please, please keep me strong. In Christ's name, Amen.*

Drew opened his presents. With surprise, he said, "Emily, I've wanted a fountain pen for years. My father and mother said they learned cursive with a fountain pen and ink. Where did you find one?"

Emily replied, "There are companies that sell several brands of pens and ink. I write with a Mont Blanc pen my grandmother gave me when I graduated from Northwestern University. She gave one to my mother, my aunt, my brother, and me. I guess it's a family tradition. I hoped you would like writing with one. Don't let anyone else write with it. The nib adjusts to your style."

"Thank you. I'll write my thank you note with it. We need to get on the road. My mother expects us at six-thirty or seven for dinner. You're my surprise."

Emily felt a sinking feeling in her stomach.

65

A s Emily packed an overnight bag for her trip back to her apartment in Indianapolis for the teachers' meeting, she called Nathan.

"Hi, brother. Just wanting to make sure you're still coming to supper after your dentist appointment on Friday. Have you spoken to the others?"

Nathan answered, "I think the whole gang's planning on being there. Permelia will ride with me. Wouldn't want to miss my favorite sister's good cooking. By the way, what's for supper?"

"Well, your favorite fried chicken, of course. I'm getting some fresh tomatoes, cucumbers, and those extra-sweet candy onions from that farmer's market north of town. Those onions are sweeter than Vidalia's. You know the ones grown by the Amish. I'll marinate cucumbers and onions in vinegar, sugar, and oil with dill weed. I'm also fixing fresh corn on the cob. I'm glad the crop was good this year. They always say, 'Knee-high by the Fourth of July'. However, this corn is over six foot already. Do you think you'll feel well enough? We can do it another day if you wish. We may even have morel mushrooms." *How nice Sally said she'd come over about four to give me directions on cooking them. She volunteered at the birthday party.*

"No, I'm only having my teeth cleaned, x-rays, and a general checkup. I'll be seeing your dentist's son. Have you met him? What's he like?"

"Yes. I've met him. He filled my broken tooth back in May. I think he's a good dentist." *Moreover, he is a good man. I feel guilty hurting him last week. I asked God to direct me how to tell Drew with kindness and concern for his feelings. My tears all the way back with him to Grovetown were from sadness. I had no choice. It wasn't right to let him think we were going to have a future. And then to tell him on his birthday. He said he loved me. I feel just awful. Should I tell Nathan the truth? Is there any reason not too? Alternatively, should I wait and tell Pastor Todd first? Of course, I'll tell Pastor Todd first. My heart is Pastor Todd's.*

"I'm glad."

"Mother keeps talking about Drew and how she thinks he and I would make an attractive couple. She won't stay out of my personal life."

Nathan said, "Yeah, I know. She keeps asking me when will I meet a 'nice' girl and get married. I don't think she likes kids that much, but I suppose she'd show off a grandchild's photo or two in a 'brag book'. I'm getting ready to ring her after we hang up. She's been driving me almost crazy calling me every other day about the estate and trying to find out what I'm doing. I'm sure it's unchristian to say that I'd like my life to be my own. I want to dress as I please. Remember she even bought me clothes to wear to the funeral."

Emily broke in, "Why she must call me on the other days wanting to know when Uncle Gussy's estate will be settled. Then she starts talking about Drew again. She calls Aunt Henrietta at least twice a week. Once in a while, she'll ask if the police have any leads on Uncle Gussy's murder."

He continued, "I think our mother may be more interested in the estate than finding Gussy's murderer. I don't like to think that it's true. She is our mother. But still...."

"Well, I do know we'll all be happier once Aunt Henrietta's administrator's job is finished."

Nathan said, "I know I won't sleep until the perp is brought to justice, I think the recent arrests are a good sign. The Chief will break them all and find the killer. Then we'll all have closure. Say, I need to call Mother so I can be the one to tell her of the recent police findings. I'll call you in Indy when I've left the dentist to give you a heads up. What time is supper? I need to tell the others. I think Patrick and Jayne are driving and Pastor Todd will ride with them."

"Between six thirty or seven. I'll see you then." *That's a whole day before I'll see my Pastor. Thank you, God for bringing him into my life.*

Punching in the numbers for his mother, he thought, *I need to be very careful what I tell her. I don't want her to jump to unfounded conclusions and spread rumors. The rest of the investigation needs to go slowly and with utmost care.*

His mother answered on the fourth ring. She said, "I always wait a decent amount of time before I answer. I don't want anyone to think I'm sitting near the phone with nothing to do." Her reasoning was a lot like someone wanting to be late to a party to show importance."Hello, is this Nathan? I thought I recognized your number and my caller ID confirmed. What is going on? Is the estate settled now that it's been so long, and no child of Gussy's been found?"

Nathan ignored the blunt questions. "Mother, how are you? Are your allergies acting up?" He wanted the conversation to stay low-key.

"Everything is fine. I keep Zyrtec in my body all the time and stay inside with air conditioning most of the time. Seems to help. I'm stressed from all my social obligations. Everyone expects me to be in charge. The volunteer work at the hospital is somewhat time-consuming, too."

"No, the estate isn't closed and we haven't found the child. Henrietta was given permission to hire a private detective."

Raising her voice, she exclaimed, "What! How much is that costing?"

"Mom, I don't know how much. I'm not privy to such info. But I'm calling with some exciting news."

Interrupting him, she said, "Tell me! Tell me! You're wasting my time with your chit-chat."

"Okay, okay, calm yourself down. I'll explain as well as I can. Why don't you get your coffee and sit down."

A few minutes later, she was back on the phone. Sitting down with her coffee and phone she said, "Go on. I'm sure whatever you say must be important. Please get right to the point."

"Well, it looks like they may have suspects in Uncle Gussy's death. Apparently Gussy was involved with the Achsworth brothers, Solomon Edwards, you know the guy that runs the American Legion, and Richard Farwell, the liquor store owner, in a scam involving fraudulent actions against the town. Remember I told you about the strange sewer back-ups. The suspects, including Gussy, cheated the town by taking kickbacks from some town officials, and selected property owners. The company constructing the new sewers was in on it too. Glenn Achsworth was the Town Building Inspector at the time of the construction of the new sewer. His twin brothers, Donnie and Billy Bob, and Uncle Gussy did the installations, or lack thereof. Even Richard Farwell and Solomon

Edwards were in cahoots. Now the fraud investigation is in the State of Indiana's hands. However, Gussy, after he became a Christian, wrote a letter telling all the others that he was going to the Town Board and admit what they all did. He told the others they should own up too."

Before he could continue, Madelyn interrupted saying, "Now, let me get this straight. All you mentioned, including my brother, ran a scam on the town with the sewer contractors, is that correct? What were their reasons and what were they to gain? I don't quite understand it all."

"Mom, it's not hard to understand. Some people want power, some fame, others love, but this was pure greed. They lined their pockets with others hard-earned cash. I don't know all the details. The company saved money. The company was paid with town tax dollars, state and federal sources for work not done and materials not used. The construction company pocketed tax dollars. Some property owners didn't have to pay for the costs of hooking up to the new sewer, like construction materials, labor, and inspecting charges. Some homeowners paid plumbing contractors for work not done. In addition, the company too. Why even the town gained by no construction charges. A very complicated situation, but in the end, people made money by the fraudulent actions of many. Greed big time! Gussy wanted to find forgiveness and wanted most of his ill-gained land parcels given to the town."

"Oh," his mother exclaimed, "so that's why in his new will he gave the town his town real estate."

"I think so. Sure explains a lot. Now, let me continue. All of the names associated with Gussy in this matter are considered 'persons of interest', meaning they are considered possible suspects in Gussy's murder."

"Have they been arrested?"

"No, just Donnie and Billy Bob, so far. The arrests are for arson, attempted arson, and burglary."

"Why?" she asked.

"Well, there are some further complications. You remember I told you about the fire at the newspaper. All those guys thought Dad and I were looking too closely into the case of the sewer backup mess. You see we were researching into the original news articles on the entire sewer project. So, it looks like the twins, Donnie and Billy Bob, set fire to the news office storage room. Billy Bob admitted to arson, implicating his brother. He told police they attempted to burn the other copies of the newspapers in the library and were breaking into the basement to do so. However, they got scared and took off. So they are both in jail for that too. The police think Jake is the ringleader. His friends, the twins, and Glenn are part of the conspiracy. The authorities believe the accomplices are Richard Farwell and Solomon Edwards. Mom, that's all I know at this point. I wanted to keep you up-to-date with all going on. I need to go. Dad and I have much to do for the upcoming articles. Lots to accomplish. Going to Em's for supper and the dentist awaits me."

"I suppose if you have to go. There's so much to process. You'll let me know when anything else happens. Bye, love you."

Nathan hung up the phone and headed to the newspaper office.

Seeing him, Raymond said, "Glad you're here. We have so much to write about to explain all that's happened to the general populace."

"Dad, no problem. I talked to Mom. She is as mystified as all of us. Here are my plans for the weekend. Tomorrow I drive to Indy for a dentist appointment with Dr. Jacobs. I'll have supper at Emily's. Em's fixing fried chicken. How nice to have someone else cooking a meal— you know old-fashioned home cooking. Permelia and Jayne will stay at Emily's apartment. Patrick, Pastor Todd, and I are getting a motel room. I'll try to be back around five Sunday. You have our cell phone numbers. Call either one of us if you need to. Well, let's get to work! "

Raymond added, "I think we should have some human interest articles. What do you think about articles showing events, people, and things from the past?"

"Sounds intriguing. But please explain in a little more detail."

"Well, I thought we might call the articles, 'Grovetown Back in Time'. For example, people are already planning this fall's Persimmon Festival. What about some photos and info on prior festival activities? We'd select various years to present."

"That sounds fine. Wasn't Mom one of the queens of the festival? The Persimmon Festival reminds me of an old wives' tale Aunt Henrietta always related to us. She said her grandmother Trinkle told her persimmon seeds predicted winter weather. You cut a persimmon seed in half in the fall. If you see a knife, the winter will be cold with cutting winds. If you see a fork, it will be a mild one. A spoon—well, a lot of snow and shoveling. Sometimes I've found the predictions true.

"Yes, your mother was a beautiful Persimmon Festival Queen, over twenty-five years ago. The festival when she was Queen would be one we would want to capture. Of course several others too. I've heard the persimmon seed theory before."

"Looks like a good idea. Let's get writing on our more pressing current ones."

*****

Emily called her mother to tell her where to reach her over the next few days.

"Hi, Mom. I wanted you to know where I'll be the next few days. I'm driving to Indy to my apartment today. I'm having dinner with two other teachers tonight. We're going to Olive Garden. I've been craving fried calamari and veal parmesan. I'll return after church Sunday. My church has a mid-summer lunch-pitch-in."

"Oh, Emily, I was about to call you to see what you thought about those suspects the police have in Gussy's murder. Nathan called and gave me some info but I wondered if you knew any more than he does. So, tell me."

Emily replied, "Nathan knows more than me. I know that the Achsworth twins were responsible for the fire at the newspaper office. Henrietta and I were at the library when they tried to enter the children's section. They had materials to start a fire. The 'town fraud', as everybody is calling it, is much too complicated for me. The police think it has something to do with a motive for murder."

Madelyn sighed, "Guess nobody can tell what's going on. At least you can tell me why Henrietta hasn't closed the estate."

"I don't know all the legal ramifications except the attorney told her she still needs to diligently search for Gussy's child a while longer. That's why Henrietta hired a private detective. If they can't find the child within a reasonable time, she can petition the court to void that section of the will and distribute the estate assets. Therefore, the private investigator is a good thing. If no one finds the child within a reasonable time she will have done all actions in good faith—an important consideration for the judge to hear. Mom, just hang in there. Now let me give you the rest of my schedule. Tomorrow, some others in the Reading Recovery team and I have a teaching day with our instructors. As I've told you, it's a program under the auspices of Purdue University. The goal is to find reading-challenged students and evaluate their reading level. Then we design an individual reading program. Each student has his or her own course of study. Remember I went to special classes to learn how to do this. After we set up the plan beginning with the level of reading for each student, the teacher instructs each student in a way each child needs to learn certain skills. Late August we take a refresher class."

"Emily, that's nice. I've seen Drew's photo. Doesn't he look luscious? I'll call Sally. Maybe she'll help by setting up a blind date. Won't that be fun?

"Maybe while you're in town. I've told you how I think you'll make such an attractive couple. The last time I talked to Sally, I suggested that you two would make a fine couple. I asked her to encourage her son to date you. What good-looking children you'd have!"

"Mother! Don't talk this way. I've met him. He filled my broken tooth. If he wants to date me, he'll ask. You really can't plan my life for me." *Dear God, please help me do better at honoring my parents.*

Madelyn responded, "I only want to see you a happily married woman who is well-supported. I don't want to tell you how to run your life, Emily. But a good-looking man with a fine income would be so nice for you, better than some teacher."

"I know you mean the best. Sorry, if I were too curt. Mother, I do have to get going before it gets too late."

"Bye, I'm hoping you get asked out."

Emily rolled her eyes.

She headed for the big city in her car, *Veggie.* As she drove, she thought about the library work they had been doing. *Boy, I hate to miss days I could be at the library. I know the computerizing of all the books is moving right along. We hope to have the system up and running by early August. I wish it were sooner. We need each patron to have a new card with barcodes. The computer will even be able to keep a track of all delinquent fines and books. We can track the whereabouts of any book at any time. The summer has been exciting.* Emily's mind went to the image of Pastor Todd. *I'm in love with him. I think he might love me too. I look forward to showing him I can cook. I've never felt like this before, and I hope it doesn't end. What will I do when I have to go back to the classroom?*

She daydreamed about what her life with him might be. *I suppose I might be able to find a teaching position in Grovetown or perhaps he could find a church in Indianapolis. Oh well, if it's God's will, He'll provide.*

66

Nathan and Permelia walked into the Jacobs & Jacobs DDS office. Permelia sat down in the waiting room. She found a *Time* magazine to read.

"Hi!" I'm Nathan Sparks here for a cleaning appointment with Dr. Drew Jacobs at one. Do I need to fill out any papers?"

"Yes," the pretty receptionist said. "There are a few forms, mainly about insurance and prior dental history. Here are a pen and clipboard with the papers. You can sit over there. Dr. Drew will be with you soon."

A tall, dark-haired, well-dressed man, with a white coat, came out, held out his hand and introduced himself. He asked Nathan to come into his private office.

"Mr. Starks, I like to talk with a new patient first, before the examination. I need to know your dental history. Please sit down."

"Thanks," he said and thought to himself, *This is a little different but quite professional.*

Nathan told Dr. Jacobs the info and answered his pertinent questions. He looked around the classy looking office. He noted the desk and lamps were very modern in oak. All of a sudden, he noticed something that looked familiar, a hand-carved wooden set of animals with Noah, and his Ark. The set looked quite like the set his uncle gave him as a baby. Inquisitively, he asked Drew, "May I ask a question about your unique carved animal set on your credenza?"

Dr. Jacob's answered, "Of course, you may. I'm quite proud to be the owner of these intricately carved animals."

"May I ask where you bought them?"

"Well, I didn't buy them. I've had them as long as I can remember."

Nathan continued to inquire, "May I look at one of the pieces?"

"Sure. Here's a giraffe. Isn't he handsomely carved?"

"It certainly is. May I inquire how you came by the set?" He nervously pushed up his glasses.

"I asked my mother one time. She said they were made especially for me by an old friend from her college days."

"Oh!" Thank you for the info. I find them very well carved. In fact, I have a similar Noah's Ark set. My Uncle Gussy made mine before I was born. Did your mother say who carved them?"

Drew responded, "No. She only said that a friend made them for her prior to my birth. I suppose they came from Bloomington while at I.U."

There was a knock on the door.

Drew said, "Come in."

A dental assistant entered, "I'm sorry to bother you, Doctor, but I'm only here until two. Shall I go ahead and do x-rays and a cleaning?"

"Of course, sorry, I held you up."

"Nathan, I'll talk to you after she's takes care of you."

Drew came into the room after x-rays and cleaning to talk to his patient. He said," Nathan, you have excellent teeth, and you are taking good care of them. Do you use an electric toothbrush?"

"Thank you for your kind remarks. Yes, I use an electric one."

"That's what I always recommend."

*****

Drew Jacobs sat in his office. He was deep in thought, *Nathan didn't mention his sister. Emily must have kept our relationship secret or at least she didn't tell her brother. Curious. My birthday last week was one of the worst days of life. I took her to my parents' house. I wanted them to meet her. Mom acted so surprised. How odd? Guess she didn't realize we'd met. And of course she couldn't have known our relationship was serious. Dad suspected, I do believe. I'm glad I didn't buy her a ring. She said we couldn't continue to see each other. She said she had also been dating someone else in Grovetown. She said she was in love with him. I missed out. Perhaps if I told her earlier, I loved her. That I wanted to marry her. First time I've been so serious as to consider marriage. What a nice girl! My loss! What if? What if? What if?*

*****

Nathan suggested to Permelia, "It's too soon to go to Emily's. Why don't we stop at Panera Bread for coffee? We can sit and talk."

"Sounds good to me. I might have some bread and cheese too. I've wanted to ask you about Baptists. I would like to know some of the tenets of your religion. I'm learning a lot by reading the Bible."

Nathan said, "I'd like to tell you and also explain what I believe." He pushed up his glasses. *Finally. I do believe Permelia is considering becoming a Christian. At least I hope she is. I have prayed and asked Jesus to come to her and save her. I want her in my life, as a Christian.*

Around five-thirty Nathan's phone rang.

"Hi, Dad, what's up?"

Raymond said, "Nathan, boy, have I found something. Henrietta went through Gussy's toolbox. She needed a wrench. She found a newspaper and a letter underneath the tools in the toolbox. Well, I'll tell you about the newspaper article first, dated Friday, April 27, 2005. I guess the police didn't look too hard. It said her name is Sally Jacobs, wife of Dr. Samuel Jacobs, DDS. Her nickname is Suze. The article talked about a benefit to raise money for the children's wing at a hospital in Indianapolis. There was no mention of her maiden name. Then there is a copy of a letter written by Gussy to Sally (Suze) Jacobs in care of Dr. Samuel Jacobs, D.D.S. in Indianapolis. I think you'll find the letter's contents revealing. Let me read the letter to you.

> *April 28, 2005*
>   *My Dear Suze,*
>
> *I was thrilled to finally locate the beautiful girl who stole my heart so many years ago. Of course, I recognized you. I carry memories of you yet today. I was crushed to realize my feelings for you weren't reciprocated. I know I wasn't much in those days, but we could have made a good life together. I see you married well.*
>
> *I assume our child was well loved and cared for. Did my baby like the Noah's Ark set? When I last saw you at the bookstore, you told me I would never see you again and would never see our child. I was devastated.*
>
> *I only found you at I.U. because you told me you worked in the bookstore. I thought I could change your mind. I hope you kept the ark and figures. I never married. You broke my heart!*
>
> *Finding you has been a blessing. I recently started to turn my life around. I found a personal relationship with Jesus, My Lord, and Savior.*
>
> *My prayers have been for you and our child. I want to be a part of our baby's life.*

I await your response so I can begin to be a part of your lives. I know we can reach an agreement.

With love and affection,
  Gussy

Nathan shouted, "Wow. That answers some questions. Dad, I met Dr. Drew Jacobs, Sally's son, today at the dentist's office. He looks to me to be in his thirties. He also owns a whittled Noah's Ark set almost exactly like Emily's and mine. This is too coincidental. He must be Uncle Gussy's son. Wasn't Sally's hair kind of reddish-blond? Drew's hair is black. Uncle Gussy's hair was always gray/white when I saw him. What color was his hair as a young man?"

Raymond said, "Jet black. He was prematurely gray. Then it turned snow white. This sounds promising. I'm calling Henrietta now."

Off the phone, Nathan revealed the details of the phone call to Permelia. They left the restaurant. Permelia said, "This may be the answer to Gussy's missing child. Unbelievable. Let's stop at a grocery store. I'd like to buy Emily a centerpiece for tonight's dinner."

67

Sally Jacobs started drinking expensive Scotch after her second cup of coffee. She hadn't dressed. Her reddish/blonde hair was advanced "bed hair." She said to herself, "I need a good strong drink!" Approaching the bar near the fireplace in the family room, she muttered, "Now, where is that bottle of Scotch? I hope Samuel replaced the one we finished last week. Oh, there it is and not even opened. There'll be enough."

Her week was getting worse by the day. She was imagining things, or so she thought. *I must be thinking the worse. Why does he want me to talk about our college days? Why does he mention our early marriage years? Is he hunting for something? Is he suspicious? Heavens, No. He can't be, can he? Why would he be after all this time?* She thought maybe he was only reminiscing, thinking of their good times. *I know our marriage is a little stale. That's it.*

She poured her scotch in the short glass filled with ice and then some soda. She started singing some words from an old Bud and Travis song from the sixties. "Scotch and Soda, Mud in your Eye, Boy, Don't I Feel High-o". She thought those were the words, but to her it really didn't matter as long as she started feeling "high-o". The Kingston Trio and the group, Bud and Travis, were her favorite singing groups. Those words were in her head from the time she had been in high school in the mid-Sixties. She tasted the concoction in her high school senior year. "Boy is this good!" she said aloud.

She finished the first drink and started her second. *Maybe he's having an affair. He has scheduled some after-hours dental appointments. Why doesn't he want me to go to that dental convention in Oregon? He always wanted me along before. We enjoyed each other on the trip we took to Guadeloupe. This enigma is curiouser and curiouser. I think I'm starting to feel the Scotch."*

Her cell phone rang. Sally walked slowly over to the desk where it set. She said, "Who would be calling me this early?"

Sally answered the phone. She cringed when she heard the voice, but being a well-bred lady she thought she was, she said, "Why, Madelyn, I haven't heard from you in a few days. What can I do for you?" She didn't want to talk to her old friend. Madelyn called at least once a week. She thought, *I assume she's calling me about Emily. Emily! Does she know Emily was here with Drew?* Madelyn extended the usual amenities, then proceeded to the real reason she'd called,

"Why, Sally, did you know that Emily is in town for a teacher's meeting? She's spending the night in town and fixing supper for her brother. Wouldn't it be nice if Drew could be there?"

Sally grimaced, but replied, "It's nice she's in town. I know her brother will enjoy a home-cooked meal. However, I believe Drew has other plans tonight. You know he is a very busy man. He has many friends. His business engagements keep him occupied most evenings. Besides, I think he has a girlfriend. He brought a girl here for his birthday dinner."

Madelyn ignored the "girlfriend" statement and continued, "I just know he would like my daughter. They would look so good together. Can't you persuade him? I just know after one date sparks would fly. We could set it up."

Sally thought, *Thank God. I don't think she knows anything.*

"Oh, Madelyn, I don't think it would be a good idea. I don't think they're suited at all."

Madelyn replied, "Oh can't you see their future? Please try to arrange something?"

"Oh, again I don't think so. Listen, I need to make some calls. I'll talk to you again soon."

Dear God, this is an impossible situation! I'm not a religious person, but if there is a God, help me. I'd better have another drink. This one she gulped down.

After another drink, she showered. She put on her blue sundress and blue sandals. The dress was a Liz Claiborne. The shoes were Anne Kline. She wanted to look classy and put together. She put on Estelle Lauder makeup. *This will certainly be a difficult evening!*

While Emily was putting the cut-up chicken in the pot of water with salt and paprika, Sally was in quite a state of mind and tipsy after another drink. She went outside to pick the white mushrooms. She muttered, "It has to be done. I know I'll rot in Hell if there is one. A second time won't make the situation any worse, but it will certainly make it better. I have no choice. I must protect my family. Should I call Emily to say I'm coming with the mushrooms or just arrive? Well, I best call Emily. I'm glad I got her number from the office when I met Samuel for lunch the other day. How easy it was. His secretary likes me. I said Emily was a daughter of a friend and I wanted to invite her to dinner with her mother."

She poured another drink. By this time, it was late afternoon. She was more than a little tipsy but used to this many drinks and could still function. She said to herself, "I'll have to stop in a while if I'm to drive to Emily's. I surely don't want to attract attention and end up in jail."

Ringing Emily, she settled herself in her favorite chair with her cell phone. "Hi, Emily, it's Sally. I enjoyed meeting you the other evening." She lied. "I have the morels defrosted. Thought I'd leave here now. Should be there in half an hour."

Emily said, "Half an hour sounds super. Nobody's coming until six thirty or seven." *I think Sally's been drinking. Her words are slurred. Kind of like the father of one of my mentally challenged students at the last parent/teacher conference.*

"I'll be there soon. With a good bottle of wine."

Ready to leave in her Mercedes, Sally first went up the grand staircase to their bedroom. She opened the drawer on the nightstand on her husband's side of the bed. She knew the pistol was loaded, but she checked the Glock anyway.

She next grabbed a bottle of French Bordeaux and the necessary mushrooms from her back yard. Sally gulped down another drink along with a big swig of green mouthwash. She drove slowly and cautiously with the bottle of Scotch, half gone, in her Neiman Marcus tote along with a pistol, wine, a corkscrew, and mushrooms. She knew an arrest was imminent if she were caught running a stop sign. At four thirty, she parked in Emily's apartment parking lot, ready for bear.

Emily greeted her mother's good friend graciously. "Thank you for coming. I want to impress my friends with morels. I know how precious these mushrooms are. I greatly appreciate the rare frozen ones from your fridge."

"It's no problem at all. I think sharing them with my old friend's daughter shows my friendship. I want to tell you what one of my college friends told me recently. She lived in Europe in the sixties. Way before you were born. She said, 'You know you're old when your ex lover's daughter wants to be your pen pal.' Isn't that hysterical? Doesn't that sound like something your mother would say?"

Emily was so embarrassed. She didn't answer. *This woman is drunk! What do I do?*

"Let's start the mushrooms. You need to soak them first in salt water. I did that for you this morning, so they'll be ready to go." Sally said, "Let's sit down for a minute."

Emily thought, *She is definitely drunk. Oh my. Dear God, please help me.*

They sat at the small dining room table already set for six.

Sally said to Emily, "Emily, I was shocked when Drew brought you to dinner. I had no idea you were dating. Well, I fear I have much to tell you. You and he can't have a relationship!"

Emily tried to speak, but Sally kept talking.

"There's so much you and your mother don't know. Drew is your cousin," she blurted out.

Emily gasped.

Sally continued, "Your Uncle Gussy was so handsome in a James Dean sort of way. That fabulous black hair. How I loved running my fingers through it while we lay naked. And Drew has identical hair. Didn't you like doing the same?"

Emily gasped again. *How can she think I did? She must think I'm a slut.*

"I was thrilled your uncle was attracted to me. Little 'ole me. From nowhere. Not glamorous like your mother—Queen of the Persimmon Festival. He was sooooo handsome, sophisticated, and exciting."

Her speech was increasingly confused.

She continued, "He could have walked off the movie screen of *Rebel without a Cause*. Oh, that James Dean look! I'd never met someone so down-to-earth and non-assuming, yet debonair." She slurred, "I was stricken."

Emily could only listen, not knowing what else to do. She found all the information difficult to digest.

"Gussy and I had an electric attraction. I met him on Deer Fly Creek. He was fishing off a bridge. Oh, we need to bread the mushrooms. Please crack a couple eggs and beat them for a couple of seconds."

Emily did as she was told. The eggs were brown—fresh free-range eggs from the Amish farmer's market.

Sally went on, "Your mother didn't notice me and definitely not us. She was totally oblivious. Gussy and I spent hours in his bachelor pad behind the big house. I think it was an old summer kitchen. He was totaling amazing. Of course, I was a virgin and in love. I didn't think I could get pregnant, and he didn't use a condom."

Emily interjected, *This is too much knowledge.* "Did my mother know about your tryst?"

"Of course not! She still doesn't. Thank goodness. If she had, she wouldn't keep bugging me all the time about you and Drew."

Emily gasped again. She trembled.

"Your uncle was so very talented. He could make anything from wood. When I told him I was pregnant, he drove up to I.U. He knew I worked at the bookstore. He made a whittled Noah's Ark with Noah, his wife, and pairs of animals. I was surprised, but I'd already made the decision to marry Samuel. I told him he'd never see the child. Time to bread the mushrooms. Take them out of the egg solution and dredge them in the seasoned flour."

Sally opened a bottle of French wine, asked for a glass. She consumed it quickly. *I need courage!*

Emily's phone rang. She saw the call was from her brother. Nathan said, "Hi, Em. I've talked to Patrick. He says they'll be at your house at seven. They're caught in some traffic on South 31. Are you busy cooking? I have a big surprise."

Emily thought, *Nathan needs to hear this conversation.*

"Oh, can you tell me? I have a big surprise too. Mother's friend, Sally, is here teaching me how to prepare morels. Tell me. Tell me."

Nathan said, "Then there'd be no surprise. We're going to Marsh. Do you need anything?"

Emily thought, *How can I tell him to stay on the line? Yes, I know.* "Nathan, I know how you never listen to me. But, you have to listen to me this time, got it? I need two bottles of white wine. Sally was nice enough to bring red, but with chicken, I need white. Remember what I say. Please listen to me." *Dear God, let Nathan know what I'm doing.* She didn't turn off the phone, but she did move the phone closer to where Sally was sitting.

By this time, Emily was confused, upset, and mortified. She was aghast at Sally's revelations. Was there more to come? She knew she made the correct decision to leave the phone on. She thought. *What is this all about?*

Nathan whispered, "Permelia, "Something's going on. How strange. Emily asked me to buy some white wine, but she doesn't drink. Moreover, I know she wouldn't serve it in her house. Shush, don't speak. We need to listen to the conversation at Emily's because I think she left her phone on so we would. I'll put it on speakerphone. We're at least thirty minutes from Emily's because of Friday's rush hour. We need to get there ASAP." He nervously pushed up his glasses.

Sally started talking faster and louder. The liquor was now doing most of the rambling conversation. "Now Emily, I don't want to hurt you but you have to understand. Gussy knew too much. I only wanted to reason with him. He just wouldn't listen. I couldn't let him ruin my life now could I? I just couldn't. You can see that. I had no choice, and I don't have now. I'm sorry."

Emily felt serious concern about being alone with this drunken woman. *What is this lunatic talking about? Would she hurt me? Surely not. Dear God, be with me. Tell me what to do.*

Sally continued her story, "I couldn't possibly marry Gussy. I wanted a good life. Samuel was a dental student. He came from a wealthy family too. I started dating him when school started. We'd been sleeping together since our third date. How easy it was. I told him I was pregnant, and we had to get married right away before I started showing. I knew the baby was Gussy's, but I wanted to marry a man with a future. I did. Your mother was my bridesmaid. We named the baby Samuel Andrew Jacobs III. We called him Drew. Okay, we'll fry a few of these mushrooms for a trial run. Don't bread them all yet, it's too soon." Her speech was slurred and jumbled.

Emily said, "Okay. *"Maybe my imagination is getting carried away. She appears harmless now. But what is she trying to say?* She pulled out an omelet pan.

Sally had more to say, "Why did your uncle have to see my photo in the Indy paper? Why couldn't the paper write the article without my photo? Everything would have turned out fine. I wouldn't have to do anything."

Sally became quite anxious. She thought, *Emily will eat the mushrooms. I'll make her if I have to do it at gunpoint.*

"Emily, your uncle sent me a letter to Samuel's office. I received it Monday. I needed to talk to him personally, so I told my husband I was going shopping Tuesday and would be gone all day. Samuel said he wouldn't be home for supper. He's playing eighteen holes of golf and he'll spend the evening with his golf pals.

"I left immediately Tuesday morning for Grovetown in a cheap rental car, wore sunglasses, tucked my hair under a big hat. I knew Gussy would agree with me and stay away. I looked at a map at a gas station in Grovetown to make sure I could find Persimmon Lane. Your uncle looked old to me. I'm happy I married Samuel instead of him. Gussy was in his workshop. Apparently, he turned his old bachelor pad where he and I experienced such passion into a workshop. Oh, I can still taste his exquisite saltiness. The lust I once felt was now anger. And where did he get that old mangy dog?"

Sally poured herself another glass of wine, pulled her tote close to her chair, and quickly drank the wine. The glass in her hand shook. She was visibly nervous.

"He called me Suze. That's the name I gave him. What a thrill to be with him. You always remember your first. The smell of his after-shave was intoxicating." She was rambling nearly incoherently.

Sally's revelations enthralled Nathan and Permelia. They were about ten minutes from the house. Nathan thought, *Where is Sally going with this?*

Sally told Emily, "Melt some butter in the pan. Real butter. Now fry three or four of the floured mushrooms until they're brown. Why was your uncle so troublesome? Why wouldn't he listen to me? I didn't want him dead, but what else could I do? He turned to open his refrigerator. I was so mad. That strange looking screwdriver was within reach. I don't remember how many times I stabbed him. A few for sure. So much blood. Oh by the way, Emily, those aren't morel mushrooms. YOU ARE GOING TO EAT THEM! These are Amanita mushrooms from my backyard, picked this morning."

Nathan screamed into the phone, "Emily, don't eat any! They're poisonous. They're Death Angels!"

Sally grabbed the cell phone and threw it across the room. She pulled the pistol out of the tote and pointed it at the frightened young woman. "Yes, you will!"

Nathan called 911 from his car. An ambulance and the police were dispatched to Emily's apartment, with instructions about the deadly fungi. The ambulance was equipped with a stomach pump. The driver put on his lights and sirens. Several police cars led the way with screaming sirens. Nathan turned his lights on and blared on the horn. The speed limit laws meant nothing to him at this point. He told Permelia, "There isn't any treatment. Pumping her stomach may help. If not done immediately, the Death Angels will slowly shut down her organs. We need to pray."

Nathan, the ambulance, and police arrived nearly simultaneously. Police, guns drawn, stormed into the apartment. Sally, stumbling fell against the table, dropping the gun. Handcuffs quickly dug into her wrist.

Nathan prayed, "Thank you, Jesus."

Epilogue

Sally's husband, Samuel, went to the jail to visit his wife. He said, "I always knew Drew wasn't my son. God told me I should marry you. I just couldn't allow you to lose your reputation." And with that, he left the jail, not allowing her to have the final say.

ACKNOWLEDGEMENTS

Sonja Wells, cosmetologist, makeup designer, Knightstown
Charlene Perry, author, Henry County, IN
Nicholas Shaneyfelt, BA, Notre Dame University
Eric Cox, Editor of *The Banner*, Knightstown, IN
John Todd, owner of Todd's Funeral Home, Knightstown, IN
Butch Baker, Sheriff, Henry County, IN
Scott Pinkerton, Chief of Detectives, Henry County, IN
Elizabeth Munroz, editor and proofreader, Watsonville, CA
Linda Addison, consultant, Carthage IN
Marjorie Wilkinson, librarian, Knightstown, IN
David Chizum, botanist, San Antonio, TX
Philana Orem, daughter of Diana Orem, editor, Rush County, IN
Autumn Orem Paul, cover designer, Rush County,
Anna Gorman Coy, senior editor, Wilkinson, Indiana

As co-author of this novel I express my greatest appreciation to my best-friend, Diana Orem's daughters, Autumn and Philana Orem, for all their invaluable help and support to make their mother's work be in print.

AUTHOR BIOGRAPHIES

Patricia Goodspeed, a retired attorney-at-law, is a Purdue and Indiana University graduate. She and her husband, Donald Goodspeed, an Indiana University graduate, reside in a small town in Central Indiana. They've lived there for over forty years. They raised three children along with three exchange students, a foster child, two dogs, and Abyssinian and other breeds of cats. They have six grandchildren scattered in Texas, Korea, and Indiana. She and her family love to travel. Patricia lived throughout the United States and in Istanbul, Turkey. She traveled in Asia, the Americas, the Caribbean islands, Europe, and the Middle East. She and her husband are active members of St. Rose of Lima Catholic Church.

Her hobbies include traveling, collecting and wearing hats, photography, knitting, Dance Orientale, and genealogy. She earlier published *Asa Lee Mattox and Nellie Frances Edwards, Our Southern Indiana Heritage.*

Diana Orem and her husband live in rural Indiana. Diana was a Purdue graduate with an undergraduate degree in English and a Master of Science in Education. She was an avid Purdue fan of both football and basketball and a strong Colts supporter. They have four daughters, one son, and two grandchildren. She loved to read and to travel. Diana felt there was a lack of novels in the Christian mystery genre. She wanted to help fill this void with this novel, she liked to call Trinkle, Trinkle, Whittle, Scar before we coined the title, Murder on Persimmon Lane. She was a member of the First Baptist Church in New Castle, Indiana. With passion she enjoyed all aspects of her life. Unfortunately, Diana passed this life and joined her Savior in 2013.

A Tribute From Diana's Family

Diana Orem is a light. Just as one of her favorite parable songs, Diana is a true light to all she encountered (children might lovingly say encroached); none the less, she is a light which will forever shine and not allow "blow out."

Diana and her devotedly loving husband, created their personal earthly heaven in rural Indiana raising five children. She often busily helped her own coop with projects or school work (albeit work with which she created and volunteered herself...that's our mother -- everyone's best friend and/or producer!) or was side to side with her soul mate in the veterinary clinic that she excitedly and without boundaries, helped create.

Her family is and will forever be her success story of done-did. She undoubtedly is almost as proud of them as they are to her for the never ending stories she prophesied without belittling her faith. Her family and friends can never forget her laugh - which can be recognized from across a movie theater - or the constant, infectious stream of singing of her favorite tunes - most of which are religious hymns or self-produced musicals. With Diana's artistic talents, she was known to transform a cold, blank slate from a damp swamp or every day run of the mill average ice cream parlor into a warm, everyone is welcome type of atmosphere. Diana is the perfect Epiphany for mercy and everything she did was with love and outwardly shined greatly for The Lord.

Known to collect and wear many hats - literally and figuratively - Diana's life on earth was nothing less than extraordinary. She celebrated Christmas every day and if nothing else, her gift to the world was sharing His love. Currently, Diana is a beautiful memory in all of our hearts while she celebrates daily with our Lord and Savior in Heaven. All the while her loved ones rejoice her memory to share with those who will listen...and likewise with those who try to ignore our obnoxiously, like-able, irrefutable personalities....like mom always said "There are no strangers here, just friends who have not yet met..."

Dearest Mother, Always and forever our love...Philana, Anjanetta, Patrick, Alicia, Autumn and MANY MANY more...XOXOXO

CPSIA information can be obtained at www.ICGtesting.com
Printed in the USA
LVOW06s0713101115

461847LV00001B/1/P